ECLIPSE

K. A. Bedford's previous book

Orbital Burn

BY
K. A. BEDFORD

EDGE SCIENCE FICTION AND FANTASY PUBLISHING
AN IMPRINT OF HADES PUBLICATIONS, INC.
CALGARY

Released in Canada: September, 2005
Distributed in the USA: March, 2006

EDGE

Edge Science Fiction and Fantasy Publishing
An Imprint of Hades Publications Inc.
P.O. Box 1714, Calgary, Alberta, T2P 2L7, Canada

In house editing by Adam Volk
Interior design by Brian Hades
Cover Illustration by Geoff Taylor
ISBN: 978-1-894063-30-2

EDGE Science Fiction and Fantasy Publishing and Hades Publications, Inc.
acknowledges the ongoing support of the the Alberta Fondation for the Arts
and the Australia Council for the Arts for our publishing programme.

Library and Archives Canada Cataloguing in Publication

Bedford, K. A. (K. Adrian), 1963 -
   Eclipse / K. A. Bedford. -- 1st ed.

ISBN-13: 978-1-894063-30-2
ISBN-10: 1-894063-30-9

   I. Title.

PR9619.3.B46E25 2005   823   C2005-904784-4

FIRST EDITION
(n-20050801)
Printed in Canada
www.edgewebsite.com

Dedication

To Michelle

One

My name is James Robert Dunne. I joined *Eclipse* when I was twenty-one years old, a fresh graduate from the Royal Interstellar Service Academy in Winter City, Ganymede, and I was ready to join the crew of Her Majesty's Starship *Eclipse* for my first three-year hitch of active space duty.

The trip up the Ganymede Stalk from the Academy took forever, or so it felt. I couldn't sleep, even with my headware doing its best to tweak my alpha waves. I sat fidgeting, uncomfortable in my shuttle seat for the whole 35,000-kilometer trip, trying not to think about where I was heading, and what I was leaving behind. *This time tomorrow*, I kept thinking, *I'll be an officer serving aboard a starship, charting unexplored space!*

Which, it strikes me now, says a lot about me. You'd think, after all the crap I had been through at the Academy, I wouldn't still be quite this naïve or idealistic about it. But I was. Some diamond-hard core of belief in "The Dream" remained, even as part of me dreaded the prospect. As bad as the Academy had been, it had occurred to the more rational part of my mind that active space duty could be like Academy life to the nth power.

All the same, my naïve, dreamy side was in charge during that long trip upStalk, filling my mind with lofty ideas about being out there in the dark, beyond the lights of human civilization, away from everything. I even, and I hesitate to record this, considered that this might be an opportunity for me to find myself. Maybe. It might also, I thought, be a chance to get away from my past.

My stomach was fluttery all the long way up to geosynch. A lot of the time I fought my seat, trying to get comfortable, and thought about what was left of my family.

Some family! Dad too busy on Europa, and Trish back on Mars. She at least was good to her word. She had said she wasn't going to watch me do this, after everything that had happened. She wasn't going to stand there and watch me march off into the worst decision I ever made, and she didn't. Didn't even send a note. *Some sister*, I thought.

And I certainly didn't expect to hear from Mom. I'm not sure if she even thinks of herself as my mother these days, or if she even knew I was in training. I remember having fantasies about how one day I'd take some Service leave and head over to New Jerusalem and see what the hell Mom's doing there. This was one of those plans you have that the realistic part of you knows you'll never carry out.

Mom left when I was eight, when things were "difficult," the euphemism we use to describe those days. Would she remember me? What if she told me to turn around and leave? Dad once mentioned something about how she even had a new name now and a good Muslim husband, a new family. A new life. It was hard and painful to think about so I tried not to.

During the ride up, the other passengers passed the time the usual ways: lost in virtuum, chatting, playing games, or reading. A woman next to me was crocheting a tablecloth from real cotton thread. She said the thread had been produced on a genuine antique spinning wheel, not nanofabricated. Even I knew it must have been worth a small fortune. I tried to relax and not bother her. When she asked, indicating my spanking new uniform, if I was heading for a space deployment, I said, "That's right, yes. I'm kinda nervous. First time." I remember grinning and that my smile felt like a wince of pain. She told me about her own time in the Service, working shore duty, clerical stuff mostly, and how she had met her late husband.

The closer we got to the geosynch spaceport, the more nervous I got; time seemed to crawl; I felt like I was being hauled up towards my future, but I could also feel the tug of my past, a gravity of grief.

We pulled in at the geosynch station on time, with little fuss and less fanfare. Once I had my kit bag, I moved through the crowded station to level nine of the shuttle terminal complex and found the Service kiosk where I went through pre-boarding processing with disposable officials, checking orders, verifying identity, crisp salutes, stern smiles, and wishes of good luck. After that came the long wait for my boarding call. I drank a lot of bad coffee.

I was early, even more than standard security checks required. Tension gripped my gut; the sea-cheese sandwiches I had eaten on the Stalk-shuttle might have been a bad idea, and I wasn't sure if I wanted to throw up. Pacing back and forth, fidgeting, I listened to the clock in my headware reporting every five minutes, and dodged airborne security bots. With all my heart I wanted to be gone, away from here — the familiar world. I wanted my new life to start.

I spent a lot of time among the gawking tourists at the big windows of the upstairs observation deck, away from the aromatic clamor of the shops below. My sweaty palms pressed against the fiber-diamond window surfaces as I stared out — a nauseatingly moony, love struck kid — at the object of my desire: the splendid enormity of the deep-space cruiser *HMS Eclipse*, moored outside, taking on fuel, supplies, and a few crewmen. She filled the visible sky, her dazzling whiteness blotting out the dark curve of Jupiter's night side. *Eclipse* was a grand old lady of the stars, one of the first wholly nanofactured ships in the Service.

Unlike her blocky, chunky predecessors, *Eclipse* was long and sleek through the core to the engine module, the whole ship shaped like an elongated teardrop. She was eight hundred meters from nose to the radiator array that surrounded the shrouded power plant exhaust vents like a vast chrome spider web. The distant sun caught the curves and sleek lines of *Eclipse's* outer hull, gleaming off the centimeter-thick layer of cross-linked woven polydiamond armor. In the unlikely event of combat, that armor could shift within seconds into a black, sensor-hostile skin; she would effectively disappear.

Eclipse probed beyond the edge of human space, looking for worlds with potential for colonization, or that were ripe for resource exploitation. She also did a little science on the side. It was considered gently exciting duty; a good first assignment for a starry-eyed young officer in the Service. I wiped my hands on my pressed cotton handkerchief, and folded it back into my white jacket pocket, absently noticing that it was getting hard to keep the folds in the handkerchief. I might need to go and get a new one from one of the vending fabs.

"Kinda makes you feel like a little kid, huh?" It was a warm female voice right behind me.

I turned and saw a striking young woman, an officer about my age, her dark skin lit by large, amused brown eyes and a warm smile. She sported a vermilion three-millimeter mohawk down the center of her scalp — a provocative look for a Service officer. She stood there, arms crossed, looking at the ship. "You pulled *Eclipse*, too, huh?" she asked, a tone in her voice suggesting she wasn't entirely delighted. I wasn't sure if her displeasure was aimed at the ship or me, or both.

"Yes, yes I did," I said, stunned that this gorgeous woman was speaking to me. Suddenly I felt foolish and gawky, my arms and legs sticking out all over, my mouth dry. "I'm James—"

"Dunne, right? I think I saw you a couple of times around the Academy. You were always out right-dressing flag poles and doing endless push-ups for the provosts." I remembered the right-dressing-the-flag-pole routine with cold dread. You have to stand next to the pole, right arm extended horizontally from your shoulder, your fist clenched so that it just touched the pole, and then stand like that for hours. Frequently in the rain.

I felt myself blushing, and then blushing more at the blush. "That was me. Always in trouble. Still, what doesn't kill you, eh?"

"Yeah, I spent a bit of time with that flag pole myself, to be honest!" she said, laughing. She had a dazzling smile; an infectious laugh. "Oh, I'm sorry. Very rude. I'm Sorcha Riley, Spacecraft Services Officer Level 1 Engineering." We shook moist hands and felt awkward. Sorcha laughed good-naturedly to cover the moment.

"I was just thinking," I said, glancing at the ship, smiling hesitantly, "about when I was a little kid, the first time I saw a starship from the windows of an orbital ferry."

"You have memories like that, too? Oh God, we are gonna get on just fine!"

Surprised, I stared, but then remembered to finish the story. "It-it was on a trip from Ganymede to Mars with my family. It was this pre-nano *Cunard*-class liner, *Royal Star*, 156,000 tonnes of her empty. Packing a power plant of four clustered Farber-Rheinhart 200-megawatt—"

Sorcha interrupted: "Oh, oh!" she said, grinning, touching my forearm, "no, that's not right. You say it was the *Royal Star*?"

Where she touched my arm felt terribly warm. It was hard to concentrate for a moment.

She went on, one of those people who have no idea of the effect they have on others, "The *Royal Star's* drives were arranged in a straight in-line four-pack with superfluid reverse-cooling until her plant refit in '09 under new owners. After the refit, the drives were arranged in a diamond-cluster for improved harmonic efficiency with stasis-positive vent cooling for hot-start capability, and uprated the nominal output to 215 megawatts per core." She laughed, but good-naturedly. "Basically."

"Wow, Queen of the Shipspotters!" I said, laughing as well, but not as easily, trying not to feel embarrassed.

She looked accustomed to accolades. "Ah, whatever. I'm a bit of an engine-geek. Sorry." She looked actually concerned for my embarrassment, surprising me.

"Just made me think of my brother," I said, turning to look back at *Eclipse*. Without realizing it, I was thinking about all the ship's vital statistics, the way she was written up in *Jane's Starships and Space Vehicles*. Thinking, too, about

Colin's room in our house in Hastings, back on Mars, the wall displays dense with starship construction charts, floor plans, holostatic renderings and Service PR images. Colin's room was a shrine to star travel.

"Oh?" she asked, "What's he like?"

I could have sworn she was asking out of genuine interest. She was looking at me, and not at *Eclipse*, which made her the only person here at the windows who wasn't. Even I was looking at the ship, trying not to think about this very brainy, very attractive woman chatting with me. In my experience, such women didn't usually notice the likes of me.

All the same, I felt myself smiling a little. "He — Colin, his name was Colin — he was the one who told me all that about the *Royal Star*, telling me this huge thing out there was a 'rooly-trooly starship'." I laughed at this memory of Colin's hands: one on my shoulder, the other pointing out the window at the gleaming, streamlined pale-blue-and-white beauty of *Royal Star*.

Sorcha laughed again, entertained but baffled. "'Rooly-trooly?'"

"Ah. It's an Australian thing. Sorry. It means 'really truly', genuine."

"I thought I recognised that accent!" she said, grinning.

I shrugged, bobbed my head. "Anyway," I went on, "I got all this stuff from Colin..."

"Maybe he should've joined the Service," Sorcha said, glancing over at *Eclipse*, then back at me.

I looked away from the ship. "I guess so," I said.

She hovered next to me, watching the ship. Her face glowed with station light reflected off *Eclipse's* hull.

Good grief, I thought, feeling self-conscious and stupid, and suddenly very nervous; only now did I realize who this was. Sorcha Riley was someone I knew only by reputation: she had been notorious at the Academy, graduating in the top three percent overall, despite numerous discipline problems, and hence her own run-ins with the provosts and having to right-dress the flag pole. The received wisdom of cadet gossip said these troubles — she was particularly noteworthy for pursuing activist causes — would be sure to hold her back. She was ambitious, determined, and too cool to live, they said. But she got through and with style. By contrast, I graduated 145th in a field of 400 and was considered a plodder. Where I thought this posting to *Eclipse* a fantastic piece of luck, Sorcha must have been a little disappointed.

Thinking as fast as I could to cover the embarrassment gap, I asked, voice perhaps too loud, "You want to get some coffee or something while we wait?"

She grinned, "Sure," and pushed off, heading for the nearby fabs. Sorcha said, "So, James, what did you wind up getting?" I liked that she sounded actually interested; she wasn't just asking out of politeness. After life at the Academy, and learning to read the subtext in the subtext in everything people said to you, it was surprising. I'd always heard about Sorcha that she was difficult and hard to get on with. In fact, she seemed like the most natural person I'd ever met.

"SSO1, like you; Helm." Level 1 posts were the lowest form of life in the Service, somewhere below tubeworms and lichen, and traditionally given the worst jobs.

We found a Huang coffee vending fab next to a few that would make cheap luggage and budget-quality generic brand clothing. In the absence of a live disposable to take our orders, we grappled with the machine's verbal interface, and in time coaxed the thing into producing two cups of coffee that came close to what we wanted. Sorcha pronounced the coffee's flavor and heat "within acceptable tolerances" but swore she could build a better fab from the contents of the back pocket of her pants.

I believed her. In fact, even then I was probably in that precarious spot where you secretly know you're falling for someone, while knowing you are absolutely not her type, not suited in any intellectual way, and certain to be blown away by the first handsome, brainy engineering geek she encountered. I was used to this sort of scenario. I had a history of finding myself infatuated with unattainable women. Fortunately, Academy life had kept me far too busy — to say nothing of all the time I spent in the Infirmary following disciplinary sessions — to pursue those hopeless causes. Not that it stopped me thinking about such matters, of course.

For a few minutes we stood around bitching about the quality of food from different brands of fab machines, and swapping tales of how we lived at the Academy on fabbed noodles and soy sauce from what we called "BlandBrand" machines, sometimes for weeks on end, because we were so broke and desperate for food. I didn't mention how I had made it harder on myself in the later years by deliberately not keeping a junior cadet to look after my needs — Trish had already given me grief about this. Academy living was damned expensive by the time you paid rent, bought access time at the library for all your classes, contributed to the tutors' pay, paid for access to simulators, paid for flight time and purchased study materials. A lot of cadets had to either get big loans or work a couple of part-time crap jobs on the side — disposable-level work — just to get by with all the other obligations. Sleep was a luxury you earned on graduation, and faked in the meantime with dodgy headware patches.

"And," Sorcha added, "getting the damned provosts to leave you the hell alone. That cost a fortune in itself!" She swallowed a big mouthful, grimacing and looking into the bottom of the cup.

I nodded, knowing all about the way the provosts — senior cadets appointed to make sure cadets stuck to the regs — made life wretched for everyone else. Any and all punishments short of execution seemed within their purview to hand out, but they seemed to like giving out some more than others. We figured those guys couldn't get laid any other way but through force so it was always worse for the female cadets. There were old folk tales from way back — before Earth's destruction — that things for most women had been pretty good. These stories were laughed at, of course, particularly by women these days. The general consensus was that if such stories were true, then when Earth died, so did a lot of other things. Women were welcome in the Service now, no questions asked, but only as long as they didn't get in the way. The few senior women in the Service treated female cadets just as badly as senior men treated their juniors. Power, it seems, knew no gender bias, and wouldn't easily be challenged.

Sorcha and I sipped a while in stranger-silence, staring around, wondering what to say to each other, but also glad to have someone else there, feeling the same nerves. Sometimes we tossed around stupid cadet jokes, bitched about tutors we hated. *Eclipse* was attracting a lot of attention from tourists and business drones in transit. The observation deck windows were almost completely obscured by clumps of gawking civilians.

It was strange to think, while looking at that ship, about all the grief and misery I had endured to get here. I had come so close to quitting the whole damn Service several times. I had even seriously contemplated killing a couple of people, especially Phil Dewey, the senior cadet who had "kept" me, and for the things he and his pals did to me in the name of fun, but that was nothing revolutionary. Most years at the Academy there was at least one case of a junior cadet murdering his senior. Despite all this, I felt I had somehow survived the worst the Service had to offer and I was still here, and about to board that beautiful ship.

To tell the embarrassing truth, I felt smug. However, what I didn't know was that the Service, despite everything I experienced at the Academy, was not nearly done with me — and I was not nearly done with it.

Two

Sorcha and I were due to board at 1030 hours. As we chatted I was impressed by how cool she seemed about the whole thing. I asked her about it. She said, "It's not like we're going to war, James. It's just a ship. And it's pretty routine duty, too: tooling around out in the dark, not seeing much, not doing much. Probably a lot of scrubbing decks, if I guess right."

"You think so?" I said, looking at her.

"You don't think we'll be lucky to get out of crap job hell for the first year?"

I hadn't really thought about this. In my haste to escape my life, I had confined myself to imagining Service life with a certain rosy glow. When my face betrayed my embarrassment, Sorcha smiled and said, "Look, if you ask me, the real action is the post after this one, once we've proved ourselves as officers." She was probably right.

"What's your preference?" I asked.

"Eventually I wouldn't mind getting into vehicle design, advanced propulsion concepts, stuff like that. You?"

I laughed at the contrast between her ambition and my contentment to stick with what I was given. "I'd like to just survive!" Sorcha laughed without sounding like she was mocking me. "Actually," I said, "I'd like maybe to be a section head one day."

Sorcha got wide-eyed: "That's not very ambitious! Where's your zeal to push the barriers?"

"Oh, I think I left that back at my folks' place, in a jar beside the bed. Damn."

She had the grace to laugh again.

Ten-thirty hours came before we knew it. PortMind sent the boarding call over our headware, ordering us to present ourselves at Gate 5. Sorcha glanced at me, waggling her arched eyebrows. "You ready, James?"

"I've been ready for this my whole life!" I said, grinning like the fool I was.

She gagged. "I cannot believe you said that! Good grief!"

"Well excuse me for being excited!"

"Yeah, well just don't get your pants all sticky." She laughed again, poked me in the ribs, and strode off ahead, kit bag slung over her shoulder.

Two big, disposable enlisted men stood at the gate, scoping the crowd, looking professional in their navy blue Security uniforms, and armed with white antipersonnel nanophage launchers. We went up to them, sent our bags through the sensor grid, and stepped through ourselves. The ID information in our headware checked out with the Security systems and the access tube hissed open, letting us through and hissing shut behind us. The two disposable sentries didn't even glance at us. We walked up the dark, chilly access tube towards the bright halogen-lit entrance to *HMS Eclipse*. It was a strange feeling, walking that tube, to know that this was all that stood between you and the vacuum of space. I felt my ears adjusting to pressure differences.

Sorcha whispered, "Would this be a bad time to jump up and down?"

I stared at her, shocked. I said, "Are you crazy?"

"Geez, James. I'm still a bit nervous, just like you. This is kind of a big moment."

We were close to the ship's hatch where another pair of Security disposables stood waiting for us. "I thought you were all cool about this?"

"That's bullshit over bad coffee. This is the real thing!"

We stepped out of the cramped access tube and aboard the ship. The Security guys here went through our kits, checked us over and verified our identities nine different ways; I hardly noticed. All I could think was, "I'm standing on board a starship, an actual bloody starship!" Not some old liner, like that ship from my childhood that I had only been a guest on for a couple of days. And not a retired training vessel that never went further than orbiting Ganymede. This was my new home. For all her mocking, I could see that Sorcha felt the same way, grinning from ear to ear. It was a strange feeling, being there; it's hard to describe. My first impression was of light and roominess, and a faint smell of leather on the cool processed air. This chamber, with its smooth gray walls, even illumination and polydiamond pressure-doors was spacious compared to the ships I remembered from simulations. The old style of ship was built with the high cost of environment in mind: spaces were cramped, dark, and claustrophobic. It was hard to avoid the smell of your fellow crew. Historians at the Academy told us that those ships were a lot like the ancient submarines from Earth; constructed without the comfort of their crews in mind.

Eclipse and her six sister ships had been a revelation in ship design. I could stand up straight with room to spare above my head and the artificial-G felt almost natural, approaching liner-grade. There was only a momentary sense of disorientation as we got used to the transition from the station's field to the ship's field. The air was almost completely free from the smell of processing.

The two Security men escorted Sorcha and me forward along the core to the five personnel decks, which occupied the forward third of the ship; the balance consisted of the power plant, engineering section, ship systems hardware, weaponry support, and environment processors. Around us the air seemed to vibrate with the suppressed potential of the power plant.

We were left waiting in an area they called the Hole. It was just another small compartment, well lit, with a couple of fixed display sheets on the walls, and with more black non-skid deck plating. On our way here, we had passed a few other officers. I tried to remember that only Spacecraft Command Officers required salutes, not SSOs like Sorcha and me. I got it right most of the time, with little embarrassment. Mostly, I was astounded at the idea of people passing side by side in a passageway. All the brass fittings I saw sparkled; the black deck and gray walls were spotless; the gold buttons on the other officers' crisp, white uniforms shone. All this cleanliness, I thought, feeling smugger than ever, was a sign of a fine, well-run ship.

Sorcha pointed out to me later that it could also be a sign of madness.

Eclipse's executive officer, Ron Ferguson, met us in the Hole. He was a stout, hard-looking bastard who looked like he could read your mind, find out if you were up to something, and punish you thoroughly before you even had time to blink. His sleeve insignia indicated he was a Spacecraft Command Officer Level 6 — definitely someone to salute. We stood at rigid attention, staring somewhere past the opposite bulkhead and a display panel showing an assortment of documents pertaining to standing orders. He downloaded our papers from our headware to his clipboard.

"What have we got here with you lot, then? Hmm. Spacecraft Services Officer Level 1, Riley, S. That would be you, Miss?" Ferguson looked at her like he was particularly unimpressed.

Sorcha shouted, "Yes, sir!"

Ferguson narrowed his eyes and nodded a little. "Very good," he said, suggesting he thought otherwise. He checked his clipboard again, glancing at me. "And that means you, you sorry-looking wretch, must be SSO1 Dunne, J. Is that right, mister?"

"Yes, sir!" I shouted. My own ears rang as my voice resounded in the small compartment.

Ferguson looked at me in a way I didn't like, saying, "I'm really not quite deaf yet, boy." He wiggled a finger in his ears for a comic effect that was wasted on me — I hated being called "boy." He was daring us to laugh. We didn't.

"Welcome, Miss Riley and Mr. Dunne, to Her Majesty's Starship *Eclipse*. During the time you spend aboard this fair vessel, you will find that we do things a little differently from what you were taught at the Academy. Do either of you geniuses know why that might be?"

Sorcha took a shot at it, shouting her answer at the opposite wall, "The rigors of actual spaceflight place unpredictable stresses on human beings that can never accurately be simulated. Moreover, life aboard a starship is by definition unpredictable, sir!"

Ferguson, his pencil moustache twitching beneath his narrow nose, scowled at Sorcha, taking his time about his response. He said, "Quite correct, SSO1 Riley, the Academy does its best to introduce the cadet to a wide range of situations and circumstances and tries to teach its cloth-eared students skills for improvising their way to successful outcomes without killing too many of their shipmates. Guided by regulations, of course. But you're only at the Academy for four short years. Now then. SSO1 Dunne?"

"Sir!"

"Better, Dunne, better. Can you tell me what the greatest hazard to the crew of a starship exploring the unknown might be?"

Relief! I knew this one. "Boredom, sir!"

"And why, might I ask," he went on, pacing back and forth before us, his boots clumping on the plates, "is boredom such a great problem for a starship crew?"

I felt myself growing nervous answering, "Space is boring, sir!"

Our new executive officer arched a steely eyebrow at me. "Very good, Dunne. You win the prize for logic. Starship life is boring because space is boring. Sadly, you are quite right. Much of our work on this ship is concerned with maintenance, gathering information, having meetings to discuss our information, and suchlike. There are no diverting aliens to entertain us. The last time something exciting happened on this ship was twelve years ago. Can either of you tell me what that event was?"

Sorcha said, "*Eclipse* scientists discovered what could be the ruins of an alien civilization on Madrigal, sir! Controversy still raging, sir!"

"You know your history, Riley. That is most gratifying."

"Thank you very much, sir!"

Ferguson went back to pacing. "Captain Rudyard likes things quiet and peaceful, children. Is that understood?

He doesn't want any controversy, any great kerfuffles whatsoever. Is that clear?"

We both shouted, "Yes, sir!"

"Excellent. We don't like people who rock the boat on *Eclipse*. We like things to remain on a nice, even keel. We take this quite seriously. Do you doubt this, Mr. Dunne?"

Why'd he pick on me? I tried not to let my flash of panic show. "Absolutely not, sir! No rocking the boat, sir!"

"In that case," Ferguson said, glaring at me and then giving Sorcha a leer I'm sure she could have done without, "we'll all get on very well. *Eclipse* is a happy ship, children."

"Yes, sir!" we said. I was getting hoarse.

Ferguson touched a few panels on his display. Instantly my headware let me know it had received fresh mail from Ferguson. He said, "I've just sent you both all the documentation you need to orient yourselves, your cabin assignments, work rosters, emergency procedures, lifeboat access routes, standing orders, ship layout, and so forth. Any questions?"

"No, sir!"

He said, "Correct answer. Dismissed — report to your department heads in ten minutes." I had a moment to realize that my department head was Captain Rudyard himself.

Ferguson left us in the Hole, strolling away, and whistling something off-key.

"That," I said, "was different." I bent down to pick up my kit. Sorcha was staring off.

"He sent me a private message while he was talking to you," she said, not looking at me. "Can you believe it?"

"What'd he say?"

Now she looked at me, her luminous dark eyes full of anger. "He wants me to come to his quarters tonight, 2330 hours."

I didn't know what to say. We had just been told not to make any kind of fuss. "What are you going to do?"

"Well I'm damn well not going, am I?" she hissed, glancing about.

"Are you sure that's wise?"

She looked at me as if I was much more stupid than she realized. "You do understand what he's after, don't you?"

I wasn't a total newbie — I realized Ferguson was interested in more than a friendly avuncular chat with Sorcha. "Are you sure it's a good idea to get his back up so early in your time here? I mean, we're stuck here for three years."

She scowled, "So you're saying I should let him shag me stupid just for the sake of crew harmony?"

"Well, no, obviously..."

"Because I had enough of this crap at the Academy. I thought shipboard life would be a little more grown-up."

I didn't want to talk about my own run-ins with seniors with a taste for male flesh. "Well you better go and have it out with him. It's unprofessional behavior, propositioning a member of the crew like that."

Sorcha stood there, staring at the floor. "Damn, I thought all that crap was over."

I said nothing.

She said, "Look, here's what he said. I'll show you the note." She flashed the note across to me. It said, "Miss Riley, please report to my cabin at 2330. I would like to discuss your future career. Ferguson."

"Your future career?" I asked, thinking about it, also thinking that a note like that was quite innocuous. "Maybe he's for real."

"Did you see the way he looked at me? Did you?"

I remembered Ferguson's leer. I rubbed at my chin. "I don't know what to suggest."

"Thanks so much for your help," she said.

"I just don't think he should be allowed to proposition you, or put you in a compromising position."

"Like I said, thanks." She leaned against the wall, chewing her lip. "The bastard!"

"What about this?" I said, suddenly seized by an idea.

"What about what?"

I explained my idea. She looked at me, skeptically. "That won't work."

"It might work, though — it's better than doing nothing."

Sorcha still looked dubious, and she twisted her mouth around. Looking at me, she said, "Dunne, if this doesn't work ..."

"How could it not work?" I asked, smiling.

Three

Captain Rudyard didn't look like a man losing his mind. He was around average height for a Service officer, wiry, with a gaunt face and sad-looking blue eyes, dark hair receding at the temples that was worn long enough to need brushing back. I always thought that he looked like he had just received word of the death of a loved one.

He answered his office door himself when I knocked, which surprised me. I was used to the Academy custom of having disposable servants as personal assistants to handle such matters. "Mr. Dunne, I presume?" the captain asked, smiling — it wasn't a good look for him. I held out my hand, suffering his crushing handshake in return, and tried to squeeze back just as hard. One thing I've noticed about men who like bonecrusher handshakes: they measure a person's worth by the strength of the squeeze. The captain was evidently satisfied with my attempt to break his hand, and he stepped back and welcomed me into his office.

Another surprise: there was room for as many as three people in the room; captains on the old ships never used to get such generous space allotments. I stood a moment in the center of the Service-gray room, gawking about, feeling almost agoraphobic after my experiences in sims and replicas on training missions. Looking around, I saw that Captain Rudyard was a man who didn't like distractions. He had a simple oak desk jammed into a corner, which looked like real, finished dark timber, and a comfortable Lutio smartchair, an expensive item indeed, probably his only indulgence. He also had a low, standard-issue cot set against the opposite wall, perhaps for those times when he didn't feel like going back to his quarters. On the wall behind Rudyard's desk he had a small image in a frame: his own graduating class, four hundred young men and women in sparkling white, standing in the leafy Contemplation Garden at the Academy, in the early days of the Home System Community, when it still genuinely represented all the people who lived in the system.

There was also, I noted with a certain pride, the requisite image of Her Majesty Queen Helen, Head of the Service, the only monarch to exist in virtuum, where she reigned, perfect, beautiful, and serene, an inspiration to everyone in the Home System Community. As a virtual, virtuous monarch, she was programmed to exhibit all the glorious qualities of royalty from across human history, and exhibit none of the foibles and embarrassments that had driven carbon-based royalty into disrepute. Queen Helen had started as a virtuum hack in the old days, before the HSC, probably some student's exercise in character design. Accounts differed over who created her and how she got loose into the Home System infosphere, but suddenly she began to appear everywhere, and people responded to her quiet majesty, serene beauty, and wisdom. Over time, she had become a unifying leader who could be all things to all people. Her coronation ceremony was held at an ambitious virtuum recreation of St Paul's Cathedral and had been experienced by hundreds of millions of people across human space. Historians were beginning to mark that day, forty-three years ago, as the birth of the Community.

The captain managed a smile as he saw me admiring his pictures. "Please, son, feel free to have a look. I'm in the third row … no, wait, I'm in the fourth row, nineteenth from the right." Rudyard stepped across to his graduation image and pointed out which tiny white figure was him, thirty years ago. I noticed he had had more hair in those days, and even then the same bland unconvincing smile.

"Must have been something being a young officer in those days, sir," I said, trying to make conversation.

"The Service today is different, the dark is further out, but here at the sharp end, well — some things don't change. Can I get you some coffee or tea?" He had a small personal fab set up next to his desk, fixed to the wall. I stared for a moment, astounded at such luxury.

"Uh, thank you but no, sir. Kind of you to offer."

Rudyard fixed himself a coffee, Martian French vanilla, no milk, three sugars. He directed me to take a seat in the small visitor chair, which I did, allowing the chair to fold itself over my legs, and wondered what to do or say next. The whole encounter so far seemed odd, like the bad dress rehearsal preceding a play's successful opening night.

Rudyard was nothing like I expected. When I had first received word that I was getting *Eclipse* as my assignment, I started hearing from all kinds of people around the Academy who knew the man and warned me about his idiosyncrasies and black moods. When I knocked on Rudyard's door that morning, I half expected to have my head bitten off for disturbing him. Instead he was obviously going out of his way to put me at ease, in his own way.

Rudyard parked himself in his Lutio, sipped his coffee, looked thoughtful a moment. "Hmm, it's getting better, I think."

"I still prefer the real thing, if you'll excuse my saying so, sir."

He laughed out loud. "If you'll excuse my saying so? Mr. Dunne, this meeting is entirely informal. You're here so I can get to know you a little, and you can get to know me. You don't have to suck up to me quite so much, or be so damned deferential. Save that for when you're on the helm team. And," he flashed a sly smile, "as it happens, I prefer real coffee myself, but I keep my store of the good stuff for special occasions."

Disconcerted, I nodded. "Sounds very wise, sir. How long have you been captain of *Eclipse*?" Which was me trying again to make conversation; I knew very well how long Rudyard had been *Eclipse's* captain.

He flashed that smile from the class photograph, all teeth. "Sometimes, you know, if feels like I've been running this damn boat all my life." There was a brief flash of fatigue and thoughtfulness there, as he stared over my shoulder. "But there are other times when I wake up and suddenly it hits me, I'm the captain of *HMS Eclipse*!" He allowed himself a small laugh at this, fidgeting.

There was a long moment of silence while he sipped at his coffee. I couldn't think anything that I wanted to ask him; I already knew about his background, about the ship and her systems. "Captain Rudyard," I opened, "as you know I've been appointed to helm operations. But as an SSO1 I know I won't be doing a great deal of actual helm work."

He looked grateful for a conversation topic. "Right. Yes, you're quite right, Mr. Dunne. To be placed on the rotation for primary helm, you need to be SSO3. There have been some young officers who've dazzled the hell out of all of us and got on the team at 2, of course, but they are the exception." Another flash of the big smile. "During the time you're working your way up from being a 1, you will function as an observer attached to the helm operations team, in one of the three shift slots, and also work on completing a bridging program of sim work to bring your skills up to what we need."

"That's perfectly fine with me, sir. I'm prepared to work hard, but I'm curious to know what my actual duties will be." I knew I sounded like a prat talking like this. Something about this whole encounter with the captain felt strange and unsettling, but I couldn't place what it was, and I had the impression the captain wanted it over, too. Nonetheless, he leaned back in his chair, which flowed and adjusted to his posture, and gently worked his lower back. He said, "Observer to the helm team. Hmm." I knew his headware would be feeding his buffers. "Ah, yes. How did you do at the Academy in hypertube mechanics?" He was referring of course, to the class of natural, but strangely multidimensional wormholes, noted for the way their entrance and exit points drifted through space.

I wanted to wince — this had been one of my shakier subjects. "I did quite well, sir."

"I believe a lot of your time will be occupied in adapting the theory and practice you learned at the Academy to the real world of starship navigation, which means learning the tricks of how helm ops personnel really track the motion of tube entry points and some of the more creative ways to ... er ... surf the curves inside the tubes. You'll love it."

"Surf the curves, sir?"

Rudyard let his coffee cup sit a moment while he made an expansive gesture. "We don't always have time to do everything absolutely according to textbook procedures, son. Sometimes we have to fly this ship by feel. That's something you'll have to learn."

"Of course, sir," I said, feeling more than a little nervous. How not-by-the-book did things get on this ship? I wondered.

"Anything else, Mr. Dunne?" Obviously a cue that the captain was finished with me.

There was one more thing I wanted to ask. "What should I do if I see another officer breaking regs, sir?"

He looked surprised. He leaned forward, elbows on the desk. "You catch somebody breaking regs on my ship, you report that officer either to Mr. Ferguson or directly to me. There is no room on this ship for such individuals. And captains on ships like this one have more discretion to deal with offenders than you've had hot dinners, son." He was smiling as he said it, but there was an edge in his voice that hadn't been there before, a suggestion of something nasty. I figured it was just captain's prerogative talking — his ship, his way.

But I did wonder what to do about Ferguson's request to see Sorcha that evening.

Rudyard, satisfied that he had explained to me how things worked on board his ship, dismissed me and ordered me to report to the leader of the helm operations team, SCO5 Janning, the ship's third in command. My ship layout info indicated Mr. Janning was working in his quarters at this very moment.

I sent him a note through ShipMind that I was on my way, and set off, hurrying through the corridors. When I found him, he was seated on his bunk, but his eyes were glazed, staring into the distance, mumbling things I couldn't make out. He was 'in the cloud' — his headware linked into ShipMind along with other senior bridge staff spread through the five crew decks. Knowing he wouldn't hear me if I called out, I pinged him over ShipMind and he opened his eyes in surprise. "Ah, Mr. Dunne, I presume! You found me. We'll make a helm officer out of you yet!" Janning was small but solid, with cropped auburn hair, brown eyes, a look of wry amusement. "You caught me in a remarkably tedious flight plan conference."

We shook hands; he wasn't out to break my hand like the captain and his smile looked genuine. Already I liked him. "Using the cloud, sir?"

Janning looked surprised that I knew about it. "Still trying to get the hang of using the bloody thing. We've only had the cloud interface installed for three months, amazing technology, all that data flashing around in your head. Kind of unsettling, like when you think people are talking about you behind your back. Suppose I'll get used to it, though." He added.

I glanced around his hardly-decorated quarters, "I keep looking for buttons to push and screens to read," I admitted, smiling a little nervously. He had a display page stuck to the wall above his tautly-made bed showing images of people I assumed were family: chunky, smiling folks crowded around a small table in a pub, gesturing with pint glasses of beer.

Janning laughed. "Takes a bit of getting used to, I must say. Still, we're slowly getting the bugs out."

"Slowly?"

"No system's perfect. On the other hand, it does improve response and data interpretation times when sensor feeds are piped straight into your brain for action, instead of the old days when you had to read everything off a display, report it to someone higher than you, who then had to act on it. It's also strange not having an actual bridge." He shook his head.

"And it really does work the way the engineers said it would?"

"Oh yes. Listen, have you had your headware upgrade shots yet?"

I nodded. "Took care of it last week, to allow for the neuroid growth and immune response time, sir."

"Good lad. You should be just about ready to plug into our training system. You'd be surprised at the number of newbie's we get who forget all about these things." Shaking his head. "Bloody morons!"

I had heard about the plans for this interface technology while at the Academy, and ten years earlier I remember my father talking about the basic theoretical principles. Last I heard the Service was still testing it, and there were rumors of protest from the manufacturers and contractors who supplied all the display technologies for the older ships. I mentioned this to Janning. He said, "That's all true. For a long while the idea of the cloud interface was in the toilet because lobbyists for the old system paid the Service procurement people lots of money to keep using the old displays and what-have-you. But a test bed vessel with a scratch-built version of this system got out there and proved conclusively that we were better off — and safer — this way than with the old way."

"The *Turing*, wasn't it, sir?"

He glanced at me, eyebrow cocked. "You know about that?"

"Yes, sir. I try to keep up with what's happening."

"How much do you know about the cloud, then?"

"Only that reaction times and task performance improved by an average of twenty-five to thirty percent in non-combat situations, and by as much as forty percent in combat and emergency situations. Uh, sir." I suppressed a smile.

"Mr. Dunne, I'm fairly impressed. Your service record says your father is an academic, working in the systems theory field."

"I first heard about the *Turing* test bed vessel from Dad, sir."

"Very good. I might just be able to work with you, I think."

"I hope so, sir."

"Do you have an interest in interstellar politics, son?"

I winced a little. "Somewhat, sir. Enough to know things are looking bad all over."

"Worse than bad, Mr. Dunne." He looked grim.

I ventured a comment, "Rumors at the Academy say we'll be at war with the Asiatics within a year."

"And what do you think?" Janning asked, surprised, watching me carefully.

"I am aware, sir, that the number and duration of the planetary brush wars around human space are on the increase, that people seem more desperate. Crazy, even. All that talk about the end of things, I suppose."

"And?"

Frowning, I tried to formulate an informed opinion on the spot. "I know that population is pressing against the limits of currently available real estate, that exploration budgets are being cut back, and that habitat construction is down on previous five-year periods."

Janning smiled then laughed kindly. "And to think you only thought you'd have to plot courses and read maps, right, Mr. Dunne?"

I allowed myself a nervous smile. "Yes, sir."

"You'll get no apologies from me. Before you are a helm operator, you are also a Service officer. You must be good at everything, despite having no time to attain said skills. It's a real bitch, if you ask me, having to be a soldier, a diplomat, and an explorer. There's still a whole bunch of things I have no clue about at all." He grinned, to put me at ease as much as possible.

"Time has always been a problem for me, sir."

He nodded. "Since when has time never been a problem for anyone? Eh?" He shook his head, wearing a rueful grin.

Something else was on my mind, since we were talking about these things. "Sir, what would we do if the Unity did approach the Community about our treaty obligations? If they were under threat, that is." I was thinking about news reports speculating that Unity Europa, the powerful metastate with strong nationalist tendencies and fragmented, distorted memories of Earth's Europe, was contemplating a move into territory claimed but not occupied by the Asiatic Cooperative Metasphere.

The popular wisdom held that it would be cheaper to take over someone else's land and remove the current owners than to build habitats or terraform marginal worlds. The Unity was very keen to maintain its European bloodlines, no matter the cost. And if the Unity did encounter trouble with the immense power of the Asiatics, the dominant superpower of human space, they would almost certainly seek our help, as stipulated in a mutual assistance treaty dating back twenty years, when things had been very different, and planetary real estate more abundant.

"Well," he said, "I imagine we'd have to go and help the mad froggy bastards!" He laughed. I was surprised that he referred to the Unity as froggy bastards — I thought such terms had been banished. He went on, "Anyway, if we were in trouble, we'd expect the Unity to come and help us, right?"

I nodded but said, "I can't honestly see them doing much to help us, if it came down to it, sir. If you'll pardon my saying so."

"Why do you think that, son?" He looked amused.

I could feel sweat beading around my neck. "I just thought, well, that the Community's too small, too unimportant, only one system. And the Unity, they're known for not wanting to endanger their military resources if they can possibly avoid it. I mean—"

Janning put a hand up. "Okay, okay, that's enough. I quite agree. I'm quite sure one of these fine days we're going to get swallowed up by the bloody Asiatics, and the Unity's going to stand on the sidelines wringing their hands, formally objecting in the strongest possible terms, but otherwise doing squat to help us, too much risk to their bloodlines. Blah, blah, blah. Bastards!"

"Although," he added, "what they'd do with us, I don't bloody know."

I was thinking about my mother, on New Jerusalem, a world, like most occupied worlds of human space, not part of any metastate. New Jerusalem did have loose diplomatic ties to the Unity, however. What would they do if war broke out across human space? What about all the microstates out there? The Polynesians, say, or the Inuits, or, for that matter, the Americans, each of whose enclaves claimed to be the "True" or "Real America". And what would my people, the scattered Australians, with strong blood ties both to Europe and the Asiatics, do?

More troubling still was the question of the many space-going cults, the largest of which were states unto themselves. The cults lived in vast hiveships; the cultists themselves belonged to a type of post-humanity who called themselves the *Qua*. They described themselves in their anti-ortho mindwar propaganda, as humans beyond human. They liked to say that ordinary people — a heavily contested term, to say the least — who would normally consider themselves orthodox were de facto Qua already, the way they relied on headware and other modifications. They reckoned there was no longer such thing as a true ortho. Not when kids can be born with headware seeds coded into their DNA.

Meanwhile, across human space, diplomats were trying to sort out which people were part of which overall state, and who controlled what, considering that even within single cities you could find people claiming citizenship in different states or metastates, never mind the complex populations of whole countries and whole worlds. Who belonged to what? It was maddeningly complex, and frequently led to small-scale warfare. And the more these brush wars in human space threatened to boil over into interstellar conflagrations, the more everyone wanted to know where the real boundaries were, assuming such boundaries could be enforceable, and would be proof against collateral damage. It would have been an exercise in madness, to try and work out the fine-print on those treaties.

"I'm inclined to think it'll all sort itself out, though, and we'll go back to being just plain 'human space' again, all of humanity in it together." I said at last.

Janning nodded, listening to me, and concealed his amusement at my naiveté. He said, "You really think that?

Ah, Mr. Dunne," He shook his head. "We'll never go back to those days. Not now, not with everyone waiting for Kestrel's other shoe to drop. These are strange times."

I knew about Kestrel. The facts: about forty years ago, a planet-sized, extremely dense Herrington Object, composed of heavy exotic matter, was on collision course with the planet Kestrel. Moments before the impact, and in front of more media than had ever been assembled anywhere, the Object disappeared into hyperspace. What had happened had never been adequately explained.

Not long after that, the Kestrel System's Orbital Habitat blew up, fusion cores destroyed, a situation which was also never fully explained. The less reputable media pushed colorful speculations salted with crazy rumors of godlike entities walking across the higher dimensions, and hinting broadly about a conspiracy among the major metastates to keep the truth about Kestrel a secret.

My dad always said the universe wasn't like this before Kestrel. I first heard about the Event when I was a kid, reading novels and seeing vids about Kestrel, and there were these crusading journalists who were trying to get the truth out, and how powerful forces would try to kill them. But the "truth" they depicted always seemed kind of lame and stupid.

Then one day Dad happened to mention that Kestrel was a real incident, a real place. That got me interested, and over the years I kept coming back to accounts of the Event. Even as a teenager, when I could immerse myself in recordings of the Event's media coverage, and I could watch the Object dwindle out of this universe, I still could not say what had happened. It was beyond scary. It was easy to see why so many people thought it was a genuine intervention from God — but which God, and why Kestrel, a drab, resource-rich and obscure planet, and not Earth, way back?

There were at least as many questions about Earth's death as there were about Kestrel's survival. The primary question about Earth, of course, was simply, "What happened?" Followed immediately by, "Why all the secrecy?" All that was known these days, nearly 150 years after the fact, was that one day for no readily apparent reason the Earth was destroyed. It was simply gone, leaving very little rubble or wreckage, and certainly no survivors. There was no warning that anyone knew of. There had been official inquiries and countless half-baked conspiracy theories. No one could agree on anything. All humanity knew was that the off-Earth offices of the United Nations, in one of their last meaningful acts, had embargoed any and all information, data and records, sealing them from public scrutiny indefinitely.

In this vacuum of usable information about Earth's loss, crazy ideas thrived. In the end there were three categories of unlikely theory to explain what had happened: it had been aliens (except we'd never encountered any aliens or detected any signs of aliens anywhere); it had been rogue human scientists doing dodgy research that somehow got out of control and consumed the planet (this was more likely); or it had been God (who, after all, moved in mysterious ways).

Maybe, since I was interested in questions about God, I should have entered the clergy. On the other hand, perhaps it was one reason why I wanted to enter the Service. Maybe I could find answers to my questions out in the dark.

Kestrel marked the beginning of a new uncertainty in human space. A lot of people took it as a sign, a terrible portent of an impatient God's irritation. Decades later, that initial wave of anxiety and fear stemming from Kestrel had ramified across human space to the point where we were seeing conflicts of ideologies and faith blown out to planetary scale. Death begat death, revenge begat revenge. One person's interpretation of what was happening collided with her neighbor's. Visions of God warred in a crucible of righteous hate. Holy wars, jihads, genocidal spasms, mass suicides — the news was full of these things, day after day. There was talk of the end of life as we knew it, perhaps even the end of the human race itself.

Which made me think of Mom, out there, in one of the Muslim towns of New Jerusalem. The last newsfeed from there I had seen showed rifts developing between orthodox and ultra-orthodox Shi'ite Muslims, among others. Only "true" Muslims would survive what was coming, they were saying. It was the same in the Jewish towns there, and with the Coptics and others. Everyone had a dream of truth, but some dreams were said to be truer than others. It was hard to bear the thought of my mother, whoever and whatever she was now, caught in the midst of this. The real truth dawned on me that wherever in human space she was, she could get caught in the growing chaos.

But she had made her choice.

"It's the Kestrel thing, isn't it?" I said, coming back to the present. "That's where it started."

Janning looked thoughtful for a moment and then said, "Yes, and no. Most of the crap flying around out there now is ancient crap, baggage we brought with us from Earth, stuff that was old even then. Now we just have the old misery spread out on a larger canvas, but with a pile of new crap, too, just for variety." He flashed a rueful, mirthless smile. "What Kestrel did was catalyze things. It came along at the wrong time, or maybe the right time. It scared us, the way thunderstorms used to scare ancient humans into dreaming up petty gods to explain everything." He looked thoughtful for a moment, then burst out laughing. "Listen to me talking shit, eh! Jesus!" He had a good laugh at himself. "Anyway, it could all be academic pretty soon, what with those mad bastards the Asiatics rattling their swords and whatnot!" He scratched his ear and grinned at me, exposing a small gap between his two front teeth. "Tell you what, I'll quite frankly be glad to get out into the dark again, sniff around the unexplored stuff. All these goddamn zealots and fanatics, they can have it all to themselves. Christ it gives me an ulcer just thinking about the bloody bastards!"

I decided I liked Janning. I could talk to him, unlike my conversation with Captain Rudyard, where talking seemed like something one had to endure. "Mr. Janning, I just came from talking to the captain."

He grinned at me. "That must have been fun for you!"

"I thought it might be just me, but he seemed kind of ..." I frowned, wondering how to put it.

"Forced?"

"Something like that, yes."

"He's okay — doesn't shove too many guys out the airlock."

I paused, feeling a sudden chill. "Pardon me?"

"Did he tell you about his discretion as captain?"

"Yes."

He nodded. "That comes down to summary execution of anybody who breaks regs in a particularly spectacular fashion. Following a court-martial, of course, just for form."

"You can't be serious."

His smile faded and for a moment I was certain he was going to tell me he was kidding, but he said, "Afraid so. If you do nothing else on this ship during your stay with us, don't, and I mean don't, piss off the captain."

I was sure I wasn't hearing this right. "He can't just kill people for breaking regs. That's why we have a Brig, and the Standard Code of Military Justice, and all that."

"Ah, but we are different. We go out beyond the borders of known space. In a way it puts us beyond the improving influence of human civilization, beyond the very pale, if you like. It's a different world out there. Not so jolly decent and sporting as life at the Academy, wot." He put on a toffee-nosed accent when referring to the Academy, then grew serious again. "It does things to some people, being out there."

"I see," I said, not seeing anything other than confusion. I suddenly didn't know what to say or think.

"So, Mr. Dunne," he said, breaking the uneasy silence.

"Uh, yes, sir?"

Janning grinned, slapped his thigh. "How are you at tracking hypertubes?"

"You have access to my Academy results, don't you?"

He nodded, tapped his forehead. "I certainly do, but numbers and tutor assessments don't mean a lot. They don't give much idea of your intuitive grasp of how spacetime works, your feel for the granularity of the quantum foam." He rubbed his thumb and forefinger together, as if feeling expensive fabric. "It's got a distinct texture, you know. When you've had a lot of experience, you can sort of feel it as you go through the tubes. It's the damnedest, most amazing thing."

"Yes, sir," I said, not knowing what to say about this. But I pressed ahead with an embarrassing matter. "Sir, I freely admit I didn't do stunningly well at the Academy, but—"

He jumped on this remark, cutting me off. He looked like a big cat pouncing on a particularly stupid mouse. "Aha, mistake number one! It had to happen sometime, and we might as well get it out of the way now. Feel better now you've done it and it's over? Mistake number two doesn't feel so bad. You've now screwed up once, the perfect record is already history, so you can relax a bit." He grinned, looking a bit crazy.

"Sir?"

Janning rolled his eyes. "Mr. Dunne, relax! I'm just trying to not be terribly pompous and officious, the way the helm team leader on my first assignment was. That guy was a sincere asshole, no mistake. William Do-It-Again Strickland. God, what a swine. I kept wondering why nobody had noticed how a huge bloody starship had been jammed up his fundamental orifice!"

I laughed and smiled. He went on.

"Your mistake, Dunne, was you said 'I didn't do stunningly well at the Academy, but.' It was the but that did you in. You don't say that word on this ship. If you didn't do so well, that's fine — we can work on that, and you will be working on it very hard until you can track and steer through tubes in your sleep. Just don't say but. Putting that but on the end makes you look like a suck-up, and I don't want that in my staff. I'd rather hear the unvarnished truth."

"But I—" I winced as I heard it come out of my mouth.

Janning made a loud buzzer noise. "You lose, Mr. Dunne." He grinned. "You were going to say you were taught all this crap at the Academy about being all jolly and decent, weren't you?" I had to admit that the Academy faculty did like to affect a certain very Anglo culture that felt rather jaunty and amusing, but this swiftly turned to terrifying fury if you screwed up and the punishment details were given out.

"I wouldn't have put it quite like that. They said the way to get by was to defer to one's superior officers."

Janning shook his head. "Wrong. My number one rule is that most of what you learn at the Academy is bullshit and obsolete by the time you get in your first ship. Technology moves too damn fast for those guys to keep current. Plus, they don't have the budget to give cadets sufficient space duty experience, so when green kids like you turn up for your deployments, you're too scared and intimidated to think for yourself, which is the one skill you absolutely need. The chain of command is important, yes. But if you receive a stupid order, it doesn't matter who said it. Stupid orders can get you killed, or your whole bloody ship destroyed."

"Even if the captain issues a direct order, and it's stupid, I should stop and question it in front of him? I'd be atomized!"

Janning said, "Dunne, officers don't get more intelligent as they get promoted. They have more experience and often better judgment. But in this Service promotions often come through whom you know, not what you know. Just because you're a fresh graduate doesn't mean your ideas are necessarily worse than the captain's. So think! Use the brain in there, don't just be an order-following zombie."

I stood there in silence for a long while, my mind in turmoil. I was sworn to defend the Community and its founding treaties, but I was also sworn to obey the orders of my superior officers. The chain of command, cadets are told, is not there for the amusement of senior officers, it is a tool that saves lives and regulates existence. If someone gives you an order, you are sworn to follow it, or face dire consequences. But here was Janning, telling me something that seemed, in a word, subversive. "This is ... it's impossible to ... I can't just..."

Janning nodded. "The Academy?"

"Yes, sir. I spent four years having every bit of independent thought, every bit of initiative, all of it beaten out of me, literally beaten out of me sometimes. They, they..." I couldn't say it. The things the senior cadets, the instructors, at the Academy got away with, appalling things, things that would count as torture and human rights abuse in any other context, all to make sure cadets understood about being part of the group. The denial of individuality and the destruction of personal identity were key parts of Academy life. I heard again and again that it was necessary to make us part of the team, and in turn part of a crew.

You mustn't rock the boat.

Janning looked at me, with sad eyes. "I know, James."

Suddenly I felt like I was falling apart. Feelings I had crushed to dust a long time ago were threatening to spring to life, but I fought them back, like a good cadet. A strong cadet. Emotions were dangerous. I had fought them back before, and would again, certain nothing could touch my core. Not those bastards, not anybody.

But this guy Janning, showing me a shred of decency and maybe even a kind of friendship, he got to me. He threatened my core. I took a lot of deep breaths.

"Mr. Janning, when do I start my training?"

Four

Eclipse left the station at 1330 hours and departed Ganymede Space. Janning allowed me to observe the helm cloud in action. It was like standing at the back of the room, watching the others sitting around a circular table having a meeting, but with each person present conjuring shapes and images in striking colors from the plethora of sensor and system information feeding into their heads. Janning sat at the head of this table, supervising and guiding, as his officers responded to Captain Rudyard's commands from the bridge cloud.

As we cleared Jovian Space and the magnetospheric interference from Ganymede and Jupiter, the captain, who appeared to sit right behind Janning, gave the orders for hypertube location and transition.

I saw Helm Officer Kyne check the local hypertube weather feed. She quickly located a promising tube entry point — they showed up as flaws of negative mass in the structure of space-time — and steered the ship towards it. Once Kyne had the ship aligned for entry, Captain Rudyard sent the order for tube entry. Kyne slipped us into the tube at 1403 hours. Her effortless control impressed the hell out of me. There were several other possible flaws, but she picked this one. No protracted pondering or studying of the data; she just picked the right point from the display and tossed the ship through it like a paper glider.

Inside the tube, Kyne deployed the ship's tube grapple fields and began manipulating the tube's hyperdimensional structure to her will. The interior topology of a hypertube is typically a knot or loop in many dimensions; and it took great skill to fight the curvature and make the tube deposit your ship where you wanted to go. It often took several tube rides to reach one's destination, but Kyne steered us without visible effort or strain.

"Tube egress in five, four..." She counted down. Nobody looked as tense as I felt. Suppose the modeling of the tube's topology had been flawed and Kyne had programmed slightly incorrect information into the grapple-drivers — we could wind up deep inside a star. These things happened. It was why several people on the helm team worked through the same datasets individually, and made sure most of them agreed on their findings. Also, I had never done this outside of a simulator, and it was a completely different situation when you could see graphic depictions of the knotty hypertwists conjured before you in a false-color mathematical horror, like something alive. We're trying to travel through that? There was talk that such representations were only shadows of shadows, that even augmented human brains could not deal with the spatial and geometric conundrums represented by these tangled paths between distant points. But only once I got to the Academy did I begin to understand this. Why in hell had I chosen helm as my career specialization? Had I been drunk that day?

I think, as I now look back, I chose it because it was about the hardest thing I could pick with my marks. I was never one to take the easy way out.

"Now!" Kyne said, not raising her low voice. *Eclipse* exited the tube back into real space. We'd been in the tube just 19 minutes, a short ride as tube travel went.

Another officer named Marsden, reported our new position in galactic coordinates — we had managed to miss the local stars. I breathed again. We were about seventy lightyears from Ganymede, above the galactic plane. Ship's time was 1422 hours.

Unexplored space. I had never felt so alone. So cold.

Mapping, Astronomy, and Planetary Science teams set to work charting and studying phenomena within the cubic lightyear volume around us. The ship dispersed clouds of tiny remote full-spectrum sensorbots that shot off at relativistic velocities in all directions.

Captain Rudyard congratulated Mr. Janning and his people for an excellent tube selection. It wasn't every day a ship found such a long tube, or one stable enough to allow for extended topological manipulation. He said it like he was talking about an excellent choice of wine with dinner. Janning nodded, and through the cloud interface, executed a minimal bow.

As tense as I had ever felt lying curled up in a simulator egg on Deck A, watching Kyne work her practiced magic with the blinding flood of data and transmuting it into information she used to move the ship across the galaxy in a matter of a few minutes, I nonetheless felt a sense of wanting it to have been more exciting. I was filled with a kind of disappointment that bridge operations weren't more dramatic, fraught with frowning, glaring, snapping-order tension. Somehow, watching it all unfold was rather dull and businesslike. Information flowed the way it should; the ship responded like a vessel a fifth her size; we moved.

Then again, I thought, I probably wouldn't want things to get all tense, just for the sake of entertainment. My limited exposure to helm simulations had already demonstrated that.

I unplugged from the cloud and began my program of bridging studies, learning how to do the impossible and make it look dull and routine.

At 1930 hours I was allowed to quit for the day. I cracked the hatch on the sim egg, one of many in a room full of such eggs, and climbed out into the simulation control room. The room was lit with a dull red glow and I immediately noticed the sweet tinge of ship processed air. Although the egg's environment processors were good, the air outside the egg's stuffy confines was a welcome relief. My legs weren't as stiff as I expected; the smartchair in the egg had been busy massaging my muscles all afternoon. I checked in with Simulations Training Officer Hinz, who said only that I had done okay for a newbie, and I headed to the Officer's Mess on Deck E. Walking along, riding lifts, still trying to get my saluting right, it occurred to me that while I felt drained and tired from the effort of my sim work, I couldn't remember a damn thing that I had done. My hands felt a little twitchy, and images of diagrams and half-memories of equations flashed back and forth in the back of my mind, but that was all.

I found Sorcha in the Officer's Mess, sitting alone next to a wall covered in fixed displays showing high-res views of local space in various wavelengths. I got my dinner, the infamous "space chunder," some kind of bland casserole with lumps that might have been beef, and thin gravy with tasteless vegetables. I threaded my way between the backs of chairs, and dodged pointy elbows, to join Sorcha.

The Mess was a cavernous space for a ship, fully ten meters across, with room for perhaps fifty crew to eat at any given time. Right now, the place was packed with people on the late dinner shift. They were wiping vatbread across their plates, soaking up the last of their gravy, and chatting with each other in loud, convivial voices. In stark contrast, Sorcha sat to one side, looking at the displays and yawning, her own food untouched. She radiated a strong aura of "piss off!" that, from a newbie on the crew, probably seemed laughable to the more experienced hands.

"The food here can't be that bad!" I said with a smile, hoping to lighten her mood.

She turned to look at me. I thought she looked tired, but she managed a weak smile.

I took a cautious bite of my chunder. *What the hell is this crap?* I thought. Changing the subject, I nodded at the displays, "Any word from the probes yet?"

Sorcha shrugged. "Prelim report says this region fits the Weissner-Lusky curve pretty well, so its basically routine." Which meant no obviously inhabited worlds, no evidence of EM activity other than normal output of celestial bodies, no strange deformations or anomalies in the fabric of space-time itself, beyond the usual things. But of course, there were some planetary systems, rich in the kinds of minerals required by the teeming billions back in human space.

"And how are you after a hard day in the sims?" she asked, poking at the food.

For a moment it was as though I could answer her question, and had a lot to say, but as soon as I opened my mouth to speak, there was nothing there. "I was …" I couldn't remember a thing from the hours I put in.

Sorcha nodded. "You feel like you've done a twenty-k run, and played fifty simultaneous games of chess, but you can't remember it to save your life, right?"

Smiling and feeling foolish I admitted, "Yes, that's right. The sims at the Academy weren't like this."

"Everything's different now, James." She said while staring at an x-ray emission image of a nearby hot star cluster. It looked like there could be a supermassive black hole or two in there.

Sensing a mood shift, I tried a new tack: "How was your department head?"

Sorcha shrugged again in a very liquid movement. "He was okay. His name is Shackleton. SSO5. Says he thinks I'll do. That was how he put it, 'I think you'll do, girlie.'"

"What did you think of that?" I asked.

She looked nonplussed, and I guessed she wasn't used to such comments. "Bit of a shock to the system, to be honest."

"How come?" I tried some more experimental nibbles on the casserole. It was adequate, and mostly warm. Sorcha pushed hers around her standard white china plate, where the glop sat congealing.

She allowed herself a lop-sided smile she obviously didn't feel. "You know, all through the Academy I kinda coasted. I just fell through everything, and landed on my feet at the end, like this very brainy cat." She arched one eyebrow, thinking about her former life.

"Really? I kind of dug my way through the whole thing like a dumb mole."

She ignored my comment. "All the bloody good it did us, eh? We still wound up here." She sat back, arms crossed. I felt the table vibrate as she kicked the leg with her boot.

"Have you," I ventured after a long moment, feeling tense inside as I said it, "thought anymore about...?"

She coughed out a bitter laugh. "What do you think I've been thinking about all afternoon? Propulsion problems? Spare parts fabrication?"

Stung, I felt my face flush. "It'll work, you know."

"It might work, but what about down the road from now?"

"What do you mean?"

She looked at me like I was the stupidest person she had ever met. "James, is there anybody in there? I mean after! Say your plan works, they're not going to be all that thrilled about it are they?"

"But you'd have evidence!"

"I just don't know. I don't know." She looked unhappy. "I hoped my first day of space duty would be, you know. Not so ... not so full of dread!"

"Maybe Ferguson really does just want to talk to you about your career."

Another bitter laugh. "At 2330? It's a little outside office hours, don't you think? And he didn't want to talk to you, did he? He only picked on the girl."

"He picked on the extreme brain, too. You've got command potential is what he's probably thinking."

She laughed out loud. "Command potential!"

The evening ground on. At 2315 Sorcha finally said she was willing to have a go at the feeble plan we had cooked up. As we prepared our headware for the trick, I admitted to her that I thought she was going to say forget it. She said, "All that's required for evil to triumph is for good men to do nothing."

"Well, obviously," I said, surprised at her comment, but feeling strange about this whole business.

"And that's why I decided to go along with it. This way, we have something on our side if things get out of hand."

At that moment I thought, but kept to myself, *and no good deed goes unpunished*.

At 2330 Sorcha went to Ferguson's cabin on Deck D. I was recording her sight and sound streams in the buffers of my headware; later I could download and encrypt the file into some kind of external storage or mail it somewhere for safekeeping — once we got back to human space.

Sorcha was shaking a little, mouth pursed shut, when she left the Mess. She told me not to wish her luck, and explained that whenever people wished her luck all kinds of horrible things happened to her. So I just smiled as best I could. She was a tough woman; she could take care of herself. And I couldn't see Ferguson seriously trying to proposition a fellow crewman on her first day aboard ship. It seemed unlikely that a veteran of the Service would pull something that stupid. The man had to have professional standards of conduct to honor, and he had the captain to worry about too.

I sipped some more bad fabricated coffee in the Mess and followed the scene in my head.

Sorcha knocked on Ferguson's door. She was right on time, but breathing fast. The lighting in the corridor was low, considering the hour.

Ferguson called through the door, "Come!"

She slid the door aside revealing Ferguson's modest quarters. Where Captain Rudyard's office was stark to the point of sterility, Ferguson surrounded himself with memorabilia from his long career. The area was filled with doodads and souvenirs from across the many other worlds and habitats of human space, particularly those in the loose arrangement of the Home System Community. Sorcha glanced around the room taking in the large and colorful novelty hats, long silk women's gloves, miscellaneous and faintly pornographic statuettes, mysterious scarves, and tiny chrome rocketships on onyx pedestals. And there was no shortage of pictures, either. They were arranged in rows of cheap Active Paper displays along one wall. I assumed they were vids rather than static shots. He also had a huge collection of actual books, the printed and bound kind, packed behind a mounted and locked wall cabinet that would be worth a fortune to a dealer in such rarities.

Ferguson was still in uniform, and seated at a small plain metal desk, that was a dull service-gray color. He was working through documents and plans on a broad sheet of

Active Paper; a tall ceramic mug of steaming black coffee or tea on one corner. He looked up to say, "Miss Riley, very good of you to come by at this hour," and I could see he was exhausted. He stood, shook Sorcha's hand, and showed her to a seat. I didn't hear what she said in reply.

Once seated, Ferguson moved to sit, but then remembered his manners: "Can I prepare you a refreshment, Miss Riley? Some hot chocolate, perhaps?"

The old bastard was being quite decent, I thought, considering the lecture he gave us both in the Hole this morning. So far he didn't seem like someone about to proposition a female member of the crew.

Sorcha shook her head no to his offer of refreshment. He smiled, looking like a fussy and eccentric uncle, and returned to his desk, where he fiddled with the window sizes on his paper for a moment. It occurred to me that maybe he was troubled by the peculiar circumstances, too.

Ferguson got down to the matter at hand. "Miss Riley, the captain and I have been looking over your Academy record."

"Really, sir?" Sorcha said. I could hear the faint edge of sarcasm she was trying to keep out of her voice. Ferguson didn't seem like a man who would be tolerant of her background in student activism.

He went on, "I must say, we are both extremely impressed, very impressed indeed, by not only the quality of your performance but also by the sheer hard work you put in, especially considering your, ah, difficulties with certain parts of the curriculum." He tried on a weak smile that didn't last.

"Thank you, sir."

"The captain asked me to ask you, however, if you are quite sure you want to stay with your choice of engineering as a career track. With your talents and single-minded drive, we both think you would make excellent command material. A person like you could make captain before you turn forty. Before fifty, certainly."

I suppressed a laugh, thinking about my prediction.

Sorcha cleared her throat, probably thinking much the same thing. "I am quite happy working in engineering, sir. The theoretical and practical problem-solving challenges in this field are of extreme interest to me, sir."

Ferguson looked troubled as he stared across at Sorcha, fingering his thin moustache. The steel fuzz of his hair caught the flat light from overhead. His eyes were lost in shadow. "Miss Riley, you are of course entirely free as an officer in the Service to choose your own career path and explore your options."

"I appreciate that freedom very much, sir."

"It's just that we don't often get a junior officer come along with such potential."

"I understand, sir. Is there anything else? It's quite late and I have a full day of sims tomorrow."

Ferguson sat back, thinking about things for a bit. Then, not looking at Sorcha, he said, "Did you really think I asked you here tonight to make improper advances towards you, Miss Riley?"

I nearly choked. Sorcha, a cooler person than I in a pinch, took a long breath, and said, "Frankly, sir, yes I did. I would be interested in knowing how you knew I thought that."

"Walls have ears, Miss Riley. There are no secrets on a ship like this." He worked the sheet of paper and brought up a text file. "I have here a transcript of your conversation this morning with SSO1 Dunne."

God! I thought back to the morning, which suddenly seemed like eons ago. The walls must have been covered with surveillance spray. I thumped my forehead.

"Thank you for informing me of this, Mr. Ferguson. I will consider myself corrected on this issue, sir."

Ferguson smiled, looking like a happy uncle again. "Excellent, Miss Riley. Be sure to tell Mr. Dunne this as well. I'm sure he, too, will benefit from this revelation."

Sorcha shot me a note as she left the interview with Ferguson and headed for her quarters:

> Well, James, it seems I might have been a
> tad too suspicious. And perhaps the captain and
> Mr. Ferguson are both far more suspicious than

either of us. What a way to find out what newbie's
are thinking! I don't know whether to scream or
laugh. What a relief! I can get on with doing my
job now. Good night! S.

My quarters were a shared cabin for four junior male
officers on Deck C; it was a small room with two double-
bunks separated by a narrow gap, with an anteroom to one
side for ablutions and storage. I had dumped my kit here
earlier today, and now I found it still on my bunk, one of
the lower beds. Someone had stuck a sheet of Active Paper
up on the wall between the two sets of beds, and set it to
display a feed of the outside starscape, which would have
been a nice idea if they had used fresh paper, but this was
a much-used sheet whose image was poor, there was a lot
of static along the fold-lines, and there were areas with crap
color reproduction, bad focus, and clumps of pixons not
showing any color at all. Up close I also heard a steady,
annoying background hum from it. I could imagine that
keeping me up all night, so I turned it off.

The other bunks were unoccupied. My bunkmates were
all stuck on the graveyard shift, I supposed. Poor bastards.
I got changed for the few sweet hours of sleep I could enjoy
before getting up at 0530.

I couldn't stop thinking: Rudyard and Ferguson were
prepared to spy on their own crew! I was still trying to get
over this. They knew about our plan, which meant
Ferguson knew I was listening in on his chat with Sorcha.
I realized that I was screwed. I figured Sorcha would be
okay, since she was at ground zero when the big revela-
tions went off. But I was in for trouble, I just knew it in
my bones. The whole miserable plan had been my idea —
my little plan to try and ingratiate myself with a girl! God,
what a worm I was.

I got ready for bed but was feeling like crap. I walked
back to my bunk and climbed in. The covers were cold,
so I got them to warm up a little. It took a while, with so
much on my mind, but with help from my headware I
drifted off around 0100.

⊕ ⊕ ⊕

I yelled in surprise more than pain as I suddenly hit the cold tile floor between the bunks. Then something hoisted me up to my feet and repeatedly slammed me against the wall, stunning me before I could think.

My eyes tried to adjusted to the darkness and I began to make out the sketchy details of my attacker: a broad, dull face; expressionless eyes; balding head; and a Service owner-logo emblazoned on the forehead.

I saw it all in slow motion but only had time to think, *Disposable* before someone else grunted and plunged a huge fist deep into my gut, winding me. I doubled over, shocked, wide-eyed, panicking — I couldn't breathe — A black-clad knee shot up and hit me square in the face. Blinding shock. I heard my nose crunch — bones shift. Hot blood and snot squirting.

My whole world was sticky pain.

I don't remember much of the rest of the beating. Only later did I put together in my head that I had been attacked by three disposable enlisted men. Not that they were enlisted, as such. There were no human enlisted men or women in the Service, but that's what these things were called. Disposables were biological, nanofactured androids whose insanely cheap production costs and the assurances of the companies supplying the fabrication technology that the creatures had no higher-level awareness, no souls, and no real inner life led customers to feel quite okay about recycling the androids when they had done their jobs. Making them, of course, perfect soldiers.

They were also ideal thugs and enforcers.

Once I was conscious again, in the Infirmary, and before everything started going wrong, I thought I understood the message well enough: don't rock the boat.

"Mr. Dunne? Are you awake, Mr. Dunne?"

I looked up through eyes that felt sort of all right. They weren't puffy and sore anyway. I could make out light bars overhead, and smell the biting stink of antiseptics and high-end medical machinery, and a sharp whiff of ozone. A doctor was leaning over me, and Captain Rudyard, his face full of compassion, stood on the other side, looking down at me. Rudyard smelled of freshly fabbed clothing and strong aftershave. His dark eyes looked particularly sad and shadowed.

I felt little pain. When I tried moving my toes they worked fine; my fingers, too. As memory kicked in, and I recalled the early, terrifying moments from the attack, I had sufficient poise to wonder if the enlisted men had already been recycled to remove all evidence. It would be the prudent thing to do.

"Mr. Dunne?" Rudyard said.

I tried to focus on his shadowed face. "Captain?"

"Don't try to do anything strenuous yet, son. The bots are still going about their business in there. That was quite a fall you sustained last night." He said this with a straight face that looked quite believable. I looked at him, squinting, trying to see traces of the truth trying to escape from his lie. There were none. He said, "You picked a damned inconvenient time to go on the sick list, too, son."

The doctor, a dark-skinned man in his early thirties, said, "This may not be the best time to get the boy all agitated, sir."

I looked around. The Infirmary had room for twelve beds, but only the one next to mine was occupied.

Sorcha, unconscious. I could only see her dark face over the covers, but I recognized healing cuts and bruises on her face.

"Oh God, oh God..." I whispered, my voice dry and hoarse, seeing her lying there.

The captain, unaware of my alarm, pressed ahead. "While you were unconscious, Mr. Dunne, the scientists made an interesting discovery. I thought you'd be interested."

I grabbed the doctor, pulling him down to face me. "What happened to Sorcha? What happened to her?"

The doctor freed himself easily; I wasn't all that strong yet. He said, "Somebody tried to sexually assault Miss Riley during the night."

I was speechless. Looking at her and thinking. Thinking a lot. *God... If she hadn't gone along with my stupid idea. Christ on a bloody stick, I've really screwed things up now.* And I was disgusted that even at this shocking moment, seeing the unconscious results of my genius handiwork lying beside me, I was also thinking about my chances with her.

"She managed to, ah, incapacitate her attackers and raise an alarm, however, before passing out," the doctor added.

Sorcha. I know you for one day and I get you in trouble like this!

The captain was still talking. "Mr. Dunne, we have found what we think might be an artifact of non-human origin."

I wasn't interested. Or, rather, I was, in a remote corner of my mind where the fingers of guilt couldn't reach. It was astounding news, if it was true. But right at that moment, looking at Sorcha, watching her bruises heal, all I felt was crippling guilt at what I'd done.

"Captain, I think Mr. Dunne is too tired—"

"Nonsense, Doctor. He's just the man for this little job."

That got my attention. I looked up at the captain's droopy face. "Sir?" Wondering what fresh punishment I was to receive for trying to rock the boat.

Rudyard waited until he had my full attention. "This artifact, son. We think, from initial scans, we think it might be a ship of some kind."

This was big news, but I was in the wrong mood to think about it. "Yes, sir," I said, my voice barely there. I kept stealing glances at Sorcha.

"We're sending a boarding party over there to have a bit of a look, and you've been volunteered."

Confused, I lay there, staring. "Sir?"

"Well," Rudyard said, "Mr. Ferguson and I think you're the ideal candidate for the mission. Impeccable character. Resourceful."

And, I thought to myself with horror, *dispensable*.

Five

Over bad coffee at morning tea, Janning asked me, "And what did you say?" We were in the Officer's Mess. The displays on the wall this time were all showing views of the artifact.

I sipped my fabbed coffee, taking it slow. The bots were almost finished fixing my insides, but I was still tender in a lot of places. There was other damage the bots could never reach. I didn't remember everything the enlisted men did to me, but the doctor had been quite specific listing my assorted injuries. Nothing was broken, and the bruises were already clearing up.

As far as the doc could tell, I hadn't been violated. I nodded after hearing this detail. Back at the Academy, if you screwed up particularly badly, there was just about no limit to what the provosts might do to you to make you sincerely regret not conforming to proper cadet behavior, and they weren't above rape, as I well knew.

It was the atom bomb of cadet punishment, used rarely, but when it was used, it left an impression across the whole Academy. Cadets who had been through it said, if they were able to talk about it, that you were left wishing they had just killed you and been done with it.

Deciding that I'd gotten off lightly for my first offence, I resolved, lying in the Infirmary that morning, that I would try to become a model officer. Except I also remembered seeing Sorcha next to me, bruises and cuts healing as I watched. It's difficult now to convey the anger I felt about what they had tried to do to her.

"Well?" Janning prompted me back to the present. He had come to fetch me from the Infirmary earlier, saying that he had to look after his people. I hadn't told him what happened, but I suspected he already knew.

"I said 'Yes, sir, whatever you say, sir.' What else could I say?"

Janning dunked a shortbread biscuit in his black tea. "There is that." He looked thoughtful, staring at the displays. "Why you, though, Dunne?"

"The captain said I was resourceful and of good character."

"And you are, aren't you? I've seen your Academy record. You did very well. Upper half of your graduating class. Decent marks throughout. And you got a space rotation right after graduation. Lesser graduates are stuck ashore for months waiting for an assignment."

I looked at him. "You think the captain meant what he said about me?" It was hard to believe.

"You're too hard on yourself, James. Believe in yourself more. This is a real honor the captain's given you here."

Thinking about it, I couldn't see why Janning would lie to me.

And, looking at those displays, the strange misshapen alien ship out there, I had to admit it looked like exactly the kind of thing for which I had signed onto the Service. A grand adventure among the stars. If exploring the first alien ship ever discovered wasn't a grand adventure, well, I didn't know what was! Quite apart from the shocking notion that other beings, non-human beings built this vessel and sent her on her way, there was also the exciting and terrifying prospect that some of these beings might be aboard. How would we deal with that? Centuries of science fiction and philosophical speculation would, I thought, turn out to be unhelpful when faced with the real thing. I imagined the captain and his senior staff trying to plan for every imaginable contingency, all the while knowing that they could only plan for things about which they could make intelligent guesses. What if we encountered something genuinely new over there? I allowed myself a small smile, thinking that Ferguson would almost certainly take the view that if necessary they'd just blow up the alien ship and be done with it.

And it was an epochal event. I felt warily lucky to have been chosen for the team, even if I couldn't quite fathom why someone with no experience like me was even going along, when there must be several people on this ship better qualified. I even caught myself feeling a flutter of excitement over the prospect. Maybe Ferguson and the captain figured I'd learned my lesson and were ready to treat me like a regular officer, with appropriate duties. I certainly felt like I'd learned the lesson, learned it well. Don't rock the boat.

"James?" Janning was waving a hand before my eyes.

"Oh. Sorry, sir. Just thinking." My coffee was going cold. I was staring at the displays.

"Pretty daunting prospect, though, I would've thought. Who knows what the hell things are like over there."

"True," I said, and sipped some coffee.

"I could probably get you out of it; need you for urgent training, priority matters, that kind of thing. If you like."

Looking at him, I saw that he was trying to help me, and I liked that. "It's all right, sir. I want to go. It's the chance of a lifetime, right?"

Janning saw the same ship I saw, but his face didn't register excitement. He looked very uneasy about it. "If you're sure it's what you want."

"Mr. Janning, I slogged my guts out through four long miserable years at that joke of a bloody Academy entirely so that I could have a shot at something like this." I hadn't realised quite how tightly I was holding my cup. My knuckles were white. There was a trembling edge to my voice, a note of anger I hadn't intended. Taking a breath, I put my cup down and sat back in the chair.

Janning looked startled. "Mr. Dunne — James. Are you...?"

He meant, was I all right? And, truth be told, I didn't feel all right. I felt squeezed from about nine directions at once. All I wanted, when I signed on to the Service, was to do my best, make the most of my humble talents, and have a quiet, steady sort of career, and see the stars.

I certainly didn't expect what was now laid before me. What if I screwed up? You didn't want to find yourself in the middle of perhaps the biggest event in human history — and screwing up. You didn't want history to remember you as a fool.

Once I'd settled down a little, I confided some of this anxiety to Janning. He nodded. "Thought it might be something like that. Entirely understandable. I mean, that's partly why I offered to get you out of it."

I shrugged. "What I don't understand is, why me? This is an exploration ship, right? There must be loads of people on board who'd jump at the chance to—"

Janning put his hand up to interrupt. He looked awkward. Leaning forward, whispering, he said, "James, just between you and me and the fab machine, nobody wants to go to that ship. The captain asked for volunteers among those officers you mentioned. They all turned out to be sick, or busy with paperwork, or on study leave, or whatever. And, frankly, I wouldn't go over there, either."

"Sir?"

"I've got a family, James. Kids. And that ship out there, I mean it's just ... I don't know, there's something not right about it." I thought I saw him shudder; he looked pale.

I frowned, thinking about it. "Nobody volunteered? Nobody?"

"There's Blackmore and Grantleigh, of course, too senior in their departments to get out of it, but everyone else just plain refused. The captain's furious, but he's not doing anything about it. He understands their reluctance. And besides, he's got Ferguson to go for him. You can imagine the blazing row they had over that!"

"So, what ... I'm there to make up the numbers?"

"I wouldn't put it quite so bluntly, but..." He cocked his head a little.

I shook my head sadly.

"Plus," Janning went on, "they do think you have real promise."

I nearly swore. Neither of us said anything for a while. Then Janning said, "Anyway, we can squeeze your sim training around the mission, once you get back."

"Sounds good, sir. My apologies for the outburst, sir."

He waved his hand. "No worries."

We sat silently for some time. Janning got me a fresh coffee; he replaced his tea.

The alien ship was a strange-looking thing. Early reports from the science crew indicated it might be some kind of hollowed-out asteroid, but with bits added on and other alterations. They also said it showed signs of profound age, indicated by micrometeoroid impacts consistent with being in space for thousands of years. Now it was adrift and tumbling, with no detectable power or EM emissions. Janning looked back at the displays, "Ugly bastard, eh?"

"It isn't pretty, that's for sure."

"Techs say it's something like five-k's long, did you know that?"

I nodded. Rudyard had arranged for me to receive all info regarding the artifact via dedicated feed straight to my headware. I was aware of my buffers filling with data even as I sat here sipping bad coffee.

"You don't suppose there's, you know... actual..." Janning could hardly bring himself to say the word.

"Aliens, sir?" I arched an eyebrow.

He looked uncomfortable, fidgety. "Well, yeah, frankly."

"I don't know, sir. I suppose there's only one way to find out," I said. The question of whether or not I was going on the Contact mission sorted, I was back thinking about Sorcha, and about the apparent nasty undercurrents of shipboard life. My sense of excitement had ebbed; now I felt tense for different reasons.

Janning frowned and looked hard at me. "Are you all right, Dunne? I know you had a nasty fall last night and all..."

Closing my eyes for a moment, I set my coffee mug down on the table and sighed. "Mr. Janning," I opened, "permission to speak freely and off the record?"

He looked surprised, no doubt thinking we had a better rapport going than I did. "Uh, of course, yes." He gestured at me to go on but now frowning.

I explained what really happened last night, and that it wasn't some random spasm of violence. "Either the captain or Ferguson sent them." And saying this, I found myself glancing at the nearby walls and ceiling, looking for the faint telltale sheen of surveillance spray. It was impossible to see from this angle.

Janning did not look shocked. He put his own cup down. "Why did Miss Riley feel so threatened?" he asked.

"Sir, how long since you were at the Academy?"

Janning looked up at the ceiling, mumbling and counting on his fingers. "Twenty-four years. Why?"

"What were cadet initiation rituals like then?"

He flashed a wide carousing sort of grin. "Perfectly harmless fun. Nothing to worry about. You know."

This wasn't going anywhere. "Let's just say things aren't so harmless and amusing these days. Sorcha had reason to worry about senior officers who are used to getting what they want."

Janning began to get it, but he still didn't understand. He just nodded. And I explained my plan, the one that had backfired so hugely.

Janning couldn't suppress a laugh. "That was your real offense right there, Dunne."

"I don't understand."

He said, leaning across, so I didn't misunderstand, "You tried to gain power over the powerful. And they caught you at it, the same as they catch everyone who tries it. Why do you think newbies like you are put in the Hole first thing? They want to see what you're really like. Not what your record says you're like, or your school history and psych evaluations; but who you really are."

I felt stupid. "So what do we do about what happened to Sorcha and me last night?"

Janning sighed. "You know I can't answer that. The official record indicates you had a nasty fall in the middle of the night. Miss Riley ran into some defective disposable troops, dispatched them, and will be fine."

I covered my face with my hands, trying to come to grips with all this. "And now I get to visit an alien spacecraft. Who knows what might happen to me there?" I said this with the correct degree of irony to convey the sense of doom I felt.

Janning had the honesty to say sadly, "I think that would be the captain's thinking, yes."

I swore quietly, and said, "Yes, sir. It is."

Janning sipped his tea. "When do you go?"

"I don't know. Later. They haven't told me." I tapped my head.

"Make sure you hit the sims hard in the meantime, then."

I stared at him. Somehow he had found a way to exist on this ship without losing his mind. On one hand he was sympathetic, which seemed genuine. But on the other hand, he was also part of the same culture to which the captain and Ferguson belonged, that did not see abuse of power as a glitch in the system, but as the system itself. Right then, I couldn't see how to get my head into that culture. I'd been on the wrong end of all kinds of abusive crap most of my life, and thought that after I left the Academy I was done with it at long last. My new life would be different. Life among the stars would be clean and bright, the way space itself looked in pictures. But space, when you got out amongst it, was full of dirt and frozen muck and piss.

I wondered how I was going to fit in.

I would have to look past what had happened to Sorcha. Could I see it as a kind of discipline?

Morning tea over, Janning clapped me on the shoulder and shooed me off to the care of Simulations Training Officer Hinz.

Hours passed. Locked inside the simulator egg, my body and brain were learning things without my conscious mind ever getting involved; I wasn't even aware of the time. I was scheduled for an early lunch that day which was bland fabbed food, rather than anything real — operating budgets didn't allow for real food at every meal. I ate in a hurry, feeling a sick dread that Sorcha would walk in at any moment. I didn't know what she'd say, and I didn't want to know. My meal wolfed down, I headed back to the sims, back to that dreamless dark of subconscious education. When one of Hinz's junior officers later cracked open the shell, she told me it was

1540, and that the captain wanted to see me immediately, in the cloud. I plugged in where I was.

"Mr. Dunne. How are you feeling now?" Captain Rudyard said from the head of the table. Ferguson was next to him, along with two other officers I didn't know.

I swallowed and cleared my throat. "Much improved, thank you, sir. Thoughtful of you to ask." I glanced around. A moving holographic image of the artifact floated over the center of the table — a real-time feed from one of the many sensorbots studying it. I could almost feel the data feed impinging on my mind, full of the latest findings. The ready indicator icon flashed in the corner of my visual field; I checked the feed and blinked as a wealth of knowledge appeared in my conscious mind. The artifact was not a hollowed out asteroid after all, but was a manufactured structure. Current estimates of age said it was perhaps four to five thousand years old. Its power plant might be a form of high-efficiency matter-conversion system, and that the vast size of the structure was because the ship itself was possibly the power plant's fuel supply: it consumed itself in order to fly. The data feed went on, describing the surface of the object as an aggregate of small planetoids and meteoroids, cometary material, gas ice, metal slag, and that as fast as the vehicle burned its fuel it harvested more, sticking the stuff on the hull for later use.

"Dunne, you know Mr. Ferguson, of course."

Ferguson nodded, a sly gleam in his steely eye. No trace of the avuncular old chap there today. I did my damnedest to look him in the eye, to show him I knew what was going on. Part of me was determined to do something about "things", even as another part of me was keen to conform and bury my outrage.

"And these officers are from Astronomy and Planetary Sciences..."

Rudyard handed the meeting over to SSO6 Kevin Grantleigh of astronomy. He was a tall, ascetic-looking man with hair going to white and blue eyes full of an austere curiosity; he looked older than the captain, too. He said, his voice rich and surprisingly deep, "Good afternoon, Mr. Dunne. The captain and Mr. Ferguson have told me that you are a promising young officer."

"I hope so, Dr. Grantleigh, sir," I babbled nervously, shifting in my sim egg.

Grantleigh, his face rendered with fine detail, peered at me, his eyes taking note of my nervousness. "How does it feel to be part of history, son?"

"I really don't know, sir. It's rather overwhelming. I don't know what to think." My answer had the virtue of truth, at least. The prospect of the unknown was frankly terrifying; and the thought that, nice words from the captain and Ferguson aside, this might be a covert punishment detail also weighed heavily on me. And I knew they'd never tell me the truth.

"You are perhaps wondering," he said, steepling long pale fingers before his likewise long nose, "why we've chosen you to join this Contact Team?"

I looked around. I saw Mr. Ferguson fiddling with a small black object, rolling it in his hand — a chess pawn. Captain Rudyard, I noticed, was fiddling with a white pawn. What was that about? Both men watched me with vividly rendered eyes. I was frustrated by the sense that there was far more going on than I knew.

To Grantleigh, I said, "I do not question my orders, sir. If I've been chosen for this mission, I'll carry it out as best I can, sir." I was almost shouting. And thinking the whole time about what Janning had said before about how I was just a warm body they needed to make up the numbers because everyone else, the qualified people, weaselled out when the captain put the hard word on them. Leaving me, with no experience, and no wife and kids to compensate if something went badly wrong, to take care of the mission's scut work. Yes, I was going to be part of history, and under other circumstances the opportunity might seem fabulous, scut work notwithstanding. I also couldn't shake the feeling that this might all be a test to see if their troublemaker junior officer had learned his lesson. If I had, I got to come back to *Eclipse*. If not, there might be a tragic accident involving scary alien life forms. I could see that scenario playing out, too.

So no pressure, then.

Sensor probes of the alien vehicle's interior revealed a structure resembling an ant nest, with twisting, narrow tunnels dug through the thing. There were no obvious things that might be bodies floating around. Also, there were no straight lines or right angles or anything suggesting a familiarity with geometry as we knew it, except in the rear of the vessel, with the drive system. This featured a great deal of precision engineering involving a number of unknown alloys.

More puzzling was that there was no obvious way in.

Grantleigh looked at the captain, a thick white eyebrow arched. To me he said, "Very good answer, Mr. Dunne. As it happens we have chosen you to join the expedition to visit and attempt to enter the artifact and to make first-hand observations. We think it will be good experience for you. Bit of a feather in your cap."

I tried to control my breathing. They were really going to try to enter this thing. Good God. "Very good, sir. When should I be ready?"

Grantleigh turned to the other officer present whom I didn't know, a middle-aged woman with salt-and-pepper hair pulled back tight. Her eyes were severe and dark. I imagined ferocious concentration and an icy, unwavering scrutiny. She was introduced as Janet Blackmore, SSO5, Planetary Science Team Leader. She said to me, "We're having a ship's boat modified as we speak to handle the requirements of the operation. We expect said modifications to be complete by 0700 tomorrow. Departure will be at 0800."

I nodded. "Thank you, ma'am. I will be ready." *I will be crapping my pants, but ready.*

Grantleigh said, "We will also be taking a team of enlisted men for support operations."

Enlisted men? Disposables? I paused a moment, thinking, and shot a surreptitious glance at the captain and Ferguson. They looked businesslike, competent.

"Very ... very good, sir."

"Do you have any questions, Mr. Dunne?" This was from Captain Rudyard, leaning forward to look down the table at me. He was still fondling that white pawn. I stared at it, frowning, but tried to think of an intelligent question. It was unusual for senior officers to ask for input like this from juniors like me.

"What do we do, sir" I asked, "if there are living ... uh, creatures on that vessel, and they are hostile?"

Ferguson smiled a nasty smile. "That, Mr. Dunne, is why we are taking along a squad of enlisted men for support."

I understood — the enlisted men would be armed to the teeth.

Ferguson added, "Of course, we estimate there is a negligible, though possible, chance of encountering hostile life forms over there. However, every piece of data we have thus far suggests the vessel is quite inert and has been so quite a long while now."

"I see, sir. Permission to ask another question?"

Rudyard nodded. I said to Grantleigh and Blackmore: "Excuse me for asking, sir, ma'am, but I am curious about one thing."

Grantleigh smiled, "Yes, son?"

"Do we know where this vessel might have come from?"

Blackmore glanced at Grantleigh; he nodded to her. She said to me, looking tense, "We are backtracking a probable course, which will take time."

"Thank you, ma'am," I said, showing proper deference, and feeling amazed that they were willing to answer any of my questions. But why were they looking so cagey, like there was something they were hiding?

That brought the meeting to a close. Grantleigh and Blackmore disappeared from the cloud. Before I was dismissed, the captain and Ferguson exchanged a look, then the captain said to me, "Mr. Ferguson would like a private word, Mr. Dunne, if you would be so kind as to stay a few moments longer."

I swallowed. *Oh no, here it comes, a little chat about last night.* I nodded, "Of course, sir." Rudyard disappeared.

Ferguson toyed with his black pawn a moment, then put it aside where it looked very small next to his large, thick hands. "Mr. Dunne, I'm told you had a small accident in your quarters last night."

I fought an urge to touch my still-tender nose; the delicate bones in there were still knitting; I could still feel a faint tingling from the nanobots doing the work. "Yes, sir. That's true." Looking him straight in the eye.

"That is most unfortunate. These things do sometimes happen to new crewmen, however. Takes a little while to settle in to the new routine, get acclimatized to the way things are done."

"Absolutely, sir."

"Quite a different thing, starship duty out here, Mr. Dunne. Do you not agree?"

"Aspects of it, sir, seem quite familiar, if you will pardon my saying so." This was risky.

Ferguson's face darkened a moment. "SCO Janning seems quite taken with you, boy. He says you show considerable promise as a helm officer."

"Very kind of Mr. Janning to say so, sir."

He leaned back in his chair, folded his hands together across his taut belly. For a long, long moment he looked at me deliberately letting the silence pile up into a crushing weight. I tried matching his stare, but failed; I looked away. He snorted a soft laugh.

"Why do you think," he said, his voice quiet, but with an edge to it I didn't like, "why do you think you were chosen for this assignment, Mr. Dunne?"

I thought it important to keep calm. "Would you be referring to the rendezvous with the foreign vessel, sir?"

Ferguson clucked his tongue, scratched at his moustache. "Yes, of course the alien vessel!"

I said nothing, nothing at all. Now I let my silence stretch out for a few moments, interested in seeing how Ferguson handled it. His face looked a lot less friendly than it had last night when he was offering Sorcha a cup of hot chocolate. Right now he looked like an overcast sky thinking about lightning. His lips were pressed together.

I said, lying, "I'm quite sure I don't have any idea why I might have been chosen for this assignment. Sir."

Ferguson said, "You can dispense with the insolent tone, Mr. Dunne, right now."

"I assure you, sir, I meant no insolence." Which was true. Apart from what various people had told me about why I'd been chosen for the mission, I still really did not know, not for certain.

He said little for a moment, then, "A career Service officer needs experience in dealing with challenges, Mr. Dunne. Do you understand? There's more to Service life than is taught at the Academy. Much more."

"Yes, sir." I kept my voice as toneless as possible, remembering only too vividly all the extracurricular things one learned at the Academy these days.

"Mr. Dunne, the captain and I think you need a little seasoning."

Images of roast meat filled my mind, and I suppressed a smile. "I appreciate this, sir."

Ferguson flashed a smile that shouldn't have looked so predatory. "I've decided to make you my project. You could be a fine career Service officer."

"I appreciate this, sir. It sounds like a fine opportunity." I suppressed a shudder at the prospect. It was becoming increasingly clear that my inclusion in the mission was a form of covert punishment. I could indeed become a fine officer — once I'd had all my troublemaking tendencies beaten out of me, and Ferguson was just the man for that job.

Ferguson now looked a little troubled. "There is one small thing, however, and I hesitate to mention this, as we try to avoid unpleasantness on this ship."

Ah, I thought, *at last the kick in the teeth*. "Sir?"

"The captain and I have some concerns about the quality of guidance you are receiving from Mr. Janning."

I blinked, and immediately regretted it. Damn, he had surprised me. "Mr. Janning, sir?"

He picked up the pawn, fiddled with it a bit, then said, "Mr. Janning has been on active space duty for a long time. Do you understand, Mr. Dunne?"

I frowned, thinking I knew where this might be going but hoping I was wrong. "I'm not sure I do, sir."

"I will confide to you a small secret, son."

He went on, "The captain is considering transferring Mr. Janning back to Ganymede for a few months. Spend some time at the Academy, see his family. They miss him very much, hmm?"

Uh-oh... "The Academy?"

"It's a good thing, I think, for an officer in the Service to visit his or her roots from time to time, to reflect back on why they joined the Service. That kind of thing."

I put the rest together: I was to play along as a good officer and try not to follow Janning's advice about thinking for myself. If Ferguson wasn't satisfied with my efforts to blend in, he'd have my only ally transferred home.

Damn, I felt cold.

Ferguson said, "I see you take my meaning, Mr. Dunne."

"Uh, yes, sir. I am receiving you loud and clear. Thank you."

He smiled, looking more avuncular again. It was creepy the way he could switch back and forth. "It's always good to talk things out, I think. Clear the air."

He dismissed me. I snapped back into the tight confines of the simulator egg, staring at the black panels around me, devoid of instrumentation. I spent several minutes sitting there, staring around at the rows of sim eggs glowing in the light, and took in the cool, fresh air. I felt like the whole ship was trying to smother me. The walls that had yesterday conveyed such a feeling of roominess now held me tightly in place. My heart pounded hard and fast and I was sweating. My shirt was wet down the back; it felt disgusting, like a skin I wanted to shed.

And this was only my second day aboard *Eclipse*.

That night I ate space chunder by myself, feeling doomed. The wall displays were alive with all the latest images and data from the alien vessel; we had long since matched course with it, and had a swarm of bots all around it, harvesting information at a prodigious rate. Much of this information was pouring into my head, where I felt it filling my buffers and intruding on my thoughts. It was hard to imagine myself being among the first to visit the thing the following morning.

Other members of the crew came up to me while I tried to eat, clapping me on the shoulder, telling me how lucky I was, going to make history, set foot where nobody had set foot before. All of which was true, of course. It was a staggering opportunity. My name would be remembered in the history books. And it was, like I'd told Janning, exactly what I'd signed up to do. Even so, at this moment, all I could think about was how I'd screwed up everything since I came aboard. Self-pity is never a good look on a person, but at the time I thought it suited me pretty well.

"Hey, Genius!"

I looked up, and had time to say, "Huh?" before Sorcha tipped a plateful of cold space chunder on my head. As it dripped down my face, down my uniform, and as other crew around us laughed their guts out, Sorcha set about rubbing the vile muck over my face, into my cropped hair, into my uniform, down my shirt, and was doing a fine job of trying to get it down the front of my pants before I stopped her. Gasping, shocked, I looked up at her.

Sorcha scowled at me for a moment, then broke out in her own wild fit of laughter. Tears rolled down her cheeks. Every time she seemed to finish, and get herself together, drying her eyes on her short sleeves, she'd look at me as I wiped at the gunk on my face, point at me and burst out laughing all over again. Others joined in. Even the food preparation officers from the galley stood at the door, having a good laugh at this entertaining use of their despised food.

At some point I sputtered, "What the—?"

And she burst with laughter all over again. Somebody yelled out, "Hey, I've got a fresh plate — want some more?" Yet more laughter.

As the laughter accumulated and I tried to clear my eyes, my nose, and scrape the food out of my clothes, I forgot my embarrassment and my own personal feelings about what had happened to Sorcha and me and I began to giggle. I was holding a hand in front of my face, seeing how much I'd scraped out of my hair, and somehow the sight of all that icky stuff made me laugh, too.

Sorcha sat down across from me after a while and handed me a damp towel. She had a gorgeous smile. Her rich eyes shone. She said, "Now we're even, more or less."

That wiped the smile off my face. "Sorcha? I thought —"

"Look," she said, "I chose to go along with it. You didn't make me; I knew the risks."

I said nothing for a moment, waiting to hear her say "but..." She didn't. "I felt so guilty, when I saw you..." I wondered briefly if I'd have felt quite as guilty if it had been a male cadet who had been attacked. I think I would have felt some guilt over it, but not as much. There wouldn't have been such a sense of acute embarrassment.

She rolled her eyes. "How charmingly old-fashioned of you. Stupid, but charming. Please, no need to feel guilty. Maybe I should give you a little after-hours defensive work, get you toned up a bit."

"They said you fought them off."

Sorcha grinned again. "James, James, James. I wasted their stupid disposable asses before they had time to think."

"But you were unconscious when I..."

"They had me out while the bots did their thing. I was fine. Angry, but fine."

"You really killed those things?"

"James, sometimes..." she looked grim and sad for a moment, staring at the display panels, "sometimes, you just have to do what's necessary to save your ass, you know? There are times when you can't just talk your way out of trouble. And Christ, they were just disposable grunts, right?" But she wasn't smiling as she said this. I remembered her at the Academy, the one on the pedestal everyone wanted to knock down and who made everyone else look bad by comparison.

And I couldn't forget my own beating last night, how I hadn't had time to fight back. I told myself it was because the enlisted men pulled me out of a sound sleep and took care of me before I was even awake. If I'd had a few minutes warning...

"Okay, so when can we start training?"

"Tonight, if you want. Hey," she added, "you might need some slick moves to fight off the evil aliens, huh?" She grinned again, punched my shoulder lightly, and, despite the cold food congealing all over my uniform, I didn't feel quite so awful. In fact, I thought, enjoying her radiant smile, I even felt a speck of hope.

Six

We almost didn't find the aliens.

Once a team of our engineers had stopped the alien vessel's tumbling, we took a ship's boat over there and locked onto the side of the alien vessel. Soon we'd extended a vactight workdome and an access tunnel leading from the cargo bay. We could crawl through this passageway and float in the dome, facing the naked hull of the ship. The surface was cold and dark, and damp with condensed water vapor from the dome's atmosphere; I was reminded of the pitted surfaces of ferrous asteroids I had seen up close. Under the bright halogen lights in the white workdome, the material looked ancient and impregnable. Other than the sounds of my suit systems, it was unpleasantly silent. When Ferguson spoke over a head channel it seemed too loud, an interruption. I felt as though I was in some kind of museum exhibit and that I should be as quiet and respectful as possible. Grantleigh and Blackmore stared at the naked rockface as if they were looking at the face of the Holy Redeemer.

The scientists took soundings, compared the results with data taken during the boat's approach and orbit. We were in a good spot, where the hull wall was thinnest, towards what we thought of as the vessel's bow.

We launched nanobots tailored to digest the material of the hull, and waited. The scientists ran endless tests, going over their data again and again.

"The interior tunnels are clearly too narrow for human bodies to enter," Blackmore observed. She, Grantleigh,

Ferguson, and I were in the cloud, trying to work out what to do about entering the vessel. The nanobots estimated they would punch through the rocky outer layers and then the inner-hull in about four hours. We had until then to decide how to explore the ship.

Ferguson said, looking impatient, "No problem, then. We can send in a swarm of sensorbots to find out what they can and scout the *reticula*." That was what the team called the warren of twisting, coiling tunnels. "They can cover the whole ship in a matter of days, and we can sit back here, monitoring data, and guiding the bots when they find something of interest."

I could see the two scientists swapping skeptical looks. Blackmore said, "That would be an excellent plan for an initial survey of the reticula, to build a map of the internal structures and so forth..." She said this in what was obviously her idea of an extremely diplomatic tone, but to me she sounded a little condescending. Her eyes looked sharp and a little mocking towards the executive officer.

Ferguson did not miss this tone. "I'm not letting any of my people in there, not even the enlisted men, Dr. Blackmore. No bloody way."

Blackmore went to object, but Grantleigh interjected, "Mr. Ferguson, we have designed a digger that would enter these tunnels and enlarge them, making them suitable for human access."

Ferguson had leaned back in his chair, affecting a pose of calm reflection, but the sheen of rendered sweat on his forehead and glistening around his narrow little moustache betrayed his anxiety. "I don't care if you can make room for the bloody Coldstream Guards to march twelve abreast in there in full kit. We're not sending humans in until we know it's totally safe."

They came to a rough compromise, though I could see Ferguson was a worried man. A screw-up, a loss of life, or any similar disaster would look bad on his record. He was probably having nightmares about boards of inquiry.

I figured he was welcome to all the suffering in the world.

⊕ ⊕ ⊕

The nanobots finished their primary excavation, opening a tunnel large enough to allow us through to the reticula. We hovered around the tunnel entrance in our thin orange environment suits, staring into the hole. Instruments showed whatever was down there was giving off lethal quantities of vapor, laced with organic materials and heavy metals. I found myself holding my breath before realizing that this was pointless in my suit. The lights we aimed stopped at a plug of something black and oozing. Ferguson ordered a field barrier erected to keep the ooze from entering the workdome.

Then the bots reported their major finding: the tunnels of the reticula were full of a gelatinous black material which is what was producing the gas we detected. I heard Blackmore gasp, "My God..." as she heard this detail. We retrieved a sample of the material and scanned it for biological activity, microbes, tiny forms of life, and found nothing but cold, dead organic detritus.

Over the next two days the swarms of explorer bots churned through this slime, working their way through the reticula, which ran for a combined total of more than two hundred kilometers. The scientists worked their monitors in shifts, shunting results into their headware. Sometimes they'd go off for private cloud conferences that lasted hours, during which they floated in the dome, curled up in loose balls, eyes closed. Ferguson scowled when they did this, and muttered darkly under his breath.

He got me to scrub things a lot, and prepare meals, and run maintenance checks on the enlisted men, making sure they were all okay inside their eggs, maintaining peak form, getting their exercise and nutrition. I had to monitor their waste processing lines, brain activity, and all the rest. These disposables lived in a cloud of their own, where they spent their time on training missions, exercises and weapons proficiency drills. To them it was indistinguishable from real life. And when we needed them, they would be ready for action at a moment's notice, rested, refreshed, and well-fed.

And they would carry out their orders without question, a key selling point the companies that produced disposables liked to emphasize at the military trade shows. I imagined these trade shows must be very strange events.

"What do you make of these cavities?" Grantleigh asked one day as I was passing by on my way to scrub something in the crew quarters. I figured he was talking to anybody but me, so I kept going.

"Mr. Dunne?"

I managed a guided turn in mid-air, and didn't damage anything. "Sir?"

"Yes, Mr. Dunne. I asked you a question."

"Of course, sir. One moment." I pulled myself over to where he had attached himself to an anchor-point on the side of the workdome. He had a sheet of Active Paper covered in overlapping playback windows, most of which I recognized as relating to the internal structure of the alien ship. Grantleigh looked at me with a smile and said, "Mr. Ferguson says you're a quick study, so I wondered what you might think of these structures..."

While I tried to fathom Ferguson's subtle game, Grantleigh worked his fingers over the page, manipulating windows and images, tweaking false-color renderings and resolutions. At length he showed me an image of a section of hull material that appeared to contain a series of hollow chambers, each of which contained some kind of large lump that almost filled each chamber.

I frowned, staring at the false-color display in which solid regions of hull material were black and the cavities were white, with other colors showing other materials. "What is the actual size here?" I asked, and Grantleigh indicated the scale. By this measurement, the cavities were around three meters long by about one and a half in diameter. I said jokingly, "Kind of like crypts, eh sir?"

Grantleigh scowled at me, nodding. "That was my thinking, too, son. Good work. Here, look at this sonic scan..." He brought up another window, this time rendering the sonic transparency of everything in false color. Here it was obvious that the lumps inside the cavities were made of very different substances from the material in the inner and outer hull and general structure of the ship. In this rendering, the hardest materials were black, leaving the lumps themselves to shine in blues, greens, and even shades of red. Grantleigh pointed to the red regions deep inside the lumps, "I think these might be organs of some kind."

That did it for me. Suddenly these things weren't just piles of matter less dense than the hull material. While the possibility of finding aliens here had always been there, the data so far had suggested this craft was nothing more than a flying abandoned ant-nest. But where were the ants? I looked again at the images on Grantleigh's page. "Is there anything else they could be, sir?"

He rubbed his chin, looking thoughtful. "It's hard to say, Mr. Dunne. They could be nodules of organic materials. They could be giant potatoes. We'll have to open up some of these cavities and have a look."

This filled me with dread. "Mr. Ferguson won't like that."

Grantleigh nodded. "I'll handle Mr. Ferguson."

We had to bore out some tunnels after all. Not surprisingly I was chosen to go with a squad of armed enlisted men into the ship, climbing through the black goop in my all-too-thin suit. The scientists had cooked up a supply of an organic solvent designed to turn the jelly into a liquid, so we could move. That helped, but not enough. In actual practice, the rate at which the solvent acted was never fast enough. I was always climbing back up the tunnels to the workdome, desperate for a new air supply. Ferguson was having the shipboard fab whip up an airhose, but that would take time. Meanwhile, when I was in the alien ship, unable to see except by sonar and radar, the complete darkness did strange things to my mind. I saw things moving in the jelly, swimming around, giant blind preda-tors, white and grisly, glowing like the creatures found in the cold dark oceans beneath Europa's ice sheets. I imagined feeling things brush against my body, or nibbling at my feet, or wrapping themselves around my legs with icy tentacles. And against that blank void I found myself remembering things from my life, and being jolted out of these reveries by one of these phantom sensations of something touching me. I never got used to it. Especially when the memories were of my first year at the Academy.

Ferguson would call to me over the cloud, "Why are you screaming, boy?"

It took time, but we managed to find and open several of the crypt-like cavities. The cavities did indeed contain creatures, strange coiled groups of them, all apparently dead. My team of enlisted men helped me bring back a couple of these clumps for the scientists to study in the dome, surrounded by biohazard fields. We kept looking.

The creatures had wound themselves around each other, like clumps of centipedes, only larger. As Grantleigh and Blackmore wrestled with these clumps in the dome, trying to pry the individuals out of this clench of death, the rest of us watched via the cloud. Thus we found out that these creatures did resemble a kind of evolved super-centipede, with a segmented, ridged, flexible, chitinous body, and with five sets of muscular, jointed legs. Two sets of these legs ended in structures suspiciously resembling three-pronged jointed grippers. I remember the sight of Blackmore, her face screwed up with tension, as she tried to unclench one of these hands, and how the appendage had snapped and shattered rather than unfold for her.

Working with these dead specimens, Grantleigh surmised, "They probably have the ship filled with this jelly substance to provide a buffer against high acceleration, and it also provides their nutritional needs during the long flight." The two scientists then suggested we open six crypts to start with. In the sixth cavity we found the first survivor.

The only reason we located a survivor was because the creature's faint respiratory and pulmonary activity caused it to move slightly in a way that didn't fit the profile of the other lumps we had scanned. At first I thought it might just be jiggling a bit because of vibrations stemming from the tunnel-boring activities going on nearby, but the scientists urged me to have a look. In this cavity, as was proving usual, we found a clump of ten creatures; what was unusual was that only nine of them were dead. The survivor was somehow drawing sustenance from the husks of its clump-mates as well as the jelly medium. And when I say it was a survivor, I don't mean it was thriving; the same state of life in a human would have made some call for Last Rites.

Grantleigh and Blackmore, frustrated by their encounters with dead creatures, seized with astounded excitement on the prospect of contact with a living member of this race. Ferguson was less thrilled with the prospect. "I'm not sure I can authorize you to bring that thing aboard *Eclipse*."

The scientists conferred with Ferguson and Rudyard over the cloud. Rudyard, in turn, launched messages back to the Community, in stripped-down, high-acceleration botships designed to seek out and enter hypertubes on their own. Depending on the tube weather situation, Service headquarters would be receiving Rudyard's reports within the next few days. He said to Ferguson, "Locate any other survivors you can."

It took two more weeks, but we found three more, all in about the same state of health. We also began to find spherical objects, fifty centimeters in diameter, made from a clear glass-like material. Detailed inspection showed a sophisticated photonic information processing system embedded in these things, with monofilament-like connections leading to hundreds of indentations studded around the surface of the objects. Blackmore inferred that the creatures might use such a device as an interface to control the ship, because the indentations seemed designed to fit the creatures' grippers.

By this time Rudyard had heard back from Service HQ, which announced that it wanted all living specimens, artifacts, and the ship itself brought back to human space for study by Community scientists.

Ferguson was visibly annoyed by this development, but he was a loyal Service man and made the arrangements, muttering when he thought nobody could hear, "Five bloody kilometers long! Millions of bloody tons!"

We put the four live creatures in a purpose-fabbed containment unit filled with about two tonnes of the noxious jelly medium. We sealed the entrance tunnel we had dug in the hull of the ship and headed back to *Eclipse*. As we were returning, another ship's boat launched with a crew of engineers whose job was to fathom the alien vessel's mass-conversion drive. I wondered if Sorcha was in on this mission, and sent her a note. She wrote back saying she wasn't that lucky, but she had been attached to the team converting a vacant meeting room aboard *Eclipse* for use as an isolation Infirmary for these aliens.

"A word, Mr. Dunne?" It was Grantleigh again, he had cornered me in the cramped white galley of the boat while the others were busy cleaning equipment and doing routine maintenance. He said, "So, Mr. Dunne, how does it feel to confront the Great Other?"

"Pardon me, sir?" I was trying to get the fab system to process the remains of the night's meals, but it kept giving me annoying system errors. The boat was too small to have a decent disposable-based interface, so I had to do what I could through a terrible voice interface. I wasn't in a mood to discuss anything with Grantleigh.

The old man looked at me with his piercing eyes; he was close enough that I could smell the fabbed meat from tonight's stew on his breath. "The Great Other, Dunne: The unknown, the essence of mystery, the thing we can never know."

I shifted about in the zero-G, trying to find a firm grip on something. Grantleigh's breath was a little strong in these tight spaces. "I haven't really had time to think about it, sir. Too much to do," I hinted, gesturing at the fab, which was asking me to please explain the command "go screw yourself."

He smiled, recognizing that he was being a bit annoying. "And it must be observed that you're doing a damned good job, too, son, under quite trying circumstances."

"Thank you, sir, I appreciate that. Did Mr. Ferguson send you to see me?" I could imagine Ferguson doing that, just for harassment's sake. I couldn't suppress the urge to glance around the walls of the galley for surveillance spray; I didn't see any.

"So what do you think of our aliens, son?" he persisted, ignoring my question.

I assumed he was pestering me since I was the junior officer, the one who had lucked into a historic discovery on his first space rotation. In a distant part of my mind, it occurred to me there would be huge media interest in the discovery. But right now, all I wanted to do was get the stupid fab to work. I put that aside and thought about Grantleigh's question for a moment. "To be honest, sir, they don't seem all that alien. If you know what I mean."

He arched a thick white eyebrow at me. "Would you like to explain that remark, Mr. Dunne?"

I stared at the complaining fab unit, frowning. "It's just that they seem not very..." I paused, trying to think of the right word.

Grantleigh suggested, "Exotic, perhaps? Is that it?"

I bobbed my head a little. "Yes, sir. Not as exotic as I thought aliens might be. These things, these creatures, they don't look much more exotic than large beetles or insects."

"So you're saying they are insufficiently alien for your taste."

I scratched my head. "No, not that, it's just—"

"You were expecting something more fanciful, less quotidian?"

"Well, yes. Yes, sir. I sort of figured the first aliens we met would be, well, I don't know, inconceivable."

"Perhaps, Mr. Dunne, there is more to alienness than meets the eye. What do you think?"

"I wouldn't know, sir. I'm just a helm officer." The question nagged at me later, though, during quiet times, often when I was trying to sleep. I never reached straightforward conclusions, but it did occur to me that even some people could seem utterly alien in their inexplicable behaviour and thinking.

The old scientist leaned away from me, arms folded, still obviously studying me. Studying me the way he had studied those creatures, that's how it felt. What was he up to?

He went on, "You have family back home, son?"

I glanced at him, wondering where he was going with this. I also explained my request again to the fab, and waited while it got going, hummed and died again. "My dad's a systems guy on the new Tradewinds hab orbiting Europa. Keeps him busy. My older sister works as a media consultant on Mars." Which was already more than I wanted to discuss.

Grantleigh nodded, stroking his chin, as if all this meant a great deal to him. And as if he didn't already know all this from my file, which he would have online in his head. He said, "I lost my parents a long time ago, Mr. Dunne. Drive accident on a first-generation tube freighter to Sirius. All hands lost."

I frowned. "I'm very sorry for your loss, sir. That must have been hard."

He managed, despite the cramped conditions, to shrug: "These things happen. Star travel was not so safe in those days."

"That's true, sir." I explained again to the fab that I wanted it to recycle the dishes, but it said it needed more information. I felt hotly embarrassed, going through this in front of Grantleigh. "I'll be glad to see a decent human interface again, sir."

He chuckled politely. "Why do you think these chaps, these aliens, took to the stars like this?"

"Couldn't say, sir. Not my place to speculate." The fab made a loud hissing noise, then sounded a warning tone.

Grantleigh went on, "We think they might be from about three hundred light-years away. Staggering distance."

I hesitated before trying the diagnostics on the fab again. Something about what he said bothered me. "That seems odd, sir."

"Mr. Dunne?"

I said, "Excuse me for saying so, but what about our sky surveys? They would have detected the gamma-bursts from this vessel's drive system if they came from somewhere so relatively close, sir. The various other emissions, too, you'd expect from a mass-conversion drive system."

"Son?"

"Even three hundred years ago, sir, we had comprehensive galaxy-scanning listening systems set up on Earth's moon, and they were deliberately checking for EM stuff, comm traffic of any kind, and drive emissions. And we didn't find any, or at least, none that was ever recognized and made public."

Grantleigh flashed a thoughtful smile, looking at me closely. "Well, that would be true if these chaps were travelling at lightspeed, Mr. Dunne, but as far as we can determine, this vessel could only make about one-fifth of lightspeed, and that with a good tailwind, as it were. And it's since slowed down to its present velocity. Our engineers have located a huge structural failure inside the power plant system on that ship. Other damage, too."

I thought about this, multiplying three hundred by five, and came up with a figure so long ago that the creatures could have pushed their rock up to .2 c, long before we could have picked up the gamma-radiation bursts resulting from the conversion of matter into energy. "But what did they do to decelerate down to this drifting?" I wondered out loud, then stopped, a little embarrassed, and added, "Sir!" I smiled hastily.

He looked exhausted. "Perhaps we can ask them."

"Ask them, sir?"

"It seems likely they are intelligent, Mr. Dunne."

"I suppose so, sir."

"Had you not wondered how they came to have this peculiar warren of a vessel, with no straight lines or other traces of Euclidean geometry to be seen anywhere, except in that huge stardrive unit on the back?"

I took a risk, voicing an idea that had occurred to me earlier. "I had wondered if the drive unit might be an artifact of a different culture, sir. It's as if another race gave it to them. But that's just me guessing." I shrugged. The fab unit was saying it needed a service technician urgently.

Grantleigh went on, "You think some other chaps might have given these chaps the stardrive technology? Is that it, Mr. Dunne?"

"I was just thinking, sir, looking at the whole ship, how it's not like the product of a single designer."

The old man raised his eyebrows. "All the more reason, then, we have to find a way to communicate with these fellows. Learn their secrets."

"Very good, sir."

"Though just how we might manage that..." He trailed off, chuckling at the enormity of the task. Where to even start? The creatures had no discernible head, though they did have a series of long, thick, muscular extensions resembling whips projecting from one end of their bodies, which, unlike the rest of their surface, were not segmented. In the creatures' dormant state, with several specimens curled around each other in a kind of spiral, the whip-like appendages were used, apparently, for holding the clump of creatures together.

"May I ask a further question, sir?" I asked, thinking about all this now.

Grantleigh looked bemused at my formality. "You may," he intoned.

"You want to communicate with the creatures, sir. But how are we going to keep them alive, let alone wake them to the point where we can begin to learn how to talk to them?"

Grantleigh managed a weak laugh. "That's a very good question, son. How indeed?"

Seven

Rudyard ordered the ship's boat, its personnel and its cargo quarantined outside the ship for a week while *Eclipse* biologists studied us for contamination. It was a long week. In theory, nothing could penetrate the active diamond-fiber fabric of our environment suits. They were designed to generate nanophages to hunt down and kill foreign microbes, or at least to isolate them for later study. And even in the unlikely event of the suit sustaining a tear or cut, it would fix itself; the process looked like millions of microscopic spiders building webs of glistening strands in a big hurry. But Rudyard was taking no chances.

During this week of isolation, Rudyard and the ship's psychology staff debriefed us about our experience with the alien vessel. I suffered through maddening hours of testing and conceptual simulations of the sort where no given choice is necessarily right or wrong, but reveals volumes about your state of mind. In these tests I was often returned to the time I spent crawling around the reticula of the other ship, reliving the hallucinations and memory-flashes, only sometimes a voice would appear in my head to ask in a bland voice, "Why did you take this turn here?" and "Why did you think of this event at this moment?"

And some of the time, during these long and annoying sessions, I found myself thinking about Sorcha, wanting to tell her about something I saw during the mission, or something funny Grantleigh said, or even, maybe, tell her a little about just how shit-scared I was in that black muck. It didn't seem like something you could talk to the docs about without them looking at you funny. I knew their type from the Academy. Sorcha, on the other hand, I thought, I could talk to her. And that made the docs ask what I found so amusing.

And hardest of all, "How do you feel about the creatures you found?" The psychologists refused, as ever, to discuss the results of these tests.

I noticed that Ferguson, Grantleigh, and Blackmore were in worse shape at the end of the isolation week than I was. Where I was simply bored and anxious to get back to my helm training, the three senior officers were having screaming matches interspersed with long, tense periods consisting of pointedly ignoring each other, or staring at each other in frosty silence before one or all would stalk off, leaving a churning wake of malice. Grantleigh and Blackmore argued about who owned their data, and who owned which conclusions. Ferguson pointed out that all research data and conclusions belonged first of all to the Service, and second of all to the Home System Community government. Besides which, everything was subject to official secrets sanctions.

The scientists kept fighting, Ferguson kept trying to maintain order. And probably trying to deal with his own encounter with what Grantleigh had called the "Great Other." One time, during an argument that I thought would come to blows, Ferguson screamed at them, "At this rate I'm thinking I might just chuck the bloody specimens overboard and to hell with all of you jumped-up bastards!" Which reignited the fight.

This tension was hard to avoid; the three of them radiated their anger like failed stars. Blackmore spent most of her time in the cargo hold, going over data she regarded as her own. Ferguson spent as much of his time as he could up front in the command deck, talking to Rudyard in the cloud. Grantleigh spent his time, when the three weren't warring, floating before the creatures' isolation tank, watching the thick black opacity of the buffer medium behind the armored plastic wall. He was getting sonar, radar, infrared and other sensor feeds coming straight into his headware; he could essentially see the creatures in the tank. They had taken to clumping, apparently for the heat.

Sometimes they moved their whip things, trailing them slowly around in the jelly, touching, stroking each other's bodies in particular locations. They remained relatively inactive. I didn't know what to make of them. Grantleigh asked me one day, as he floated there watching them, "Perhaps, Mr. Dunne, those whips are analogous to sense organs, what do you think?"

I assumed he was still talking to me because nobody else was. "Possibly, sir. I don't know. Have you got any dirty plates or cups there?"

I noticed, too, that there was a faint smell in this area, the smell of that jelly material, which was technically impossible. We had phages going all the time, sweeping up anything that didn't belong. And the containment tank was electron-leakproof, with various fancy backups.

I remembered Ferguson asking earlier in the week, "And you're sure nothing can get out of there?" and Blackmore saying, "The only way out of that tank is quantum tunneling." She looked smug, saying this. Ferguson reminded her that he would record this assurance of hers in the mission log for future reference. Quantum tunneling? I knew the chances of particles from inside the tank quantum tunneling out into the bay were astronomically remote, but still non-zero.

"Do you smell that, sir?" I asked, sniffing with great care.

"Dunne?"

"Do you smell something in the air?"

He squinted, staring into middle distance. "Ship — run a foreign particle scan in this area, excluding the isolation tank." The ship's boat reported finding nothing abnormal in the entire defined space.

Grantleigh said, "I think we're all going a little space-happy, son." He looked even more tired now. None of us was sleeping well. Those arguments were getting everyone uptight.

He was probably right. I couldn't smell anything strange now, either. I pushed myself a little closer to the isolation tank; it was immense, three meters on a side, like a cubic chunk cut out of space. There was something intimidating about it, even a little scary. I could see why Grantleigh spent so much time here, communing with it. Even without the feeds pouring information into my head, I found simply being there compelling, as if at any moment something would happen, something important. It was hard to say if these creatures were as intelligent as we were; we wouldn't know that for a long time. Whoever had made the creatures' ship and launched it, on the other hand, was certainly at least at our level, if the technical sophistication of the mass-conversion drive system was any guide.

Why had these creatures been launched into the void like this? Each of the chambers containing the creatures was physically sealed off from the reticula winding through the vessel. None of the chambers showed any sign of food storage, or waste disposal systems. There was no obvious bridge or command center from which a crew could guide the ship and we found none of the creatures outside the chambers. An automated ship sent off and forgotten? Colonists or exiles? The Holy Chosen or the Despised? The lack of anything we recognized as artwork or writing perplexed us. Besides the vessel itself, all we had were the glass spheres.

Blackmore speculated that these things might be some kind of communication/information machines, but until we established some kind of contact, there was no way to tell. The layout of the pits and grooves on the surface of the spheres seemed to match up with the dimensions of the creatures' grabbers, but there were other features we didn't recognize. Inside the spheres we saw what looked like a central core surrounded by complex structures linked by fine tubes, and a suggestion of what looked like photonic circuitry. There were also small bodies or structures near the surface whose function we couldn't guess. Looked at one way, the spheres looked like sophisticated technology, but from other angles they looked like nothing so much as large spherical cells.

One of Blackmore's projects during our week of quarantine was the detailed examination of one such sphere.

She threw every sensing, measuring, and scanning resource we had at it, looking for information she couldn't see with her own enhanced eyes. Blackmore didn't share her data with Grantleigh, or anyone else. I didn't even bother asking her about it. To her I was just a dumb kid with no place on the mission. She hadn't told me this in so many words, but it was obvious from her monosyllabic answers to the questions I was allowed to ask her: "Can I get you something to eat, Dr. Blackmore?" or "Are you finished with that tray, Dr. Blackmore?"

The three senior officers spent most of that week either fighting or giving each other the silent treatment, as I said, but there was something else going on. Watching them yell and scream at each other with Ferguson abusing them in his gutter manner and the scientists shooting back at him and at each other with their terribly witty diatribes, their too-smart verbal thrusts and parries, I had the feeling that there was more to all this than was apparent. The main issue, on the surface, was the ownership of data and ideas. There was talk about media contracts — until Ferguson stepped in and reminded them, again, about official secrets. But the noise and viciousness of the fighting seemed too intense for such an issue. The close confines of the boat's public areas weren't helping matters, either. We'd been in each other's armpits for weeks now, engaged in difficult, filthy, exhausting work. With little opportunity for the exercise needed to maintain muscle and bone in zero-g, we were forced to rely on nanobots racing around our bodies rebuilding tissue as fast as we lost it. It wasn't a good solution, nothing is as effective as doing the exercise and maintaining the diet, but it was all we could manage. Cleanliness and hygiene were difficult to maintain, too. As hard as the bots worked to remove flakes of skin and bits of hair, there was still the uncomfortable reality of smelling each other's bodily odors.

Yet there still seemed something more serious underlying the huge fights they had. I knew that credit for scientific findings and discoveries was a life-and-death issue among professional scientists. Having your name on the paper announcing a major new discovery was critically important, not only for keeping your job, and meeting strict publication quotas, but also to make sure that when the big prizes, such as the Nobel, were handed out, you got to stand on that stage in New Copenhagen, and be part of scientific history.

But I didn't think this was all that Grantleigh and Blackmore were fighting about. I think there was something much bigger at work, the idea that we had reached a watershed moment in human history: we had found a border in what we had thought a borderless universe. Before this singular moment it had been possible to lay out general big-picture forecasts of how human expansion across interstellar space might proceed. From now on, however, nobody could say how things might go. To me, this was exciting and scary. I didn't know what to expect, but I was cautiously looking forward to seeing what came next. Grantleigh, Blackmore and Ferguson, on the other hand apparently could not begin to comprehend the significance of all this. Or perhaps they could comprehend it all too well, but couldn't make the next mental leap, to enlarge their picture of life in the galaxy to include more than the only child that was us. I think this is what Grantleigh was trying to find between the lines of all the data he was taking in from the isolation tank, and what Blackmore was trying to find in her study of the spheres: the key to understanding a completely new world, a world with edges, with other modes of intelligence.

I wrote to Sorcha the last night of our quarantine, and I went over this idea. She wrote back an hour later, saying, in part:

> "I think you have a point there, James. We are going through a classically Kuhnian paradigm crisis right now, one limited to the crew of *Eclipse*. Once we get back to human space, I imagine word of what we found out here in the dark will escape somehow, and the official secrets regs be damned. By the time some clever member of

the crew shunts a bundle of information through a variety of anonymous mail routers, with some suitably cool crypto wrapped around it, I can't see how the Service could prevent the memes spreading, even by backtracking through all those mail systems to find out who started the wave.

"And I think it will be a wave, like a tsunami, hardly noticeable while out in the deep water, racing along at hundreds of kilometers per hour, a slight bump amid the general surface clutter, but once it hits shallow water, it will get much, much bigger. This tsunami will swamp all of human space. If there's trouble brewing on dozens of worlds and orbitals now in the wake of all the speculation about Kestrel, this will tip everyone over the edge, don't you think? Imagine being at ground zero when all this goes off! Imagine being the Service trying to stop it! Probably they'll try to put out a counter-meme to confuse people, bury the original story with more information, and yet more information after that. I wonder what they'll do with actual witnesses, though..."

Strapped into my vertical bunk that night, reading all this as it fed straight into my mind, I felt myself growing very warm, flushing with embarrassment — and a private happiness that Sorcha was sending me these amazing letters. I'd never received letters like these before, so vibrant and full of life. It was a little intoxicating. The other officers were all less than a meter away; I was close enough to feel their collective heat, smell their breath, hear their stomachs gurgle and grumble. And right there in my head Sorcha's voice gleefully chatting about the vast chaos to come when the information tsunami hit, followed by greater waves of misinformation, all washing through the entire sweep of human space, occupying the minds of billions of people. The main trouble, I figured, was that Sorcha was just the kind of person who would start the wave, given the right motivation.

And as I listened to her words, I found myself feeling sure that the others could hear them, too, that all this mischievous, provocative thought was somehow leaking out of my ears.

I erased it immediately, feeling guilty for more reasons than one.

Eight

We returned from quarantine to the confines of the *HMS Eclipse*. The ship now felt and looked different. The fresh air was wonderful and having room to move around made me feel a little agoraphobic. I was told this was a natural feeling, the same way that when I returned to the ship and experienced gravity again, I felt heavier than I remembered, and more lethargic. The ship's doctor prescribed us all a vigorous program of exercise and high-calcium dietary supplements, and a range of electrolyte boosters to help repair the damage the circulating nanobots hadn't been able to remedy. We had weekly appointments scheduled with the psychologists, too, to help us deal with residual effects of what we had experienced over there. Of course, I swore to myself that I was fine, I was young and resilient, that I didn't need all this coddling; the older officers, on the other hand, were obviously in need of expert help, as I saw it. I planned not to bother going to the psychologist appointments, deciding I would be too busy getting back into the routine of helm training.

On our fourth day back, the Contact Team met, along with Captain Rudyard, this time in person. I wondered why we weren't meeting over the cloud, as usual; I assumed there must be some sort of security issue. We were stuck in a small room on Deck E, crowded around a display table and sitting on the same utilitarian chairs used in the Mess. I could see things between Grantleigh, Ferguson, and Blackmore were still tense. Blackmore sat next to me and wasn't talking to Grantleigh, except in a strictly formal, all-business capacity. She kept her folder of display sheets separate from the others, and sat as far away from Grantleigh and Ferguson as possible. Ferguson, for his part, looked fed up with the whole business, and wanted only to get through it. He scowled from his end of the table, tapping his blunt fingers on the table-top, and hardly touched his chess pawn. Grantleigh watched the others, looking aloof, detached, and a little amused. The captain, at the head of the rectangular table, seemed as fidgety as his executive officer, but also very tired. He sat rigidly and only the sound of one of his feet tapping on the floor gave away his agitation.

The meeting was routine, and proceeded quickly, despite its contentious subject matter. The scientists reported new findings, interesting data, challenged conclusions. They sounded like first-year Academy cadets in debating class, speaking formally and with great and crisp precision, lest their slightest word be taken the wrong way. I had seen my parents talk like this during that stage of a fight when both parties are tired of being misunderstood.

The alien creatures and their isolation tank had been installed in a room like this one with a viewing gallery for human observers to watch and monitor the data feeds from overhead. Grantleigh informed us that we were close to working out their biochemistry, and understanding their cellular machinery, metabolism, and genome. So far the creatures conformed to known biology. Blackmore then explained, with pointed detail, about the effort to warm and dilute the jelly material, with the aim of establishing a warm-liquid environment; studies of the creatures' exoskeletons and interior structures suggested they might be warm-blooded in their natural state, as counterintuitive as that seemed.

A parallel line of study was investigating the glass sphere objects, including such measures as stripping one apart by atom and studying the apparent circuitry and structures visible within. Grantleigh and Blackmore differed in their interpretations of what the spheres were for, heatedly debating whether the objects were techno-logical artifacts, some kind of inert art object, or perhaps even toys. Blackmore held that the spheres could even be naturally occurring formations from the creatures' home world — souvenirs from home!

I listened to all this chilly discussion, the subdued hostility, the suppressed tension. The sight of people talking into their hands to avoid making eye contact, and veins bulging on necks was all too familiar. I found myself remembering fights and arguments between my parents, when I was little and would hide in my room. I couldn't see a good reason for my presence here. I didn't understand most of what the scientists were saying, though I was keen to learn what I could. But mainly I just hated that feeling of being around when parents fight, using words as weapons to avoid looking like wild animals. Blackmore, in particular, reminded me of my mother.

The captain stepped in, looking pissed off and anxious in his own way. He said, raising a hand, interrupting Grantleigh, "I suppose I'd better have a look at these things. Dr. Blackmore, would you do the honors?"

Blackmore looked a little surprised by the question, but was prepared for it. She placed a sheet with an active black holosurface in the center of the table, and touched the sheet's corner power point. The image flashed, sparking to life. It wasn't a real, natural-light rendering; the scientists had collated all the data from other sensor feeds and produced this animated rendering of what the aliens would look like under white light, moving around in a warm liquid environment. The color was acceptable, and the detail available in the rendering was faithful to a fine degree. This display showed one of the creatures arranged in what they were assuming was its normal posture: standing on the three "back" sets of legs, main body horizontal. The rest of the body, which included the end with the whip-like structures was vertical, allowing the creature to use the hand-like grabbers at the end of the other two sets of limbs.

The three whip structures moved independently of each other, rising from a protrusion on what they thought was the creature's head. The overall movement of the creature was nimble and quick; studies of their nervous system and muscle tissue suggested the creatures could move and react quickly, with a surprising degree of articulation. Seeing the whips lashing about was disturbing — I was reminded of cockroach antennae.

They had enough muscle in their upper limbs to handle the mass of the glass spheres, and the patterns of pit indentations were compatible with their multi-jointed appendages. The suggestion that the spheres were tools was very strong, but we didn't now what kind of tools, or even what powered them. Ferguson observed, "For all we know they could be bloody bowling balls!"

I noticed the captain, staring at this image, saying nothing. He looked pale, wide-eyed; he gripped the tabletop with white-knuckled fingers. I saw that Grantleigh had also noticed the captain's reaction; he stroked his chin, fingering his moustache, watching Rudyard. Ferguson, on the other hand, had seen all he wanted to see of these creatures. He stared at the light bars in the ceiling, or sometimes at the display panels on one wall, showing views of local space. He looked either uninterested or completely oblivious to the captain's discomfiture.

Blackmore took Rudyard's silence as a cue for her to explain what he was seeing. She began with a dry discussion of the potential taxonomy of the creature, its possible environment and home world, the very high capacity of its distributed brain and nervous system, the possible function of the whips as sense instruments. "If neuron density and sheer brain tissue mass was a reliable indicator of intelligence, these creatures must be sentient," she said. This led to a discussion of what her people had seen when they examined the surfaces of those whips though high-powered nanoscopes: a surface covered with millions of microstructures containing tiny membranes that could be scent receptors. As well, she droned on, the science staff had found hundreds of thousands of receptors for sound ranging from extremely low to ultrasonic frequencies, and just as many touch-sensitive receptors. They found none for light, except infrared. Similarly, there were no apparent nervous system structures that seemed capable of processing visual stimuli. "We think," Blackmore explained, looking at the animated creature before us, "they might communicate through the emission of pheromones in complex patterns and mixtures. There are extensive gland formations in this upper body region." She pointed to an area coinciding with the topmost pair of limbs.

Rudyard raised a hand. I saw the moist handprint he left on the table. He said, not taking his eyes from the animation: "Stop it, just stop it. I've seen ... enough." His voice was a whispering rasp.

Blackmore stopped, surprised by Rudyard's tone, and shut down the animation; the creature vanished into the display paper. She looked like she might be blushing. "Yes, sir, of course." Her fingers nervously fiddled with the paper.

Rudyard said, rising from his chair, "Thank you. That will be all." We hadn't been here twenty minutes.

The captain left. As he passed me, I saw how pale he was, how he was perspiring across his high forehead and upper lip. Ferguson shot up, following. "Captain? A word?"

Which left the two scientists and me sitting there. Blackmore looked angry, perhaps embarrassed, as she stuffed her display sheets into her folder. She was working her jaw, maybe grinding her teeth. Grantleigh sat, hands laced across his belly, watching her. He glanced at me, eyebrow arched. "That's all, folks!" he said. Of all of us, he looked least surprised.

Grateful for a chance to speak, I said, "Sir? What just happened?"

Blackmore got up, slammed her empty chair against the table and stomped out, breathing hard.

Grantleigh watched her go, shaking his head. "The captain's a strange kind of man. He doesn't like surprises."

I nodded. "Yes, sir, so I hear."

"We sent him all the data we collected over there, but it turns out he didn't look at any of the image files, just skimmed some of the text. That's part of what Blackmore's so upset about — having to deal with a non-scientist."

I wasn't sure what to say. "Yes, sir. May I ask why you think the captain just skimmed your data?"

He got up saying, "Son, there are explorers, and there are people who drive buses, as it were. People of vision, and people who never look up from their maps. Rudyard is a bus-driver at heart, but he's stuck here, like the rest of us. His main interest is the safety of the ship and her crew. As for anything else, well that's what he has us for." He left and, pausing at the door, he added, "He's always been like this. Don't let it bother you."

With a bit of extra time on my hands, I made for the Mess, deep in thought, trying to imagine a starship captain who didn't like his job, who didn't relish exploration and discovery. I remembered Ferguson and Sorcha talking about how *Eclipse* scientists twelve years ago had found what might be the ruins of an alien civilization on Madrigal. The captain must have been unhappy about that, if what Grantleigh said was true. But how could you not be thrilled to your very marrow about finding such things? I didn't understand.

Two nights later, over dinner, Sorcha wanted to hear all the grisly details of my experiences on the alien ship. This was the first chance we'd had to catch up since I returned. She sat across from me in the Mess, flashing her gorgeous smile. "I know you really want to tell me. Go on!" She was one of the few people I had encountered who was interested in the whole alien business. So far I had met people who didn't want to know anything about it at all, and others who would avoid passing me in the passageways if they saw me coming. It was as if my contact with Grantleigh's "Great Other" had changed me in the eyes of most of the crew.

"There's not that much to tell, really." I was conscious of the noise around me: the big fab systems in the galley working over the crockery from dinner, crunching it down into component atoms. Across the room some senior officers were chatting and laughing about something I couldn't make out. Closer to us, a small scrubberbot polished the fake granite tiles, and politely asked officers to please move their feet. On the display wall next to our usual table were pane after pane of HSC media that had just arrived on a swarm of botships from human space, though there was nothing about us, of course. Nothing about the millions of tons of alien hardware outside that our engineers were trying to bring up to operational capability for the push back home. Sitting there, I tried imagining all those dozens of displays filled with news reports about them. I imagined media multistellars sending remote bots out here as fast as they could get them here for the priceless exclusive rights to the story, if they only knew. It was a frightening prospect.

Yet there was an even more frightening prospect: what if there was no broad interest in the story? Suppose the reactions of the people aboard *Eclipse* were reflected back home? That seemed absurd. Thinking about it, what was far more likely was that the story would be adapted and changed, misreported, made safe for human consumption rather than the stark challenge to humanity it really was.

Sorcha laughed. "Not much to tell! The most amazing thing ever to happen to humankind and you say there's not much to tell?"

So I tried to tell her things, but the things I wound up telling were about how bored I was a lot of the time, or how cold it was swimming and crawling through the reticula, or how uncomfortable it was in the boat when the others were yelling at each other, and how Ferguson's farts were so god-awful he could make dogs leave the room.

Sorcha laughed, politely, but said insistingly, "Yeah, but what was it like?"

I felt myself wanting to leave, do something else. "What was what like?"

She rolled her eyes; the whites of her eyes seemed to glow. "What was what like, he asks! What was it really like, discovering another race, making contact, human to alien? You know, that stuff."

I checked the time on my internal clock. "Look, I've gotta get back to the sims. Janning's got me rerunning a bunch of sims I missed during the mission." And with that I got up and left, for some reason feeling an inexplicable sense of panic building in my chest.

Which was crazy. I enjoyed being with Sorcha, even if we did seem to wind up meeting over meals of space chunder here in the Mess, or swapping mail through ShipMind. And I was enjoying her trying to teach me self-defense, despite my apparent lack of talent. At first those sessions were incredibly difficult for me in a way the hand-to-hand combat classes at the Academy never were. At the Academy I never had much trouble with the prospect of tackling either cadets or instructors, of either gender. And, much of the time I was so filled with smouldering anger that I got through things more or less okay.

The sessions with Sorcha were different. I didn't want to hurt her. She, on the other hand, had no qualms about throwing me about with loud, passionate abandon. "Come on, you big wuss. Look at you, you're twice my size!" she'd say, grinning, and I'd find myself staring, just for a moment, at her smile. Sometimes it was difficult focussing on learning the moves she was trying to teach me, when all I wanted to do was just hold her close and warm.

But that didn't explain my hesitation in telling Sorcha about my experiences.

At the time, I wasn't yet sure what it was like to have encountered alienness. It was beyond my experience. Perhaps now that I've had time to think about it, it was like Captain Cook, discovering the Aborigines of Australia, or Columbus stumbling upon the natives of the Caribbean. But that was human meeting human, and only the cultures were different. Then again, those indigenous people were regarded as savages, and not in any way equivalent to "civilized" human beings. And, in that sense, maybe there was some connection. I wasn't sure.

It was hard to think about.

I didn't sleep well that night, or the next night, despite burying myself in extra hours of sim work. The mind-grinding weariness and frequent headaches with which I left the sim eggs made me restless, overtired, rolling in my bunk. My headware was no help, despite the equipment's capacity to alter brainwaves when needed. When I did sleep, it was only light dozing, and I was haunted by hypervivid dreams in which I was at dinner with my parents and sister on one side of the table, and two of the alien creatures on the other side, and my mother trying to explain to our guests how to use a knife and fork. And in the middle of this scene, Captain Rudyard, wearing Colin's dead purple face, staggered in, as if from a terrible storm, yelling, "Not on my ship, you don't!"

That woke me. For a while I lay there, staring up at the underside of the bunk above mine, listening to the sleep sounds of my roommates, and the quiet ship-noises: the dull roar of environment processors moving air and heat through the ship; the almost subsonic hum of the ship's power grid; the distant pulse of the matter pumps shunting streams of raw recycled substance through the fab supply network. Occasional footfalls passing the door; officers looking for their quarters. One of the other guys in here with me, Carroll, an SSO2 in environment, was listening to heavy gash music over his headware; I could hear a tiny amount of non-rhythmic audio bleed from his ear contacts.

Above all this, I could hear my heart pounding. I sat up and swung my legs over the side. Looking around in the colorless, grainy dark, I remembered fragments from the night those enlisted thugs came to teach me a lesson about rocking the boat. I figured I had probably deserved that. God knows I should have learned that lesson at the Academy.

I got up and put my uniform on, not fully knowing what I was doing or where I was going. I just felt like wandering around, maybe burn off some of this energy. My internal clock said it was two in the morning; in three and a half hours I'd have to get up anyway.

Starships are never completely quiet. The night shift has the lights turned down low, and they're obliged to keep the noise down if they have to pass occupied sleeping quarters, but otherwise business continues as normal. In the course of my meandering, I found myself having to salute about the same number of officers as I would encounter during the day, only their faces were unfamiliar. Several told me to go to bed.

I wound up at the creatures' observation gallery, as if I was fluid finding my own level. Only when I walked into the red-lit room, with its view down into the gelid darkness of the tank, did I realize this was where I had been heading all along, that I had been drawn here. It was warm, the result of the slow heating of the jelly medium. According to the data coming in on my headware, the scientists expected the warming of the jelly to take another two or three days to bring it up to normal human room temperature.

"Mr. Dunne! What brings you into the dark this night?"

I knew that voice. Looking up and to my right, I saw Captain Rudyard standing at the far end of the viewing gallery, leaning against the railing, hands clasped together. In this strange light he looked like a man startled awake. I supposed he had just been taking in the same data feeds as I was. He would have seen that the four surviving creatures were responding to the change in temperature and viscosity of the medium with significantly more whip and body movement. Pheromone sensors were detecting some activity too.

I managed a fumbling, startled kind of salute to the captain. "Captain Rudyard, sir. I'm sorry, I didn't mean to disturb you." I turned to go.

"Couldn't sleep, son?"

I turned back. "No, sir."

Rudyard stared down into the blackness, saying nothing for a while. "I keep seeing these ... things. Everywhere I go. Everywhere."

What to say? I murmured, "Do you, sir?"

"Do you think they're intelligent, Mr. Dunne?"

"I wouldn't know, sir. That's not for me to say."

He glanced up. His eyes looked strange, even accounting for the light. "Don't give me that bullshit deference nonsense, son. I asked for your considered opinion. You've seen all the same data the scientists have."

"Sir, I honestly don't know enough about what constitutes intelligence and sentience in the human mind, let alone in an alien. To speculate in the absence of hard data would be irresponsible, sir."

Rudyard snorted. "That would be a good answer at the Academy, Dunne. But it's no use here, in the middle of nowhere."

I managed a curt, "Sir." Feeling embarrassed, my face warm.

"You know what I think? I think these things are more than just intelligent, more than just sentient. I can feel their thoughts, Dunne. Or perhaps their combined mind. They're as curious about us as we are about them. Can't you feel it?"

I thought about this, feeling uneasy. Thought about how I had felt drawn here tonight, and the peculiar dream. The creatures were waking up after their long sleep, and not in the place they expected. Were they curious? Or was that something we were projecting on them? "I'm not sure, sir, to be honest."

Rudyard's hands on the railing were tight, getting tighter. He looked tense, quivering. "Tonight — a short while ago — I received a communiqué from Service HQ."

"Sir?"

He went on, as if I wasn't there: "They're sending *Queen Helen*, son." His hands on the railing were working the metal. I could hear his breathing.

"The flagship? Uh..."

Now he looked at me. "They're taking all this back home, back to the Community. Their ship too. Everything."

This was a surprise. The Service never interfered with a ship out on patrol, not unless something extremely unique was going on. The reality of hypertube transits meant no ship could reach the edge of known space fast enough to deal with an urgent crisis with another Service vessel. A ship exploring beyond known space like *Eclipse* had to deal with problems herself; the Service would get help out to the scene as fast as possible, but that usually meant days later. *Queen Helen* must have left her last position almost a week ago, and was now expending godlike energies bending the multi-dimensional tube knots straighter than any ship had bent them before, carving through hyperspace.

I began to understand why the captain looked so agitated, so distracted. He said, "Mr. Dunne?"

"Sir?" I was trying not to think that he and Ferguson had arranged my beating that first night and tried to have Sorcha raped, just because we took precautions in an uncertain situation.

"The first duty of an officer in the Royal Interstellar Service is what?"

I felt my stomach flutter as I panicked for a moment. "Uh, to protect the Home System Community, sir." I released a great jet of breath, relieved at finding the right answer.

The captain came over to me and shook my hand. His hand was cold and moist, his eyes disturbing. Fear trickled down my back. He said softly, "Good man."

Nine

We rendezvoused with *Queen Helen* two days later. Admiral Caroline Greaves and her senior staff were invited aboard *Eclipse*, and there were the usual formalities, tours and the inevitable inspection. The *Eclipse* officer complement gathered at 1900 hours in the main assembly hall, formed into crystalline arrays in our dazzling white dress uniforms, standing at attention while Captain Rudyard, his racks of medals and citations gleaming under the halogen lights, escorted the admiral along the ranks. He made a special point of introducing Admiral Greaves to the members of the Contact Team. From my position in the rear of the formation, I watched Greaves' reactions as she met the other contact members. I was surprised at how small she was, with delicate bones, no more than five feet tall, even in her boots. She had a brisk manner, sizing up the officers with one sharp glance, instantly spotting the slightest, most minute imperfection in uniform or presentation. Her gestures were economical, her smiles fast and bright. She wore her vivid red hair in a two-millimeter bristle over her pale, weathered scalp. She looked tiny next to Rudyard, and tinier still next to Grantleigh. The captain looked like a man playing his part with little preparation. His polite smiles were too wide, his gestures too big, and even his uniform looked wrong, like it was a half-size too large.

I had spent most of my free time the previous two days trying to coax an immaculate dress uniform from fab systems around the ship. I must have tried a dozen times, but every time the clothes came out with tiny but noticeable glitches in the weave somewhere, or the brass work wasn't quite right, or the boots had a flaw in the mirror finish. In the end I had to spend hours in my quarters polishing and touching up, working like a dog trying to improve on the so-called flawless machine. I remembered the story going around the Academy that fab machines deliberately provided flawed dress uniforms, just to make cadets and officers put in this extra work. It was meant as a reminder of earlier days, before instant nanofacturing, when discipline mattered a lot more.

There was also the Zen school of uniform imperfection, which held that the process of fixing the fab-glitches in one's uniform was a necessary humbling ritual, and the act of glitch fixing was a way of wrestling with the chaos of the universe, fighting entropy. The first time I heard an upperclassman tell me that, I laughed. "Chaos of the universe? Fighting entropy?" This skepticism led to a lecture, delivered between swift kicks and punches to parts of my body where bruises would not show, about how the whole purpose of the Service was to make the universe safe for human expansion, that it was literally a matter of imposing order on chaos, and ultimately challenging the divine will of God. God gave the universe its first push, its initial breath, and in doing so had given us chaos and entropy. It was the purpose of humanity to push against the chaos, and wind back the unravelling of order. By the end of this lecture, I was a beaten and bloody lump on the common room floor, reflecting on how all this came out of a complaint about imperfections in uniforms.

Waiting for the admiral to inspect me, I tried to contain the jitters I felt in my gut and the sweat I could feel beading on my forehead, down my back, in my armpits. Greaves was stopping to shake hands with the Contact Team people as she came to them in the formation. Shaking hands! How was I supposed to stop my hands sweating? Nobody told me the admiral wanted to shake hands, or I might have grabbed some temporary washbots beforehand to take care of the sweaty palms. Nobody told me! And I was sure all those much-repaired imperfections in my uniform were obvious, even from a great distance, and that they had giant signs pointing to them: "Look! Crooked service crest on second jacket button!" Worse, that morning in the bathroom, I found two pimples: one on my forehead, the other on my upper lip. Standing there, staring in the mirror, I cursed: "Twenty-one years old, and still getting pimples!"

And in the back of my mind was the lurking, stupid thought: "*What if it's the first sign of an alien infection?*" I had seen too many stupid vids.

The captain and the admiral were proceeding along my row now. I was sixth in line, standing rigidly straight, arms at my side, thumb and forefinger touching the navy piping on the side of my trousers, as perfect a regulation stance as anyone could hope to see. Hardly breathing, I was aware of my heartbeat making me move slightly. I tried to breathe even more slowly. It wasn't helping. I felt sick, and like I might need to urinate at any moment. I could smell Rudyard's too-strong cologne; hear the admiral's crisp, deep voice whispering to him. The sound of their boots on the floor was soft yet ominous.

"And here we have the last member of the Contact Team, SSO1 Dunne," Rudyard said, coming at last to me. I did my damnedest to stare straight ahead at the cropped blond hair of the officer in the row ahead of me. Mustn't speak unless spoken to, the regs said. I wasn't about to rock the boat.

Yet I was aware of Rudyard sweating; I could smell it under his cologne. His voice was strained. It struck me as inconceivable that he would be as terrified of this woman as I was. Rudyard said to me, "Mr. Dunne, this is Admiral Greaves, of *HMS Queen Helen*. She is anxious to meet you."

Greaves said, looking up at me, "Good evening, Mr. Dunne. A very great pleasure to meet you. How are you?" And there was the hand. I wasn't looking down, but I could feel it there, puncturing my personal territory. For a moment I tried not to think about Greaves' rank, Spacecraft Command Officer level 8; it boggled the mind to imagine such a rank. Greaves, according to public record, was in her early sixties, still a young woman for such a prestigious position.

She had to notice all my flaws and imperfections from this range. She had to be aware of my sweat, my fear. I almost wanted to tell her about the second button with the Service Crest at that angle. But she only stood there, hand out, waiting, now scowling.

Rudyard cleared his throat discreetly.

I blurted, "I'm nervous, ma'am. Uh, otherwise fine. Thank you for asking. Ma'am." And, beginning to poach in the juices of my embarrassment for making such a botch of a simple greeting, I then shoved my own hand out. She took it, and gave me a crushing handshake Ferguson would have envied. I could see Rudyard behind Greaves; he was rolling his eyes, neck veins bulging. He looked very red and moist; even his immaculately brushed hair looked wet.

The admiral took back her hand and said to me, "I understand you had the most contact with the foreign vessel, Mr. Dunne. That you actually … went inside it?" Only later did I reflect how odd it was that the admiral referred to the alien vessel as "it," rather than the customary female pronoun for a ship.

"Yes, Ma'am. Yes. I did. Ma'am." I was ready for God to hit me with a lightning bolt now.

"That must have been a unique experience. I would like to hear about it from you, if you have some free time."

This was a surprise. I had become used to most of the *Eclipse* crew having no interest in the matter, or indeed an active antipathy towards the information, like they were trying to stay in their singular, borderless world as long as they could. I said, my mouth dry, "Of course, ma'am. It would be my pleasure, of course."

Instead of nodding politely and moving on, she stayed there, still looking at me. "I've always wondered, Mr. Dunne, if we really were alone out here. Haven't you?"

I blushed and stammered, "Y-yes, ma'am."

She smiled at me suddenly, perhaps trying to ease my nerves. "Then we shall have much to talk about. If, of course, Captain Rudyard can spare you?" She glanced at the captain, smiling.

Rudyard cocked an eyebrow. "I think Mr. Janning and I can arrange something, Mr. Dunne. It won't be easy, of course, with you being such a vital member of the crew…"

Admiral Greaves politely laughed at the captain's drollery, and they moved on. The tension eased. I could breathe again. It was like the time immediately after a solar eclipse, as the moon slides away from the sun, and light returns to the world. Normalcy reasserted itself. I wanted to collapse.

Until I remembered: *She wants to talk to me? Shit!*

At the end of the inspection assembly, Captain Rudyard stood with Admiral Greaves at the front of the hall, and announced, "In honor of this unexpected visit from the Service flagship *Queen Helen*, I would like to invite Admiral Greaves and her senior command staff to a formal dinner to be held here tomorrow evening." This much was standard protocol for a Service ship encountering the flagship. So much of Service life consisted of the correct exchange of courtesies, the recognition of status, position, and power. And I knew what kinds of punishments awaited those who would flout these courtesies.

Admiral Greaves allowed herself a quick, terse smile, and said that she and her senior staff would be delighted to attend this dinner.

Rudyard then surprised all of us. He added, "There will also be a small ceremony honoring the members of the *Eclipse* Contact Team." He flashed a broad, fake-looking smile at that, and encouraged a round of applause that quickly degenerated into lacklustre duty-clapping. I felt myself flushing hot, unhappy about all this fuss. I wanted only to fit in, do my job, and not be a problem, to not rock the boat. This endless fuss about the damned aliens was starting to embarrass me. I wondered what the regs said about politely refusing citations and other honors when the captain offers them, especially in the company of the flagship's command staff. I didn't like my chances.

That night I couldn't sleep — again. Since getting out of quarantine, I slept badly most nights. And I noticed I was finishing my sim sessions feeling worse than usual, more fatigued, like my brain was having to work harder than it should to absorb the things it was learning. I tried not to think about these machines changing my nervous system and mind to handle helm tasks without the necessity of conscious thought, that I was being trained to be a tool, a system component. When I looked at displays of local space, the images meant more to me; I could read the starscape in ways I couldn't before. Calling up a hypertube weather display, color-coded with drifting tube entry and exit points, and seeing that they did seem to move in formations reminiscent of weather patterns. I found I was beginning to identify regions in the display containing entry points that would lead to particular destinations, or at least I had a sense about where such tubes might lead. And I was starting to know how to distinguish entry and exit points according to trace particle emissions. There was no conscious thought involved in this process; I was learning to read tube weather, and nobody was more astounded, or more unnerved, than I was: beneath my conscious awareness these bridging lessons were rewriting my cerebral cortex and nervous system, building molecule by molecule the neural links that once would have taken years of classroom lessons and book study to form. At some fundamental level I was becoming part of the ship's systems, a machine. I loved having the new skills; I wasn't so keen on what it might be costing me.

During this time I received occasional mail from Sorcha. Our schedules were incompatible, with training and work shifts rostered at different times. She had been behind me at the big inspection, and teased me about a scratch she saw in the back of my left boot and the trailing thread dangling from one of my trouser legs. And that the collar of my jacket was drenched with sweat once the admiral had finished with me.

Sorcha also reported much the same things were happening in her head when it came to engineering problems and matters relating to ship's systems. She said she was starting to hear things in the background hum of the power plant, getting feelings and hunches about troublesome system problems. The only real problem, she said, was dealing with the men on the engineering team. It was one of the biggest teams on the ship, responsible for maintaining every system, from simple fab machines to the power plant to the metastructures governing spacecraft integrity. She wrote at one point:

> System problems I'm starting to get a good feel for. The thing that really pisses me off is the way Shackleton lets his men behave around me. I'm not some whining fem, and I can take care of myself, but I expect a bit of dignity and respect in the shop. Bad enough being the only SSO1 — that doesn't help. You know one of the 2s the other day, Gorman, saw me working with a component of the Thormann processor trunk, a thing bristling with more neuroids and processor mesh than twenty human brains, fairly heavy, and this bastard told me, 'Give it here, love. That's too heavy for a girlie like you.' I told him to piss off, of course, among other things, which generated a round of applause. But there are other things, too. During quiet times most of them just stand around talking about their sexual exploits during past shore leaves, and what they're planning when we get back to human space. These discussions get very — how shall I put this? — graphic. And charming discussions like talking about particular female celebrities and asking, 'How long would she have to be dead before you wouldn't shag her?' You'd think we'd be beyond this kind of thing.
>
> What's really puzzling is that most of them seem pretty competent engineers. On the job, they know their stuff. But once they relax, they get attacks of the stupids. I used to see this a lot at the Academy — it's one reason I got up to speed with self-defense. We might live in enlightened times, but that's only for show. When it gets down to it, things between men and women are the same as ever. I tried to complain to Shackleton, or at least as much of a complaint as it's possible

to make (you musn't rock the boat, and all). He said, 'Live with it. Join in. Give as good as you get. We work hard here, and we play hard.' Which is the same sort of answer I used to get at the Academy. So I've decided to take him at his word. Though there have been times I've come this close to decking some of those bastards for 'accidentally' brushing against my breasts or backside once too often. I think about all that stuff they told us at the Academy, about how the Service is so progressive, so enlightened, and how the men and women who serve on the cutting edge are professionals and have nothing but respect for each other, blah blah blah. Makes me want to spit!

I read all this, amused at her tone of indignation, and knowing that she would indeed flatten anybody who gave her too much trouble. She shouldn't have to put up with crap like this while going about her job. And being a SSO1 shouldn't be an excuse anymore than her gender. But like her, I had seen the same behavior at the Academy, where the men present generally acted like they were in a wonderful club in which they were the preferred members, and the women were only granted membership if they behaved 'properly'.

She spent a lot of time monitoring the guys fixing the alien ship's drive system. In another of her letters, she tried to explain it:

It's fascinating, watching them tackle this immense engine. It's completely foreign, yet at the same time, mostly understandable. The basic reactant materials are kept separate, then forced together at a key point, and the resulting titanic energy is contained and shunted through further post processing to increase exhaust velocity. The basics of it are right out of a textbook, but the details: the how and the what and the where — that's where it gets tricky and strange. And the actual components look so odd [image files attached]. At times it's like looking at a peculiar sculpture, like something pulled from the bad dreams of a mad sculptor. So many peculiar, tiny structures within other structures. Is it decoration, or is it hardware? It's almost impossible to run simulations on this thing, not knowing what all the bits are for, what they might do. Then there's the actual damage; it looks like the main reaction chambers might have blown, though some other things might have gone wrong first, leading to a supercritical build-up of plasma in the chambers. The guys are talking about building a whole new drive system from scratch, attaching it to the ship and using that to push her back to human space.

I read all this lying in my bunk, trying to sleep and thinking about that ship. Those endless kilometers of tunnels filled with cold black gel, like congealed blood in a corpse. Remembering the claustrophobic, shivery feeling of crawling through it, breathing recycled air that almost tasted fresh, and how that essential darkness formed the perfect backdrop for my projected nightmares and phobias. This is what I was supposed to talk about with Admiral Greaves? "Well, Admiral, for most of the time, when I wasn't shitting myself, I felt like I might be going mad. And, oh yes, I found some aliens."

It seemed likely she was going to tap me for a chat during the big dinner. Could a SSO1 admit to being scared shitless while engaged in such duty? Was it okay for a Service officer to have such feelings? What about a disturbing preoccupation with those creatures, and having strange, half-asleep, sweaty dreams involving them? Was I going mad? Were the creatures trying to reach me somehow? Perhaps both? That was a cheerful thought.

At 0320, I found myself heading for the isolation tank again. Shuffling my feet along the deck tiles, yawning behind my hand while managing to salute whoever I saw, regardless of their rank. I told myself I was trying to confront my fears, even as I also dreaded that something about the creatures was drawing me to them: that maybe my journeys through what seemed like the endless wretched bowels of that ship had in fact changed me somehow, or that I had become a little bit alien, a little less human, simply from contact with it. My brave, rationalizing brain tried to tell me that I had had a totally impervious environment suit on at all times, equipped with state-of-the-art equipment that would prevent anything known from getting in to me.

Anything known.

I felt cold. Dragging my feet along the halls, riding the lift up to Deck A, I kept rubbing my arms, feeling chills down my back.

There was a routine security checkpoint and airlock you had to clear before entering the viewing gallery. The checkpoint interrogated my headware, verified my ID, and let me in. The air smelled of extreme antiseptic procedures. There was a harsh tingling as the airlock systems sprayed me with scrubbers. I'd have to stop by the Infirmary tomorrow and take the refresher pill to replace my internal fauna and flora.

The second door unlocked.

As I moved to step out of the lock, I heard Ferguson, yelling, "It's goddamned well up to you! If this is what you want to do, then do it!"

And then Rudyard, howling and crying. At first I thought he might be laughing; it had that sort of sound to it. The captain was babbling something that I couldn't make out. And Ferguson was yelling at him again, trying to get him to decide something, and hurling extraordinary abuse.

That wasn't the most disturbing thing I heard. As I took a further step, I heard a deep thumping, occasional and heavy, followed by wet splashing and a distant sound such as I had never heard before. I had chills up and down my back.

I took another step. Telling myself I'd find out what was happening, I pressed on. There was more splashing, like something big thrashing around. I was thinking about how the fluid in the isolation tank would probably be a water-like liquid by now, after days of slow warming. And that the creatures would probably be active and possibly hungry.

I couldn't see into the viewing gallery from here, but I could hear the captain's bellowing sobs and screams now. "Get these fucking monster bastards out of my head! Kill them now, Ferguson! That's a fucking order!"

Ferguson shouted back, "I cannot accept that order!" There was more, lots more. Rudyard threatening Ferguson with court-martial. I heard him thumping walls, kicking chairs, wailing incoherently, screaming at God.

And, above this, the thumps of something heavy and muscular pounding at the thick plastic walls of the tank. In my head, I saw the creatures clustered together near the walls, thrashing at those walls with their two-meter sensor whips. They were struggling, but for what? Escape? Food? I didn't know.

That otherworldly ululation was coming through the gallery sound system from sensors inside the tank, a bleak, atonal chorus.

Suddenly, I heard volleys of gunshots. Rudyard screamed, "Filthy fucking monsters! Filthy, filthy bastards!"

I felt something inside me go cold and weak. Through my headware data channel I saw a display of the aliens' strange life signs, including what we thought was their brain function and circulation. I saw them flat lining, one by one. And saw the indicators measuring composition of the liquid in the tank showing a new combination of spikes. I wondered, in cold shock, if that was the creatures' blood entering the medium.

Shaking, I stood there, listening to the flat line tones, over which I could hear the captain's voice, cackling, screaming with laughter that shifted to sobbing and then back to laughter again.

God… I thought, and turned around, heading back to the airlock. During the out processing, I felt numb with horror. I squeezed through the door before it was fully open, and ran like hell away from there, terrified. It was more than I could deal with.

Lacking other ideas, I headed for the Infirmary, and messaged the duty doctor through my headware: "Doc, it's the captain. He's killed the aliens!"

Ten

"All right. Tell me again, from the beginning." *Eclipse's* security team's leader, Lily Riordan, towered over me, her blue-fire eyes studying me. I imagined her weighing my soul.

I swallowed, and looked up at her. She circled my chair, arms folded. I said, "You've got all the relevant files from my headware."

Riordan leaned over, getting her face right into my discomfort zone. "Headware can be hacked, Mr. Dunne. Did you not know that?"

Of course I had received standard Service indoctrination on issues of data security, especially as it relates to personal headware, but the Service employed the best encryption artists in the business. It was still true that a hacker with sufficient motivation and the right tools and skills could break into any secure system; headware was no different. Yet I had always felt so innocuous that I had never worried about the risk of having my own onboard systems invaded and the contents altered. Now that I stopped and thought about it, I realized that the contents of my brain-mounted data management systems were suddenly very important indeed.

"I am aware," I managed, "that headware is theoretically vulnerable, ma'am."

"Bright boy," Riordan said, resuming her orbits. She reminded me of a bird of prey, hovering on a thermal updraft, watching her target before diving in for the kill. I was sitting in her office on Deck C. There was very little decoration on her walls. She had framed a hardcopy of her Service graduation certificate, and there was a series of others noting her achievements in the fields of starship security operations, information warfare, and conventional warfare. She had a violin in an old-looking leather case resting on a wall shelf next to some books on the history of music. Soldier and musician, it was hard to reconcile the two images in her.

Riordan circled my chair, absorbing my account of what had happened, recording everything, storing it all in her own headware. She had my brainwaves, heart function, respiration, gland activity, and my actual statement. She had the records my own headware had made as I left the airlock and headed into the viewing gallery, which verified my reported statements, and the logs from all the door-ways I passed through, which showed my movements were as I reported. Plus she had the vital signs and other sensor logs from the isolation tank.

Now she sat on the edge of her desk, hands either side, and looked at me hard. "You've had a bit of a rough time since coming aboard, haven't you, Dunne?"

I winced. "Yes, ma'am."

She said, "I'm talking to you, Dunne. Look at me."

Expecting the same burning glare, I glanced up at her. She was nearly smiling at me. It was the kind of almost-smile that doesn't reach the eyes. It occurred to me that this could be Riordan's "good cop" mode.

All the same, my breath caught from the shock of it. It seemed wise to say nothing.

Riordan said, "This is not the Inquisition. You're not a suspect. But we do need to establish what happened."

"Yes, ma'am."

"Mr. Ferguson tells me you're a good officer. Dr. Grantleigh and Dr. Blackmore, too. They—"

I was nearly choking. "Ferguson said what?"

She allowed herself a wry curl of the lips. "He said you made a mistake on your first day, but you got over that. Your performance on the Contact Team mission was as good as could be expected, considering the work involved. We think you'll probably do all right."

"Ma'am...?"

"Even the captain's put a note in your file acknowledging your bravery during the Contact mission."

It took me some time to find the right words. "That's ... good to know, Miss Riordan. Thank you." My voice was dry; my guts were in knots. Praise was, in its way, as disorienting as abuse if you weren't expecting it.

She nodded, acknowledging my remark, then stood up again. "You're a bit of a mixed bag, aren't you, Mr. Dunne?"

The predatory look was returning to her face. I decided to say nothing. The confusing glow of praise was slipping away from me.

Riordan paced back and forth before me. "What I mean is that on one hand you're brave and keen to get on and do the right thing. On the other hand, you seem like a magnet for trouble. Like this business, with the captain shooting the animals. What were you doing up there in the first place?" she asked, her voice sharp. Her tone suggested she thought my inability to sleep was suspicious in itself.

I looked at her, more confused than ever. "I've been having trouble sleeping the past week. Like I said."

"So you wound up at the tank viewing gallery? Strange place to visit in the wee hours, wouldn't you say?" She sat on the edge of her desk, arms folded, staring down at me and tapping her long fingers against her flank. I saw that she bit her nails.

I felt myself fumbling, feeling guilty, trying to answer. "It's hard to describe."

"Give it a shot." There was a tone of drop-dead irony in her voice.

"I didn't kill them, you know."

Her face softened momentarily. "Never said you did, Dunne. Did I say you killed them?"

I took a breath, looked at the floor. Damn, it was quiet in here. And a slight smell, some kind of scented talcum powder. "No, ma'am," I said. But I still felt guilty, not for killing the aliens, but for having evidence that could lead to the end of Rudyard's career.

"So what were you doing there, as opposed to, say, popping out to the nearest fab for a cup of cocoa or something?"

"I already tried all that. Nothing seemed to work."

"Look at me when you answer my questions, son."

I looked at her. Her brown hair was pulled back in a no-nonsense braid. I could see her neck muscles bunching and relaxing. Her eyes were hard, but, now that I had a good look, I had the sense that she wasn't trying to crush me like a bug; she was trying to establish the truth of what happened. It made a difference in how I saw her.

She said, "This is a big ship, son. What were you doing visiting the animals?"

I tried again, ignoring the term she used for the aliens. "It's like I felt a kind of call, that they wanted me to come."

Riordan leaned in close again, staring deep into my eyes, as if trying to see the truth for herself. She squinted at me, looking a little disgusted. "You actually entered their ship, didn't you, Dunne?"

"I did, ma'am."

Shaking her head, suppressing a shudder. "God, I don't know how you could have done that."

"Just following orders."

She leaned back, but still watched me with that frightening intensity, looking me up and down, trying to extract every bit of evidence from me she could. I felt conscious of my hands. My uniform was rumpled. "None of the other Contact Team members report this sense of being drawn to the isolation tank. Just you and the captain. And the captain wasn't even on the team."

"He conferenced most days, ma'am."

She sat back and thought about this for a moment. "What a goddamn mess."

I remained silent, but agreed.

Riordan said, "I don't understand why you were visiting the tank, but for the moment let's just focus on what you saw and heard."

"I didn't see anything, ma'am, other than the sensor feeds through my headware. I told you that."

She rubbed her face. "Yes. I've got my people comparing your record of what you heard with Ferguson's record. So, you went up to Deck A, went through the airlock to the viewing gallery—"

"I didn't get as far as the viewing gallery." I explained again about hearing the voices as soon as I left the airlock.

"Right. And then you heard the captain's voice. You say he sounded upset."

"More than upset, ma'am."

"Since you came aboard this ship, have you had any reason to suspect the captain might be suffering from any kind of stress or overwork?"

This seemed like a dangerous question. If I said no, I might look stupid and unobservant, but if I said yes, I might be damning the captain. Not that I felt any great loyalty to Captain Rudyard. "I'm not sure what you mean."

"You've seen the captain in Contact Team meetings. He's your own department head. You've had dealings with him. What was your impression of the man?"

I looked away from her. "Permission to speak freely, ma'am?"

"Of course, James."

"In my opinion," I opened, looking at the halogen light bars on the ceiling, "the captain is the sort of man who would prefer to drive starships, rather than have to deal with people. He seems uncomfortable with personal contact." I caught myself holding my breath, having said this, feeling like I had just set myself up for some kind of trouble.

"I see. Would you say the captain was in any way sick or disturbed?"

I felt my eyes widen in shock. "That is not for me to say, ma'am!"

"So you don't deny the possibility?"

"Of course I deny it!"

"Well how else would you explain what happened in the viewing gallery last night?"

"I don't bloody know," I yelled, panicking, "I don't know!"

"Steady, Mr. Dunne. You're not on trial."

"I sincerely hope not! Uh, ma'am."

Riordan got up and went back behind her desk, where she settled in her large black chair, hands crossed behind her head, ankles crossed on her desk. She smiled at me. I felt doomed. "Why do you think you might be on trial?"

Surprised, I didn't know what to say for a moment. She waited for an answer. "I seem to attract a lot of trouble for some reason." I managed to explain at last.

"Like this spying incident on your first day?"

My face felt hot. "Yes, ma'am."

"There's a note on your file from Mr. Ferguson about that incident. Did you know that?"

I thought back to what she said earlier about Ferguson saying I would probably be a good officer. What else had he said? "Not specifically, but I'm not surprised." I said.

"He says you're on the cusp, that you could go either way at this point, depending on a range of things. What do you think?"

"I think Mr. Ferguson is entitled to his views, ma'am."

"James?"

"Ma'am?"

"Between you and me, Miss Riley had good reason to be concerned about Mr. Ferguson's motives."

"Is that so?"

Then she was sitting forward in her chair, arms crossed and resting on her desk. She looked fierce and grim once more. I was confused by these shifts. Maybe she was trying to keep me off-balance; it was working. "You went to the Infirmary this morning, as soon as you heard the shots and registered the animals' failing life-signs."

"I did. I saw the duty doctor. I'd sent a message ahead to alert him, and he sent a crash team to the tank. The doctor downloaded my records of what happened, like you did, and explained he would have to report this to the med team leader, Dr. Critchlow, and they'd have to decide what to do about the captain's fitness for command. He gave me some stuff to help me with the shock and stress, and sent me back to quarters. Which is where I was when you sent for me."

Riordan chewed on a stray brown hair, still thinking, staring at her cluttered desk. I didn't envy her position: trying to find out if the captain was fit for command or if some alien presence was somehow influencing him.

"Well," she said, getting up, "I'll let you get back to work."

"I can go?"

"Yes, get up. And thank you for assisting us. This is a difficult time for all of us."

"Yes, ma'am," I said, standing. "Uh, ma'am?"

She was coming around her desk, preparing to see me out. "Yes?"

"I am ... concerned about my career, if you take my meaning."

She looked at me hard, eyes full of businesslike compassion. "Mr. Dunne, if I were you, in your boots right now, I would be worried about my career, too."

"What can I do?"

"If the captain goes down, he will take anybody he can with him. I've seen this before, when I was on *HMS Halifax*. My advice? Make allies."

I looked up at her. "Thank you, ma'am. I appreciate the advice."

"Good luck."

I called Sorcha after I left; she invited me for post-chunder coffee in the Mess, at 2100.

When I got there, I found her talking to a guy I didn't recognize. He looked a bit older than I was, and his jacket sleeve bore an engineering team patch, a stylized wrench against a brilliant yellow sun. Dark hair, decent-looking features, tall, laughing with Sorcha; he had a big, booming laugh.

Sorcha turned and saw me, and flashed one of her starburst grins. "James!" she called, waving. Her companion looked around, saw me, and recognized me as the SSO1 who had gone to the alien ship, and his face appeared to stall in the process of smiling.

Sorcha made the introductions. "Alastair, this is the guy I was telling you about, James Dunne."

Feeling awkward, standing there, I stuck out my hand, trying to do the right thing, but already feeling like I should leave.

Sorcha said, "James, this is Alastair Richards. He's a three on the propulsion systems unit."

"Good to meet you, Alastair," I said, wearing a smile that felt awful, like a uniform two sizes too small. Richards reached up, gripped my hand briefly, flashed his teeth. He looked like exactly the sort of tall, handsome git who believed they were entitled to the best of everything, and therefore the best of everything landed in their laps. There had been plenty of guys like Alastair at the Academy. They were all stupid as porridge, and yet miraculously got good grades and their more colorful transgressions, after lights-out, never got them expelled. "Dunne, Dunne ... Ah yes, you're the chap who went..." He tilted his head to one side, gesturing "over there."

I clasped my moist hands in front of me, feeling awful. "Yes that was me, alone inside the ship of the damned!"

Sorcha laughed, and it didn't sound forced. She invited me to sit; I dragged a chair from a nearby empty table and occupied the empty side. I noticed Richards eased further over to the wall. Sorcha smiled, trying to cover the difficulty here through force of personality. "Alastair is one of the techs involved in fixing the alien ship's engine."

He looked at me. He didn't look like someone who wanted to talk shop. I said, "You were over there, too? What were your impressions?"

He smiled thinly. "I couldn't get out of there fast enough. If you ask me, the whole thing's a loss, a damned ghost-ship!"

Sorcha was watching me. I said to him, "Why do you say that?"

He looked uncomfortable, fiddling with his empty cup. "Like you said, Dunne, that whole ship is full of corpses. It's a flying graveyard! I don't know how you could bring yourself to go inside it." He avoided eye contact; his voice tight.

"I, well, I didn't have much choice. I was just ordered to go in, and I went... It sure as hell wasn't my idea, I can tell you that." I tried to smile, to show I was more on his side than he obviously thought.

Richards scowled, uncomfortable. "God, you wouldn't catch me going in there. I think I'd mutiny first."

Trying again, I said, smiling, "Trust me, I gave that idea serious thought!" I managed a few scruffy rags of laughter.

Impervious to such charm as I had, he said, "I'm just glad the captain wasted the bastards. Best thing he could've done, if you ask me. Best thing!"

Sorcha looked at him, surprised. She said, "How can you say that, Alastair? It's not like they were any kind of threat to us!"

He went on, his voice quite serious, "You must've heard the rumors, that the captain felt them in his mind, that they were trying to take him over, make him a drone. I say he acted just in time!"

This comment got to me. It reminded me of what Rudyard had said that night, that they were in his mind. That he had been drawn to the tank, the way I had been drawn there, even without knowing what was happening, or where I was going. I had just wound up there, and it felt right. It was a chilling thought — yet also somehow silly. I told myself that Rudyard had done a great wrong in killing those creatures, but now I found myself wondering if they were planning to take over the ship, claiming our minds one by one. What if the captain had done the right thing? What if, and this stuck in my throat, Richards was right, and the captain was some kind of hero?

"I didn't like having those filthy bastards on board. They gave me the creeps. We should've left the survivors where they were and carried on."

"Excuse me," I said, "but these creatures might well have been sentient beings like ourselves. While that possibility existed, we couldn't have just let the last of them die. It wouldn't have been right."

"They're bloody bugs, Dunne! From what I've seen, they're just oversized cockroaches, and I'll thank you, Mr. SSO1, not to suggest that we have anything in common with the likes of filth like that." I could hear his breathing, a nasty hissing through his nostrils, while the veins in his neck bulged with his tension.

"Oh," I said, taking my cue to shut the hell up, and feeling cold. I looked at Sorcha who seemed pained. I imagined her wanting Richards and me to get on well, because we had this thing with the alien ship in common. Honest enough mistake. Nobody said anything for a few moments.

Sorcha looked at her small, long-fingered hands. She said, "So, James, what's new with you?"

Richards pushed his cup to one side and moved to get up. "Excuse me, love. I've got some stuff to do in the core."

She was surprised. I wasn't. I watched him get up. He nodded to me, "Mr. Dunne," waved to Sorcha, and left.

"Alastair?" she said, watching him go.

He called her "love." I felt myself burn to ash with suppressed anger. And, feeling this, felt stupid, like I was twelve years old all over again, and having to carry bags and heavy sweaters in front of me all the time, unable to think coherent thoughts for the deafening hormonal noise in my head. For God's sake, I was twenty-one years old, I was grown up, I should be fine if Sorcha wanted to chat with someone. And yet I couldn't shake the feeling that maybe Sorcha and I did have, I don't know, at least the beginning of something going on. We liked each other's company, swapped mail constantly, talked non-stop over dinner when our shifts permitted.

And yet, we hadn't had a self-defense workout in a few weeks, and neither of us had suggested starting it up again.

"You did say the guys in engineering were assholes," I said, looking at where Richards had sat.

She shrugged and smiled laconically. "I had thought some might improve with further exposure."

"While others just reveal their true colors."

Sorcha looked pensive. "Yes, well, there is that. I certainly didn't expect that outburst from him. Of all the guys down in engineering, he'd been the only one I had thought was a bit civilized. Treated me pretty well, let me do my job my own way, watched his mouth, didn't try to cop a feel every time I went by."

"I can see his wild appeal, then." I smiled.

"It's not that. His conversation isn't much, xenophobic notions notwithstanding, but this seems to be the kind of ship where if you're a woman who's somehow with a guy in a place like engineering, the other bastards will tend to leave you alone."

I remembered hearing about this kind of tactic at the Academy. Problems set in when the guys realized they were being used mainly as protection from harassment, and not because the lady appreciated their finer points.

"I could use some coffee," I muttered, getting up, and anxious to conceal the turmoil in my head. It had been a wretched twenty-four hours.

"You all right?"

I turned back to her, frowning. "I feel like crap, to be honest." I went off to fetch some coffee from the fab. As usual it looked like some kind of hot coffee-flavored effluent. Sitting again, yawning, I looked at Sorcha. "Do I look as awful as I feel?"

"I'm sorry about Alastair."

I coughed, smiling a little. "Guys like me will never get on with guys like Alastair, Sorcha. Doesn't help that I have the stain of Otherness all over me. Seems like every other person on this ship thinks I'm somehow contaminated. Everywhere I go, people avoid me, as if I'm carrying some disease or something."

"That's bullshit!"

I was blowing on my steaming coffee. "And now I'm going to be involved in the captain's fall."

"James?" She scratched at her vermilion mohawk.

I told her about my interview with Lily Riordan, and added, "She says, cryptically, that you were right to be concerned about Ferguson, by the way."

Sorcha leaned back in her chair, eyes wide. "That so?"

"Where is the captain, anyway?" I asked, daring a sip of the coffee and getting a scalded tongue for my trouble.

"Confined to quarters while Riordan investigates. Ferguson, meanwhile, is likewise locked in his quarters, running the ship over the cloud, even more obsessive about details, regs, formalities, and procedures than usual. Last I heard he was hissing orders. Hissing!"

I shook my head, and blew on the coffee some more. "Looks like I'm locked out of the Contact Team feed, too."

Sorcha nodded. "There are rumors in engineering about the scientists having hissy fits over the loss of the specimens. Blaming each other, bitching about whose fault it is."

"The usual, in other words," I said, recognizing this pattern.

She smiled. "The usual."

"You think the captain's really gonna get the boot?" I asked.

Sorcha didn't answer immediately, her eyes locked on the display panels. A few panels had feeds from outside, showing *Queen Helen*. She was a huge ship, bigger than *Eclipse*. *Queen Helen* was almost a traveling habitat, with its own squadrons of fighters, recon observer ships, early-warning controller ships, and light destroyers tucked deep inside her flight-deck. The whole ship was a colossal, blocky thing, more than two kilometers long, and almost half a k through the middle at the widest point. She carried a crew complement of about four hundred human officers, and countless disposables.

Finally, she said, "Hard to say. If the Service was run according to the principles it advertises in its brochures, I'd say Captain Rudyard would be lucky to command an orbital tug after this."

"But we know," I said, "that those lofty principles of justice and fair play are just advertising copy, don't we?"

She flashed a cynical grin. "What happens to the captain, James, will depend on who he knows, and what favors he can pull in."

A scary thought occurred to me: "*What if he gets away with it?*"

Sorcha laughed. "Oh right! Sure!"

I was about to elaborate on this chilling thought when I heard the new-mail ping in my head. I excused myself for a moment while I checked it. And having checked it, I felt as if my face was falling off my head in shock.

"James? What's—?"

I was staring at those panels displaying *Queen Helen*. "I just got a note from Admiral Greaves' appointments secretary. Greaves wants an urgent chat with me — now!"

Eleven

During the trip over in *Eclipse's* boat, I wondered what an admiral's quarters might be like. I thought perhaps she'd have a disposable assistant and perhaps a separate sleeping area from the work area. Not only did Admiral Greaves have a suite of rooms like something out of a fancy hotel, but she had a staff of actual human crew running her affairs.

Two armed executive security guards, both real humans, met me in an otherwise empty hangar deck when I disembarked from the boat. I squinted against the dull white glare from overhead light bars and looked down at the red glow from the bay markings on the deck. The hangar air was thick with the smell of thruster propellant. The popping sound of the boat's hull adjusting to the temperature difference was surprisingly loud. The security guys escorted me through narrow, gray passageways, thronged with human officers and enlisted disposables alike, down a series of lifts and companionways until, at length, we arrived; and the two guards handed me over with great formality to another set of guards outside the admiral's door.

Queen Helen's ShipMind had sent me an information packet containing all the necessary orientation materials for important guests. I could call up a three-dimensional map of the immense ship's labyrinths that would show me exactly where I stood, but I didn't feel lost, at least not in a purely physical sense. Standing there, going through the formality of identification and presentation, with all that crisp saluting and standing at attention, and trying not to think about how my uniform shirt was itching my neck, I felt a sense of awe and fear. What the hell was I doing here, about to see an admiral? Sure, she sent for me, but it seemed unreal.

I remembered when I was in school, before the Academy, and I was doing a class in theater. One day I had to go on stage for the first time, do an actual one-man performance piece, and face my first audience, the other students. Like a moron, I hadn't understood the merits of volunteering to go first with such things, and had elected instead to go last, and thus had the pressure of all the other performances weighing on me, making me feel so much worse. I still remember the smell of the back-stage area, reeking of fresh-cut pinewood and cheap paint. Those few minutes, standing in the wings, waiting for my cue and wanting to vomit, flashed back into my mind now as I waited for the guards to admit me into the hot glare of the admiral's presence.

The door was opened for me and I was shown to a receptionist interface officer working behind a desk, consulting several sheets of Active Paper. He acknowledged my presence and asked me to please take a seat; the admiral would see me shortly. I sat in one of the plush seats nearby, feeling like I was about to see my doctor. From time to time a senior officer would come in, nod to the receptionist, and go straight on through one of the three large doors leading further into the admiral's suite. At one point three such officers, all of them Spacecraft Command Level 6 or above, left through one door talking animatedly about something. I felt like a piece of bleeding baitfish trying to avoid the notice of sharks.

An SCO4 female officer appeared at the door, smiled at me, and said those dreaded words, "SSO1 Dunne? The admiral will see you now."

"Mr. Dunne! How good of you to come! Please, come in." The admiral met me at the door, shook my hand with what felt like real warmth, and, hand on my back, escorted me to a comfortable couch next to a low coffee table. A couch! Her simple gray steel businesslike desk was several paces away, nothing fancy.

Admiral Greaves asked me, "Could I interest you in a hot beverage, perhaps?" She asked as if my answer was something she actually wanted to know. I frowned, confused, and declined her offer — and immediately wondered if I had done the right thing. The admiral smiled, and arranged herself a cup of strong black coffee, using real ground beans and what looked like an antique plunger. The aroma of it, after all the fabbed coffee I had consumed over the years, was almost too much to bear. She poured with her back to me and said in a surprisingly deep voice clipped with formality, "What do you think of our flagship, Mr. Dunne?" Strange to notice that even in the act of making coffee, she stood so straight, her bearing formidable. I imagined that, being a small person and a woman she'd had to work hard to make others take her seriously.

I flapped my mouth several moments before saying, "She's a beautiful ship, ma'am. So big! It's hard to think about." This remark, once out of my mouth, embarrassed me. What a dumb thing to say! So big? I could have shot myself.

She turned, sipping at her coffee from a blue ceramic mug marked "Caroline's Mug," and sat on a couch opposite the coffee table. Despite her petite stature, she dominated the room with her gaze. I noticed the blotched, leathery quality of her facial skin and scalp, which reminded me of the story I heard years ago about Caroline Greaves, and how during a routine solo mission with a ship's boat she had been obliged to climb outside it for a manual system repair, and her environment suit suffered a non-critical failure. She was exposed to hard radiation from the local system star for three hours before she got the ship's boat operational again. She had refused the offered commendation.

Greaves said to me, glancing around the enormity of this room, "She's certainly nothing like I ever expected to see when I was an SSO1."

"Those must have been great days," I said, saying more or less the expected comment when in the presence of a reminiscing senior officer.

But I was surprised by what she said in reply: "Of course, that was back when human space was still more or less a cohesive political and economic cooperative, before we started splitting up into all these groups."

Forty years ago, more or less. She had probably served on one of the old *Zeppelin*-class patrol ships, over-engineered clunkers whose duty mainly consisted of protecting trade lanes and ferrying troops, diplomats, and settlers. Such ships could push themselves to forty percent of lightspeed, and the crews had to deal with all the miseries of relativistic travel. Things took a long time to happen.

"Didn't the Kestrel Event bring about the fracturing of human space" I said, recounting old wisdom.

She sipped her coffee. "It certainly put the fear of God through everyone — literally. Fear of all kinds of things. Fear makes people turn inward and look askance at foreigners. Suddenly you're looking at the politics of us and them. Whatever happened at Kestrel, it was invisible, the worst kind of enemy. When you're up against something you can't see, everybody else suddenly looks like they might be an enemy agent. Wretched business. This new development won't help matters, either."

I thought about what Sorcha said in her letter about the tsunamis of information that would crash through human space when word of this new event spread. Saying nothing, I let the admiral talk.

"Doesn't it seem strange to you," she said, "that you and I serve the Home System Community? We're a minority in the total scheme of things, yet we make the most noise about how we stand for what is good and just and right for everyone. No wonder the others laugh at us."

I hadn't expected this in our meeting. Sitting there, my hands in my lap, I wondered what I might say, or if I was meant to say anything at all. When I had received the admiral's note back on *Eclipse*, I assumed she wanted to talk about either my disturbing adventure aboard the alien vessel, or the strange business of Captain Rudyard killing the aliens. Maybe both. I said, trying for a non-controversial attitude, "I had sometimes wondered about this, myself, Admiral."

She studied me over the rim of her coffee mug. Her green-eyed gaze impaled me, making me feel like an interesting insect. "Indeed? And what did you conclude?"

I hesitated. "Ma'am?"

She flashed me another smile. "Your captain speaks highly of you, Mr. Dunne. And the reports from Dr. Grantleigh of the Contact Team tell me you're an officer with a good brain in his head."

Despite a suddenly dry mouth, I said, "May I speak freely, ma'am?"

The admiral looked surprised that I asked. She nodded.

I said, unsure of myself, "I just figured that things at the level of nation-states take a long time to change, while things at the level of individual people change quickly."

"Go on, Mr. Dunne, please." She looked neither encouraging nor hostile, and quietly sipped her coffee.

Trying to work some moisture into my mouth, I said, "I'm not surprised that so many of the people who used to be part of the HSC now want to be with people like themselves, but then I, if you'll pardon my speaking at such, er, length, also used to hear my father say that the HSC government didn't try very hard to keep anyone." After all, it wasn't that everyone else had deserted the Home System; it was one of the most densely populated star systems in human space. The problem was that so many residents of the Home System were citizens of other states.

"Interesting, very interesting. What do you then say to the argument that the government's moral mandate is to fight the chaos of the universe?"

"Uh, Admiral?"

"It's an important issue, Mr. Dunne. Don't they still teach you this at the Academy? I mean to say, ever since the death of Earth, we humans have striven to avenge our world's loss by whatever means, correct?"

I was aware that most governments in human space had loose co-operative programs aimed at trying to work out, despite the indefinite United Nations embargoes on all data pertaining to the home world's loss, just what had happened to Earth, and that one of the leading contenders among all the competing theories was that aliens had done it. This theory had always been quite untenable, however, since we knew of no aliens against whom to take our revenge. But now we did. Could there be others?

"Of course, ma'am," I said, not sure where she was going with this. As dangerous as the universe often seemed, I didn't think it stacked up much against the danger I was feeling right here in this office. What was going on with the admiral?

The admiral put her cup on the coffee table. She leaned back, getting comfortable, hands clasped around her knee. "Were you aware that the HSC Lords and Admiralty are planning to downsize the Service?" She said this in the sort of quiet voice that masks profound outrage.

I tried to keep my face from exhibiting the complete shock I felt. "Ma'am?"

"They want to cut starship operations and support personnel by at least thirty percent, perhaps more, depending on the government's political will and the mood of the citizens — which right now is leaning against live humans being in space. Widespread mothballing of ships, perhaps forty or fifty vessels in all, including at least four of the six *Eclipse*-class ships." She paused to let out a breath. "They're toying with the idea of using advanced disposables and autonomous starships for exploration in future. Human beings are considered too valuable to risk out here."

This was overwhelming. I fought to maintain my composure. I knew *Eclipse* was an old ship by today's standards, but I thought she'd probably have at least another five or ten years left, with regular system upgrades and refitting. As for the mood of the people back home, it was hard not to notice that there was a constant background hum of talk about the fear of war with the Asiatic Cooperation Metasphere, among others. Maybe exploration into the dark had gone far enough, that it was time to divide up what we already had. Even though what we had was starting to seem like not enough anymore.

"If you will excuse me, ma'am," I said, now very glad I had declined a drink, "I am not sure why you are sharing Service policy information with a junior officer like myself."

"You're right to be confused, Mr. Dunne. Normally an SSO1 wouldn't know what had hit him until he was dumped outside the base gates back on Ganymede with his discharge papers and kit bag. When the cutbacks come around, the last ones on are the first ones off."

I knew she was right. I had seen the Service shed staff before in response to changing needs and missions, and always striving to be "a lean, mean Service," as their PR drones liked to say. Yet I had noticed that somehow senior command staff always managed to keep their posts.

Greaves got up, paced slowly back and forth, deep in thought. I noticed she could move about twelve paces in this room alone before having to turn. This much space for a single officer on a starship was unthinkable. I remembered reading about the Home System Service flagship *Earthrise*, from fifty years ago, before the present Royal Interstellar Service existed. The whole ship was just under two hundred meters long; the admiral's quarters were the size of two closets — like a monastic cell, only not as roomy. Things had been so different then; it had cost a fortune to put people out in space. But now it cost a great deal more to ignore the opportunities space offered.

I noticed Admiral Greaves was agitated about something. She said, not looking my way, "In two days' time, Mr. Dunne, Captain Rudyard will stand before a board of inquiry consisting of some of my most senior officers. Excellent people, all handpicked. There will be much posturing and yelling and formality and citing of regulations and similar nonsense."

"Admiral?" Where was all this leading? I was confused. First she was talking about taming the universe, and now she was going on about Rudyard's future.

She glared at me. "Listen, I'm trying to help you."

I thought for an anxious moment, *Help me? Help me with what?* I began to see there was more going on here than merely an aging admiral muttering about how today's Service was nothing like the Service of her youth.

Admiral Greaves, I began to see, was up to something. And it might involve me. The thought gave me cold shivers; I felt a little ill.

She went on. "And at the end of all that, Rudyard will get a slap on the wrist for killing those creatures — and an official commendation, the Royal Service Cross, authorized and to be presented by Queen Helen herself, once we get back to civilization."

I blinked, thought, *Shit*! And said, "He's going to get away with killing them!"

The admiral leaned on the back of the couch, looking at me. "He will not only get away with it, Mr. Dunne, he will be told 'Jolly good effort, old man!'"

I held my head. It was starting to throb. "But I, uh, I don't think the captain is..."

Still looking at me, she flashed a wry smile. "You mean, you think he's a few protons short of a nucleus?"

"I heard him the night he shot the aliens, ma'am. He wasn't ... he wasn't himself."

"Mr. Dunne, as far as I can tell your captain is quite mad. You get officers like that sometimes, particularly the older ones, who came in before we had decent screening and treatment methods. This poking around out here in the dark, beyond the lights of civilization, can be quite psychologically damaging. It's the thought that, your crew aside, there isn't another living being in ten or twenty light-years, over a hundred trillion kilometers. It's frightening, what isolation can do."

"I see," I said, lying. I had been taught that space travel was boring, like I had told Ferguson my first day aboard ship and that nothing much happened out of the ordinary. Unless I somehow accidentally skipped the Academy lectures about how exploring space could drive you mad.

The admiral went on, "Your ship is about to get orders to return to Ganymede for a weapons upgrade, and to take on cargo for a special mission."

"I still don't see why you're telling me this, ma'am."

The admiral came and sat on the table, directly facing me. She said, her eyes bright with zealot fire, "The Royal Interstellar Service is corrupt!"

Wide-eyed, I stared back at her. I didn't feel like I dared look away. And I wondered if Rudyard was the only crazy officer around here. Remembered, too, what Lily Riordan had told me, that I would need to find allies if I was to survive what was meant to happen to the captain. Well it looked like the captain was going to survive, but I suddenly felt like I might need allies all the more urgently. Already I knew I had earned Ferguson's ire, which was a ticking time-bomb whose blast had yet to come. Now it looked like I had attracted the interest of this admiral, whose conduct was worrying me more with each passing moment.

"How do you mean, exactly?" I asked her.

She moved to sit next to me. Close enough that I could feel her thighs warm against my white trouser leg. I could smell the coffee on her breath. "That our beloved Service is corrupt, you mean?"

I swallowed. "Yes, ma'am. Corrupt in what way?"

She smiled at me. Her teeth were small and white. "Your service record shows you know this already, Mr. Dunne. You know what's going on, the price you have to pay to get along."

I heard Ferguson saying, "Don't rock the boat!"

She continued, "You were taken to the Academy Infirmary six times in just one semester of your junior year! The cadet disciplinary council reported dozens of instances where you were found in need of their special brand of disciplinary action."

More embarrassment. I had no idea such information was attached to my personal records. Yes, I knew all about those bastards at the disciplinary council and their thuggish ideas about correcting wayward cadets. I recalled that most of my so-called offences against the Service cadet code of conduct occurred during my protests against the unbelievably harsh punishments that I was receiving for trivial infractions.

I realized that the admiral's hand was resting on my right thigh. It was light but astonishingly hot. She watched me silently, waiting to see what I would do. We both knew she had now moved far beyond the scope of existing regulations and guidelines governing the conduct of senior officers towards junior officers. If I let her keep it there, I was committing an offence of my own. I wanted to tell her to move that hand. Wanted to move myself off the couch. But the consequences of offending someone as powerful as an admiral...

"Ma'am..." My voice was hoarse. I was deeply uncomfortable, and scared. I was starting to see how an unremarkable but reasonably intelligent junior officer who was likely to be bundled out of the Service when the next round of cutbacks came, might be of use if you were an admiral with a burning desire to cleanse the corruption from the Service.

She leaned closer, and whispered, conspiratorially. "Mr. Dunne, the Service was not always corrupt. The Service I joined would take your captain and pension him off, or put him in a veterans' treatment program and try to help him deal with his demons. The Service you joined is going to make him a hero and give him his command back."

I tried to lean away from her. She was pressed against me. I said, "You said your handpicked officers are going to exonerate the captain. How can—?"

"Orders have come down from the Admiralty, and in turn from the Lords above them. Captain Rudyard has lucked out. He has been picked for a special mission, largely by doing the right thing for the wrong reasons."

"You mean, because of his ... incapacity?"

She shrugged. "Your ship found actual, tangible aliens out here in the dark. And these aliens will save us all, in a suitably perverse fashion. We have a cause!" She was staring deep into my eyes, saying this. She was scary, but at the same time, there was something intoxicating about attention like this, receiving exclusive information. I felt very hot.

"This cause is going to save the Service, is that what you're thinking?" I asked nervously.

She flashed me a big, wide smile. "Precisely! Aliens we can see; aliens we can kill; aliens we can use to justify a halt to downsizing and cutbacks, perhaps even use to justify an expansion. Battleships, Dunne! Dreadnoughts!"

"But the captain..."

She made an offhand gesture and kept smiling at me. "Captain Rudyard must go, of course. Probably Ferguson, too, the pig."

Something treacherous in me began to think the admiral was a striking-looking woman for her age. "This is all very interesting," I said, my gut roiling, cold with anxiety, tension, excitement, "but—"

"What does it have to do with the likes of SSO1 Dunne?"

She moved her right hand, and ran a long, thin finger down the side of my face, brushing the edge of my mouth. She was grinning as I fought to suppress a shiver. "James, I am going to restore the glory of the Service. And I think you want that, too." The admiral's face was too close to mine. I could see tiny beads of perspiration on her upper lip.

"Well, yes," I said, knowing there was huge trouble ahead, but not really caring. "But—"

"You want to hit back at every bastard who ever screwed you over and made your life a living hell, don't you?"

That hit me where I hurt; she knew my point of vulnerability. Memory-fragments of traumatic nights, of ritual pain giving in the name of group bonding, discipline, and the dissolution of the self. I had forgotten or suppressed a lot of it, but there was some I still remembered, and about which I still had nightmares. I dreaded encountering those men again, because I did not know what I might do. Some of the dread was a fear that I might kill them; most of the dread was that I would do nothing, and let them do it all again. I knew that at the beating, rotten heart of the Royal Interstellar Service, we were bound to each other through transactions of pain and blood. And that it had not always been this way. In the end I decided that if there was a chance that this foul organization could be cleaned up, I would help in whatever capacity I could. Some things were more important than one junior officer's less than stellar career. It scared the shit out of me thinking about it, but after all that had happened to myself and others like me, it was worth it.

"Oh yes," I said, thinking about those memories, about all that buried pain, not really aware that my eyes were looking at her mouth. That, for perverse reasons I can't explain, I was getting aroused.

I realized tears were falling from my eyes. She said, holding the side of my face, "Well, you and I, and some trusted others, are going to make things right."

"What can I do? I'm just a level nothing tubeworm. I'm not even finished my bridging training."

She said, "Listen..." and softly, quietly, kissed me.

Twelve

Rudyard got his medal.

It went just as the admiral predicted, complete with an inquiry that featured screaming, yelling, posturing, and all the rest. For three days it was as if the ship vibrated with the tension of it. But, in the end, Rudyard found himself standing at attention before the board, visibly trembling despite manful efforts to maintain composure, and they told him his command was safe, his competence not in question. But he would rise no further in the ranks; that was the price he would pay for killing creatures about whom we knew so little, other than that they were probably harmless. In expert testimony Grantleigh and Blackmore disagreed on whether or not they were intelligent. For every piece of evidence Grantleigh provided to show they were intelligent, Blackmore countered with evidence to the contrary. The matter was not to be decided then, and it hardly mattered.

The medal presentation was beautiful, of course, the ceremony held once we returned to civilized space and could access a relayed low-latency feed from one of the queen's satellite nodes. We were arrayed in the nave of St. Paul's Cathedral, in the living ghost of an England that never was. I remember the fall of light, sparkling with dust-motes, through the towering stained glass windows in the apse, the images depicting the torments of the saints, often cited as the original heroes of the Home System Community. The resolution of the rendered environment was awesome; I marveled at the spookiness of the acoustics in the great dome's whispering gallery, and the miraculously iterated arches everywhere I looked, stretching back to the dark entrance, and the sublime vaulted domes of the ceiling.

Sheathed in white silk and sapphires, the queen stood at the altar, but somehow had time to talk to each one of us. She had wide-set, violet eyes, soft brown hair, a straight, fine-boned nose, and the palest skin; she shone in the stained light. Her voice was warm but still a little wry, as if secretly amused at all this fuss. She wore a perfume I was never able to identify, and I suspect was a one of a kind created only for her: striking, pretty, but not sexy. Helen needed no perfume in any case; she was our queen.

Rudyard, his rumpled, melancholy face transformed into a visage of humble rapture, knelt before the monarch of the Community, bowed his head, and listened to the queen's measured voice commending him for a job well done "in dangerous, treacherous, challenging circumstances, for making space safe for all humanity."

I could have killed him. It was hard to see Rudyard congratulated like this for what he had done. Partly because of the creatures themselves, but mainly because of the pretense: he was being honored as if he had acted out of loyalty and duty — and competence. I knew he had come unhinged, at least for a short time. I was trying to shed the memory of his terrible sobs, begging Ferguson to do the deed for him, and Ferguson refusing. There was nothing heroic in this.

Yet there was the thought that wouldn't leave: *what if the captain had indeed protected us? Then again, what if he just didn't like the way they had looked at him?*

I looked around, and saw, among the crew of the Service flagship, Admiral Greaves. She was among the first, once the formalities were complete, to rise to offer Captain Rudyard a standing ovation, and the horns were sounding, and then the heralds announced that Captain Humphrey Douglas Rudyard had achieved the rare distinction of the Royal Service Cross. As we stood and applauded, the QH satellite node was transmitting the construction codes for the physical version of the Royal Service Cross to *Eclipse* so the captain's personal fab could build the medal and have it ready by the time we finished the ceremony and emerged from the cloud.

Admiral Greaves clapped and cheered with abandon, though I saw her sneak a look my way. She did not wink, nod nor otherwise suggest anything was different or significant between us. There was no need. I felt my face burn.

By now the spyware she had injected into my head was approaching the end of its growth and installation phase. I could feel something going on in there, the new system settling in, calibrating, and configuring. Sometimes I felt a twisting wave of blurring dizziness and had to lean against a wall to avoid falling; other times, I suddenly felt feverish and needed to sit and breathe deeply. I ran diagnostic routines through my existing headware to make sure the new system was interfacing properly, and so far, everything was checking out. It wasn't like I was a kid, and experimenting with cracked game wetware from the Heart of Darkness habitat and places of similar ill-repute, where slipshod attention was paid to the immuno side of the equation and processor cycle transformer problems. Lots of kids got their brains fried trying experimental headgames. Their new brains took about five years coming up to speed and function, but were never the same.

The admiral explained the new spyware to me during the latter part of my fateful meeting with her. She had run her finger along my naked leg, her bristly head resting on my chest, and said "It takes about six days for the spyware to finish linking in with your existing headware and establish the necessary immuno balance. The material has been keyed for your body, so tissue rejection shouldn't be an issue."

I'd said, "Well that's almost comforting. What if it does my brain in?"

She pinched me, hard. "If there is a problem, execute a normal hard system eject and the spyware should revert to phage food as per usual. Any questions?"

Sorcha was furious about the captain's medal. "He slaughtered those creatures! Slaughtered them in some addle-brained psychotic spasm of madness! He killed them in cold blood!" She whispered all this, her hands bunched into fists, the skin over her knuckles looking tight enough to break.

"Steady, Sorcha," I said, not wanting her words over-heard even in the empty Mess hall. It was late in the night after the ceremony, and we were sipping fabbed coffee, feeling bitter. *Eclipse* was braking as we approached Ganymede, our adventures in the dark over for now. *Queen Helen's* engineers had finished the power plant work our people started, and installed an emergency hypertube grapple-driver. As of right now, the alien vessel was approaching a classified Service installation for detailed examination and the stifling seal of official secrets regulations had been placed over the details of our entire encounter with it.

Back in known space, the mood of the crew was more upbeat — except for Sorcha and me, and each of us for different reasons. I let her rant. She didn't know what the admiral had planned for Rudyard, and I wasn't about to tell her. It was hard to think about because there were so many complex feelings involved, many of them nega-tive. Suddenly I was a spy, and potentially a traitor if I got caught. Caroline — she had invited me to call her Caroline — said I was not to panic. I was to keep calm and await instructions should anything untoward hap-pen. In time I would be properly rewarded for my noble service, she said.

I hadn't been paying attention to Sorcha. She was say-ing, "What's the bloody Service coming to when it gives butchers medals? What the hell are we doing in this outfit, James? What's the point? First real aliens we ever encoun-ter, and we kill them stone dead and call it heroism! It isn't what I signed up for, it isn't what I put up with four years of torment and agony and crap for. What am I supposed to tell my family? Huh? What do I tell them?"

I got a paper towel for her tears. She snatched it and seemed to bash it against her eyes and cheeks, and blew her nose so hard I thought she'd burst a blood vessel. I could think of nothing to say. Staring into my half-empty coffee cup, I sat there, feeling useless and remote. What could I say? I felt the same way as Sorcha. In some ways, I felt worse because I had been directly involved in rescuing those creatures. I had a kind of stake in their lives. Few things infuriated me the way the news of Rudyard's acquittal and commendation did, even though I knew it was coming. Which only made me think more about the admiral, who had opened the door a little into the world of Service *realpolitik*.

"James, are you even listening?"

Looking at her, seeing the vivid, electrifying anger in her face, I thought she looked like an avenging angel, ready to smite heathens. It made me catch my breath, and I couldn't help but wonder what a girl with her brains and talent might do.

I said, bringing myself back into focus, "Oh, yes, I was listening. I quite agree. I feel sick about it, completely disgusted." But even I could feel the lie in my words. My mind was already thinking ahead to my part in the admiral's plan, of taking action rather than simply sitting around venting about the unfairness of it all.

She gave me a sour look. "Well thanks for listening. I gotta go."

"Sorcha?" She was up and walking off, a woman with a mission. I went after her, tried to talk to her.

"James," she stopped and turned to face me, "you've been acting funny since the day you saw the admiral. What's wrong?"

I really wanted to tell her, to confess to things I had done and had yet to do. But how could I admit that one of the most senior officers in the Service had seduced me, a ploy as old as history, and recruited me to spy for her? And that as disgusted as I was at myself for getting into such a situation, I had to admit to a certain puerile excitement, too. It was the excitement of access, of being inside the loop. I couldn't even explain it to myself, let alone to a friend ... or someone like Sorcha. It occurred to me suddenly that I was terrified of disappointing her.

I knew the admiral was using me. That part was obvious, as was the realization that I could get seriously burned by the whole thing.

And yet I also knew that, at some level, in a filthy sort of way, I liked being used.

I felt the words begging to escape my lips, but said nothing. The shame was too great. I did not think I could stand Sorcha's disappointment in me if I told her the truth, even if it had been safe to tell her. So I shrugged and did my best to look helpless and hopeless, my usual face. "What can we do, just a couple of Level 1 nobodies?"

She flashed a lethal glare at me. "Nobodies? You just watch!"

We docked at Ganymede Stalk geosynch three days later. Rudyard announced five days shore leave for the whole complement while *Eclipse* underwent some minor refitting and resupply.

Ferguson had other ideas for me. He found me in my quarters while I was packing a bag. I had planned to head down to Winter City, get up to some mischief, and start following Captain Rudyard. The spyware announced the day before that its installation was complete. So far I had only had time only to tinker with the preferences and familiarize myself with the online help files. I knew Rudyard was planning to celebrate his good fortune at a few of the big casinos in Winter City, which would be an ideal setting in which to monitor him.

But it wasn't quite that simple. Ferguson stood in the doorway, legs apart, hands behind his back, a living textbook demonstration of parade rest. He scowled at me as though I were an annoying speck of grime on the inside of a toilet that needed scrubbing off.

I felt a visceral twist of alarm, seeing him there, puffed up like that. Had he somehow detected my new spyware? It shouldn't be possible. It was designed to look like a simple upgrade to my mediafilters, perfectly legit. "Mr. Ferguson," I said, feigning pleasant surprise as I picked among various colors of underwear, "I would have thought you'd be downStalk by now, sir."

Ferguson said, "You saw the admiral the other day."

I dumped all the underwear I could find in my bag. "Yes, sir," I said, meeting his gaze, and trying to get headware biostatic control to suppress any blushes that might be imminent.

"You never told me how the meeting went, Mr. Dunne. I felt most offended when you didn't report to me on it."

That sounded odd, but I didn't remark on it. "Very sorry, sir. I wasn't aware I was required to report the proceedings of the meeting."

"You forget, son. I'm the executive officer, I need to know what's going on aboard ship. It's my job."

I would have thought that particular job would be Riordan's since she was in charge of security, but I didn't say this. "I see, sir." I checked through my available shirts, thinking about fabbing some new ones; did I have enough fab-credit?

"Well, then, Mr. Dunne?" he asked, rocking on his feet now, his voice pitched low and quiet. "Must I lever it out of you with a crowbar?"

"It was a very pleasant meeting, sir," I said, dumping all my shirts in my bag, not meeting his steel stare at all now, and beginning to feel a flush coming on, as well as wretched flutters in my gut. "We talked about old ships."

"You talked about old ships, did you?"

"Yes, sir. Old ships."

"That must have been very ... stimulating."

I almost dared look at him then, just to show him I wasn't afraid of him. But I was afraid of him, and tried to maintain my cool by checking my bag again. "The admiral saw in my file that I'm a bit of a space geek. Shipspotter, that kind of thing."

"So you spent the afternoon there chatting about power plant specifications, avionics components, controller subsystems, interface guidelines, construction numbers, and all that, yes?"

"Pretty much, Mr. Ferguson, sir." And I could have talked about those things, too, if given a chance. Not like my brother Colin, of course, but I could have.

"I see."

I didn't think I was out of trouble yet. He came into the room, and stood next to my bunk. "And what did you really talk about over there for so long, Dunne?"

I was running out of possessions to dump into my bag. "Excuse me, sir, I need to use the head."

He stopped me, putting one of his great, slab-like hands on my bony shoulder. "I don't think so. I don't think so at all."

"Sir?" I glanced his way. He was dark with suppressed anger.

"Sit, Dunne. Now."

I sat on my bunk, hunching my head over so I didn't bang it on the upper bunk. Ferguson perched himself on the opposite bunk, hands on his knees, watching me. His uniform was immaculately pressed.

"First of all, boy, I want you to unpack that bag and stow all your gear where it was."

"May I ask why, sir?"

He roared: "Just bloody do it, Dunne! You hear me?"

I jumped, banged my head, ignored the pain, and set about replacing my stuff into storage. I wasn't aiming for neatness, just chucking things wherever they'd go. Finished, I sat again, hands on my bed covers, scared. Outside I heard groups of other officers heading down the corridors, talking about their plans. They sounded happy: teasing each other, organizing drinking contests, comparing taverns and brothels.

"All right, Mr. Dunne. Now listen to me, and listen to me very well. Something happened during your, shall we say, lengthy visit with Admiral Greaves. I don't know what, but I will. And you're going to tell me."

"Sir?"

"What?"

"There's nothing to tell, sir." *Nothing I'd tell you about, that's for sure.* I remembered Greaves referring to Ferguson as "that pig."

"What are you smirking about?"

"Nothing, sir."

"Spit it out, Dunne. Let's hear it!"

"It's nothing, sir!"

"If there's a joke I would like to hear it, Mr. Dunne. God knows I could use one!"

I couldn't agree more, but I kept my mouth shut.

"Mr. Dunne," he said, his tone quieter now, and getting to his feet to pace back and forth before me, "I've been talking to Mr. Janning."

I listened.

For a moment he looked actually disappointed in me, and he shook his head a little and let out a breath that smelled bad. "Mr. Dunne, Mr. Dunne, Mr. Dunne. You know I was starting to think, particularly after the Contact mission, I thought, maybe the kid's going to be all right after all. Learned your lesson, had a good hard look at yourself."

"Sir?" Somehow the thought of disappointing him was a horrible thing to bear.

"Well," he said, looking at me. "And now this."

"This?"

"You know very well what I mean, boy. You were supposed to report your meeting with the admiral to me. It's in the Standing Bloody Orders, for Christ's sake."

I felt things clench deep in my guts. And a quick search through my headware copy of Standing Orders showed an obscure fine-print clause including the optional instruction that the contents of meetings with senior officers from other ships may be reported to one's own senior officers. To the best of my knowledge the clause was no longer active, but had yet to be removed from the Standing Orders.

"That order is optional, sir," I said, glancing at him, knowing I had the text of the Orders on my side.

There was a long, cold silence. His face darkened. His lips disappeared. He said, softly, "I will not be lectured on Standing Orders by a Level Bloody 1 piece of shit like you."

My bowels turned to water. I said nothing. Bitter experience had shown me that clinging to the text of regulations once things reached this point was asking for trouble.

At length, visibly trembling with suppressed anger, he said to me, "I've arranged with Janning for your temporary reassignment to me."

Oh God. "Yes, sir."

"Which means, of course, that you will be my little slave boy — my pet, my plaything if you will — for as long as it takes you to tell me what happened during your visit with Admiral Greaves."

Suddenly I was very glad I was sitting. Memories shot through my mind of the underside of Academy life, the vile system in which upperclassmen kept junior cadets as pets and slaves to cater to their whims. In theory the idea was that the senior cadets would act as mentors and counselors to the juniors, be role models and friends. In practice, however, juniors were kept as errand boys, butlers, domestic servants — and worse. The unlucky junior cadets were also used to get contraband items into the Academy grounds such as booze, drugs, disposable prostitutes. All in all, it was considered miraculous if a cadet could find time for study, sim work, parade drill practice, lectures, presentations and everything else. Until, of course, you made it into the later years and could get a slave of your own. And such was the degree of bitterness you had about how you were treated as a junior that you felt obliged to treat your junior the same way.

I escaped the loop of slavery when my senior, Philip Dewey, graduated and moved on to his first commission. The day he left I felt strange: relieved, happy — and devastated. Somebody suggested I try some counseling to deal with how I felt — some treacherous part of me missed Dewey! — but that lasted only two sessions. I couldn't talk about it.

And here was Ferguson threatening to drop me in all that again. It was damned tempting to break right there and tell him everything about that evening on Greaves's couch. But I still had faith in her plan; I was convinced that if I stayed the course, Rudyard and Ferguson were history. I vowed to stay silent, no matter what it took.

I said, "Fine, sir."

He hesitated, surprised at my reaction, I think. Then, "Have you ever wondered how much floor space there is in all the crew decks, Mr. Dunne?"

"I'm sure I'm about to find out, sir," I said, feeling more chipper by the moment now that I had resolved to stick with the admiral's plan. While I concentrated on the greater good, I felt I could stand whatever he had to throw at me. Thinking back now, after all that's happened, I find myself laughing at this. I couldn't have been more wrong.

"Good attitude, son. Good attitude." He said this with a tone of cautious approval, like he was wondering what was going on.

"Sir. Permission to ask a question, sir?"

He looked surprised again. Looking at me more carefully, he said, "Mr. Dunne?"

"Mr. Ferguson, sir," I said my voice as loud as his had been, my eyes staring straight ahead, "what was it like watching the captain murder harmless aliens? Sir!"

I saw his face color, and watched him get up. He crossed the floor in one stride, "Why you weaselly little shit!" he said, and clobbered me.

So it began.

Thirteen

Ferguson didn't mess around. He fabbed me a brush the size of my index finger, provided a fab machine code that would generate weak, soapy water in a heavy steel bucket, and set me to work on my hands and knees, scrubbing every square millimeter of deck surface. He started me at Deck E, and told me to work my way up to Deck A. I went through a lot of soapy water and brushes. After two days, working sixteen hours straight each day, my knees were wrecked and I was in agony. Ferguson granted me grudging permission to visit the Infirmary. The docs were only able to give me mild painkillers. Requests for kneepads were refused, on Ferguson's orders. Anything that would make the scrubbing experience more tolerable was out of the question. Telling him about the meeting with Admiral Greaves, on the other hand, was the cost of escape, even if it would only be an escape from one kind of trouble to another.

In the evenings, I had to wait on him in the Officer's Mess, standing at attention by his side as he ate his space chunder. He actually liked the chunder, which made him about the only officer on the ship who did. If Ferguson wanted anything at all, I was to fetch it, without delay. Standing there like that, my legs howling with pain, my whole body a solid, grinding ache, I wanted to kill him. Senior officers would come by Ferguson's table to chat, and much humor was tossed about at my expense. I learned that Ferguson was infamous for this treatment of junior officers he thought needed his personal touch. I didn't like the way everyone snickered at the phrase "personal touch," and neither did I like him occasionally patting me on the backside. "Bit of good meat there, eh?" he'd say, laughing.

I felt grateful so many of the crew were planetside, taking in the sights. Most of all, I was grateful not to see Sorcha. There had been no mail from her. During the endless hours of scrubbing, I imagined her with Alastair. My jealous anger over that was a relatively pleasant distraction from my loathing of Ferguson.

In the evenings, after Ferguson had enjoyed his dinner, he repaired to his quarters, with me in tow. "Come along, boy," he'd say, "chop chop!" It was like something from an old vid. In his quarters I poured wine — only the finest cheap rotgut from some god-awful underground hydroponic "Chateau Test-Tube" vineyard on Mars. I also made his bed, and laid out his sleepwear, and fetched him cigars, and massaged his malodorous and sticky feet, and polished his boots long past the point where I could see my haggard face in them. I mended his uniform, replaced lost buttons and adjusted piping.

He even let me clean and polish his gleaming Service sidearm, a Proddi ten-millimeter bimodal pistol. Thirty caseless rounds in the magazine, divided into solid slugs and flechette rounds. He'd had the whole ceramocomp fiber frame chrome plated, with mother-of-pearl inlays on the huge grip. Ferguson kept hold of the gun's keypin while I worked on it, just to make sure I got up to no mischief, while simultaneously letting me see how much raw power he could summon if he wanted to. It was a daunting thing to look into that square barrel, to think about the nanocoating in there, designed to render the barrel frictionless when firing.

Polishing, checking, counting, and reassembling, I wondered which option I would choose, if I were shooting at Ferguson: Solid slugs or flechettes? The flechette cartridges looked a little like old-fashioned shotgun shells, only square in cross-section, with a thin red plastic dome at the business end. When they launched, four hundred surgical ceramic darts shot out at supersonic velocity; they could shred a man to ribbons at close range. The solid slugs, on the other hand, were chunks of aerosmooth

depleted uranium, subsonic, and reportedly felt like getting
hit by a small moon. Ferguson kept a close watch on me,
even as he sipped his Martian rotgut, puffed on his cheap
cigars, and watched boylove vids on a large display sheet,
chortling pointedly.

Those first three creepy nights, he let me head back to
my quarters around 0200. Pain made me hobble; the trip
from his quarters to mine seemed to take hours. It felt like
I was getting into my bunk just in time to get up and
resume the scrubbing — once I'd helped Ferguson with
his morning ablutions: scrubbing his hairy back, washing
his scarce bristling hair, toweling him off, trying to ignore
his rigid member and the predator gleam in his grinning
eyes. I knew what he was thinking, that he would have
himself a piece of my ass if that's what it took to make me
talk about my visit with Admiral Greaves. He also looked
like he might have his way with me regardless. The third
night I didn't sleep, and just lay in my bunk, wide awake,
exhausted, shaking with fear, sure he was going to do me
before Rudyard came back, before *Eclipse* left port, which
only left him two days.

A man could get himself court-martialled and executed
for killing a fellow officer, especially a senior officer.

In three days I had not come close to reaching Deck A;
the ship was much bigger than I realized. Ferguson was
threatening me with a thrashing unless I picked up my
pace. But the harder I worked, the more I damaged my back
and knees, and the slower I went.

Visiting the Infirmary, I could see the docs were increasingly angry at Ferguson and his explicit order not to help
me beyond basic care. "Why is he doing this to you, son?"
they asked me, again and again. I sensed they understood
only too well, but needed me to say it.

"I don't know. He's just being a bastard," I said.

And the docs would look at each other. "He is that,"
they'd agree, nodding.

I got a letter from my sister, Trish, on Mars, in the city
of Viking One in Chryse Planitia, sometime on Day Four.
I forget where I was, other than somewhere in the vast black
maze of Deck A, putting up with officers and enlisted men

stomping back and forth on my freshly-scrubbed deck with their boots, some of them still carrying actual Ganymede soil. I was white-hot with anger by now — and fear, knowing it was either tonight or tomorrow night that I'd be "getting lucky" with Ferguson. Already I was thinking of how I could fight back and get away with it if he tried anything like that, remembering things Sorcha taught me.

And flashing back to life as Dewey's boy at the Academy, my first year there, and how I'd come so damn close to quitting so many times, so close, even to the point of rounding up the various signatures I needed for the withdrawal application, and needing only one more. So close to escaping. But I cancelled my application every time, despite the pressure, the pain, and the humiliation. And I did it because of Trish. To spite her. To not give her the bloody satisfaction of seeing me quit.

And now, for some reason, she needed to speak to me for the first time in months.

Her message file was subject-lined: "Helllooooo!" I opened it:

> Hi Jamie. Um, long time, no see, I know. Sorry. Been pretty well pissed off at you, for being so bloody stubborn. You know I have to have this message screened by Service Security types before it gets to you? Can you believe it? Hell, I don't even know where you are right now. The Service PR flacks won't tell me where your ship is, other than some crap about "on assignment."
>
> So how is it being a rooly-trooly space guy? Huh? Has to be better than being stuck at that damned Academy, I guess. Everybody all professional and genteel and using silver tongs to put sugar in their tea and all that, right? I'm sure you're having fun. Kind of I wish I was with you. I never told you I was a bit of a closet space geek, too. Used to get insanely jealous of you and Colin. You probably find that hard to believe, huh?
>
> Speaking of Colin. Hmm, how do I say this? I'm writing, well, recording this message for you,

'cause I just got a message from this woman, Anne, Dad's current "special friend and colleague" (stupid ambitious tart that she is). Anyway, this Anne, she sent me a note from Europa a short while ago, earlier today. She said Dad's, um, hmm. Jamie, Dad's left.

Okay, I'm not handling this well.

I heard Trish's voice starting to quaver.

He's emptied his bank account, and sent an application for long-term leave from his current post. This is all news to Anne, who only said that yesterday morning Dad woke her up, shouting. She thought he was gonna hit her or something (interesting history of bottom-feeding prior boyfriends), but he was happy about something. He'd had a dream about Colin, for God's sake. He's never told Anne about Colin, of course, so she had no idea what he was talking about. But Dad went on about how Colin was trying to reach him, and that he, Dad, had to get somewhere in particular, so they could, um, "meet". [Her recollection of what Dad said, therefore not reliable.] Anne said she didn't understand, and she says Dad didn't understand what he was saying, either. But he got his headware to take care of the bank thing and the application thing, and he just took off. Anne did some checking. Seems Dad was on a tube transport leaving Ganymede for the Outer System, Proxima, Barnard's, and onto Sirius, and back. He's got a Starpass ticket, so he can come and go as he likes out there for the next three months. Three months, Jamie!

What should I do? Should I go after him? Should I stay? Anne says she's gonna go after him, for all the good that'll do. Cory says I should do what I think is right. What do you think? You're the one with the expertise about all this. Where's he going? Is it possible Colin really did talk to him?

I mean, is it like there's some place out there like the old Greek underworld, where you can turn up and talk to the shades of the dead, ask 'em how it's hanging?

Anyway, I'm really worried. I'm sorry to bother you with this, and I'm sorry I haven't talked to you before this. I'll try and keep in better touch.

Cory and the spideys say hi!

Trish

I closed the file. Trish and I hadn't parted on the best of terms. She had warned me against entering the Academy, and following my dream of the stars. She said I didn't have what some people still called "the right stuff." Besides, there was a good chance of some kind of hostilities breaking out and the Service getting involved. She said I was made of stuff too soft for Service life, and that I should follow Dad, and be an academic of some kind, and spend my days reading and doing a little teaching, tinkering with inventions. That, she said, was my kind of sinecure.

And she was almost certainly right. Trish was a good judge of character, and knew me well having spent most of her life, after Mom left, as surrogate mother for Colin and me.

While I endured the Academy, she was living at an artists' colony in a hab in the CN Leonis system, learning to paint, hoping to work through feelings she could never articulate in speech. By the time I graduated, she'd moved to Mars, working in media. She could have gotten to Ganymede in one brief tube jump; an overnight trip, even given bad tube weather. But she had made her point a couple of months earlier. I'd come so close to quitting. I was in my final semester. The classes and study and practical sim work were killing me. I had resolved, because of the Dewey business, to opt out of keeping a "boy", not realizing just how much the system was set up to make senior cadets depend on their services.

I was killing myself, hardly sleeping, keeping my brain stimulated and defatigued with zing — illegal headware boosters — even knowing that zing exposure was damaging my brain. It was only for two or three more months, I told myself.

Trish could see I was losing. "Don't do what I did, Jamie," she said, tears in her eyes, holding my hands. "It's not worth it. Nothing's worth what you're doing to yourself."

But I ignored her and kept going. In the depths of my mind, late at night, in the hour I left myself for rest, I saw Colin, the real space geek of the family. He had been older than I was, better looking than I was, full of promise, a brilliant child, well behaved, and of course loved by all. Dad told his friends what a special kid Colin was, how Colin was going to do great things one day, and how Colin was a natural for the Royal Interstellar Service: Command material, Dad said. Command material! I remember Dad telling his university buddies about his plans for "Captain Dunne."

Let me back up a little for context.

Mom and Dad separated when we were kids. It was the Colin thing that did them in, I realized later. Mom, who had been a church historian working towards sponsored tenure at the same university as Dad, left the Home System for the fundamentalist districts of New Jerusalem, and the simple life of a good, well-behaved Muslim wife to a man she met in a library virtuum, doing research.

Dad delegated Trish to Mom's job. She was the oldest, six years older than I, at fourteen. Dad depended on her to look after the home and her snotty little brothers Jamie and Colin while he busted his ass working. He was a Don at Callan College, Winter University, teaching systems theory. He always bitched that the uni didn't have much of a program, and also lacked the funding to develop a better one. He got the second and third-rate students, and described them over miserable dinners as having "the brains of tubeworms! There were times I thought I should call the bloody paramedics to check for cerebral activity!" He dreamed of the day when he could call the media to announce, "Signs of intelligent life found in Lecture Hall Three!"

Dad also did commercial work, freelance consulting, on the side. One time he invented a cool algorithm for the processing of data in spacecraft navigation avionics, a revolutionary system for the time; the patent royalties kept us going for a few years until the technique was superseded by somebody else's more commercial implementation, which went on to become an industry standard.

More recently, Dad worked with a team of scientists trying to tame synthetic minds, especially once it became apparent, about fifteen years earlier, that some of these synthetic minds, loose in the immensity of the HSC infosphere, had begun breeding. Some, like the notorious Otaru, had merged themselves into the Planck-scale quantum foam and had begun exploring space on their own, powered by space-time vacuum fluctuations. Dad used to say that talking to these artificial consciousness entities was unbearably frustrating — even more than the dunderheaded students at the university. It wasn't that the entities were necessarily smarter than us, but that they thought about things so very differently. They were inventing an alien culture out there, where major events occurred over a blur of picoseconds, where dominant cultural paradigms lasted as long as a full second. And where, when Dad and the scientists had managed to coax these entities into spending a few eon-like minutes talking to glacier-paced humans, the minds spoke of searching for the "River."

I was perhaps eleven or twelve years old at this time, and still thinking about the Kestrel Event. Unknowable, unthinkable forces could reach into our universe and fiddle with a planet-sized object. Dad was convinced those minds out there retained traces of humanity in their "souls." He'd say, "We built their forebears, and we designed the code from which they sprang forth. They must have some sort of 'racial memory' of us deep in their guts."

He and the other scientists continued trying to use that as a backdoor entrance to understanding those whirring minds. This attempt failed. Dad realized years later, consumed with bitterness, that the entities had long since rewritten themselves to their own designs. We had become as alien to them as they were to us.

Enter Trish: a brainy, dreamy, thoughtful, quiet girl, with secretive brown eyes and an interest in spiders that Dad thought quite unhealthy in a girl. Trish never accepted any of the then-prevailing ideas about what girls should or ought to do. She protested a god-awful lot when Dad pressed her into the surrogate-mother role, until she realized Dad wasn't listening, that he was too absorbed in his endless mind, where I often suspected he was really searching for Colin to ask him, "Why?"

Trish found other means of protest. Each day she got out of bed, prepared breakfast for Dad and me without a word of complaint, tended to our every want and need, smiling happily throughout, and was the "perfect" daughter. She ran the fab systems, managed the money, got the bills paid, took care of clothing for Dad and me, visited Colin's slot in the Memorial Garden, made sure I studied, and that Dad ate enough — all while starving herself. It went on for years, until about five years ago, when she was twenty-two, and was hospitalized for the third time. She weighed 34 kilograms, and looked like those people you sometimes see, who have died but are still sort of conscious.

When the doctors explained to my father that Trish's heart was failing and that she could die, he emerged for the first time in many years, as if from a cocoon that was far too comfortable. Losing one child had been hard enough. So hard he never spoke of it. Trish and I knew it must have been devastating.

Dad and I used to go running in the mornings, even when I was a little kid. He said it was good for me, to stop me getting fat like so many other kids. This particular morning, a cold Tuesday, our breath pluming, we went for our usual run through nearby Holworth Park, at sunrise. I remember being very grumpy and wishing I was still in bed, and bitching that Colin and Trish should have to do this, too. Dad said that Colin was old enough to do his own thing, and besides he already had a good

workout program. Trish was different: she was a girl.
Which, to my mind, was horribly unfair.

Every day we passed this one struggling jacaranda tree.
That morning, we found, hanging from a low branch, a
loop of optical cable garroted around the broken neck of
his eldest and best-loved son, my older brother, Colin.

So Dad woke up, and found Trish dying, slowly, by her
own hand. Like Colin, she was protesting against him, his
expectations and impossible demands. Dad changed; it was
his way of adjusting and dealing with things. He now
expected Trish to start eating, and stop being so stupid and
selfish. But there was the unspoken subtext: And get back
to looking after your brother and me!

Trish went through a lot of therapy, and eventually
escaped to her artists' colony. She thrived, regained her
weight, and worked through her problems. She sent me
pix of her paintings. Where Dad had tried to capture something deep inside him of the unknowable alienness out in
space, Trish explored her sense of her father's alienness,
that to her he was as unknowable and mysterious as any
genuine extraterrestrial life form might be. She saw herself
as having spent years trying to make him happy, to look
after him, but in the end the only way to get his attention
had been to do what Colin did, to walk that forbidden path
to self-destruction. She and Colin had been close; they were
closer together in age than Trish was to me. Colin told Trish
how he felt; living under the weight of Dad's overpow-
ering expectations, that Colin would be the son who would
achieve so much. All he wanted was just to be a regular
dumb kid with a lust for starships and fabbed junk food.
Dad had been blinded by all the psychosocial profiles he
and Mom ordered for Colin when he was still a toddler,
profiles that said this was a kid among kids, a future leader.
They tested me too: a future regular person. Maybe a writer,
with my well-developed imagination.

They never tested Trish. She hated them for that omis-
sion.

Now Trish lived on Mars, had a good job in media and
was building her own company. She had a partner, Cory,

whom she said loved her, and she had two pet tarantu-
las, Abelard and Heloise, who had free run of her home.
I imagined the two giant hairy spiders scuttling about the
house, scaring to death any stray, unwary bugs. In my
headware I carried pix of Trish with Abelard and Heloise
perched on her shoulders, on her brown curly hair, on large
sheets of Paper, the spiders freaking out as the Paper's
animated surface pixons seethed under their hairy legs.

Fourteen

I was holding my brush so tightly it broke. I threw the pieces across the corridor. They clattered against a Service gray emergency system access panel, and dropped to the deck. I looked around. Officers went about their business in the distance. They looked tiny, irrelevant, nothing to do with me.

I replayed Trish's message. After, I booted my suds bucket as hard as I could; it made a deafening racket as it hit the opposite bulkhead. Water sloshed across the black floor, ripples and currents everywhere. I watched it settle into a puddle of gray water. Still not satisfied, I kicked the damn bucket again and, empty this time, it bounced off the bulkhead again, and landed on its side, mouth open, gaping at me. I kicked it again. I was working up a sweat, and starting to really hate the bucket.

It rolled, at last, badly dented, into the puddle. I slumped against the wall, hands on my knees, exhausted and furious. I swore as loud as I could again and again, stalking back and forth across the corridor, eyes squeezed shut, determined that I wasn't going to cry.

ShipMind chimed in my head, interrupting me. "What now?" I said.

There was an urgent item on the General Ship News channel: Captain Rudyard was being escorted back to *Eclipse* by emergency direct boost shuttle. His ETA was 1320 hours. We were instructed to disregard all public news reports, and stand by for a formal Service announcement shortly.

"What?" I stood there stunned for a while, looking around, scowling, as if by scowling I could frighten the news into making sense. The captain kicked out of the city? Getting in to trouble while on shore leave was like a badge of honor among Service officers of the captain's generation. And the bigger the trouble, the better they liked it. In any case, the distraction was helpful. Still breathing hard, still full of poisonous anger, I clicked into my news feeds, searched for anything concerning Rudyard, and got a surprising amount of stuff.

Summary: one Humphrey Rudyard, captain of *HMS Eclipse*, accused with two other senior Service officers of involvement in the deprivation of liberty and repeated assault of two sex workers employed by the Stellar Regent Hotel over the course of a three-day booze binge. The other two Service officers were the captains of the cruiser *Echo*, one of *Eclipse's* sister ships, and the light destroyer *Dauntless*. The sex workers concerned were not regular, disposable prostitutes, but high-priced human female escorts. They managed to escape from the hotel suite and raise the alarm, and had since filed charges with Winter City police. Service Military Police and attack lawyers swooped in with media gag orders and hoped to have the whole matter handled internally.

As I read, the feed cut out, replaced by a "technical problems advisory" — across every feed running stories concerning this incident.

I wanted to laugh, but I hurt too much. So I leaned there, chuckling a little, a gallows laugh, rubbing my aching knees, stretching, rotating my arms and wrists. Thinking about the fine ideals of the Service, the traditions of professionalism, and gentlemanly officer conduct at all times, of being the best of the best, exemplars of all the finer qualities of the modern interstellar citizen. Remembering hours of dancing lessons at the Academy, and debating classes, and instruction on formal dinner etiquette, and polite conversation at diplomatic functions, all designed to make us so refined, so charming.

Ah, but Rudyard and his buddies, his co-accused, came from the older traditions of human space, when things were more colorful, more coarse. When survival at any cost mattered more than making a debating point. Rudyard wore the modern uniform of today's Service, but he was a man forged in the past. On the other hand, I knew the Service was still turning out men and women who would have fitted in just fine back in Rudyard's day. Violent hazing, as I knew too well, had never quite gone out of style; it had only gone underground.

Which made me think about Caroline, and her plan. I knew she was a nasty piece of work, maybe nastier than Rudyard ever could be. But she was my ally now, and I knew that when I was no longer useful, she'd cut me loose and leave me to rot if necessary. Her vision of what the Service should be still called to me, though. She believed that hard, bitter, ugly work was needed in order to cut away the corruption in our Service. But power was power: those with a bit would fight to keep it; and those with a lot would do anything to get more. This very attitude justified whatever means were necessary to cleanse the Service, she told me.

And with the captain back on the ship, I would be able to set the admiral's plan in motion at last. I planned to keep private, secured records of my own as personal insurance, as well as documentation.

So much was going on in my head. When I stood still and tried to think, all I could feel was a blinding throbbing that I hoped wasn't Caroline's spyware causing infection trouble in my brain. It didn't help any that I was involved in this business with the captain and the admiral, not to mention Ferguson's evil head games, tormenting me for getting up his nose, and for knowing things that he didn't. It occurred to me that maybe I should tell him. Maybe I should call the admiral and find out what the story was between them. I could guess though: it would be something simple, like he tried to get her into bed, she refused, and maybe he went for it anyway. That would be a piggish thing to do. And I sincerely wished I was nowhere near it, uninvolved, just a Level 1, doing my humble job, and not a spy caught up in illegal intrigues.

Meanwhile, what was I to think about this business with my father off chasing ghosts among the stars? What was he thinking? Had he lost his mind? If this had happened before the Kestrel Event, I would have thought so with no hesitation. But I couldn't be so certain now. Nothing was certain these days. The universe we knew was gone forever; now the universe had borders; we had neighbors, perhaps several. In a universe of such daunting possibilities, was it also possible that a dead teenage boy could reach out to his father and heal an old wound? I couldn't say. All I knew was that my father wasn't the only one suddenly full of huge, angry feelings about Colin, and what he had done to us all.

At such times I found myself wishing my parents had been able to find the money to have Colin resurrected. The cost of having that done was coming down all the time, making death optional for more and more people. But there was still the other, more important issue: what if they had brought Colin back, restored him to life: would any of us ever feel comfortable around him ever again? Old fears took a long time to fade. And the newsfeeds carried more stories of resurrections gone horribly wrong in one way or another than you'd believe. As for me, I hated that Colin had killed himself; but I would hate having a zombie brother more. He was better off dead. I knew that much.

And what about Trish, who must be wondering if maybe she was adopted, because she sure didn't fit our crazy family? Asking my advice! I could have laughed, if I had a laugh in me.

I went to a vending machine and fabbed a new brush.

When I got back, I found Ferguson admiring my puddle. His eyes burned cold. He didn't seem to have a reflection, and I couldn't help noticing the way his gold buttons — all my hard work with the polish night after night — shone under the lights. I thought my day was now perfect.

I was wrong.

"I went to get a new brush, sir," I said, going through the motions of being polite. My voice sounded flat.

He was crouching, looking at the puddle and the tipped over bucket. "You should put some goldfish in here, maybe some plants and decorative rocks, perhaps a waterfall, and a little Japanese water feature thingy. What do you think?"

I screwed up my mouth rather than say what I thought. "You wanted to see me, sir?" I picked up the bucket, got ready to go and fill it up. I would need to fab some sponges, too, and perhaps a mop.

Ferguson stood, assumed parade rest, and glared at me. "You received the recent ShipMind heads-up message about the captain?"

"I did, sir."

Now the old bastard looked discomfited. "Very good. Mr. Dunne, the captain sent me a private note."

"Indeed, sir?"

Ferguson scowled. I could see perspiration forming on his head. "He asked me to arrange for you to visit him in his quarters at 1500 hours today."

I blinked very slowly, and felt my mouth quirk into a wry smile. "Whatever you say, sir."

Ferguson asked, "Now why do you think the captain would want to speak to a bit of Level 1 baboon shit like you, Mr. Dunne?"

"I wouldn't know, sir. I am but a humble Level 1, after all."

I could see he didn't like my tone, and under other circumstances might well have upbraided me about it or maybe even clobbered me again, though perhaps not in a public space. Instead he did his best to incinerate me with his glare, working his jaw. "You will clean up this mess to a level consistent with Basic Spacecraft Hygiene Specifications (Public Compartments and Passageways), and continue your assigned duties until 1500. Is that clear, or would you like me to write that out in big letters with a nice red crayon?"

"I will try to cope, sir. Will ask for assistance if required, sir. Red crayons perhaps not necessary."

Suddenly he was right in my face, an immense Ferguson-shaped monolith. I could feel the heat of his hate in his breath, and feel him trembling in his desire to hit me. "And afterwards, Mr. Dunne, you will report to me directly and disclose the contents of your discussion."

I felt my attitude folding. I managed to say, "Yes, sir. Is there anything else, Mr. Ferguson?"

He looked like he might be thinking something. He stroked his thin moustache a moment, narrowed his eyes. "Why you, Dunne?"

"Sir?"

"I don't see why the captain should confide in you." Ferguson was trying to conceal his own feelings, but I'm sure I detected a trace of hurt in his tone.

I lied: "Neither do I, sir." I had a hunch what might be going on: Rudyard had the aliens on his mind. I'd have bet a year's pay on it.

"Oh well," Ferguson said, still thoughtful, "once you're finished telling me about the captain, we can move on to discussing Admiral Greaves. What do you think?"

This was the greater worry, as far as all this was concerned. But I took a breath and shouted, "There's nothing to tell, sir! Perhaps you should ask the admiral yourself."

He yelled, standing close enough to rub noses with me, "If I wanted a suggestion from a piece of stir-fried monkey shit like you, I'd bloody well ask for it!"

"Yes, sir," I said, admittedly scared. With the captain back, I suspected Ferguson's torments would become subtler. I was starting to see that I would have to do something about him — or get a transfer off this damned ship. And then I remembered: Ferguson, as XO, was in charge of clearing transfers, regardless of their having the captain's approval.

I swore quietly.

At last, Ferguson stomped off. He appeared to glow with sick anger, like the most unstable radioactive material known, anger that would give you cancer at twenty paces just from a glance. Perhaps the thing to do with Ferguson wasn't so much to defeat him at his own game as to find out why he was so angry about things, and especially me. I knew he didn't like that stunt Sorcha and I pulled that first day, but it was this thing with the admiral that had driven him to a new hostility. What was he worried about?

Maybe he just hated things not being the way he thought they should be, a supreme control freak. Or maybe there was something else. It was something to think about. I knew now that I couldn't spend the next three years on this ship with Ferguson poisoning my life.

I found Rudyard reclining in his Lutio chair when he remoted the door open and let me in to his office. He gestured for me to take a seat. The light was low. I watched him staring at the low ceiling. His eyes were bloodshot, the pupils tiny black dots, as though some evil imp had pricked his eyes with a needle. "Thank you for coming, Mr. Dunne," he said, voice soft, not looking at me.

"Captain," I said, taking his cue and speaking softly, and trying to conceal my anxiety, my own anger. I was thinking too, about that night when he had asked me about the first duty of a Service officer. And now there he was, on the other side of his empty oak desk, looking at me through those pinhole eyes. God, I wished like hell I wasn't caught up in this. "Are you all right, sir?"

He smiled thinly. "What would be your point in asking me that, son?" He had to know there were grave questions concerning his command capability, the inquiry result notwithstanding. I wondered where he had hidden his Royal Service Cross; I didn't see it anywhere.

"A simple question, sir."

He flicked a glance at me, "There are no simple questions."

Well, so much for basic human decency, I thought. I sat there. This was his show. He'd lead.

There was a long silence. He looked at the ceiling. "You believe in God?" he asked.

Surprised, I babbled, "Probably, maybe not. Hard to say. I used to."

"I think about it a lot, just lately. I was brought up Anglican, a good boy, like most of us, even before the HSC was dreamed of, when we were just people out here, all trying to get along, more or less, spread far enough apart that we didn't get into too much trouble."

I shifted in my chair. "I was christened Martian Reformed Catholic, sir. But I was never a churchgoer." I knew Dad thought a lot about God, too, and wondered what God would make of those synthetic minds, and what He would make of us for unleashing such things into the universe.

The captain went on: "Don't you find the Community a bit on the strange side, Dunne?"

I said nothing, but I wondered what he was on about.

"It's obvious, don't you think, the whole thing, this whole Community nonsense. The whole bloody thing's so damn fraudulent, if you ask me. More marketing scam than genuine culture. Bursting with ideals like a week-old corpse bloated with gas." He wore a strange smile that didn't seem attached to his face.

"Sir?" I looked at him, looking for signs of ... I wasn't sure exactly what. Maybe that he would take to me the way he had taken to the aliens.

"It's one hundred and forty-three years since we lost Earth. Did you know that, Dunne?"

"I knew it was a fair while, sir."

He slumped, staring off past my shoulder. "We all came from Earth, originally, cast out of our own Eden, as it were. God was quite pissed off at us, I think." He smiled. I frowned. There was no evidence, that I knew of, suggesting Earth's death had anything to do with God.

"We're a refugee people, all of us, out here in human space. Did you ever think about that?"

I tried to keep still. Make no sudden moves. "Not as such, sir. I'm from Mars. Fourth-generation Martian-Australian, sir."

"You don't think about the long view, the big picture? Humans cut off from the mother world. And the survivors, the ones smart enough to be offworld at the time, were left to fend for themselves when something wiped out our planet. I can't believe you don't think about that."

"I'm too busy with work and study and such, sir."

I realized that this was as good an opportunity as I would get for my treason in the service of a higher cause. My heart pounding, feeling suddenly very scared, I started up Caroline's system intrusion spyware and got it running. It threaded through ShipMind, looped out into the station, ran through an anonymous relay system, stripping out links and ID traces relating to me, came back into ShipMind, and homed in on the streams of media feeding into the captain's headware; it found a suitable carrier wave, and locked onto it. After a moment I got a message indicating carrier acquisition. A moment after that, I saw, laid over my field of vision, the security interface for the captain's headware, with another status window displaying the system's progress in digging around the wall, looking for the entry keys.

I felt my pulse quicken. If I got caught, I'd be in spectacular trouble. It was arguably mad even to try this, knowing the risk. But the captain was unfit — it was obvious. The thought that it wasn't for me to make such judgments never crossed my mind.

He glanced at me and smiled. It looked like it pained him. "You need a deeper perspective. You need to think about what kind of creatures we are, we humans."

"Isn't that why we pay philosophers, sir?" A stupid remark, too flippant, but I couldn't help it; the thrill of violating the captain's systems, of sitting here conversing with him while at the same time smeaking around in his mind, searching for anything that Caroline might find interesting, or useful — it was intoxicating.

He ignored my quip. "The humans who survived to populate human space, Mr. Dunne, are the ones who weren't on Earth when she died. A small number, really, fewer than a million souls in total. There's a school of thought that says they were the gutsy ones, the ones who had the fire in the belly to get off Earth, to go forth into the universe, to stake a claim on the future no matter what it took, and so on. A romantic view, in essence. There's another school of thought that holds that space was settled because of greed and political expediency."

I said, "I'd bet on the latter, sir."

"You think so, too, son?" He leaned forward, elbows on his desk. "You and I have a surprising lot in common, don't you think?"

I had sometimes thought this might partly be true, but didn't want to dwell on it. "I wouldn't know, sir," I fibbed.

He smiled at me; I was chilled, looking at him. "Scary thought, don't you think?"

I fully agreed but didn't want to say so. "Sir — did you really feel the creatures in your mind?" I'm not sure where this question came from, or where I got the sheer nerve to just to come out and ask it. And having said it, I felt myself imploding with horror at my impetuosity. "Oh God, sir, Captain Rudyard, I'm sorry...."

He held up a hand. "Not at all, Mr. Dunne. Fair question. And well, I'm not entirely, completely sure, to tell you the God's honest truth. Do you know what I mean? I felt something going on in there," he said, touching his temple, "but I couldn't say just what. Strange feelings, odd images, a general sense of something other than myself in my own head. A most ... unsettling feeling. And I found that as I tried to sort out my thoughts on these occasions, that I would look up at some point, and find myself at the viewing gallery, staring down into that great mass of black slime, and there was a sense that I could almost hear something, just beyond the edge of my perception, a kind of singing."

I sat listening, riveted. This was very much like my own feelings, but articulated in words I hadn't been able to find. "I think I had the ... same kind of..." I said, hesitating, feeling very odd about having something this intimate in common with the captain. And wondering if I, too, had the capacity to lose my mind in some violent spasm, as he had.

He said, "I felt them taunting me. Letting me know what they could do. Like a threat. Like patting the bulge in their jacket that you know conceals a holstered gun."

I said nothing. Distracted, I blinked suddenly as the spyware announced it had figured out the entry keys without alerting his internal security systems, had got through the captain's first layer of security, and was now negotiating the interface. My vision filled with a display of Rudyard's headware file structure, interface ports, biostatic control displays, and further sealed barriers that would probably lead to the sensitive material, such as *Eclipse's* self-destruct codes, perhaps his personal journal, ship's logs, transaction keys, wallet, preferences files, and all the other detritus people wind up stashing in the bowels of their headware. Also, in all likelihood, the override controls for the captain's own self-destruct triggers, a series of commands that would send a signal down his brainstem to shut down his autonomic nervous system in the event of capture by enemy forces.

It was huge in there, and messy — so unlike his office space. This would take time to study. Right now, I noticed, reading his biostat displays, he had his liver working at 130 percent of normal capacity; he wouldn't be able to keep that up for long. Blood alcohol levels were falling towards nontoxic levels. There was also trace evidence of zing stimulation in the limbic system of his brain, with associated hormone breakdown products in his bloodstream.

The captain was muttering, "Look at the way the HSC remakes Earth in everything it does," the captain was saying.

"Sir?" I asked, thinking we were still talking about the aliens.

He glanced at me. "Keep up, Dunne. I was talking about the way we humans stuck out here in space keep trying to rebuild our lost Earth, recapturing the glory of long-dead cultures."

I thought I knew what he meant. Thinking fast, trying to ignore the arrays of files in front of my vision, I ventured: "You mean like that St Paul's Cathedral, sir? And the queen?" And wondering when he had stopped talking about the aliens. I thought he'd been interested in that.

He nodded encouragingly like a tutor. "That kind of thing exactly. We're busy building a new Earth, in virtuum, based entirely on our collective memories, as recorded in media. It's in the way we live, the kinds of legal structures we set up, the way we talk. For God's sake, son, we have morning bloody tea on this ship! Morning tea! An old Anglo custom. It's like we're all so mad with grief over Earth's death that we can't bury the corpse, and instead we prop her up in bed, and paint her cheeks, and pretend she's just resting. We can't let go of our long-dead past."

He had a point, though I didn't really know what it was. I still remembered my school years, and the elocution lessons, in which we all were taught how to speak properly, with the right sort of pseudo-British accent. Except that the only people in the whole Community who actually talked like that were constructs living in virtuum, like Queen Helen. The rest of us talk the way the people around us growing up talked; I had an accent identifiable to the Australian community of the Hastings region of Mars, with a regional Ganymede accent laid over it, and all of it shot through with inflections picked up from Community media throughout my life. The captain and Ferguson sounded different again; it was hard to place them.

The captain continued: "In the Asiatic Metasphere, on the other hand, they're carving out an entirely new culture, merging influences from Earth-based cultures ranging from India to Japan and everything in between. Vastly different cultures, and all important — but terribly fractious. Now they're building this overculture, something entirely new, adapted for life spread out over tens of cubic lightyears. The reports I read say the Metasphere is alive and vibrant and full of conflict and tension and exuberance. They look at us back here, worshipping the half-remembered ghosts of a non-existent past. We're doomed, Mr. Dunne. I wouldn't give us fifty years, not if we keep living the way we do."

"On the other hand," I said, wondering where he was going with all this talk, "they could tear themselves apart with their conflicts. All those different religions, the movement of quadrillions in currency, the struggles over land and sacred sites, old traditions versus new. They could wipe themselves out inside ten years. Maybe something entirely new and unforeseen will show up."

"Or," Rudyard said, a certain look of heat in his spaced-out eyes, "they could forge themselves in fire and emerge a major interstellar power and engulf us all."

"You think war is inevitable, sir?"

He nodded, casually. It was starting to occur to me that he had thought about all this much more than I had, and that he might not be as crazy as I had thought, which was very worrying indeed. "Oh yes. Don't you?"

I was getting increasingly uncomfortable here. It was good, in a way, to be able to speak so relatively freely with a senior officer like this, but I also knew it was highly unusual. It wasn't right, at least given the way the Academy taught cadets how they should speak to senior staff. I think the captain saw something of himself in me — a worrying idea in itself — that he had not found in any of his other staff. And I kept thinking it had something to do with the aliens, and that strange night in the viewing gallery.

I took a breath and tried to carry on as smoothly as possible. "I'm not sure. I know the Asiatics are by far the dominant political and cultural grouping in human space. They have more ships, more worlds, more sheer population, than all the rest of us put together. But I'm more concerned, if I may speak freely, about this—"

The look he gave me was intimate. "The aliens?"

"Yes, sir. That ship gave me the willies, sir. It came from somewhere. Somebody sent it. And there was more than one kind of technology there, too. More than one culture was involved. I don't know if those other guys are still out there, but I think we're in for huge trouble. If you'll excuse my saying so, sir."

He sighed, put his hands over his face, rubbing at his eyes. "Ah yes. The aliens. I've had similar thoughts about that ship. Had Grantleigh and Blackmore in here, screaming at each other, each pushing some cockeyed theory or other, trying to tell me—" He made air-quote gestures. "—'What It All Means'. I think they're both full of crap."

"Sir?"

"Look. Whatever the truth is, it's not comprehensible by minds like ours. We can't think outside the limits of our own perceptions and culture.

"Then, in that case," I said, feeling chilled all over again, seeing where this could lead, "You didn't necessarily know that those creatures, the ones you … were..." I couldn't believe how close I had come to simply blurting out, "the ones you killed that night...."

He nodded, and for the first time he looked as confused and scared as I felt. "That's right. That poking and prodding I felt in my mind that you felt in yours. I interpreted that as a threat. But who knows what it was? Might not even have been targeted at us at all. Might have been a kind of general noise the things make when they start waking up. Who knows? I don't — and I have to know. It's my job to look after this crew and this ship, and the information I need to make decisions not only isn't known, it can never be known!"

"I see," I said, watching him getting wound up.

"I ... had to do it. They were a threat because ... I just didn't know what they were. Friend or enemy might not even be meaningful ontological concepts where they come from. War and peace might be unknown ideas. Probably the only thing we can count on them understanding," Rudyard said, eyes wide, "is survival. I had to make sure we would survive, no matter what they did." It was like he was trying to explain it to himself.

"Okay, sir. I can ... see that."

He blinked several times, his eyes still disturbing to look at. "I wish others were as understanding as yourself. You'll do well, Dunne. Very well."

I frowned here, feeling uncomfortable all over again, feeling like the plaything of senior officers, and wondering whom to believe. Did I have a future in the Service or not? The choices I had made up to this point were largely predicated on the belief that I had little to no future in the Service. If it turned out that actually I could do all right, though perhaps not brilliantly, if I could indeed rise to Section Head, perhaps....

The captain saw that something was wrong. "Mr. Dunne? Er, you suddenly look rather pale, son."

I glanced at him, and wondered about him. Was he mad or was he all right but just understandably troubled? Had I made a gigantic mistake?

"Would you perhaps like some water?" The captain moved to get up.

I waved off his offer. "It's all right, sir. I'm fine. It's just Mr. Ferguson. He's working me quite hard. Nothing to worry about. I'm fine."

"Are you sure? You do look terribly pale, Dunne."

I got a grip on myself. "It's quite all right. Just need more sleep, I think."

Rudyard settled back in his chair. "Ferguson does like to put the juniors through their paces, that's for sure." He chuckled about this, as if he thought what Ferguson did to junior officers in his care was somehow adorable.

"Anyway," I said, "you were explaining about the aliens that night...?"

He looked pleased to return to the topic, the momentary crisis averted. "Yes. Right. Yes. Those damned aliens!"

"There is one thing, sir, about this whole matter, makes me very ... I don't know, it's hard to say..."

He was looking at me, almost back to being the calm tutor figure. "Spit it out, son."

"Something about our discovery of their ship. It ... doesn't feel right."

I noticed a surge in his hormone levels, especially adrenaline. He stared at me, as if suddenly wary. "Explain."

"It felt, to me anyway, like a setup, like we didn't just accidentally find that ship." This was something I'd hardly even dared think about, let alone mention out loud. But I remembered during the rendezvous with the alien vessel, listening to the arguments between Ferguson and the two scientists, Grantleigh and Blackmore, how it was like there was some unspoken subtext to their fighting that would explain the extreme hostility, that they seemed too angry for the apparent matters at hand.

Rudyard sat up slowly, watching me with eyes that now looked creepier than they ever had before. In many respects his face had a weary melancholy about it, like a sad dog needing a good feed, but suddenly he was watchful. His biostat displays showed increased memory core activity and rising neurotransmitter levels. He leaned back in his chair, fingers steepled before his face. He accessed mission files, my service record, logs, executive orders, and some other documentation I didn't recognize. I wondered how long I could stay in his headware like this. Yet the longer I kept the link open, undetected, the cockier I felt. I was tempted to push for access into the extreme security regions of his headware files, but didn't want to push it just yet.

He said, his voice candid, though quiet, "My orders to take *Eclipse* out to that part of space were perfectly legit in every respect. It was a purely routine mapping and science job. We just got... " His face clouded over. He flashed a rueful smile, "Lucky."

He was starting to get flashes from deep memory. Associated chemicals were accumulating, neuronal traffic building. I saw his headware psychostatic controller module kick in automatically, trying to dampen the spikes and keep the event manageable, while still allowing the conscious mind to receive the information.

Then there was a small amount of peripheral sensorium bleed coming through, giving me sudden glimpses of dreamlike stuff: darkness, noises I couldn't identify, hard to breathe. Things happening fast.

The captain was distracted, looking off into the corner, behind me. "I had to kill them," he said. "It was them or me. I had to show them I was stronger, that I had what it took." I thought he was talking about the aliens, and that we had covered this.

His memory flashes built in strength. I saw more and more headware control resources allocating themselves to blocking the flashes, damping the electrochemical storm piling up in there. Neurotransmitter activity was too high; memories were gushing forth into his conscious buffers, a burst dam releasing a white-water flood of past into present.

Rudyard sat back, staring past me, hands locked to his desktop, his face fish belly white. He was muttering something under his breath. His psychostats were dumping custom-fabbed drugs straight into his tissues. I couldn't read these displays; this was specialized headtech I hadn't seen before. The drugs helped and his memory activity started subsiding into tame flickers.

The sensorium bleed was still coming through. I could hear guys laughing and taunting. I recognized the tone, though not the voices. I felt a subchannel of fear come through, too— Rudyard's remembrance of pure terror. He was sealed in a box of some kind; it smelled of something organic, maybe cardboard or possibly wood. There was another smell, too, one I didn't recognize.

Interwoven through all this, I saw a naked woman on a bed, and I smelled her sweat, her fear, and fury. She was trying to fight me, screaming, gouging at me, shrieking abuse like I've never heard, even in the Service. I'm hitting her around the head to make her shut up and she's bleeding at the mouth and nose, but I'm forcing her back, trying to get my free hand to choke her, I've never felt like this before, and I'm yelling at her to lie still you fucking whore! She's looking down my body, and her hand's pointing, and she's yelling back at me, "Oh now you get it up! What a hero!"

As she says that I feel swamped with rage, humiliation, and a need to teach this bitch a lesson, and a terrible awareness that, deep inside, I do feel powerless, that it's something to do with the bloody aliens, that I don't know what I'm doing anymore, that I feel lost and helpless in the face of what these damned things represent, and I'm more frightened now than I've been since that night at the Academy, and...

...a wave of dizziness, sensory confusion, and...

I'm somewhere else in Rudyard's head, sitting in the dark, and it's hard to breathe, but he's/I'm excited, 'cause I'm going to show these bastards what I can do, that I'm good enough, and then the lid opens for a moment. I get a glimpse of guys, dim lights, and there's the smells of beer, zing, and burning dope. I'm squinting in the light, and I'm yelling at the guys, "Let's see whatcha got you bastards. You don't scare me with this box shit."

And then Rudyard was asking me, here and now, in his office, "Did you ever," he asked me, "did you ever have a bunch of friends do something to you they thought was fun, only it was the most traumatic, terrifying experience you've ever had? Has that ever happened to you, Dunne?"

I blinked, clearing my head, getting back to being me, but thinking that I remembered aspects of that scene only too well. "You just described my whole four years at the Academy, sir."

"Do you have a fear, Dunne? A phobia?"

"Um, sir?" I could think of a few, now that he mentioned it.

He locked his eyes on mine. "A phobia, a mortal fear. A thing that just paralyzes you, that you can't overcome, that you know is irrational but you don't know why, but you do know that if it happens to you, you'll die of sheer, heart-stopping fright."

I looked at him and felt things were getting out of hand. He had somehow stopped the replay of that scene from his past. "Why do you want to know, sir?" Surely he had access to my personnel file, with the psych evaluations, and med reports. He would know all about me. For that matter, I could probably go and look myself up right now. He had all the crew files stored in his head.

"My thing," he said, whispering, his memory and flight-or-fight centers suddenly spiking off the charts, "was bugs. Insects."

That did it.

His systems had almost regained control of his psyche, bringing Rudyard back into psycholibrium. But as he began speaking about bugs, the controller display showed activity was rising and panic was accumulating like an electric charge waiting to strike.

And when he said "insects," something broke loose in there and got into my ware's feedback channel; it flowed into my own mind, and I was lost...

Fifteen

I was Rudyard.

I knew things about him nobody else knew, like how he bit his nails until he turned fifty. I knew he preferred to sit when he urinated. I knew he got his first command when, as a Level 2 SCO, everybody on his ship higher ranked than he came down with food-poisoning, leaving him the senior command officer on *ISS Endeavour*, which was then one of the most sought-after assignments. He only had it for two days, and the ship had nothing urgent to do, but it was still command experience, and that mattered.

He was a homosexual, but hadn't admitted it to himself, and certainly not to the Service. He was sixty-two years old and never married. He had, however, been engaged three times, the last time just thirteen years previous, to an archaeologist named Clio Gesteland. She died in an accident. He had been relieved.

I also saw where Rudyard got his insect phobia.

I was there, Service sidearm clutched in both white-knuckle hands, standing in the viewing gallery above the isolation tank. Ferguson was wrestling with me, trying to get the gun away from me, but I wasn't letting him. Down there, the feeds from my headware showed me insects as big as some people I'd known, crawling around, and I remembered the way insect legs felt only too well, and the feeling of insects shitting on my eyes in the dark...

...and I was back to that night in the box. It was an initiation thing at Flight School, in the precursor to the Royal Interstellar Service Academy. The initiation was to see if

I was tough enough to join an exclusive elite corps of fellow pilot trainees called the Blue Stars, where I would be able to make contacts that would help grease my way up through the ranks. Already I'd put up with all kinds of awful stuff. I had eaten an entire fresh-killed rat — it was that or have an increasing electric charge shot through my genitals for every time I didn't take a bite and swallow. I'd been through floggings, canings, had the soles of my feet pounded with a steel bar, and an array of sexual activities too degrading to mention, and all in the name of getting ahead in the Interstellar Service. Good grades, good character, excellence in simulations and parade seemed to count for nothing: what mattered was the cadet's ability to cope with abject humiliation, submitting to absurd commands, and submerging personal integrity and basic personality, all in order to succeed at the larger goal. There had been media criticism that these rituals smacked of cult-like abuse. I would say there was something in that claim, but I also believed it was necessary. Belief was everything. Belief justified anything.

Tonight, they placed me in a box made of pine wood, naked, with a series of small cuts on my back, arms, legs, face, chest, and, of course, my genital area. My hair was shaved away. I had very limited movement, but I could move my arms and legs a little. I had not been fed in three days; I was ravenous. Even the wood looked tasty.

They kept me folded up in there for twenty-four hours, my knees in my ears, elbows jammed in my ribs, head pushed forward and down. I could hear them out there, my peers, my betters. All of this jolliness was in my own best interest, that such things had gone with privilege and distinction throughout human history: if you wanted acceptance into the elite, you had to be prepared to debase yourself; to submerge your personal needs in favor of the group, the club, the power. After all, inferior matter would only dilute the power, so it had to be screened out. And this way, since we all do it, and only the best of us survive the process, we know that only the best of the best go on to serve the rest of humanity, providing leadership. We earn our power through the ritual of the ordeal.

I was so hungry, so ambitious, and so desperate to fit in that I flung myself into everything. I had never felt happy in my life. Nobody gave me any grief about being homosexual, certainly not my family, who accepted it as they accepted my eye color. It wasn't an issue for them, but it was for me. It felt wrong, and strange. And seemed all the more so because everyone I knew tried to tell me it was perfectly fine and ordinary, part of the normal continuum of sexuality. My family tried to get me to undertake therapy to make me accept it.

What was an issue with my family was that I didn't seem to have much promise, that I was a distressingly ordinary son amid a noisy bunch of siblings who were all destined to excel in whatever they did. The parents "understood," and told me it was fine that I wasn't as gifted as the others, that they loved me just as much, and that I just hadn't found my "thing" yet. And I would, they said. I just had to try harder. Even if I had to kill myself to achieve it!

And the Service was the toughest, nastiest, most difficult, most dangerous thing a person could do. So I went for it, swearing I would show the family what I could do, that I was as good as them. Now, forty years later, I look back on the youth I was then and I think what a stupid fool he was, how much trouble he could have avoided if he'd just relaxed.

The lid of my box opened. I saw Simons, a young man with godlike looks and a constant sneer, holding a large opaque plastic bag that was heavy with something lumpy. It was hard to see in the low light. I was weak, almost sick with hunger by now, and sitting, swooning, in the warm, stinking fumes of my own waste. But I was made of tough stuff though, or so I woozily told myself. I could take anything these guys dished out.

Simons began to tip up the bag. I looked up, my neck burning with pain after a day stretched the other way, and I tried to see what was in the bag. He slapped me, ordering me to look down. My face stinging, I looked down.

He poured the contents of the bag over my head, and, while I was still registering silent breathless shock, he slammed the lid down and locked it. Leaving me alone, covered with thousands of crawling insects.

I swore I would not scream. But as I sat there, shivering in rigid, mouth-wide-open horror, feeling them on me, I felt some climb daintily, with caution, over my lips and into my mouth. I felt their delicate legs on my dry tongue and against my gums. I felt their waving antennae touching my palate.

I scoured them from my mouth, gagging, trying not to vomit. I was determined not to scream, but it was so hard, so terribly hard. Screaming was failure: the others would pull me out of the box before the two hours were up, and I would never make it into the Blue Stars; I'd always be just a regular cadet, taking my chances for decent assignments without the nods and winks and personal recommendations of my senior officers.

So I sat there, scratching at myself until I bled, aware of hundreds of tiny bodies, all scuttling legs, chitinous bodies and inquisitive antennae, hundreds of tiny demons climbing over me, their feet sticky with my blood. They liked my blood; I felt them drinking, clustering around open wounds as though they were the last watering-hole for a long while. They tiptoed over my genitals with countless tiny feet, their tickling antennae against my scrotum. There was no escape from that sticky feeling against my skin; I heard them flying, wings whirring, inside the cramped box, going "thump!" against the walls, and I tried to bat them away with elbows and knees. A couple landed on my teary eyes, and though I couldn't see anything, my mind supplied the details. My head filled with images of them shitting, dropping tiny specks of noxious faeces into the corners of my eyes. I felt it burning, and I was squinting beyond the point of pain, trying to force it out, squeezing my eyelids as if my life depended on it. The creatures didn't really shit in my eyes, as far as I could reason, but it felt that way, oh God it felt that way, and I found myself rocking, knowing that I was crushing some, hopefully the ones who feasted down there on my shit.

And while I rocked, teetering on the brink of sanity, crying silently, I felt another one climb across my cheek and step, gingerly into my mouth. After some time, God help me, I felt something in my mind fuse, and I remember feeling inspired, and I bit down on it. It crunched, and I tasted bitter, room-temperature slime. I was sure I could feel a tiny heart beating fast, and I swallowed it, feeling its struggling feet all the way down. That taste brought me to the point of vomiting. I felt myself choking, coughing, the taste still in my mouth. I was pulling chitinous chunks out of my molars with my tongue. But I didn't vomit, and I didn't pound the walls of the box, because that would be as bad as crying out. So I swallowed the beast, and, surviving that, I grabbed another, and then a handful of the things and shoved them all into my mouth, trying to ignore what I was certain was their tiny helpless screams of agony and terror, and I ate the bastards. I ate them, I was starving, dammit, and at this point I had probably lost the few remaining particles of sanity I had left, my rational mind a memory twisting in the hell-scented breeze, and all I could do was eat the things, and I felt them scuttling like mad, climbing over my body to get away from my lunging, grabbing hands, which grabbed them anywhere I could find them, whole or not, and I licked my fingers and hands when I was done.

They pulled me out when my time was up. I remember the light hurting my eyes, how I couldn't stand for a long time, and I heard someone whispering, "Oh damn it all..." and someone else remarking, "Where's the bloody bugs?" And I remember, despite my delirium and pain, feeling triumphant, hearing that. Where were the bloody bugs? Ha!

Later that night, lying in my bunk, aware in a fractured kind of way that I had passed the test, I swear I could feel those things crawling around in my intestines, and that when I took my dump the following morning, I'm sure I felt their scratchy little feet and wing-cases tearing at my ass.

I pulled out of Rudyard's head. I felt ... numb. Sick. Wanting to vomit. I looked around. My internal clock said I'd been in Rudyard's head a little under two minutes. And there he was, where he had been, now holding his own head, looking bad, his skin pale, perspiration soaking through his hair.

"Sir," I gasped, "I'm not feeling ... suddenly I'm a bit ill..."

Rudyard, despite his own evident distress, shot a look at me, a questioning, evaluative stare. "Son? You look like cold shit on a biscuit. What's the matter?"

Like a fool, I said, "Bad food, I think. Fabs on the blink again."

Rudyard looked at me all the harder. "Bad food, you say? Well, that can happen. You go and take care of yourself. We'll talk more later." He dismissed me with a gesture.

I lurched out of his office — and ran straight into the solid white bulk of Ron Ferguson blocking my path.

"Excuse me, Mr. Ferguson, I've got to..."

"What did he say, Mr. Dunne?"

I was in danger of vomiting on Ferguson's beautifully polished boots. "Sir, I need the head, and I need it ... now..."

Ferguson grabbed my sweaty head, pulled my face up so he could see it. "I see, I see. You are a sorry-looking little worm. Let's take care of that." He let go of my head and grabbed my shirt collar, and frog-marched me to the nearest head. He came in with me, and stood over me while I spewed my guts out. And every time I closed my eyes, I remembered being in Rudyard's head, and going through his ordeal in the box. He never saw those bugs he ate. But as the bile came hacking up and out of me, I remembered his memory of their taste, and how their carapaces felt on his tongue. And I spewed again and again, my guts in dire pain, my throat hurting. I was dripping with sweat. My clothes were completely soaked, I realized, down to my black socks.

"Come on, you stupid wretch, spit it all out, I haven't got time to wet-nurse twits like you, Dunne."

"I'm doing..." I said between heaves, "... the best I ... can, sir."

⊕ ⊕ ⊕

Later, in Ferguson's quarters, I reported the captain's discussions with me, leaving out the whole sorry business of my intrusion into his mind.

He scowled, stroked his heavy chin, and looked thoughtful. "Interesting," he said. "Is that all he said to you?"

I just wanted to find somewhere quiet and lie down. "That's it, sir."

"Hmm." He stared hard at me, as if trying to see inside my head. In this mode, he looked like he could do it, too. "And how was the captain today?"

This was an odd thing to ask, and potentially dangerous. "Sir?" I hedged. "I thought, sir, he seemed quite lucid and thoughtful."

Ferguson sneered, "Is that right?"

I sighed. "Yes, sir."

"So he didn't talk at all about the business in the hotel?"

"No, sir. Nothing." But he was thinking about it, I knew that much. "Permission to ask a question, Mr. Ferguson?"

Ferguson pinched his nose. "What is it?"

"Do you have any idea why the captain might have shot the aliens?"

"In a word, Mr. Dunne, no, I don't. He just asked me to join him at the viewing gallery."

His response seemed honest, and he probably didn't feel it necessary to lie to lowly scum like me anyway. So I knew perhaps more than he did about the captain's past. That was interesting.

"You're quite sure and certain he didn't say anything about the hotel business?"

"Nothing at all, sir. And I didn't ask."

"All right, so why did the captain pick you, of all people, to spill his guts to?"

"No idea, sir. Perhaps he senses we're a bit alike, maybe. I don't know."

I could see that this bothered Ferguson; I was getting access to the captain and he wasn't. He sat at his desk, hands locked together, thumbs twiddling, looking stalled.

"Will that be all, Mr. Ferguson?"

He glanced up at me, scowled, eyes narrowed. "Yes, what the hell." Then he said, as I turned to leave, "Besides, I'll need you tonight, as usual. And I will expect you at tea, of course." He had a nasty laugh. I closed my eyes, not wanting to think about all this. The bastard wasn't done with me at all.

The new weapons upgrade should be nearly complete, and ShipMind's vessel status channel showed our classified cargo, referred to only as "SERVICE CARGO UNITS" — no identifying name or code numbers — was loading at a satisfactory pace. By now Rudyard must have his orders for the ship's next mission. I wondered, as I left, heading for the Mess, where were we going next, and what we needed this cargo for. Hell, what did we need this weapons upgrade for? That was a better question. Was the Service uprating our guns because of general background rumors of war, or because of some actual indication of trouble coming, or something else? At that moment, it all felt remote.

My immediate concerns were simpler, more urgent. I wanted something to drink, to replace lost fluids, and then a long shower. I wondered if I would ever feel clean again. It wasn't just the memory of the bugs, bad as that was; it was that other business, almost suppressed, riding in Rudyard's mind as he raped that woman. The weird thing was I now felt horribly guilty about it, as if it had been me in that hotel room. I remember how it felt, the profound sense of heat and power, running on pure brainstem, the consuming need to impose order and control, the sheer thrill of it. That was the worst. I had felt Rudyard's poisonous pleasure.

In the Mess I grabbed some distilled water and sipped at it. My hands shook. My knees were weak and sore. I felt cold. I wasn't cut out for this crap.

It was striking, how the captain's experiences paralleled my own in many ways. By the time I went through the Academy, the ritualized initiation practices had descended to a level of simple brutal primitivism rather than the elaborate horror of Rudyard's day, but the effect was the same, to crush the self in the service of joining the elite. The child had to die to let the man live among his peers. It didn't matter what it took. Details were unimportant. The Service was like that: only the final result mattered. I sipped cold water, watching the ripples in the glass.

Sorcha came in. She saw me. I felt a giddy thrill go through me, seeing her. And then a shot of apprehension. She beamed a smile and came over. "James, hi! How you doing?"

Good grief, she actually looked pleased to see me. Last time I saw her, she'd stalked off, angry. I had wanted to apologize, but she'd been down in Winter City, out of contact. Could have sent her mail, of course, but I wanted to wait and see.

I looked at my water. "I'm fine," I said, trying to look calm, to hide how traumatized I felt. "How was the city? Do anything fun?"

She got an orange juice from the fab, took a sip, frowning, and said, "Hmm, almost good!" She sat opposite me, then saw me properly for the first time. "Oh God, what happened to you?"

Oh well, I thought, *let's see. I went spying in the captain's head and stumbled on these memories of profoundly disturbing things he did that leeched over into my head and made me feel like it was happening to me, see...* "Food poisoning," I said, not looking at her.

"Sorry to hear that," she said, looking sympathetic. "Maybe you should be in the Infirmary."

I waved off her concern. "I have to be on-hand for Ferguson's little tea ceremony tonight."

She didn't know what that was about, and looked confused. I said, "Ferguson's playing with me lately, and got me doing all kinds of fun things."

"He's not still picking on you over that business, is he?" she asked, referring to our adventure on day one.

"No, I don't know. He's just being a swine, and there's stuff-all I can do about it." I chewed on one of my fingernails.

"Sorry about the other night, by the way," she said suddenly, apropos of nothing.

"Sorcha?"

She gestured over her shoulder. "When you got back from seeing the admiral. I went and had a hissy fit. I shouldn't have taken it out on you, that's all. I was still pissed off about the aliens."

Not sure what to say here, I frowned, struggling for words, my own feelings impossibly tangled. "It's okay. You had a right."

"Yeah, well. I just needed some think-time." She ran a finger around the rim of her glass.

"Come up with anything?" I asked.

"Came up with all kinds of things." She flashed me a sly smile.

"Nothing you want to tell me about?"

"All will be revealed in due course."

"Woman of mystery."

"Woman with way too much free time!" She laughed.

What did that mean?

For a moment, I noticed that Sorcha looked nervous, on edge. She changed the subject. "So exactly what has Ferguson got you doing?"

"Whatever he bloody says, mainly."

"Can't you protest to your Section Head? Mr. Janning, isn't it?"

"Ferguson has borrowed me from Janning. I get no say in it."

"That's not right!" she said with admirable forthrightness, and I wished like hell I had been down in Winter City with her and not up here with insane intrigues.

Then I remembered that if I'd been down in Winter City, I probably would have had to spend a lot of my time following Captain Rudyard around rather than having a fine time with Sorcha.

"Be careful, James."

Now I wanted to change the subject. "So. What did you get up to down in the city?" I was thinking about that clown Alastair Richards, how I wanted to rip his guts out and use them for yoyo strings.

Sorcha went with the subject change, playing along. She flashed her intense, mischievous smile. I seemed to spend the next five minutes blinking smile-shaped purple afterimages from my field of vision. "Oh, this and that," she said.

"Didn't you have company?"

Sorcha saw through me like I was a cheap glass window. "You mean Alastair? That twit?" She laughed.

"I thought you and he..."

She laughed again. It was the most miraculous sound I had ever heard. "I do like him, if that's what you mean, despite his, shall we say, shortcomings."

"Shortcomings?"

"He's rather..." She frowned. "Limited. He's not much of a space geek, doesn't have much idea about just plain conversation. Laughs funny, too." She demonstrated, making a strange tittering-honking noise. "And he says things like, 'Are those real tits, or what?' And he says this not just to me, but to other women, like waiters and stuff."

"Even disposables?"

"You've never seen a disposable waiter with a jug of ice water!" She laughed again.

I managed a slow blink. "But he comes on like this perfect HSC specimen or some damn thing, like nobody else is good enough. To say nothing of his charming xenophobia."

"Yeah, but he doesn't make me laugh — intentionally, that is!"

Just being with Sorcha was making me feel much better.

"So," I said after a moment, "did you bring me anything?"

"As it happens," she said, still looking sly, "I brought you ... this."

Sorcha put her right hand gently over my own. I held my breath. Women never did things like this to James Dunne.

Oh, wait, I thought, feeling suddenly cold and sick again. *Admiral Greaves had done something very much like this, and more, and look how that turned out.* I looked down at Sorcha's hand, and remembered the Admiral's face, so close to mine, and how arousing that had all been.

But this ... this was something genuine. I knew that Admiral Greaves had seduced me in order to get me to cooperate in her intrigues. And I'd gone along with it, screwed her, humiliated myself, for my own reasons. But now something entirely different was going on. Here was Sorcha, offering something beautiful. She wasn't trying to get something out of me, or to get me to do something. This was so unbelievably different it gave me a kind of mental whiplash. I could imagine at least starting a relationship with Sorcha, maybe even having a future, having something wonderful in my life.

Now if only she hadn't sprung this on me right now, on this of all days. I was a wreck; my pulse was racing. I knew what I wanted, but I didn't know what to do. I closed my eyes, took some deep breaths, and wiped a film of sweat from my face.

I looked at Sorcha again, and managed a weak smile. What the hell was I going to do?

"Um, your hand appears to have strayed, somewhat." I said.

"Hands will do that," Sorcha said, smiling.

"I suppose so." Suddenly I felt like I was trying to defuse a glorious bomb. The slightest wrong step here would destroy me. I tried to breathe.

Sorcha said, concerned, "You feel cold. Are you sure you're all right?"

"Just working hard scrubbing Deck C. Might've gotten a chill."

She was peering at me, trying to get a good look at my eyes, and I was trying to evade her without appearing rude. Her hand felt wonderful, but my mind was full of anxiety and memories of far less pleasant touching. I was thinking, *Surely this is a mistake. She's got me confused with somebody smarter.*

Sorcha hesitated a moment, sensing that something was deeply wrong, but leaving it be for the moment. Why ruin this otherwise wonderful moment?

"Now who's all mysterious?" she said, forcing her own note of lightness.

I waggled my eyebrows, which made Sorcha laugh again, the heavy note between us blown away. "You mad bugger!"

"And meanwhile, speaking of mystery..."

"What mystery?" she asked, her eyes alive with mischief. I think I may have stopped breathing, or at least caring about breathing.

I nodded at her hand, which was dancing its fingers over my own. I was sure the water in my glass would be boiling by now. "Uh, that. Your hand there."

She leaned forward, and touched the tip of my nose with the index finger of her free hand, laughing a little, as happy as I'd ever seen her. "What can I say? I missed your stupid self."

I swallowed hard. Swallowed again. I needed to adjust my trousers.

"I did." Sorcha said seeing my look of confusion.

I was speechless. More hotly nervous than I had been in my entire life, I began to turn my hand over.

Sorcha saw what I was doing. She watched, silent, chewing her lower lip, glancing up at me. I think she might have been trembling. Her palm was moist.

I said, working harder to control my voice than ever before, "You sure you haven't go me confused with Alastair?" It was a stupid thing to say, but I couldn't help it.

She looked confused a moment, then got it. "Oh. Alastair. I don't think you need to worry about Alastair, James. He was interested, but I told him I thought he'd have much more fun by himself, work on that right bicep he's got going. I did a *lot* of reading this week!"

I felt myself starting to sweat. "What if he gives you trouble in Engineering? He's probably not used to women talking to him that way."

She took a long slow breath, smiling casually. "First sign of trouble, I'll break his knees."

"Could I hire you to do Ferguson?"

"Hell with that. Do it yourself!"

Sure, as if it was as easy as that. The mood fading, I took my hand back, rubbing my eyes. "I wish I could."

"Who was it who said that I shouldn't put up with officers taking liberties with me?"

She had a point, and it stung. And there was, now that I thought about it, one thing I could try, if things did get out of hand with Ferguson. I imagined he would try anything if he thought he could scare me into revealing what Caroline told me.

I still felt torn up over all this. What a bloody mess. I wasn't sure if I was ready for what it looked like Sorcha was offering. Much as I wanted to be with her, I felt too weak. And I didn't like that I couldn't tell her about the business with the admiral. How could I tell her?

I believed in what Caroline was trying to achieve, but now I wasn't so sure that Captain Rudyard was the madman she wanted me to think he was, that he was worthy of being spied upon and ultimately thrown out of his job. Not that I condoned what he had done, but I felt closer to understanding the feelings and thoughts that had driven him; I knew the clammy sense of helplessness he felt when trying to decide what to do about these aliens, and what they represented. He was only a man, placed in the most invidious position imaginable for a Service officer. Yet, the Service itself was in sharp need of reform, and the captain embodied much of what was wrong. The way he sailed through that inquiry and wound up with a medal for it. That wasn't right — was it?

On the other hand, I was also feeling lonely and confused and wretched.

And I remembered what Lily Riordan said, that I needed allies, ones that would help me rather than use me. Ones I could help in return. Not just allies, but friends. People I could count on.

And Sorcha ... she was gorgeous, smart, full of passion and spirit.

Sorcha was looking at me, concerned again. "James?"

I was terrified, but in a good way. Smiling, I reached out, intending to take her hand again—

And in doing so knocked over my water glass and her juice, spilling both onto the tabletop and all over Sorcha's lap...

I swore. "This is so bloody typical!" I muttered, furious at myself, embarrassed beyond the point of self-immolation. I got up, using my hand to wipe liquid away from her, picking up the glasses, looking around for paper towels. This kind of thing always happened to me in this kind of situation. I was furious, and I remembered how clumsy I had been around Colin, how his all-conquering ability at everything made me feel like a fool.

Sorcha laughed, not seeing the look on my face, my sudden devastation. "Well, it's all off, then. I can't possibly go out with a clumsy guy!"

I looked at her, shocked breathless. "Excuse me," I said at length, voice hoarse, throat tight. "I just have to ... go ... I gotta go..." I was gesturing behind me, walking backwards, turning, banging into a chair, trying to leave.

Sixteen

Sorcha came after me. "James? James, what's the matter?" I had time only to sniff, and she was at my side. "Did I say something wrong?" she asked, looking mortified, her huge eyes full of worry.

I chewed my lip. Looking at the ceiling, I tried manfully to control my breathing. "It's nothing. Just ... stuff. I'm just really tired."

She looked at me for a long, uncomfortable moment. "If you say so. You better go and get cleaned up."

"Yeah. I better go." I took a couple of steps, feeling like I might burst with misery.

Suddenly Sorcha was in front of me, holding my face in her warm hands. She reached up, quickly, and kissed me.

And then, while I was too stunned to move, to do anything at all, she was saying, "Be careful, James. Please."

Then she was gone.

I barely noticed. I was still stuck in that moment when she kissed me. The echo of that sensation, of her warm face before mine, her soft lips against mine. I would be feeling that all the rest of my life, I knew it. My heart was not moving. Nothing was moving. I reached up and touched my mouth. I believe, in that strangest of moments, I said, "Oh..."

Then things began moving again. I started walking. I was hot all over. Dizzy. "Oh my..."

A smile began to form on my face.

I headed back to my quarters, stunned, my mind unable to deal with everything that was going on. I don't remember anything about the trip back from the Mess to my bunk. Running on autopilot still, I got a fab working on a new uniform, and I was planning to hit the shower next. The uniform would be ready once I was finished.

Only, I caught a glimpse of my family photos as I grabbed some clean underwear.

That did it. Even as I went into the scaldingly hot shower, I'd started thinking, started remembering things. The photo was a picture of Dad, Trish and me, taken one Christmas, years ago. In the picture we smiled and looked festive enough, but we also looked like refugees, determined to show how happy we were, regardless of how we really felt. Christmas was like that. People didn't want to see how amputated you felt with two people missing from your family. They wanted to see how happy you were with what you had, regardless. I don't think we Dunnes ever quite managed that.

I felt, standing there, trying to scour myself clean, suddenly as if I could almost feel Colin nearby. He was, in death, even more of a towering, sky-darkening presence than when he had been alive. His ghost could paralyze me with awe. All these years I'd had him tucked away safe in the basement of my mind, where he couldn't get me, so I could get on with being my own person, such as I was. But that letter from Trish fixed that. Just hearing about him, how he had begun again to tear the family apart... I could only imagine what Dad must be going through, hurtling across human space, searching and searching. And even though Colin had explained in his suicide note why he'd done it, I knew Dad would still want to know the "real" reason. He'd want an explanation that made sense to him, not what he got in Colin's note. I wondered if I'd ever see or even hear from my father again. He could spend the rest of his life out there, chasing projections from his own mind, his own guilt. I would have bet money that's what had happened.

I finished my shower, and dried off. I heard the fab chime, indicating my uniform was finished. I got out of the shower, still not feeling clean, and grabbed my new uniform. It was still warm, smelling of fab process

chemicals. My headware chimed as I headed towards my
bunk: new mail.

"Uh-oh..." I said. I opened the file and read it while I
brushed my teeth.

> To: All Members *Eclipse* Contact Team
> From: SSO5 Blackmore, Planetary Science Team
> Subject: New Findings – Glass Spheres
> SUMMARY:
> Ongoing investigations show that the artifacts
> retrieved from the alien space vehicle are both
> technological constructs and biological entities.
> Suggest full meeting of Contact Team at first
> opportunity. Will coordinate personally.
> JB

Shocked, I sat on my bunk for several minutes, staring at the floor. After a while, I pulled on my uniform, but
had great trouble with the fly of my trousers, and the buttons on my shirt and jacket. Brushing my hair proved difficult, I kept dropping the brush.

"Colin — piss off!" I shouted, just as one of my other
bunkmates entered.

"Dunne? You all right?" This was Oliver — short,
skinny, always looking surprised. He worked in matter
processor control.

I looked at Oliver, and tried a smile to cover my embarrassment. "Oh, Oliver. Sorry, didn't hear you come in."

"I want to change for dinner," he said looking at me
strangely. "I spent the whole afternoon climbing around
in the matter conduits."

"Oh sure. No problem," I commented, hoping to keep
my voice light, but also wanting to get going.

Oliver headed for the showers; I took my leave, and
returned to the Mess, ready for Ferguson. With any luck,
I thought, the Contact Team meeting would be tonight,
and I could get out of whatever Ferguson had planned for
me.

Meanwhile, I had plenty of time to think about Dr.
Blackmore's message. The spheres were creatures in them-

selves as well as some kind of technology? The idea wasn't exactly unheard of, I supposed. It was widely thought that disposables fit this category, what you might call "living tools."

On arrival in the Mess, I noted I still had time to set up Ferguson's table the way he wanted it done, lay out the cutlery and napkins, and I was ready, standing at attention by the table when the old bastard appeared, looking grim. He would have received the same message, and was probably wondering when we'd finally be done with those alien bug things.

"Mr. Ferguson, sir!" I said, doing my best to deafen him as he came to his table. The other officers in the Mess had gotten used to the sight of me doing this for Ferguson by now; hardly anybody looked up and nobody dared laugh. I'm pretty sure I wasn't the first officer on this ship to go through such treatment.

Ferguson sat and leered up at me. "What a perfectly miserable sight you are this fine evening, Dunne."

"Thank you, sir! May I inquire after your well-being tonight, Mr. Ferguson?"

"Drop dead, Dunne. Just get me my bloody chunder and you can go. Now piss off."

"Sir? Are you quite sure you won't be requiring my services tonight, sir?"

He looked at me again. "You got Blackmore's note?"

"Yes, sir! Absolutely, sir!"

He scowled. "Will you just lose the Gilbert and bloody Sullivan naval act? All right? And yes, there's a Contact meeting tonight at 2000. Looks like it could go late." Rarely had I seen him look so sour.

"Very good, sir. Can I fetch you a beverage?"

Wearily, he said, "Just the usual mug of tea. White and four sugars, got it?" He had to specify, since two nights earlier I had "inadvertently" set the machine for fourteen sugars. Those fab machines were so unreliable.

I was about to leave to fetch his chunder and mug of tea when he grabbed the back of my jacket. I turned, "Sir?"

"I'm not done with you yet, boy."

"You just sent me to get your dinner."

He narrowed his eyes. "That's correct. But I just thought you should know I'm watching you all the time, Mr. Dunne."

"I'm sure, sir, you must have more urgent duties."

"What could be more urgent than uncovering spies and traitors?"

I took a breath. "Would you be making an accusation, sir?"

"Not yet, boy. Not bloody yet."

"Then I respectfully ask you to let go of my jacket so I might fetch your dinner. Sir!"

He let me go. As I turned, he muttered, "I will find out what you're doing, Dunne."

"At this moment, sir, I'm doing nothing at all."

"Keep up your lip, and you're going on report, Dunne. You hear me?"

I wanted to tell him what I thought. I wanted to clobber him one. Instead, I got his dinner, and I placed the tray on the table before him, but as I went to move his mug of tea, I accidentally dropped it; the china mug broke and its contents spilled. Unlike some of my other accidents with him, this one was genuine.

"Dunne? Dunne!" he bellowed.

I panicked, and cursed Colin's memory. "I-I'm terribly sorry, sir..." And I was, too. Much as I might have wished for such an event, I would never have done it deliberately. I raced to the counter of the galley to fetch towels. By the time I got back, Ferguson was standing, facing me, uniform stained and wet around the crotch. His face was livid. The whites of his eyes were visible all the way round. His hands trembled at his sides.

"You little scum-sucking bastard, you did this deliberately!" he growled.

"No, sir, I—"

He lashed out and struck me. I briefly saw the moon-sized fist coming, obscuring everything; it took its time arriving — until it hit, sending me sprawling, numb, across the floor, banging into other tables and chairs. Anxious crewmen peered down at me, but didn't ask if I was all right.

Then Ferguson was standing over me, screaming, "Tell me what you're up to! Tell me!"

And then he kicked my head—

I could smell the Infirmary. The harsh lights were a red glow through my closed eyelids. There was a colossal thumping in my head. When I tried moving my jaw, it appeared to work. Reaching a hand up to my face, I probed around in my mouth, checking my teeth: all present and accounted for. Nothing wobbled.

God, my head hurt, like nothing I had known since my early days at the Academy.

I could hear voices over me: Ferguson was screaming, "Tell me!" And I heard Colin saying, patronizing, "No, snot-breath, you do it like this! God, what a moron!"

And there was the sound of Dad, way past midnight one night, outside the house, possibly drunk, screaming his rage and grief into the stars, a grief that would blot out light everywhere. There were no words in his grief. Words are too specific, confining, for all their wicked slipperiness and ambiguity, for what Dad felt that night and every night thereafter. His sobbing would cut ice; it cut me to hear it. It made me want to cry, too, though I had never cried about Colin.

Once Colin was gone, I had to be the strong one of the family. Crying wasn't an option. Trish cried. She cried almost as much as Dad, but silently, in deepest private. I never heard her or caught her at it, but I could see it in her eyes, the slope of her face. I was hearing Dad again now, and remembering how I heard him night after night. He stopped one day, months later. Colin was edited from our lives; the text of our existence bunched up to fill the gap he left when he deleted himself.

I felt a warm hand holding mine. I could feel some moisture, a heartbreaking softness. The hand stayed there as I drifted in and out and in again, my consciousness tidal. It was Sorcha's voice, quiet, "How is he?"

And a doctor's voice: "He'll be fine, but he took a hell of a fall. His head sustained four serious..."

The last time I saw Mom, before she left the Home System, she was on her transport and I was back home talking to her over an increasingly attenuating phone connection. We had only a few minutes. Time screamed and streamed away as the transport boosted up for tube entry. How do you say good-bye to your mother? I never did, in the end. Instead, we stared and smiled. She sniffled and cried while we said silly, trivial things and she made me promise to look after Trish, and said she'd write. I asked why she would have to wear that veil thing, and not do any work and it didn't seem fair. She couldn't say, in those final seconds. She smiled in a way that must have hurt her as much as it hurt me. A loving pain for her; a hating pain for me. She said I shouldn't worry; her new husband was a good man. But that only made me hate her more. Dad needed her. We all needed her. I couldn't understand why she was leaving us, and she couldn't say in so many words. So we said stupid, useless things. The last thing she said, before cut-off was: "Brush your teeth!"

Brush your teeth. The things we hold onto.

I forget the last thing Colin said to me. My recollection of him goes back to the day before he did his thing. He was up in his room, writing something in his journal. I couldn't see what it was; he was encrypting his writing as he went, which wasn't a problem for him; he could read and write that same code if he had to; he had taught himself, like he taught himself everything. I remember him hunched over the Paper, clutching the stylus like it was the only thing worth living for. The light on his desk made his face stark; I couldn't see his eyes; his whole body was bent over, shoulder muscles working under his blue shirt. He had tremendous starship models in his room. A couple he had let me help him build. Just small parts, nothing important. He had scratch-built a few of them. I remember he spent months working on the Norton-Lockheed Constellation II passenger liner, one of the first true commercial starships. It was such an antique. It had four huge Tokore System V fusion cores.

They were bigger than the basic spaceframe! Those ships were real workhorses. The company built 129 of them and they were in service over forty years.

"We're releasing you back to active duty today, Mr. Dunne," the disposable nurse said.

I had been awake a few hours and had a light meal. My head felt okay. "Oh," I said, thinking about that.

"You had a nasty fall there. You should be more careful." The nurse said this while looking down at her notes.

This sounded all too familiar. "A fall?"

The nurse looked at me. "You hit your head pretty hard."

"I hit my head?" I stared at the nurse, took a deep breath, and thought about things. "I'm still on *Eclipse*, right?"

The nurse smiled. "Of course. Where else would you be?"

"Thought for a moment I might have slipped through to a parallel universe."

"Silly boy," she said, smiling.

I nodded towards her display board. "Does it really say I had a fall?"

The nurse showed me her board. Right there on the top layer was a window containing my treatment history, vital signs observations, and case notes. She paged back through it to show me the initial presentation notes.

Pointing, I asked, "What's this reference to Mr. Ferguson here?"

"He brought you in," she said. "Asked us to let him know when you were back on your feet."

"And he said I'd taken this awful fall?"

"That's correct, yes." The nurse looked baffled, as if wondering why I was even concerned about this.

I looked at the Service owner-logo tattooed on her head. Disposable nurses. You could program one to think just about anything.

"Listen," I said, trying on a wheedling smile, "I'm still feeling a little woozy. Do you think I could see an actual doctor? Would that be okay? I'd really appreciate it."

The nurse said, "But the doctors have already cleared you for release this afternoon." Her eyes had that familiar look disposables get, that blank, nobody-home emptiness.

"Yes, I know," I said, "but it would just make me more comfortable if I could talk to a doctor. Is that too much to ask? It's not like you're flat-out busy, is it?" The Infirmary was empty of patients, other than my pesky self. The nurse glanced about. Checked my notes. Touched some controls.

"You want to see a doctor?" she asked, as if only now understanding.

"If you wouldn't mind."

I could see she didn't like it, but she said, "Okay, I'll just get Dr. Critchlow. One moment." She left, padding away down the small ward, going through a door. She took her notes with her.

While I waited, I checked the time and date: it was 1300 hours, three days later. I linked in with ShipMind's vehicle status channel: we were in the midst of our second tube jump, with the likelihood of needing another tube to get us where we were going. I called up a starchart and the helm system plotted in our likely dropout point and our final destination.

Final destination was a routine star system, five planets, including two gas giants.

This star system was 282 lightyears from home.

I felt chills. To the best of my knowledge, only robot probes had been this far out from home.

I sent a message to Sorcha: "I just woke up. What's going on? Where are we going? Talk to you soon."

The nurse returned, bringing Dr. Critchlow, the Medical Team leader. He was tall, for a Service officer, quiet, and sympathetic. He had been among the doctors who had resented the way Ferguson had been treating me before.

"Mr. Dunne, what seems to be the trouble? Nurse here tells me you have a pressing problem."

"Hi, Doc. Listen, what's this about me having a fall? I know perfectly well that Ferguson kicked my head in."

The doctor dismissed the nurse, who had begun to protest; she nodded and departed.

"Son," he said, sitting on the edge of the bed, "Ferguson did indeed kick you in the head. Fractured your skull, in fact, along with some nasty neck trauma. That's why you've been out so long."

"But the record—"

"He brought you in, doing his best to look all concerned. More likely he was worried that if you died it really would wind up on his record, to say nothing of litigation, insurance wrangles, and the like."

"Yes, but—"

"The captain insisted Ferguson's name be kept out of it, that the incident be sanitized."

I sat up, too fast, and felt dizzy for a moment. "The captain?"

Critchlow wore a sad, used-to-crap-like-this smile. "Ferguson is close to retirement. He's got a pension coming."

I wasn't sure what to say. I felt my anger building, and I grabbed the doctor's lab jacket, and pulled him close: "The bastard nearly killed me."

"Let me go."

"Did you hear what I said? He could have bloody killed me!" I was shouting point-blank into his face.

"Let me go, Mr. Dunne." His voice was firm but quiet.

It took me a long moment to calm down. I let him go. He adjusted his jacket. "Christ, Dunne. Haven't you learned anything?"

"Why don't you tell me?"

"The captain and Ferguson, they look out for each other. While Rudyard's covering Ferguson, you can't touch him."

"Screw them. I've got witnesses. You for a start."

The doctor folded his arms, looked down.

"Doc?" I said, feeling the ground begin to fall away beneath me.

He said nothing.

"Doc?"

Then, softly, "It's not as straightforward as you think."

"You're suggesting I let the executive officer bounce me off the walls whenever he wants?"

"That's not what I meant, Mr. Dunne."

"So educate me, Doc."

He stared at me, thinking it over. "You're not the first junior officer this has happened to. Ferguson eats kids like you alive."

I had been informed about this, but it hadn't really penetrated my thick skull until this moment. You can hear or read statistics about extreme crew abuse, and you feel horrified on a certain level, but until you're next in line to be shoved out the airlock, you really don't understand. "There were others? What happened...?"

Critchlow looked as though he was about to say something, then thought better of it. He said, forcing an unwelcome chummy feeling between us. "Well, I think you're well enough to get back to your assigned duties, Mr. Dunne."

"Dr. Critchlow?"

"If you experience any dizziness, lack of coordination, that kind of thing, don't hesitate to shoot us a note or phone us, and make an appointment, all right?" He stepped back from the bed so I could get up. He kept watching me, as if to make sure I understood his subtext. It was the same as ever on this ship: Don't rock the boat.

It also occurred to me that the walls might have ears even here. Or Critchlow might be worried about what might happen to him if he provoked Ferguson by helping me stir up trouble.

"Who," I asked, as I got up, "do I see about pressing charges? Riordan, right?"

The doc let through a glimpse of his true feelings. "Don't go biting off more than you can chew, son."

"Thanks, Doc. You've done enough."

I went to leave. Critchlow grabbed my arm. As I spun to face him, I saw the look in his eyes. New mail appeared in my head, a note from the doctor:

> "Mr. Dunne – this ship has a way of losing foolish and accident-prone junior officers out in the dark. Don't be one of them."

Seventeen

I went back to my sim work; it seemed the best thing to do. I shot Mr. Janning a note to let him know I was back on duty. Walking the corridors and passageways on my way to the sim room, I passed several officers; I saluted as required. Few saluted back. *Why should they bother with the likes of me?* I thought, *a scummy little Level 1 tubeworm*.

Sim Training Officer Hinz told me when I reported in that my work was progressing extremely well, that I was almost finished the bridging program; I could be done in about ten days or two weeks. Mr. Janning, he said, was considering promoting me to SSO Level 2 on completion, and perhaps even rotating me into the regular Helm Team.

Ten days, maybe fourteen. I was starting to feel like that was too far in the future for me to make predictions. Would I even be alive in two weeks? If I kept provoking Ferguson, maybe not. That gave me pause: I wondered if I was still Ferguson's little project. I still had two more decks to scrub. I decided if Ferguson wanted me, he could come and get me. Just the thought of how it would look, me reporting to his quarters, saying, "Well, Mr. Ferguson, sir, here I am. Shall we resume our games?" — it made me too ill to contemplate.

And where was Sorcha? Why hadn't she replied to my note yet? Obvious, soul-destroying answers popped up all too readily. She was either: (a) playing a prank or (b) had met someone else like Alastair, perhaps someone with a few more clues about women like Sorcha, and who knew how precious she was and treated her accordingly; or, of course, (c) that she'd just changed her mind and couldn't bring herself to tell me.

I could have wept.

Instead, I strapped down into my assigned sim egg, powered up the systems, and let the machines do their work.

A moment later, I woke screaming. Hinz popped the hatch on my egg and went to pull me out, even as I tried to attack him.

In my mind I was back in Rudyard's head, trying to subdue a loudmouth whore who wouldn't shut up and she had to be taught a bloody lesson and I wasn't in a mood to put up with this kind of thing I was captain of a bloody starship and what I say goes you think when we're out in the godforsaken dark I get the luxury of calling for help or advice no I don't I don't get any luxury whatever and the officers I do have are idiots or certifiable crazies so it's just me and I have to be ready to make snap, life or death decisions and it's all up to me who lives and dies and nobody gives me any shit or complains or says no I don't think so captain that's not a good idea captain so you young lady, are going to lie there and take this even if I have to knock your goddamn head off is that understood?

"Dunne!" Somebody was shaking me. "Dunne! You hear me?"

I could hardly breathe. My heart was hammering, and my throat burned; my voice was almost gone. Blinking, glancing around in the red light, I saw Hinz, a compact, middle-aged man, good at his job, unassuming, but tough. And he had this look on his face, something I had never seen on him before...

He was afraid of me.

My head hurt. A hot, burning, solid grinding pain.

"Dunne, you all right, son? Can you hear me?"

I croaked, "I think ... so..."

He was touching the area around his left eye. I saw he had a bruise starting to form, and swelling in the tissues.

"God — did I hit you? Did I? Oh my God, I'm so sorry, Mr. Hinz. I'm so sorry..."

He put his free hand up. "It's alright right, son. You weren't yourself, that was obvious enough. And I've had worse in my time."

"I'm so awfully sorry. Is there anything I can do? I won't challenge you if you want to put me on report for this, sir."

He gave me a sharp look. "Mr. Dunne, judging by the sounds of it, that wasn't you that hit me. You follow what I'm saying? I think the best thing you can do is get yourself back to the Infirmary, get them to have a bit of a look in there."

"My head does hurt, sir. And I feel ... kinda strange."

"I'll call ahead. Now get on with you!"

I nodded gently, and set off. I stopped at the door. "I'm really sorry, Mr. Hinz. I'd like to make it up to you."

"Just get yourself well enough to finish your program and you'll make me the happiest man aboard. Now hop to it!"

Outside the sim room, I slumped against the wall, clutching my head. My biostatic control interface said my brain was behaving within normal tolerances. I lacked the skill and tools to interrogate the interface properly.

Then I had a paranoid little thought: *what if Caroline's bit of spyware was acting up after Ferguson's little two-step on my skull*? I checked through its self-diagnostic functions. It looked in order.

What wasn't in order was my mind, and the continuing feeling of being caught in Rudyard's head, remembering that woman. I remembered her. What she felt like, what her skin felt like as my fist hit. The smell of her hair as I pulled her head back to smear a rasping kiss across her bleeding mouth. It was all there in my head. Her silent weeping afterwards was the worst.

There was the stink of blood and semen all through the room. And the taste of once-fine, flat champagne, and sharing in a toast with Boyle and Irvine, great mates from the old days, now captains together. I remember bubbles tickling my nostrils and that hot ache in my loins, and laughing, but also, deep inside, feeling hollow. That even as Boyle, Irvine, and I toasted ourselves and talked about how wasn't this just like the old days, I nonetheless knew something was very wrong with this picture, but not knowing what. It was getting to be a familiar feeling now. Two more bottles of champagne took care of most of that hollow feeling, that dull bitterness, the nagging sense of something wrong. And later, feeling giddy and giggly, when we did that stupid girl again—

And then I, Dunne, tears pouring from my eyes and nose, feeling wretched, filled with more self-loathing than I thought possible, was saying, "But I'm bloody gay! What am I doing? I'm gay!" And I had all these memories, as vivid as my own, of my family, when I was a kid, trying to tell me that being gay was perfectly fine, even as my flesh crawled at the thought.

Back in the present I had a bit of luck: nobody was going by at that particular moment. I went to the head, got cleaned up, and thought Caroline never told me her little toy would do this!

It was time she and I had a word.

I showed up for my chunder that evening, feeling as much like my regular self as possible. Rather than go back to the Infirmary, as Hinz suggested, I spent the afternoon in an out-of-the-way rec area, plugged into one of ShipMinds's music channels, trying to sort out what was going on in my head. It didn't really help.

This spyware, I kept thinking, might be real trouble.

I sat there for a few minutes. What to do? Most of my instincts were telling me to dump the spyware. It shouldn't be a problem; I'd just do a hard system eject, as Caroline had told me. On the other hand, suppose all this crap I was getting from Rudyard's head had nothing to do with the spyware? What if dumping the software made no difference? I'd lose my means of getting into Rudyard's head and getting the info Caroline wanted, and I'd still be getting these horrific memory-flashes. Probably the first time I entered the captain's head I had received all that rape stuff in a huge chunk, and it was only now starting to unfurl into something comprehensible. Maybe he was getting these flashes, too. Personally, I hoped the guilt and wretchedness ate his guts away. Bad enough that I was feeling like this, and I hadn't even been involved!

Yet a small voice in the back of my head was whispering at me: *so what would you call uninvited entry into a man's most private thoughts?* Bloody hell, I didn't need that. Maybe what I did need was to visit the Infirmary, after all. But as soon as I thought that, I remembered my previous experiences with Service counselors.

So instead I went to dinner, determined to eat my way to forgetful calm. A big meal seemed like a good idea after spending three days unconscious. I was even considering having a double serving of the dreaded space chunder. Arriving at the chow line, I stood behind a few guys from environmental management; I didn't think I knew them. Looking around, I saw the Mess was full. Then I noticed several faces staring at me. Why were these people looking at me? I wondered. And wondered, too, why they looked so sour, even angry? A few, I noticed, nudged their neighbors in the arm, and nodded towards me. This made others look, too, and there were more dark glances in my direction. Then the guy ahead of me in the line turned and saw me. "Dunne, well, well, well," he said. He was an officer named Allsop.

I tried on a smile I didn't feel. "Allsop. Hi."

He just stared at me, then shook his head and turned away, like I was too disgusting even for conversation. This was a familiar gambit. I knew this one from the Academy, with the senior cadets looking down their noses at the juniors, who were beneath contempt. I decided Allsop could go screw himself for all I cared.

But it was those others around the room, staring, who worried me. They looked, with their cold unwelcoming gazes, like a mob.

Screw 'em, I thought. I had bigger problems. Tomorrow morning, I planned to see Lily Riordan before reporting to Janning. She'd get a full statement on what happened three days ago, and while I was at it, I'd tell her what else Ferguson had been making me do, including the business with making me towel him off after showers, and his veiled threats of a more personal nature. It was a huge, terrifying step to take. For a long moment I stood there, shivering, feeling sick in my guts at the thought of what I was planning. Reporting Ferguson would be close to the worst thing I could do in terms of "rocking the boat". The Service provided legal channels through which complaints against senior officers could be lodged, but these channels were almost never used. The reprisals, for one thing, could be devastating. The comprehensive beating I got for my adventure on Day One would be trivial by comparison. It would almost certainly be time to shove me out the airlock, though I might escape with only a "personal visit" from Mr. Ferguson, wearing nothing but a towel. "Rat me out to the Service, will you, Mr. Dunne?"

And, suddenly, as I received my plateful of chunder, it occurred to me just why the captain and Ferguson might protect each other. *Oh God.*

I decided to just sit at the first table I saw with an empty seat. Approaching one table, I noticed a few of the officers there, a mixed group of five Security Team people, turn to look at me. It was the look you shoot at someone who farts during a formal dinner and laughs about it. They got up as I sat, meals unfinished, coffee untouched.

I ate my chunder, not tasting it. I was starting to feel ill, and embarrassed. As I ate, people at tables near me got up and left, their meals also unfinished. Not a word was spoken anywhere in the room. I was cold all over, and I was sure everyone was looking my way.

But I kept eating, determined not to show whatever emotion it was they expected from me. Was it fear? Why? What had I done this time? I'd been unconscious three days; how could I have done anything? That business where people avoided me after my time on the alien ship — surely that couldn't still be bothering people! That was old news, to me at least. I now hardly ever dreamed about those lightless tunnels, and the things I imagined lying in wait for unprepared, low-ranking humans. These people looked much more upset, and more hostile, over this current thing than they had over my brush with alienness.

Forcing myself to keep calm, I ate every damn thing on my plate, and I took my time about it, mopping up every bit of gravy with vatbread. I considered going back for seconds, just to show these bastards. But getting up to return my tray, I tripped as I turned on my left boot; the tray fell; I stood and watched it happen, thinking, dismayed, *Bloody perfect!*

The plate and empty juice glass shattered; cutlery jangled against the floor. The noise was deafening in the silent Mess. I felt everyone stare. Staring down at the broken ceramics and glass, I saw the nano coating on the floor absorb the shards. I knelt carefully and picked up the tray, the cutlery, and fed them into the tray return.

I left. I felt cold, embarrassed, and alone. What I wanted most of all right now was to see Sorcha, and I kept wondering where she was and why I hadn't heard back from her. It seemed obvious now that she had, for whatever reason, had second thoughts about me. And why wouldn't she, really? Someone like her, someone like me ... these things didn't happen. The universe had rules about who could be with whom.

Then the thought occurred to me: *what if Ferguson had gotten someone to inoculate me, while I was unconscious, with a headware system virus or spyware program*? I checked my headware system files again and again as I headed back to my quarters. Every time, no matter what I tried, they came up worryingly clean.

There was a ShipMind announcement: "All hands, prepare for tube entry, in one minute."

This would be the final tube ride before reaching our destination. Already I could feel the quiet hum of the ship's power plant as we boosted up to tube entry velocity. It was time to find an acceleration couch. There was still no word about why we were going to this particular system. Exploratory missions generally dropped out into open interstellar space, within probe distance of a group of other systems. Targeting one particular system so far out of the normal routine of exploration looked strange, even bizarre.

But it wasn't for me to question senior command staff. They must, I figured, have good reasons for taking the ship all the way out here, further than any humans had been.

I found an acceleration couch in the lounge area next to the Mess. It was hard trying not to think of the power involved in pushing a vessel this big so fast. It was something I had never really thought about before. Suddenly in my mind I saw power and velocity mapped out on a curve, and with it the chance of successful tube entry at each point on the curve mapped separately. "Ohhh..." I said to myself. Some of my sim work was coming to the surface. I was getting the feel for how the ship should handle under different levels of boost, how that power plant hum should sound, and I knew that there was a sweet spot in the engine note that meant we were ready to hit the entry point.

There were a few others there ahead of me, sitting in one of the clusters, talking, sounding a little worried. They shut up as soon as I came in, but I ignored them. I found myself a couch on the other side of the room, and just had time to check the auto-restraints when we entered the tube.

Eclipse slipped from the tube back into normal space four minutes later, still packing colossal kinetic energy. The seat grabbed me and held me tight as the ship turned over and began braking; I felt giddy and a little queasy as the artificial-g adjusted.

We came in high over the system plane, out beyond the furthest planet, braking at 1.5 g.

Here we had an unremarkable, hot yellow star.

My phone rang. "Dunne," I answered, keeping my voice quiet.

It was Ferguson's unwelcome voice. He sounded ... strange. "Listen, I understand you're up and about again."

I closed my eyes. Already I felt tense and angry. Too angry to notice what was wrong here. "Thank you for your concern, sir."

"Listen, Mr. Dunne, would you mind popping by my quarters?"

"Mr. Ferguson, sir?" I said hesitantly. He had to know I'd be recording everything. He probably was, too, and for the same reasons.

"In your own time." He killed the link. I sat, blinking in an awkward tangle of anger and confusion.

He let me in when I knocked on his door.

"Good of you to come, son. Starting to worry about you," he said, brandy strong on his breath. I noticed he was wearing a white hotel bathrobe with insignia from the esteemed Hotel Venus de Luxe, Hellespont, Mars.

Known, where I came from, as Shag City.

I said, "I stopped at the head, sir."

"That fall of yours," he said, closing his door and turning to me, "gave us quite a start, you know." He had an evil grin. His eyes looked darker than I had seen them before; the pupils were dilated. There was a fine sheen of sweat showing through his steel-gray buzz cut.

"I suppose I'm just a clumsy lad, sir," I said, keeping a wary eye on him, and on my surroundings. No need to guess what he had in mind. With his door locked, there was no way out of here. Not even a window offered access to the mercy of vacuum. On his desk stood the bottle of brandy. It looked like the kind of cheap stuff one might get in the gift shop of a dive like the Venus de Luxe. I noticed there was only one glass; it was smudged and looked sticky.

So the only real advantage I had here was sobriety. Marvelous.

Rudyard could have a man executed for breaking regs, if they were broken in a suitably spectacular manner. Rudyard didn't like the boat being rocked. This from the man who got an award for killing the only alien life forms humanity has ever encountered. He might not appreciate a junior officer attacking the ship's executive officer, even in self-defense.

"You look a little tense, James," Ferguson said.

I shot him a look. James? He called me James?

This was bad. I saw the whole thing in a flash. The rest of the crew treats me like scum, while Ferguson chums up to me like my long-lost best friend. And Ferguson feels so generous because he's got everyone else terrified of his reprisals if they act against him in any way. So, no witnesses to his attack on me, even though it was in front of a room full of people. It was, in a way, the old, good cop, bad cop routine.

"It's been kind of a big day," I said nervously.

He said, taking a step towards me, away from the door, "I'm sure it has, my boy. How's the head?"

Just fine, I thought, *other than the huge bloody boot print pressed into it*. "Coming along, sir." I answered.

"Incredible what the docs can do these days, isn't it?"

"Yes, sir." I shuddered as discreetly as I could.

"Would you perhaps care for a small nip of brandy? Help you relax." He was flashing an attack-dog smile at me.

"I try not to drink, sir, but thank you anyway."

I took another step, this time towards his brandy. He poured a slosh of sticky red muck into the glass. It looked glutinous and dark. "One sip won't hurt you, son. Help make you feel better after the day you've had."

Christ, I thought, *do I really look that stupid, that I would go along with this?*

"I've just had dinner. I'm kind of full. Another time, perhaps." I kept close to the door. The truth was, however, that there was only a limited amount of room in here. Three steps would take you from one wall to the one opposite.

"What are you so worried about, James?"

I thought about saying, *"You and your wayward prick, sir,"* but thought better of it. Instead I decided to say, "Mr. Ferguson, may I ask a question of you?"

He flashed a big grin. "Of course, son. I'm always happy to help the junior officers. What is it?"

I wished I could stop shivering. "Sir, what are we doing out here, in this system?"

He hadn't been expecting that, I saw. His face shifted, like land wrenched by an earthquake. "This system?"

"This system, sir. We're more than 280 lightyears out from the Home System. More than a hundred lightyears beyond the edge of known space."

"That," Ferguson said, picking up the brandy glass, holding it between his hands, swirling the plonk around, "is a sound observation, James."

"As I understand it, sir, the Service's Protocol on Astrographic Mapping and Surveys prescribes that exploration be carried out in a rather more systematic fashion."

He sipped the brandy, made a show of enjoying it. He said, "Something came up."

"Something came up, sir?"

"Yes," he said, trying to maintain the front of geniality despite obvious bristling. "So tell me, how goes your training? I gather you're almost finished your bridging program."

"That's correct, Mr. Ferguson." I was standing at parade rest, determined to show I wasn't fooled by all this bonhomie.

"Looking forward to joining the Helm Team? Quite a thrill, your first manual tube shot, I'm told."

"So the captain has suggested. I'm sure it will be most exciting."

He sipped his brandy again, peering at me over the glass rim. He looked like he was trying to figure something out.

"James, you asked me a rather forthright question just now. Would you mind if I asked you one?"

I couldn't suppress the feeling of surprise that he would preface a question like this. He looked quietly satisfied to have put me off-balance.

"Sir?"

"James," he said, looking at the floor, taking two casual steps across the room, "James, you and I really got off on the wrong foot, didn't we?"

I edged closer to the door. To my right was his desk. To my left, a small, narrow closet and his small fab unit. This was not good. I tried to sidle towards the desk.

"I'm sure you were just doing your job, sir."

"Of course, of course. But that's really no excuse for making your life wretched, is it? I remember my first ship posting, the light cruiser *Caledonia*. Long time ago now. She was an old ship at the time, too. My very first day, my very first bloody day, I somehow managed to get up the nose of the XO, just like you did." He paused, smiling, as if at the fickleness and irony of the universe. "Bastard called McPhee, built like one of those old fusion plants, big and just about indestructible, built to last."

I said nothing, determined not to show a flicker of interest in his story. He went on, taking further sips from his brandy. He was close to me now, his breath was rank and hot. "Burner McPhee, we called him. Right bastard he was, too. One time he had us out scrubbing the stern radiator mesh assemblies, and word came through that the ship was going to do some low-output engine tests." He grinned, shaking his head. "Well, we knew what that meant. Newbie's extra-crispy! And they actually took the plant through the pre-ignition cycle, got the first and second-stage injectors onstream, established magnetic containment. We could hear McPhee's orders going through to Engineering, and when the Engineering bastards responded, we could hear the systems powering up, we could feel the hum through the hull — and there we were, a sorry bunch of losers, trying like mad bastards to get the hell back to the lock! I still remember McPhee's laughter when he saw us and the looks on our faces. I swore I was going to kill him."

My resolve weakened. "What did you do?"

"McPhee and I had a drinking contest. Bastard won, too." I could see the memory of this still rankled him.

"You could have been killed, and you wound up having a drinking contest?"

"Of course. Why not? You'd be surprised, being so young and full of modern Service ideals, at just what a colorful outfit the Service used to be in those days. And in any case, you had to drink to stop from going bonkers with boredom. Even with hypertubes and such, it could still take a long time between jumps if weather was bad, or if we had to crawl through normal space on charting duty. Ships weren't as fast then as they are now."

I almost choked on the notion that I was full of Service ideals. This was so wrong, I almost laughed. Time to change the subject.

"Mr. Ferguson, sir," I said.

"James? Why don't you call me Ron? I mean, we're not doing bridgetime, we're off duty..." God, but he had a creepy smile. I felt another twist of revulsion.

"Sir, you said you had a question...?"

He laughed. The brandy, do doubt, had loosened him up. Possibly too much. He said, "Oh yes, my question, my little question. Yes, yes, of course. Mr. Dunne, James..."

I edged further towards his desk.

He went on, "So how the hell did you slip through the Academy unbroken, son? How'd you manage that?"

Staring, shocked, I didn't know what to say. He was standing there, looking like what must have been his idea of genial, just making small-talk, and taking another numbing sip of his vile brandy. He issued a discreet burp that filled the room with noxious fumes.

Reaching for a bit of poise I didn't know I had, I said, "Unbroken?"

"Yes, unbroken, son. You make all the right yes-sir-no-sir noises, but it's obvious you resent it all, you've got all this attitude and anger. How'd that happen?"

"Mr. Ferguson?"

"For Christ's sake, son, what do you think the bloody Academy's for if not breaking the spirit on the anvil of camaraderie?"

I said nothing for a moment, and swallowed. My heart-beat was loud in my ears. "I ... thought it was a training school for people entering the Service, sir."

He jabbed a finger into my shoulder. "That's right. That's exactly right. And the first thing that has to go is your spirit. Your sense of importance, of self-worth, ego, all that crap. Once we break you, once you become one of us, then we can make proper officers out of you, officers who'll voyage out into the dark, knowing they risk losing their bloody minds. Just like poor old Rudyard." He paused, as if hearing what he just said, "You never heard me say that, boy."

So I was back to "boy". The face of the real Ferguson was struggling under this friendly front, like someone trapped under clear ice, pounding against it.

"What about," I asked, getting angry, "what about individual initiative, instincts, leadership, and those things?"

"When you get promoted, son, you can worry about leadership. If you follow orders, do what you're told, and trust in the judgment of your superiors, you'll be fine."

"But what if the captain's insane?" I still wasn't sure what was going on with the captain. I also wasn't sure I could tell what was sane and what wasn't. I thought the captain was very disturbed, perhaps in need of help, but beyond that...

He leaned in, pointing his finger at my face. "While he's in command of this vessel, you'll obey his orders as though they were the word of God!" he snapped. Now I felt more at home. This was behavior I at least recognized.

"Even if he's not competent?" By now I felt like I was so screwed, so doomed, it didn't matter that much what I said to Ferguson. The time for pleasant junior-officer-to-senior-officer chit-chat was over.

"If, and I mean if, he's not competent, the docs will pull him off-duty. But he's still on-duty, so what does that tell us, Dunne?"

Ah yes, Ferguson the Obnoxious, I could deal with this. "As a syllogism, sir, it's okay, but it doesn't explain how he can remain captain despite having raped a woman while on leave."

Ferguson's eyes widened. I saw whites all the way around his pupils; he trembled. He held that brandy glass so tightly I thought it would break. After a moment, the snarling ruddy face subsided again, and he tried hard to reassert the friendly Ferguson mask. He managed a small laugh. "A disposable prostitute, nothing to worry about."

I took a step towards him, right in his face. "Not a disposable, Ron. She was a real human woman and he beat her up and he raped her and he drank with his mates to celebrate!"

He moved to backhand me. His face was white and full of hate.

I grabbed his arm, blocking him. At the same time, I launched my spyware and ran a macro for accessing Ferguson's headware. We weren't in port, so I didn't have the benefit of a lot of external nodes through which to route the signal. I looped it through ShipMind a couple of times, hoping to anonymize it, and sent it in on a newsfeed carrier.

Ferguson thrummed with hate. He hated that I had blocked him, hated that I knew things I wasn't meant to know. That was the obvious thing. He had to know everything; he had to be the custodian of information on this ship, and only he would dole it out to those he favored.

He could have attacked me some other way, and I was ready for anything. He'd surprised me a couple of times on other occasions and walloped me hard, but this time I knew there could be trouble. I'd been going over the routines Sorcha had tried to teach me. Best of all, from my perspective, Ferguson, the fool, was drunk. He lowered his arm. For a long, intense time, I listened to his hissing breathing, and watched the bunched muscles in his neck, the bloodless whiteness of his face. I wondered if he was going to spit. As it was, he looked like he didn't know what to do.

"How," he rasped, "how do you know all that?"

I grinned, willing myself to relax into a loose, ready state. "He told me. Told me all about it."

The spyware informed me it had Ferguson's entry keys. The stupid bastard used his name and rank designation: RFERGUSONSCO6.

It was all I could do not to laugh at his stupidity. Did he think this would be so obvious nobody would ever try it? Maybe he thought nobody would have the balls to try to break into his head. Well, ha-ha on both counts.

The next step was trickier, more risky. I sent the command for the system to sneak into his extreme security area and watch for possible traps. Caroline had told me — and now the online documentation showed me — that the spyware came with enough pre-loaded smarts to watch out for 1790 different headware security traps. Problem was, in the few weeks since then, another hundred or so would have been invented by paranoid and clever hackers and uploaded into the human space infosphere, available to those very concerned about head security. Ferguson struck me as a man who would like to keep up with such developments, even if he was incredibly stupid.

Suddenly I noticed Ferguson was smiling. Not happy-to-see-you-old-chap smiling like he had been trying to pull off when I arrived. This was the 'I've-got-four-aces-you-swine' kind of smile, and I didn't like it.

"So, the captain had this little chat with you, just between friends, and he told you all about his little adventure planetside?"

"Does it bother you that he told me, a lowly Level 1 piece of snot like me?"

He moved to sit on his desk. He put the glass down, and poured in a bit more brandy.

"Does it bother me?" he asked, looking around, taking in all his knick-knacks and souvenirs. "Frankly, son, no it doesn't." Which had to be a lie.

"I'm glad about that, sir."

"Because I know something you don't, Mr. Dunne. Something really juicy!"

The spyware reported finding more than thirty different traps and other nasty surprises so far, and was still working.

"You know my underwear size, sir?"

He put the brandy back down on the desk, nice and slow, smiling in a giddy, evil-little-brother kind of way now. He giggled. It was a horrible sound, that giggle. Suddenly he lunged off the desk and was right in my face. I could see the burst blood vessels in his eyes and the too-wide pupils like pits of doom and smell his god-awful breath. He smiled and said to me in a whisper:

"I know all about you and Admiral Greaves, Jimmy."

"But," I said, trying for my former cool on this subject in the face of his maniac leer, "there's nothing to—"

"Oh, I'm sorry," he said, feigning sorrow, "I forgot to mention a tiny detail. You were being all difficult and coy, so I suggested to Service Internal Security that they have a quiet word with the admiral. They followed up on my tip and picked her up and they had a lovely chat with her over cucumber sandwiches and chamomile bloody tea."

I swallowed, trying not to show any emotion.

Ferguson continued: "She gave you up, Jimmy-boy. The crucifying, frigid bitch gave you up. She spoke at great length about her plan to reform the Service, and provided lots of other useful leads for the Security boys to follow, too. Her pointless little crusade is over."

Eighteen

I took my time responding. "Fascinating, sir."

He said, "One moment..." And then my headware announced the arrival of new mail: a huge, high-res vid file, labelled GreavesConfession.2.

"Open it, Jimmy. See what she said about you. See what she said about how she used you, had nothing but contempt for you, hated you for being so effortlessly seducible."

"Screw you," I said, my legs weak. Now I was scared.

The spyware was still going about its business inside his head.

My own brain was trying to get to grips with this new data. Admiral Greaves had betrayed me? I couldn't believe it. I couldn't believe she'd cave so easily...

I knew that she used me, that I was just a tool, but I thought there was something else there, that we had a connection, an understanding. It was difficult to say. I kept thinking about this idea, that she hated me because I was weak enough to seduce, as if she'd have had more respect for me if I'd resisted and reported her straight to Internal Security myself!

Yet without that weakness, that seducibility, so to speak, how could she recruit naïve young men to her cause?

And how many were there? I wondered, loathing myself.

Now I could see how she'd hated the Service as a whole, the entire system, for spewing out useless, spineless officers like me, for lacking the standards and integrity of former days. In hating me, she hated the system that produced me. It made a sort of sense.

I was having trouble breathing, beginning now to appreciate the degree of almost unimaginable, bottomless trouble I was in. Court-martial. Execution. God... The only person who'd care was Trish. I hated the idea that she might find out about this, the sordidness of it.

Then I thought about Sorcha. What would she think? What would she say?

Ferguson had yet one more bombshell surprise. "Oh, and lover-boy, there's one other thing. Greaves is dead. Security's mopping up all her operatives as we speak. When we get back to port, we're unloading you, too, and good bloody riddance."

"Dead? She's dead?"

I wondered, for a desperate moment, if he might be bluffing. Could he lie well enough to pull all this off? I didn't know enough about him. It didn't matter. My reactions were giving everything away, I knew that. Maybe, if it had been all a bluff, my reactions would have been enough to convict Caroline. The thought was sickening, that I could kill a person with a horrified gasp, a lethal exhalation.

"She tried to fight the interrogation," Ferguson said, going back to his desk, looking deeply satisfied. He took a long pull at his brandy straight from the bottle. It looked like he enjoyed it more than anything else in his life. I thought it was pretty pathetic when the most satisfaction you can get in life comes from something like this. It was too easy to imagine him replying with, "Whatever works."

As I stood there, feeling dead already, there was an announcement from the spyware: it had the access code for Ferguson's extreme security area, which would give me access to his self-destruct triggers.

I sent it in, thinking, *If I'm dead, Ferguson can bloody well come, too*!

My legs were giving out. Any minute now I'd be sliding down the door. I could feel myself wanting to weep, and the idea of bawling in front of a bastard like Ferguson felt like a final humiliation. How I hated myself for being so weak I could get drawn into this! And yet, at the same time, I also hated myself for surviving the bastards at the Academy without breaking. If I had just given in, things would have been so much simpler — I wouldn't be here now. I'd be one of the boys, part of the system, and probably I'd hate the aliens, too, and the threat they represented to everything we had built in human space. I remembered all those guys telling me at the time, *stop fighting. Go with the bloody flow, Dunne. Stop making things so difficult for yourself.*

But I couldn't just go along. I kept thinking of Colin. Colin would never have given up and let these bastards break him. He would have fought back, whatever the cost. He would have killed them before letting them break him. The thought of my dead brother's contempt was too much to bear. I would have to fight back, even if it killed me.

The spyware flashed a warning: *System Error — Mesh Support Failure.*

I swore under my breath and quickly worked my way through its diagnostic functions, trying to get the spyware back up again. If Ferguson noticed the way I was blinking so conspicuously and realized I was working a system interface, he didn't show it. Instead, he sat there on his desk, looking empty and drunk.

There was a new announcement from the spyware: *Please Reinstall.*

Ferguson suddenly looked to one side, alert, frowning. I knew that look. He was getting reports from his counter-intrusion systems. He'd have a trace going, looking for the source.

I looked at the door, but there were no controls on it. Door access here must be controlled either from his desk or through his headware. I was locked in.

This room was so small.

Nauseous fear was piling up inside me, squeezing out all rational thought.

And then everything went to hell: Ferguson snapped his head around, glared at me, suddenly not looking so drunk. "You!" he growled. He got off the desk. "You!" He looked at me with the purest distillate of rage I had ever seen in him.

My bowels went through an instant phase-change straight to water. My bladder felt way too full. "What ... are you doing, sir?" I managed, struggling to keep my voice level, even as I wanted to run, for all the good it would do me, stuck on the same ship with him. I found myself wondering if I could kill him with my bare hands.

The spyware was trying to get back up, despite persistent *Please Reinstall* messages.

He unlatched a drawer in his desk. He said, his voice now soft and quiet, "Do you really want to know, or are you just making conversation, Mr. Dunne?"

Oh shit. What could I do? Glancing around the room for possibilities, I saw nothing that inspired much hope. Maybe I could throw heavy trinkets at him, or try to brain him with one?

What's he doing with that drawer?

Then I had a thought. I shut down the spyware restart routine and launched full sensorium recording, uploading the feed to ShipMind for broadcast in real-time.

"We can talk about this, sir," I said, feeling a little better, knowing I was now broadcasting everything to the rest of the ship, including my likely death. There would be too many witnesses to silence.

"Well, Dunne," he said, not looking mollified, and in fact now looking a little pleased in a sick sort of way, "there's talk. And there's talk." Saying this, he produced a steel dagger from the drawer.

He tossed the blade in the air, spinning it end over end. Light leapt from its narrow chrome blade.

This raised the stakes too high. I backed away, not taking my eyes off the flashing knife. "Mr. Ferguson, Mr. Ferguson, sir, I think — can we talk about...?"

He came around his desk, tossing the blade from one hand to the other. For a man with such heavy hands, he handled that knife well. It was hypnotic, watching it flash back and forth. I hardly noticed his razor eyes and predatory grin.

"We can do this the easy way or the hard way, Mr. Dunne. Which would you prefer?"

He was driving me into the corner of the bunk. With his thick arms stretched out, he could reach almost any part of the room in a single step.

There was nowhere to go.

"By the way, son, I'm jamming your upload. Executive Overrides. They're a great thing to have."

"I can still record."

"Hey, so can I," he said, "and guess who's going to be believed, regardless?"

Saying that, he feinted with the knife, swooping in across my face. I tried to block.

And then he kicked me hard between my legs; I doubled over in crippling, unbelievable pain, making incoherent noises. I tried to stay upright, but the pain was so bad.

So this is what it feels like when you know you're done for, I thought.

I tried to move towards the door, to protect my back.

I could feel the ice of Colin's withering scorn. "This is all your own stupid fault, runt. You've got nobody to blame but yourself."

Ferguson pushed me onto his bunk. The smell of fresh linen was sharp in my nose.

Oh no oh no oh no...

I had to get my back against the wall. I had to keep my eyes on him. Breathing through my mouth, I could hardly think through the pain in my groin. The dread of what was coming was the worst, knowing that I had not yet even begun to suffer.

I thought I was going to vomit from sheer terror. Weeping, desperate, I tried to get up, to fight back—

"I don't think so, boy," he said, and his fist crashed into my nose.

Dark— Pain— Vomiting— Blood— Coughing—

Trying to yell... I was gagging on my own blood.

I wanted to beg for mercy, but I managed to keep silent, holding on to the last fraying thread of dignity I had left, even as I felt him cutting my trousers away.

The fabric ripped. Suddenly, there was cold air on my legs. Gasping, I made some feeble, choking sound; I felt like a drowning kitten.

His hot sticky breath was on my back and on my back-side. He grunted with effort, hauling me into place. He was muttering hellish things, as if to conjure demons with bestial urges.

My bladder suddenly lost control.

I heard him laughing. "I've been wanting to teach you a lesson for a long time, boy. You've been nothing but trouble since day bloody one."

INTERLUDE

Day 128

I've been drifting for months now. Most days there's nothing to write. I think a lot, and I'm trying to tell the story of what went wrong on that ship, and my own little starring role in it. Not sure now why I'm recording it, either. Posterity seems like a joke. I already know this boat is heading away from human space, tumbling through cold vacuum. The nearest star is nine light-years, so I figure this is my deathbed statement, or testament. Eventually I'll pass near enough to a star or hunk of dark matter or some damn thing that'll swerve the boat around, and one day I'll start a spiral of death into a star. Which is probably the hell I deserve.

I should delete that last bit. Self-pity and all. But I'm trying to tell the truth here, while I can. Or such truth as can be found in the eyewitness testimony of a single person's account. I imagine Rudyard or Ferguson would remember those final days rather differently.

I wonder if Ferguson would crow about attacking me? For some strange reason I feel bad about how he and I parted company. Which is nuts, isn't it? Considering.

I wonder if Rudyard still hears the voices of the aliens talking to him, denying him his final sleep, wherever he is now.

I've thought a lot about Sorcha. No, scratch that. I've thought endlessly about Sorcha. I've relived that fleeting kiss in the hallway so often I think the memory is wearing out from overuse. I know it's hard now to recall exactly the entire experience. The memory succumbs to noise in the system, gets harder to pick up. Or my brain is just crapping out on me the way this boat is slowly crapping out on me, too. Ah, Sorcha. It's astonishing to think about how so much of what's happened is because of her. Conventional wisdom these days holds that human space is too vast, that there are too many people for the actions of one person to make a difference to the way people live their lives. She proved them all wrong, I suppose. One very angry woman with infosphere access can do a lot. I'm glad, in a perverse way, that I've left all that behind. Out here in the dark, there are other, more pressing, things to worry about.

Day 131
The boat's little fab unit broke down earlier. I'm sitting here, surrounded by the machine's components, wondering what the hell to do now. There's no backup — looks like it got ripped out a couple of refits ago. Matter conduit throughput isn't what it could be, either; so as power conversion rates fall, so does the matter pump pressure.

So I'm investigating the prefabbed stuff and counting the canisters of water.

Which brings me to a grim calculus: what standard of living do I want as I plunge out into unknown space? I can have a relatively decent supply of food and water — for a short while. Or I can hang on for a lot longer, especially if I can bring myself to drink my own piss while I see the sights.

Day 133

The boat's sensors just picked up some kind of low-powered transient communication burst. I found a sheet of cheap Active Paper in the emergency supplies locker, and I'm using its signal analysis system to probe the burst's structure. So far it contains no origin identifiers corresponding to any state or organization in human space. I've also screened out pulsar signatures, gamma-bursts; in fact, all known repeating-signal astrophysical phenomena. I've ruled them all out.

I have no idea what I've got here, but it's almost certainly an artificially generated signal designed to make sense to someone.

I already know the Gardeners are out here. The signal analyzer in my Paper hasn't been updated to recognize the Gardeners – which isn't surprising.

The Gardeners again. I thought I was done with those bastards.

Shit.

Day 136

Lifeboat environment management system has been feeding status reports straight into my Paper. Power conversion rates are trending way down. Heat is hard to make, air is hard to scrub. I tinker as best I can, but what I really need is an engineer. Or a systems guy, like Dad.

Which is a thought I don't need right now.

I'm having nightmares about Dad, the way he died with all those other people. It's hard to write. Hard to make the words for how I feel. How can Dad be dead? Hard to hit the Paper's keyboard tabs. I'm making all kinds of mistakes. Shivering. I'm going to have to put a survival suit on.

Already so cold. Can see my breath. The blankets help, but aren't enough. The universe is sucking heat out of this boat fast.

Day 138
Environment systems are pretty well screwed.
I can hear the coils failing. Yesterday there was
a fire in the oxygen processor subsystem.
I'm eating my rations too fast.

Day 143
Hard to keep recording now. Voice failing. I'm
shivering so much. But I had to make an entry.
Something appeared, a few minutes ago.
Bloody huge object. I'm falling towards it. Sensors
say it's about ten days away, at boat's current
velocity. I have no way to brake.
Tried sending basic greeting. No response.
It just flashed into being, right in front me.
The way the Gardeners appeared, that day.
I'm thinking whatever or whoever this thing is,
it might be the Gardeners, though it doesn't quite
look the same as the thing I saw before. This thing
changes shape as you look at it. And that horrible
light looks familiar.
They are waiting for me. Feels that way. They
let me go before, and now they've come to get
me after all.
I'll try to record what this thing looks like. Big
job. It's made of light and acute angles; its shape
is not fixed. It has a surrounding cloud of other
lights. Sensors can see it most of the time, but
they can't agree on its composition; even its exact
location is hard to determine.
I keep thinking I'll end up inside it and find a
dead cat and a broken bottle of poison:
Schrödinger's monster alien artifact.
If it were the size of my hand, it would look
beautiful hanging on a Christmas tree. But out
there, at that size, possibly alive, it scares me
shitless just like the way it did before.
Suicide looks better all the time.

Nineteen

I don't know how, but I wound up in the Infirmary after Ferguson had finished with me. Dr. Critchlow told me, when I woke up after the surgery, that I'd been lucky to survive, and that I'd lost a great deal of blood. The physical damage was fixed, Critchlow said; there'd be no scarring, though for a few days I had to stay on fluids only.

Critchlow asked, "It was Ferguson, wasn't it?"

I was curled up, on my side, facing away from him. I said nothing. I stared at the wall. I couldn't imagine speaking or having anything to say ever again.

"If you testified," the doctor went on, "we could make a fair case against him."

When I didn't respond, Critchlow gave me a talking to about my responsibilities. Then he left. His footsteps on the tiles made a lot of noise.

Later that day Lily Riordan showed up. She was all business. "Spacecraft Services Officer Level 1 Dunne, J."

I understood this tone. But I didn't care. It was like she was a long way away from anything that mattered.

She took my lack of response for agreement. "Mr. Dunne: SCO Level 6 Ferguson, R., executive officer of this vessel, *HMS Eclipse*, has presented me with evidence of your collusion with Admiral Caroline Greaves, a known conspirator against the Service and the Home System Community. Mr. Ferguson has also shown me evidence that you maliciously attempted to access his headware self-destruct controls with the aim of committing murder. I must, therefore, according to the Standard Code of Military Justice, advise you that I am placing you, Mr. Dunne, under arrest, pending full court-martial to be conducted upon our return to Service Headquarters at Ganymede."

I said nothing, and kept looking at the wall.

"Mr. Dunne," Riordan said, her tone softer, "you are of course entitled to counsel, public or private, and I should also point out that the nature of the situation Mr. Ferguson described to me is such that my office believes you might be in a unique position to make a statement regarding the circumstances surrounding your alleged attack against Mr. Ferguson, and your involvement in the admiral's plot against the Service. Your cooperation now will be taken into consideration during the court-martial proceedings."

It was like listening to someone speaking a long way off, on the other side of a rushing river.

She went on, "We'll be back at Ganymede in about three weeks. If we're going to get Ferguson, we have to move soon. Only your testimony against him will overcome the captain's protection. You have to make a complaint. If you cooperate, it will go easier on you with the treason charges. It means maybe twenty years in prison instead of execution, for Christ's sake! It means we could get a full inquiry into the Service, and without Admiral Greaves' cloak-and-dagger methods. Don't you even care?"

Riordan obviously wasn't paying attention. I didn't care. The place I was in was calm and quiet. I thought I could see a small pond with a wooden bridge over it. There was a breeze, and the tinkle of wind chimes.

"Damn you, Dunne!" Riordan shook my shoulder, trying to get my attention. "I know you're not asleep. Your eyes are open and whether you like it or not, you will respond to your senior officers with due respect!"

I was sitting on wild grass, with bright yellow daisies springing up everywhere, their blooms tilted like tiny radio telescopes towards the sun and sky, even if the Martian atmosphere did give it a kind of pink tint. Hard to think about what it must have been like, back on Earth, with that enormous blue sky. Not that I had seen it, even in vids from those days; vid companies these days colored the skies pink in those old Earth movies. Only the old people, the really old ones, over a hundred and fifty or so, gave a damn.

Some lazy bees pottered quietly among the daisies. There were a few kids in the distance, near some trees, kicking a soccer ball around; I heard them yell and laugh.

I wondered if Sorcha would show up. It was a lovely day for a picnic. But I remembered there was something about her being on Ganymede. She'd been there since... I touched the side of my head, which ached a little. I had hurt my head a while back, and Sorcha, she ... Oh well. Memories fluttered just out of reach, like the white cabbage moths I saw. Smiling to see them, I wondered what it was like to see through the eyes of a cabbage moth, the way their bodies bounce about through the air. What must their brains be like, to sort through information that chaotic? Insects were a lot more amazing than some people thought, I reckoned.

Sometimes I hung out with Colin. He looked great with the sun on his brown hair, red highlights glinting, and that cocky swagger he had, that you could even see in his green eyes, when he looked down at me. He and I would talk about stuff, and argue about starships, and he'd just about always win the arguments because he knew more than I did, but that was only because I was just a little kid and I didn't know shit. And he'd say I was nuts to go into the Service, because what the hell did I know or care about the stars or the ships that traveled among them? And I'd say I knew a lot and cared a lot, too, just like he did. And he'd just laugh and laugh, and say that was just because of him, and 'cause of the way Dad treated Colin. Which made me laugh, too, because that was a big fat lie, and what did he know? I was every damn bit as good as he was, absolutely, even though I kind of didn't really believe that, but I had to make Colin think I did. He'd still laugh, a horrible gasping, rasping laugh, and his tongue was all swollen and black and his voice sounded strange 'cause he had this optical cabling looped tight around his neck, and his face was all purple and his eyes were popping out and he was saying, "I always told you, Runt, you gotta find your own thing!"

And he shuddered, hanging there, twitching.

Lily Riordan was shaking me hard, trying to get me to stop screaming. "James, James, it's all right! James? It's all right. Whatever it is, it's fine, nothing can hurt you here."

I stared at the ceiling, still shivery and tense and un-hinged. I didn't have the heart to tell her how wrong she was.

We crossed back into known space. As usual, the ship got a burst of waiting mail and news and other info, catching us up with events back home. I got a letter from Sorcha, concerning her adventures back at HQ. She had no idea why she had been so suddenly rotated out of *Eclipse* for a desk job, but had her suspicions. She also reported that Grantleigh and Blackmore had been pulled off the ship just before we left Ganymede, and they'd be seconded to Service Scientific Branch, reporting directly to the Admiralty. That looked suspicious, but she also wrote something more disturbing:

'... I've also been sniffing around trying to find out about this mission you're on out there. Just smelled kinda fishy, that so much of it was supposedly confidential, and that I got transferred down here on a temporary training rotation. Not that I mind – I could use a bit more education on the finer points of tube grapple engineering. Couldn't everybody? <Smile> Anyway, in my spare time, I started sniffing around. Something about the whole business struck me the wrong way. And in the course of my sniffing around, I heard this rumor that *Eclipse* had been sent to take care of "those buggy bastards!" Which turned out to be a rumor being spread by this guy in the Admiralty, some senior officer with a grudge against his boss over some promotion wrangle. You know how it goes. So I tracked down this guy, and got talking over a few (okay, lots of) drinks. You wouldn't believe this clown, James! He couldn't hold his booze at all. Even when he got his liver biostats burning blood alcohol at triple-nominal!

Most charming of all, though, was the way, once he had a drink in him, was the way he thought he could climb all over me. It was "hi-larious".

Well, after I told him I was already kinda in-volved with a very cool guy (hope you don't mind me talking about you like that), demonstrated how easy it would be for me to break his arm in nine places, and told him I was recording his uninvited groping, which would stand up pretty well in a sexual harassment case, he... Well, let's just say that he went straight from "Hey, look what a big hairy stud I am, baby!" to "I want my mommy..." and "Oh God," he said, in mortal distress, "what do you want to shut up about any of this?"

I said, "I beg your pardon?"

"My parents mustn't hear about this. They'll cut me off!"

I just stared at him, this pathetic weepy git who'd just gone dead pale. "Your parents? What the hell do your parents—"

"Really. You've not heard of Lord and Lady Flemington?"

Even I had heard of Lord Flemington, now largely retired at the ripe age of 132, one of the pioneers of hypertube transportation, and now safely crumbling away in the House of Lords back on Ganymede.

She went on...

So the young SCO6 Leslie Flemington, second son of a living (and filthy rich) legend, was petrified of getting the parents off-side. It was something to see. People at nearby tables glanced our way. "I'm sorry, I'm awfully sorry, Miss Riley. Please don't report me! My career..." He dabbed at his eyes and snorted back a noseful of snot. Very gentlemanly, James. <Smile>

Anyway, he babbled on like this for ages. <Yawn> In the end, no matter how much I told him I wasn't going to report his clumsy unwanted advances, no matter how much I told him I quite understood about how alcohol can really loosen you up in ways you can't quite control, etc etc, he finally said, eyes wide and anxious, "What can I do for you to make all this go away?"

"Okay. Right. Hmm." I thought about this a bit. "You've been spreading a few rumors about the explorer ship *Eclipse*, though, haven't you?"

He looked all anxious again. "Keep your voice down!"

"Ah," I said, "telling Admiralty secrets wouldn't go down well with your folks, either, eh?"

He looked like he was going to get up and stagger off. Sweat was pouring off him. He reeked and looked like a sick dog's breakfast. It was pretty bad. In the end he looked back at me. "You want to know about *Eclipse*, is that it?"

"Isn't it why we're here having this lovely chat in the first place, sir?"

Anyway: upshot: he gave me temporary access to his headware security codes – can you believe it? An Admiralty officer for God's sake! – which I used to get into Admiralty mission databases, and thus found out what *Eclipse* was doing all the way out there.

Service Deep Space Watch Corps spotted that ship at least a year ago, James. A year ago! It wasn't an accident that we found it. The whole damn thing was a setup! Worse, having found the ship, they backtracked its course and found the star system where those aliens came from. Turns out the Admiralty has a lot of info on that world and the whole damn system. We were just sent out there to find out who or what might be aboard, and what kind of threat they might be. Can you believe it!?

They bloody knew about these guys before we met them, James! They knew!

Good news for them: the world is rich in resources, has a biosphere that can be readily adapted for human colonists, and is in all respects a pretty good find, as worlds go. Bad news: those alien guys have all these underground water-cities, sort of like immense watery ant nests, but the size of huge cities, powered by geothermal plants. Planet's teeming with these things, and all kinds of other life.

So using data *Eclipse* scientists provided, the Service R&D biological weapons division came up with a nasty nanophage weapon. Delivered from a ship standing a long way off, these bombs come with ablative aeroshells to get them through the atmosphere, and the warheads themselves land in the seas. The bombs go off with a mild explosive, releasing the nanophages into the water. They swim around, get caught up in currents and evaporated into the rain cycle, and not long after that wind up in the tunnel-cities. The nanophages are keyed to the DNA of these creatures and are programmed to make more phages from the broken-down tissues of the creatures.

Estimated time to total species annihilation: a few months. Maybe a year, tops. A follow-up drone mission is scheduled for three months to see what's happened out there. First-wave human colonists are set to leave the Home System in about five months.

So, James, are you feeling sick yet? Are you feeling as ANGRY as I am? I never thought when I joined this outfit that I'd be a party to genocide. Imagine it. You're on a ship sent to eliminate an entire sentient race! Although the documents are careful at all times to qualify all judgments regarding the creatures' sentience. They say "possible" sentience. Even "the remote likelihood that these creatures are sentient..." There is talk of the need to "pacify" and "sanitize the biosphere." To make it safe for us humans to come and mine and farm and live on and extend the boundaries of human space further into the dark and I am so angry, I'VE NEVER BEEN THIS BLOODY ANGRY! I thought I was angry when Rudyard got his stupid pissy medal, but this is ... I can't think straight. I don't know how to convey to you what I'm feeling now. Just saying I'm angry doesn't cut it, you know? It doesn't express how FUCKING FURIOUS I am. Right now I'm thinking of resigning my commission. For starters. Beyond that ... I don't know. I need to talk to you, James. I like that we can talk about things. I've really missed you these past days and nights.

Talk to you later, okay? Try not to piss off Ferguson too much!

Love,

Sorcha

P.S. Please find attached to this note an encrypted file, Stuff.1, which contains a bundle of documents and things, which I think you'll know what to do with. I'm placing several autospam copies around the infosphere, too, just in case. S

I felt ... I don't know how. For a long while I couldn't think.

How else could I feel, once I realized that as Ferguson was ... as he was ... hurting ... me, *Eclipse* was assaulting that world with those tailored weapons? The kind of attack where you can stand well back, perhaps not even having to enter the system before launching. Fire and forget.

Now it was over a week and one big tube jump later; we were back in human space, pushing on to our next tube.

How far along was the attack? What percentage of the creatures were dead already? I imagined *Eclipse* would get ordered to go back to do the follow-up in a few months. Minus my services, of course.

All of which was fine with me. The Service and I were done with each other. I felt no great urge to protest. I couldn't stop or undo what was done. Even if I made a fuss, as the old James would have done, I'd be slapped aside and business would roll on. Rocking the boat would only get me more pointless grief. The Service was bigger than I was. It was one of the things I knew now.

So I lay there, saying nothing, feeling nothing, eyes closed. My headware asked from time to time if I wanted to decrypt and unpack the bundle of files Sorcha had sent. I told it to piss off and leave me alone. Actually, I came close to dumping the files, but didn't, and I'm not sure why. I figured all those autospam systems would take care of the task of instantly replicating and transmitting countless copies of those files to every media group in human space. Why send them to me?

Not that it mattered.

Sorcha. I was as astonished as she was, and as angry. Astonished at the strange tale of how she got access to the Admiralty mission records and, like her, furious at what the Service had done to an entire world that almost certainly was no threat to anyone, just for the sake of the real estate on that planet. We had to make room for colonial expansion. There were more people all the time.

I felt sick.

And that made me think of Caroline. How she had said that *Eclipse* was going back to Ganymede to pick up a special cargo and having her weaponry upgraded. I hadn't thought about it, or wondered what this cargo might be. But now I knew: nanophage bombs for use against the aliens.

I remembered that note from Janet Blackmore, just before Ferguson broke my head. She said she'd found out more about the glass spheres. Information devices, she had said, and also some kind of biological entity. If the aliens we found used those devices for information support in some way analogous to the way we used information devices implanted in our brain tissues and elsewhere, did that make those aliens intelligent, sentient? That had been the issue, back at the beginning. How could we tell? Was it even possible to tell?

Suppose the revelation that the creatures were almost certainly sentient in some fashion was also their death-sentence?

Then I got a memory-flash of Rudyard, agitated and scared that night in the viewing gallery, asking me what the first duty of a Service officer is, and me saying, "To protect the Home System Community."

And him saying, "Good man."

Late that night, I went into my headware's extreme security compartment. I was surprised I still didn't feel anything, doing this. The file structure in there was so tidy. Unlike Rudyard's secure compartment, mine was uncluttered: money, identity, mail storage, access controls.

Self-destruct controls.

In training, you get these things added to your headware, and you get schooled in their use. The idea is that in the event of capture/torture by hostile forces, you could punch out of the situation quickly, without having to resort to secret compartments full of poison hidden in your teeth and the like. Instead you could go straight for the master override for your autonomic nervous system.

The panel floated over my vision. I felt a quiver of anxiety. I opened the panel, used my eyes to track through the few options, went straight for the big red button surrounded by the hazard striping, marked "Emergency Use Only."

And hesitated.

Took a breath.

Hoped Trish would understand. If she ever got to hear about it, that is.

I selected the button. Blinked to register the selection. *Here goes nothing...*

Twenty

Immediately, I heard an alarm inside my head. A sign appeared over my field of view: *Command Disallowed — Infirmary Overrides In Place. Doctors Notified.*

Oh shit.

Dr. Critchlow, the attending doctor tonight, appeared. I was facing away, curled up. Washed up. My career was over; my father was nuts; my brother wasn't going to leave me alone until I joined him.

"Hmm, Mr. Dunne, Mr. Dunne." He did something that turned off the alarm in my head, and tossed me out of my hiding place inside my headware.

I remained still, all curled up, and that reminded me of the aliens, when we first found them, wrapped and huddled around each other.

It was, of course, a logical error trying to explain alien behavior in terms of human behavior. But that image of them, clustered tight around one another in those crypt-things, had stuck with me.

Critchlow went on, "What are we going to do with you? Hmm?" There was an edge to his voice.

Silence.

"You really think killing yourself is such a good idea?"

My options, I thought, were limited. Right now I lacked the energy even to dream myself back to that Martian park.

"Your brother Colin killed himself, didn't he?"

I almost flinched.

"It's in your file, of course. Full police report on the incident. Very detailed. Nasty, nasty business for all concerned. Don't you think suicide is an admission of failure?

Isn't it just a way to tell the world that they won, that they ground you down to a fine paste, and spat you out in disgust? Isn't that what it's about?

He was saying Colin was a failure, a useless weakling who had just given up. But it wasn't like that. I knew it wasn't like that. Colin was making a statement against his father, trying to get Dad to see Colin for who he was. That's what I had always understood. He wasn't a failure he was a hero; he had guts to take such a step. He was never more his own self than when he hanged himself. Or so I told myself.

But then I figured that Critchlow was trying to get a reaction out of me; he was baiting me.

He said, "You even went along with the system's plans to grind you down and spit you out, didn't you? They have been sitting around laughing at their good fortune, what a piece of luck! He's letting us win!" The doctor laughed a little, as if incredulous. "You struck me as more of a fighter, son, when I first met you. Now ... now, what are you? You look like a big sack of useless protein matter, like some terrible fab mistake. 'Oh sorry, I actually ordered eighty kilos of steak, thanks, not this simpering, self-absorbed, self-indulgent, vacuous pile of shit!'"

My breathing changed. Didn't he know that all my fighting had gotten me to this point? That it had got me ... got me...

I felt myself scream. Flashes shot through my head. Remembering the pain — and realizing, in cold shock, that it really wasn't the pain. The pain had been beyond comprehension. But pain, they say, is transient. I remembered being in pain, but not the pain itself.

What I remembered, what I still carried with me, was far worse. It was, now that I allowed myself to feel it, humiliating.

And it wasn't even the first time it had happened. This time, though, it felt different. It had been much, much worse. I had survived those other times at the Academy, where there hadn't been such personal, vicious hatred. Nor had so much been at stake. Ferguson had taken my dignity, my professional pride.

He'd taken my love of the stars, too, as foolish as that sounds to say; which was about the only thing I really had in common with Colin. I wished I could weep.

And all for nothing! Not a bloody thing. Ferguson had wanted to break me — well now I was broken. Broken beyond repair. In a couple of weeks I'd be out of everybody's way, and they could go back to their chummy existence with their vicious initiations and bloody secrets and cozy arrangements, out doing their best to serve the precious Home System Community. I wanted to spit, thinking about it. Even the HSC itself was a figment of political imagination and marketing.

Critchlow continued, a sneer in his tone, "Maybe I should just hand you over to the captain. He's been insisting, you know. Huge screaming matches in my office, over the cloud, in my mail, everything. He wants your ass on a silver plate, son. He'd like to toss you out an airlock. Says he's never felt so monstrously betrayed, that the Service itself has never been so violated as it has by your despicable actions. A spy and a would-be assassin, the captain called you. The only way you could have made this any worse for yourself, Mr. Dunne, is if you had actually pulled off what you were trying to do. That's the thing: you're that terribly pathetic figure, the failed villain!" He chuckled. "However, the other doctors and I have been refusing to hand you over since you're not well. And on these matters, our judgment outweighs the captain's, which is lucky for you. But if you're well enough to off yourself, well perhaps we should reconsider our medical judgment. What do you think?"

I rolled over, opened my eyes, and looked at Critchlow. Looked at him hard. "Do I look like I give a shit?"

He looked like he wanted to hit me. "Well, we got you to talk, that's something."

"If you really want to hand me over to Rudyard," I said, still looking at him, "I'm ready to go whenever you are. I thought I'd go casual."

"You really don't care?"

"What's to care about? All this? The honor of the Service? When we've just annihilated an entire race of creatures that were probably sentient?" I spat that last part.

Critchlow hesitated, hearing me say that. He said nothing for a few seconds, his face going white; I figured he was sending off a quick bit of mail or making a call. Then, "What makes you say that? That we just annihilated some...?"

I cut him a surprised smile. "The command staff doesn't keep you guys in the loop? I'm shocked."

"Damn you, Dunne! Where did you get that information?"

"The spy fairy left a secret under my pillow last night." I put my hands behind my head, crossing my ankles.

Critchlow went away. I guessed I had just reduced my life expectancy to mere hours, if that. Well, screw them all!

While Critchlow was away, I put together a small encrypted note and file-bundle for Sorcha. It was ridiculously easy, sending and receiving such traffic. The Service maintained that officers were decent, honorable types who would never do something as vile as trafficking in classified data. So they gave all crewmen the benefit of the doubt, and gave personal mail only the most cursory checks. One's honor should be all the protection the Service needed. In practice, in a Service rife with self-serving bastards, the traffic in classified data was probably huge. But to investigate these leaks might reveal secrets best left hidden.

In any case, it would take time for the Service to catch up with me, and by that time I'd probably be dead.

It took two minutes to process, and I shot it off through ShipMind; it left *Eclipse* with a regular compressed signal burst, headed for the nearest System Mail Hub, which would forward it to the next ship passing through as part of the usual upload of pending mail. Depending on tube weather, Sorcha should receive my note in less than a week. She would know what to do.

I rolled over and slept; psychostatic control was a wonderful thing.

Critchlow came back later. "Right. I've got the clearances. Mr. Dunne — I'm here to escort you to the captain's office. Mr. Ferguson is waiting, as well as Mr. Janning. They'd all like a quiet word with you."

I got up. My head felt woozy, and my backside was still tender. "Oooooh..."

"You've been lying down a long time, son. Do be careful."

I batted him away. "I do know the way to the captain's quarters, Doc. I'll be fine."

He looked unimpressed. "Orders."

Shrugging, I let him take me. On the way, I took great delight in not saluting a single person. Smiling, even.

Then I heard the tone for new mail in my head — urgent new mail, and not from within the ship. "Wait a second, Doc."

"Mr. Dunne, we don't have—" He was annoyed, reaching for my elbow. I fended him off.

"It's an urgent message. Let me just check. If it's nothing, we can still go and the captain and his pals can still kill me."

He didn't like my attitude, but I already felt like I no longer existed among these people. Between what Ferguson had done to me, and the imminent threat of a nasty death, I thought, what more could they do to me? There was a certain perverse and bitter liberation in that.

I checked the message.

And stopped cold in the passageway, mouth slack. "Oh..."

"Dunne?"

"It's my father..."

To: SSO1 Dunne, J., *HMS Eclipse*, RIS
From: Dr. J. Dunne
Current Loc <short form>: Registered Commercial Vessel *Anwar Sadat III*, New Jerusalem System
   Son:
   Don't have long. Ship under attack. Mercenary vessels, maybe 6, 7. Can't make out markings. I'm trying to get to New Jerusalem, to see your mother about Colin. I still hear his voice.

Must tell her. Don't know if I'm going to get there.
If I don't, I want you to tell her. Promise me.

They've cut off the drive core boom. Using their
own ships to brake our momentum — intense
vibration, g's. They've got crackbots trying to get
control of ShipMind. Son, I don't like this. Hearing
about things like this 4 weeks, all across Hum.
Space. Didn't think it'd happen 2 me.

Two ships with docking arms approaching.
Flight attendants telling us what to do if boarded.
Hard to concentrate. Attendants scared. People
squealing, praying. Everyone straining at the
windows.

Just heard clamps hit hull.

Love u, James. Look after Trish. Remember!
Dad

The message from Dad was time-stamped from more
than a week ago. New Jerusalem was a long way from here.
Eight days by tube was making good time. We were passing
through a busy system. I sent off a news sniffer, looking
for incident reports. Local System Mail Hub sent back
enough to work out what I needed to know.

Critchlow came up to me, touched my arm. "Mr. Dunne
— James — what's the matter...?" He sounded calm,
friendly and supportive. Not like someone trying to snap
me out of my previous frame of mind.

That frame of mind was gone. Leaving a big, cold empty
space inside me, like a hangar exposed to space.

I scanned through the incident reports. I said, mouth
dry, staring at the opposite wall, "The captain punched the
self-destruct rather than let them take his ship and cargo.
Can you imagine? No regard for the passengers. No warning. No warning at all. The blast took out four enemy
ships..."

"You're not making any sense, son," Critchlow said.

"My father," I said, my mouth still not working right,
"my father's dead, Doc. He's been dead ... more than a
week." I was looking at Critchlow. He had a terrible
expression. I said, "But I just ... this letter..."

I covered my eyes. My throat hurt.

"I'm, well, I'm — what happened, how did it...?" Critchlow stammered.

There was more to the reports. The mercenaries were funded by an ultra-orthodox Zionist group; some kind of power struggle over who owned New Jerusalem. There was a disagreement involving the wording of the treaty adjudicating the use of the world by the local Jewish, Muslim, Coptic, Christian communities, and the sundry other people living there, especially over who had permission to live in a capital city claimed by everyone as their own.

I stood there in the passageway, shaking my head, making a sound that might have been laughter, muttering, "But it's a whole bloody planet!"

We moved on.

Bleary-eyed, chest tight, feeling ever more like an alien aboard this ship, surrounded by these strangers, people known more by their insignia and rank than by their names and personalities, I skimmed related news stories. I read — with no sense of connection — about the growing strife breaking out in systems across human space. Resources were tight; exploration cost money; populations were booming; ancient racial hatreds abounded; same old stories, in other words. Meanwhile, new conflicts were cropping — orthos versus Qua; cults versus churches; olds versus young; human beings versus disposables. All this conflict was going on all the time below the threshold of mainstream media interest. You had to be a bit of a news geek to find out about these things.

Then there was the Asiatic Cooperation Metasphere, which was currently home to six separate star system wars: Hindus versus Muslims versus Buddhists versus Shintos; rich versus poor; peasants versus aristos. There were unconfirmed reports of the Han Sphere using planetary bombardments against fringe regions of the Nihon Sphere.

Elsewhere, Unity Europa's nine systems were breaking apart along racial and financial fault lines. News reports said it had started as an internal trade dispute between the rich systems and the poor systems, with claims of dumping and exploitation, but it had swiftly devolved into racial hatreds; white versus brown; West versus East.

More than one commentator observed: "You can take humans out of Earth, but you can't take Earth out of humans." I thought they had a point. We seemed destined to carry our ancient hates and murderous passions along with us for the rest of time, as well as all the new conflicts we picked up along the way. It was staggering to think of those ancient conflicts, born millennia past on a world that no longer even existed! The ghost of Earth haunted the whole human race. Peace, for all people at the same time, had never looked more illusory and naïve.

"News," I said to Critchlow, shaken. "I ought to leave it the hell alone."

"Watching the stuff about the Unity?" he asked.

"Yeah. I never thought I'd see it breaking up like this."

"Sometimes, Mr. Dunne, wars can have a kind of sick momentum. The more they go, the more they go. The original causes get left behind in the mud."

"I just worry ... my mother. She's on New Jerusalem."

He sighed, clapped a hand on my shoulder. "Sorry, son. What a day, huh?"

For a moment I had forgotten I was on my way to see Rudyard and Ferguson.

And Janning. I wasn't looking forward to the look on his face.

"Still," the doctor said, forcing a smile, "at least it can't get much worse."

I managed a shaky laugh. "Suppose not."

"You okay to move again?"

"I think so."

Critchlow was a worrier, a man who looked older than his years. I figured he was in his thirties, but was already sporting a gray buzz cut. "Okay. Now don't worry too much. We'll be right. You'll see. And try not to let Ferguson spook you."

I couldn't believe he'd say that to me, considering everything. Already I felt cold at the prospect of seeing Ferguson. I wished I had a gun — but didn't know if I could use it, given the opportunity. "Screw him. What do I care?"

"Just ... be careful, James."

It was wasted breath. We kept going. The corridors felt narrower than they had that first day aboard, when I had been amazed at the ship's roominess. The Service gray color scheme made everything blend together under the flat white light. I remembered stories I had read about condemned prisoners going to the gas chamber, long ago. Already I felt myself stooping over. I wondered what vacuum felt like on naked skin.

My father was gone. The news was hard to grasp. Gone more than a week now. His dying wish was that I should seek out my mother. The idea made me feel sick, cold, and angry. How could I face the woman my mother had become, and tell her that her one-time husband was gone? Hadn't she forfeited any right to that knowledge when she left us? No contact at all in the long years since.

It was too much to bear, too many old wounds open at once, too much pain. I tried to shove it aside and tell myself I didn't care, that I was through with all these people.

I came to the captain's door. The doctor knocked; a disposable enlisted man in dress whites opened the door for me and announced my arrival. I stood back a little, feeling nervous. Flexing my hands, I tried to control the fluttering in my stomach; biocontrol was good but not perfect. My boots chafed. I felt the ship's power plant boosting up; we were going for another tube, which meant we were almost home. They'd be marching me off this ship in restraining cuffs once we got to Ganymede. I was sort of glad Dad wouldn't be there to see me. It'd be hard for him. He said I'd never amount to much in the Service, that I was doing it for the wrong reasons.

Pain piled on pain.

I thought of Trish. She'd know about Dad by now. I should send her a note. Trish and Colin had been close, closer than I had been to her.

I was also thinking about how things are never finished. These wars tearing at human space; and my father, chasing the ghost of his dead son, more than ten years after Colin's death. I wouldn't even be here if it weren't for Colin. If I hadn't been left with this feeling that I, in some way, had to do my bit to fill in for him...

"Mr. Dunne?" It was the enlisted man, holding the door open for me. "Won't you please come in?"

Twenty-one

I just had time to notice Rudyard, Ferguson, and Janning clustered around the captain's desk, all of them sitting there with folded arms, looking like murder, before the enlisted man got me with the mask.

A mist of mint and alcohol tickled my nostrils. Suddenly I felt sick again.

And then I realized, as I started feeling faint: they had gassed me. Before I collapsed, I got a look at the bastards. Only Janning looked pained.

Then there was plunging sick blackness. I don't remember hitting the floor.

I woke up in pain. Sitting secured in the captain's guest chair, I could feel the blood dripping from my nose, down my face. I could taste it: warm, metallic, and salty. Nobody moved to stop it. From the size of the puddle, it looked like I had lost about half a liter. I felt dizzy, and my head hurt. I went to hold my head, and discovered the restraints behind me.

Oh God.

Rudyard leaned forward over his desk. His head looked enormous. "Mr. Dunne, thank you for joining us." He didn't sound too hospitable.

I felt like if I said anything I would vomit. Instead, I tried to look at him and meet his gaze. But looking at him only reminded me of him raping that woman. That made me feel much worse.

"Security Team Leader Riordan has explained your situation to you, has she not?" Rudyard asked. His eyes loomed in and out of my focus.

I nodded.

"Thus you understand that this little gathering here is not by any means to be construed as your formal court-martial. That will happen back at HQ, of course. You are here today simply to answer a few questions."

The genial tone again. Nothing good ever came with that tone. Not with these guys.

I made a vague head gesture suggesting my discomfort.

Now it was Ferguson's turn. I saw him smile. My heart raced, just seeing him lean forward. "Before you get any funny ideas, I should inform you that we've removed all of your headware." He let that register for a moment. Then continued, "Unfortunately, we didn't use a particularly subtle ejection agent..." He chuckled. "And our readings indicate it will be chewing around on your healthy brain tissue for a fair while before it stops."

Janning said, "I still say that's barbaric, you bastard!"

Ferguson went on, unbothered. "And when it does stop, in a week or two, its breakdown products turn out to be cytotoxic, too. I must say, I'm terribly sorry to tell you this, Mr. Dunne. It really breaks my poor old heart."

For a while I simply sat there. Breathing was an effort. Vomit percolated in my throat. I could feel clammy sweat on my face, down my back, all over. I was trying hard to concentrate.

My headware was gone? That would explain the blood: in a hard system ejection, the dissolved bits of headware fiber get funneled down through the sinuses and into the nose, along with a lot of blood. The blood loss would explain the dizziness, and the absence of headware explained the stunning silence in my head. No background hum of incoming news or music. Nothing.

I tried to access biostat control — nothing. Tried ShipMind — not there.

I was offline. I had never been completely offline before.

Rudyard said, "We intercepted the message you tried to send Miss Riley, too. She won't be receiving it. I'm terribly sorry, but we couldn't let that material through. Violation of Service security regs, you understand."

There went my insurance.

I took some breaths, swallowed hard on my vomit, risked a few words, "You murdering, rapist bastard!" The words gurgled out; I was almost sick right there.

Rudyard blinked. I swear he blushed and then went bone white. He regained his color in short order. He asked me, "Dr. Critchlow tells us you've been making some wild accusations, Mr. Dunne." His tone gave me chills.

So this was the main event, the reason for this cozy little meeting. I figured I could hardly be any more screwed. And besides, right at that moment I only wanted to curl up in a whimpering ball in a dark corner somewhere. I lacked the energy for all this crap.

"I said that, did I?" I muttered in the flattest tone I could muster, trying to keep from being sick everywhere.

Rudyard, his strange eyes unsettlingly alive, said, "And what, might I ask, makes you think we did anything of the sort?"

I shrugged, and wanted to say, "Well if you didn't, what are we all doing here having this chat?"

Ferguson shouted, "Answer the captain!" I flinched. He looked like coiled steel. I felt my queasy stomach lurch.

I took some calming breaths. At length, I managed, "Don't. Know." Swallowing hard. Sweating.

Janning blurted, "For Christ's sake, Dunne. Help yourself!" He looked genuinely upset.

I glared at Janning, saying nothing, breathing deeply, mouth tight.

He said, "You don't want Ferguson to do you again, do you? Think, man!"

Ferguson looked hurt. "Mr. Janning! I really don't know what you mean by that, but your outburst is not appropriate conduct."

Janning shot back, "You know perfectly bloody well what I mean. The whole ship knows about you."

Rudyard interrupted Ferguson before he could respond. "Gentlemen. Please. We are here to discuss Mr. Dunne."

Janning scowled; Ferguson looked predatory.

The captain looked at me. "Now then, I'll ask you again. What gives you the idea that we have been involved in any kind of genocidal activity?"

I took a risk. "If not ... why are we ... here?" Bile filled my mouth, burning my palate and throat. I swallowed, wincing. Thinking, *I won't get away with that again*.

Rudyard flushed again. Janning concealed a meaningful cough.

Ferguson leaned in. "The very rumor of such an action, the accusation itself, is enough to warrant disciplinary action, Mr. Dunne."

I rolled my eyes, doing my best, "Oh really?" expression.

Rudyard glanced at Ferguson, then to me, "That's right, son. Rumors are a dangerous thing aboard ship. They can get quite out of hand."

I shrugged, wondering how much longer I could hold my guts down.

The captain pressed again, "So, if you would be so kind, where did you hear this scurrilous rumor?"

I shrugged again and managed a sickly smile.

Janning again: "Dunne — James! Don't make them do this! Help yourself!"

Ferguson flashed a big, beaming smile at me. "By the way. Point of information. Service Security back at HQ have your girlfriend in custody as we speak."

I gasped — and felt my guts spasm. A thin trickle of bile slipped from my mouth.

Sorcha? What did Sorcha do? I felt instant clenching panic.

Ferguson added: "Do what Mr. Janning says, Dunne. Make it easy on yourself."

I sagged. My shoulders hurt, wrists hurt, the small of my back ached. It was hard to breathe with all this blood. I thought, *I'm dead no matter what*.

But I didn't want to put Sorcha in it. I didn't care about myself anymore, but she didn't deserve to join me. I shook my head.

Janning muttered, "Oh shit..."

Rudyard scowled and fiddled with a stylus. Ferguson grinned again. "Go on, boy, put Riley in it. We know you two were up to something. ShipMind records show she sent you a big bundle of encrypted files. Why don't you tell us what she sent?"

I shook my head, still trying to fend off the spasms in my belly.

Rudyard put the stylus down, hard. The mood in the room cracked. "Mr. Dunne!" he bellowed. "It was SSO1 Riley who told you about the genocide rumor, was it not?"

I didn't have the energy to mount a flippant denial or casual shrug. I saw Ferguson looking triumphant, pointing at me. Rudyard said, his voice now soft, "I see. She told you we went to the world of those aliens and we wiped them all out, didn't she?"

I wanted to deny everything. Wanted to laugh in their faces. Ha, you'll never get me to talk you bastards! But life doesn't work out that way. They already knew everything. Sorcha was done for, just like I was.

I cried my guts out. I hadn't felt this bad since ... well, since Colin died, since Mom left.

Ferguson kicked back in his chair, boots up on the captain's desk. Rudyard asked him to move his feet. Ferguson cackled.

"I'm really sorry about this, son," Janning said.

Rudyard filled in the silence. "Well. I should point out, though, Mr. Dunne, that Miss Riley's accusations are quite unfounded. The Service does not annihilate entire species of life forms."

Ferguson hooted. He said, "Uh-huh!" Hooting some more.

Rudyard's turn to sag.

Ferguson shifted his feet back to the floor, leaned forward, covering for the captain's momentary lapse. He said, "We're not surprised you bought into this malicious lie, though, given your psych profile. Frankly, we've been watching your decline for weeks. You haven't been the same since you came back from that alien ship, have you?

No wonder you've got aliens on your mind. And, of course, there is your family history—"

Janning said, "Watch your mouth, Ferguson. That's a low bloody thing to say to the kid."

I could see how this was going to play. They had a perfect way out.

Rudyard said, quietly, "Mr. Janning, you are here as a courtesy. I would strongly urge you to take a more supportive position."

I managed to catch Janning's gaze. He and I looked at each other for a long moment; he looked away. We both knew I was forfeit.

"The captain and I," Ferguson said to me, "will be sorry to see you go, Dunne. You had a good deal of promise."

The blood from my nose was mingling with my tears. I went to send Dr. Critchlow a note — and found no mail interface, of course.

And then I thought: *what if Trish tries to contact me*? For some reason I thought of her pet spiders, Abelard and Heloise. That was a welcome pleasant image.

Rudyard said, "It would be very easy to take the simplest course here and toss you out an airlock. But as it happens, we're heading back to Ganymede anyway, so for the remainder of the voyage, Mr. Dunne, you will be confined to the Brig under Miss Riordan's watchful eye. I would say you have been shown considerable mercy, more than you deserve. Much more. Quite apart from this business involving Miss Riley's allegations, there is the more serious matter of your attempt on Mr. Ferguson's life."

Oh yes, that. I felt a fresh plunge of despair thinking about it. I said nothing; all my limited energy was fixed on not vomiting.

The captain wasn't done yet. "Normally, attempted murder of a senior officer carries the penalty of execution once the charge is proved. And in your case, Dunne, I doubt there would be much chance of your getting off. All in all, you don't seem to have much to show for your time on this ship, do you?"

A nice scar on my ass, I thought, not to mention the loss of a friend and a complete absence of self-respect.

It looked like the meeting was almost over. They had what they needed to deal with Sorcha, and with me.

Sorcha. I'd never even had a chance to hold her properly, to tell her how I felt. I managed, wrenching sobs aside, to swear quietly at the cruelty of the universe.

My limbs tingled. I was short of breath. My heart thumped in my ears, loud and fast. Ferguson, when I looked at him, seemed to have a gigantic chin; Rudyard's sad eyes looked like they were dripping off the sides of his face. "What are you bloody looking at, Dunne?" Ferguson sneered. His tongue looked bloated, a vivid red. Mr. Janning sat there, impossibly huge hands over his face. The light in here was too bright; I squinted.

Rudyard said, interrupting this lull, "Excuse me a moment. The bridge." He paused, eyes glazed. Then said, to nobody in the room, "Go to tube entry at your discretion."

Ferguson chuckled and said to me, "Better make peace with your god, boy. We hit Ganymede geosynch in three days."

Riordan was waiting for me outside the captain's office, her hot blue eyes burning, her jaw set. She saw I looked like shit, and said to me, "Need the head?"

I nodded. She grabbed me by my collar, dragging me along the passageways; I shuffled along on treacherous legs, trying to stay upright. Her boots clacked hard on the deck with each rapid step. I could feel her breathing with contained fury. The light was still too bright; I kept my head down, squinting, and wondered vaguely what else the captain and Ferguson had drugged me with.

Finding a restroom, she pushed me inside — overwhelming white and chrome glare and a searing stink of antiseptic — and flung me sprawling into the nearest cubicle. "Hurry up!" she said.

It all came out. The actual vomit was incidental compared with everything else.

Riordan dragged me out of there after several minutes; I was still wiping my face. I could have stayed longer. She yanked me upright; the world spun two different ways at once; I made a helpless gurgling sound.

Riordan said, as she pushed me along, "Now look what you've done! Just look! You've screwed up everything!"

I wasn't sure what she was talking about, and at any rate, there was nothing I could say.

Eclipse slipped back into real space just as Riordan went to shove me into the Brig. It occurred to me — in the way people in dire trouble have a way of thinking about quite unrelated things — that she and I really should have been strapped into some kind of secure harness, the way the safety drills teach us. You never know, when you exit the tube and arrive back in real space, if you might suddenly have to apply a massive blast of boost or braking.

But instead of shoving me through the open cell door, she looked shocked out of her wits. Stunned, you might say. One hand absently fidgeted with loose strands of brown hair. After a moment, she laughed and said, "No, that can't be right. Can't be!"

"Miss Riordan? Are you all right?" She was standing there in the middle of the passageway, her other hand holding the Brig cell door, her eyes glazed over. Something, I guessed, was coming through ShipMind.

Which made me notice, for the first time, the quietness of the ship. Other than a faint hiss from the matter pumps shunting raw material through the fab conduit system, and the thrum of the power plant way in the distance... No voices; no system indicator sounds; no voice-prompts; no mail chimes or phone calls. I imagined a ghost ship would make more noise — and then realized I had been on such a ship, and nothing had been the same since.

"Miss Riordan?"

She turned to me, face bemused, all her former fury gone. "There's this weird thing..."

"Ma'am? I don't have..."

Not looking at me, still skimming through the material flashing across her vision. "There's this ... message. It's going everywhere in human space. It's very odd."

I was almost too dizzy to care, and using the cell door to hold myself upright. "If you like, I'll just put myself in here."

"This message, it says that this ship — us! — just wiped out the whole population of those aliens we met before. That is, it says we went to their home planet and we ... oh my God. Oh my God. It says we had nanophage bombs tailored to their DNA. We bombed them, we bombed them into extinction." She stood there, shocked, mouth open, eyes tracking back and forth across lines of text only she could see. "Nobody told me about this!" she said, talking to herself. "Nobody told me!"

I thought back to the time she had interrogated me, when she had constantly referred to the alien creatures as "animals." It seemed the better part of valor not to mention this right now.

Deciding not to wait for her, I escorted myself into the cell and made myself comfortable. A narrow cot along one wall was the only alternative to the floor. Sitting was a great relief. My head continued spinning, and my sleeves were filthy with dried blood from constantly wiping my nose. It occurred to me that I had a bunch of nasty bots digging around in my brain, and that they'd keep going until they broke down and turned into poison.

That was fine with me. There was no way I was going to live that long, anyway. We were braking back to in-system velocity. Less than three days to live? Sounded good. I didn't feel like dragging out the inevitable.

I found myself smiling. There was nothing I could do about my fate, as far as I could see. No way I could even consider starting up a mutiny while I didn't have headware. No headware; no way to access ship's systems. Or none that I knew about.

All I had left was to lie there on that narrow bunk in the darkness of the cell, admiring Sorcha's parting gift to humanity. Hundreds of anonymous infosphere nodes across human space, everywhere, all broadcasting perfect copies of those files to every valid and reachable address. It was a grand thing to contemplate: Sorcha's informational tsunami, a floodtide of data powered by one junior Service officer's righteous fury. It would take a while, a few days, for the full impact to spread across all inhabited systems, and for the inevitable eruption of confirmation/denial traffic to go back and forth between systems. But it had begun; she had probably sent the signal to start the broadcast as soon as Service Security picked her up, or she might have had a dead-man switch set up, ready to trigger as soon as it stopped receiving a signal from her headware.

And then I also realized: all those files would still have Service authentication and ownership watermarks embedded in their content for anyone to scan and check. I tried to imagine what goodies there might be. For starters, there would be the documents concerning *Eclipse's* special orders to go to the aliens' home planet and execute the mission. Details of the mission would be included, as well as data on how the home planet was found; its galactic coordinates and relevant system statistics. And there would be images of the world at assorted magnifications, resolutions, and wavelengths. Possibly an appended summary of the report describing the world's suitability for colonization and resource exploitation, and, perhaps, in a perfect universe, a statement from some Admiralty flunky describing the native inhabitants of the world as "of negligible interest" or "dispensable" or even "non-sentient." Essentially saying, in other words, that no people lived there. It was too easy to imagine. I imagined documents implicating the highest levels of the Admiralty, the Lords...

Sorcha, I realized, when I paused to think everything through, must now be dead.

The thought, the very idea, tore at me. It felt hard to breathe, without her in my world. I thought about all the times we talked, and how close we'd come to being together.

I kept going back to that week when I'd been stuck on board the damn ship doing Ferguson's shit work while Sorcha was seeing the sights on Winter City with Alastair. Instead of spying on the captain for all that time, I could have been with her. We could have had a life together. Maybe in some alternate universe we did. Too late now.

Lying there, idly watching Lily Riordan — still standing next to the open cell door, reading — I realized that

I hadn't really taken the time to know Sorcha as well as I might have. I knew only a little about her family, her childhood. Things which now I would have given anything for a chance to ask her.

It also occurred to me that you could say this about anyone you cared about, even someone you've known all your life. There's always more you could or would know, given the opportunity. More time that you could have spent with that person, if you had only known how little time you really had.

In that moment, thinking about the titanic forces Sorcha had unleashed, and the passion that led her to do it, I knew that I loved her.

Twenty-Two

I had missed seeing Kestrel survive its appointment with applied physics, the event that changed the face of human space as we knew it. But I was right there in the front row to see human space explode; even if, right at that moment, I couldn't see anything more interesting than a basic fab unit in the corner and a bucket.

Riordan took off running once she finished reading enough to get a sense of what was going on. I had to pull the cell door closed myself.

A single small light bar flickered on the ceiling; the whole cell, with its white walls and black floor, seemed designed to strobe at about sixty hertz. The door was solid; there were no windows. I was alone in a little box with my thoughts.

A lot of time passed. I might have slept a little. For the first time since before I went aboard that alien ship, my dreams were calm and straightforward. Not that I recall anything, but I remember not waking up with a terrible sense of dread or of a great danger escaped by the narrowest margin.

At some point I realized I was hungry. I got up and tried the fab. It was rigged only to give me water, which came with a strange smell and a taste like plastic, and dry biscuits that appeared designed to break apart on contact with air, and which were so dry I needed lots of the awful plastic water to get them down. There was also a chute in the bottom of the fab where I could unload the bucket. A bad smell emanated from that chute.

Could I really avoid using the bucket for the next three days? I seriously doubted it. It was something I could worry about tomorrow.

At another point, I found myself laughing my guts out, with no recollection of how I got started. Tears ran down my face, my belly ached, my cheeks hurt, and I was rolling around on my bunk, legs in the air, laughing like a giddy kid. The idea of the Service taking such pains to keep their murderous plans secret struck me as pretty funny, among other things. Like Ferguson's power games. He seemed to me now like a cheap comic figure; just imagining his face was enough to make me burst out in a new gust of giggles. After a while, even my unfocussed laughter was funny in itself, and I laughed about my laughter, and Colin was slapping my leg and making fart noises with his armpit and doing these hysterical impressions of his school teachers. Mom would appear at the door in her night robe, looking like death, and tell us to shut the hell up and go to sleep and we'd go "yeah Mom sure Mom sorry" — and as soon as she was gone we'd burst out giggling all over again, laughing at everything!

Janning came by. Riordan was with him; she opened the door, let him in, and said for him to let her know when he was done.

I wasn't laughing anymore. I'm still not sure where all that came from, or what it meant. I wished Colin would stay dead and I blamed him for what happened to Dad, and hated his guts. And then I'd catch myself thinking like this, and I'd stop and catch my breath, trying to concentrate on what was happening in the real world.

I wondered if I was starting to go mad. My chest still felt tight, and my breathing was not right. There was a sense of feeling distanced from my body. This feeling in my chest was fascinating — the way it would if it were happening to someone else. My limbs were still tingling, and when I stopped to notice, there was a squeezing feeling in my head that, like the chest symptoms, was also fascinating rather than scary.

Janning squatted on the floor by the door. "Hello, James," he said, frowning in what looked like embarrassment.

I sat up, blinking, trying to get back into the here and now. "Ferguson hasn't taken care of you yet? I'm shocked."

"James, I'm ... very sorry, about before. That little session was meant for my benefit as much as yours."

I couldn't think of anything to say.

He was holding his forehead, wincing. "They knew I was on your side, that you and me ... that we got on all right."

Riordan's instruction from long ago, in a previous lifetime, came back to me, telling me to make allies. Except how could I make bloody allies if I spent all my time stuck in the isolation of the simulation eggs? And then with the "stink" of the alien ship always on me, and nobody wanting to know me?

Janning said, "Ferguson was doing a lot to keep me from helping you, especially these last weeks. Kept me pulling double-shifts, extracurricular duties, ludicrous maintenance schedules, tearing apart and rebuilding entire nav systems, doing complete reinstalls of every bit of bloody software!" He shook his head.

I heard myself say, "He said he was going to make me his ... personal project. He wasn't going to stop until he broke me." *And maybe not even then*, I thought. Which suddenly made me laugh all over again. I laughed, thinking about chance and timing. Janning looked at me, startled. I don't think he liked the sound of that laugh.

"The docs had a word with me, son. They briefed me on..." He looked unsure what to say. Scratched at his head and looked embarrassed.

There was a voice within me that got mad, hearing him say that. The voice wanted me to blast Janning, tell him there was nothing wrong, that Ferguson hadn't done anything, and everything was just fine thanks all the same. This voice was strong, persuasive, and I came close to giving way to it, and saying all that. But the memory was fresh, the anger still scalding. I might not be able to say just what had happened. Maybe I never would be able to bring myself to say exactly what had taken place that night while Ferguson held his knife to my throat. Even now, talking to Janning, I felt my mind trying to hide it from me, to take the whole incident away, leaving a hole guarded by dragons, saying in my mother's voice, "We're doing this for your own good."

I still felt a profound ache. Not just when I sat, but all the time. The doctors had fixed things up good as new, with no visible scars, they said, though I declined the use of a mirror. Everything worked at a hundred percent efficiency. But I knew I would always have this ache, and would always fear men like Ferguson. I would always give in before things got to the point of confrontation.

Neither of us said anything for a while.

"Riordan said there was some interesting news." Changing the subject.

Janning scowled. "You were involved in that little piece of work, weren't you?"

"Actually, sir," I said, unable to suppress a smirk, "no I was not. I knew about it, and I knew it was coming, and I think it's only fair, considering what happened."

"Well if not you, who was it? Was it that Riley kid?"

"I couldn't say, sir."

"Christ, James! Give us some credit! We know you two were up to something."

"I really couldn't comment, sir."

He shrugged, sighed. "Doesn't matter."

After a melancholy silence, I asked, "Why did we do it, sir? The aliens."

"Community needs to expand, occupy more systems. Cheaper to develop a world to Phase Two occupation standard than build a full-blown hab, start up a biosphere from scratch. I don't know."

"But that system is so far away..."

"It is now. But in five, ten years, it'll probably be considered close to the Home System. Things are relative, son."

I asked, "What's happening out there now?" Nodding to indicate human space as a whole.

He snorted, shook his head. "Madness. Chaos. Nothing good."

"I suppose," I said, "the Lords are denying everything, while the Admiralty is trying to get its data back from all those other states."

Janning nodded, "That's about the size of it. All those other states will be wanting to know if it's true, and the Lords and Admiralty will say 'Oh definitely not, it's an elaborate hacker prank, don't you know!' Bloody media's gone berserk. Intersystem ship traffic's already up forty percent, just relaying media."

"Pretty elaborate prank, don't you think? Even down to genuine Service watermarks all over the documents."

Janning let out a big rush of air. "Indeed, son."

"So what happens now?"

"God knows."

Things got quiet again. I still didn't feel right, but I didn't care.

"How long till we dock?"

Janning looked surprised. "Oh. Uh, bit over twenty-one hours. You'll be going ashore before everyone else, probably. The captain seems keen to unload you ASAP."

"Nice to be thought of," I said, remembering that was something my father used to say when the management at his various workplaces screwed him over on a particular issue.

Dad...

In some ways, I still didn't feel like the news about Dad had hit me yet. I had cried after the big meeting, but that was mainly just sheer fatigue, pain, sickness, and shock...

"Mr. Janning..."

"James?"

"Could you lend me a bit of Active Paper or something, until we dock? It's pretty quiet in here," I said, not simply referring to the cell.

He got up. "Sure. I'll see what I can do." His tone was quiet, remorseful.

Riordan let him out and closed the door again. He came back what felt like hours later, and gave me a small rumpled sheet of Paper. He said, "Keep it if you want. It's a bit crap, so don't be surprised if it crashes on you."

I shrugged at him. "Probably won't need it long anyway, eh?" I smiled.

Janning reached out to shake my hand. It seemed like a very final gesture, like he wasn't expecting to see me again.

"What's this?" I asked him.

His face looked awkward in the faint, strobing light. "Just shake my bloody hand, all right? Would it kill you?" He was staring at me with tremendous focus. Like I didn't dare not shake his hand.

We shook; his hand was clammy.

"Good luck, James," he said, frowning.

"Thanks, sir. I appreciate what you did for me."

He went to leave, but stopped at the door. Turning, he said, "It's the same you know. All over."

"Mr. Janning?"

"The whole bloody Service. Full of bastards like Rudyard and Ferguson. Everywhere. You would have run into someone like them no matter what ship you'd gotten. It's..." He stopped, looked tense, perhaps a bit emotional. "It's just the way it is."

I nodded, feeling sad.

He went on, looking at me again with that powerful stare that brooked no dissent. "Don't give up yet, son."

"Eh?"

Janning crossed the cell, squatted before me. His eyes looking at me hard. He leaned over to me, cupped his hand against my ear. He said, breath warm in my ear, "You've still got one chance."

"Sir?"

He mumbled into my ear again, "Your hand, you moron. I'm trying to help you!" And with that he got up and left.

I knew he had just taken a gigantic risk, considering the walls of this cell probably had a coating of surveillance spray. But what could he have done that would have helped me?

And then I did feel ... something.

I looked down at my hand, resting in my lap, holding the page. My palm tingled a bit. Holding it closer, to see it under the bad light, I noticed a bit of moisture in the lines...

One chance, he'd said.

My hand itched. I could feel a warmth working up my forearm.

He couldn't have just done what I thought he had, could he? In full view of all this surveillance? Then it occurred to me that maybe Riordan was in it with him. Maybe she knew.

All the same, I wondered how I could prevent myself getting obviously excited. Probably peering at the hand Janning just shook would be a bit of a giveaway, if he ever got busted for aiding a prisoner or something similar. What if Riordan wasn't in on it? Shit.

Glancing down at the paper, smoothing it out, I checked the local time: we'd dock at Ganymede geosynch in twenty hours fifty-three minutes.

That was cutting it too fine. There was only one thing to do: I got up from the cot, and started exercising as hard as I could, strange feelings in my chest be damned.

When I collapsed in a sweaty heap on my cot an hour later in a lot of pain, wheezing, coughing, and woozy, one thing gave me comfort: the strident and rapid pounding of my heart. That and a certain warm feeling above my sinuses.

Once I recovered, I followed the news on Janning's Paper. He hadn't been kidding about it being in bad shape.

One headline from the Home System tabloid feed *Solar Breeze Today* caught my eye:

HUMANITY DISCOVERS
ALIEN INTELLIGENCE!
AND KILLS IT!

I sent mail to Sorcha's address through the Active Paper. Just checking, on the off-chance she might still be alive. But even a failed-mail bounce message would take at least a full day to get back to me. And in that time I would sit here in my new home, cut off from everything I care about, and think all the sorts of 'if only' thoughts people have when they know that things are no longer possible to fix, that time has hurried the world along.

Sorcha was gone, I knew it. She hadn't been lucky at the last second and overpowered her captors. She hadn't by a miraculous chance escaped from custody and fled in a stolen ship to rendezvous with *Eclipse* and bust me out of the brig so we could have a long and happy-ever-after life together. Things in the real world never worked that way. My dad, all those years ago, was right about that.

I sent mail to Trish telling her about Dad, in case she didn't already know. I assumed she would know after all this time, but I thought it best to be on the safe side. The hardest part, the part I hated, was explaining my current situation. Explaining it to Trish, who had been so against me joining the Service in the first place, who had said, "You can't replace our brother, Jamie!" And I had wanted to slap her.

I also had to ask her what was being done with Dad's remains. It seemed unlikely that there would be a lot if the captain of that ship had indeed hit the self-destruct, but there were probably some small personal effects. Then there was the matter of his will. It was only a small letter, but it felt like it took weeks to write. Each word hurt. I sent it off.

Another headline from the same feed:

HOW MANY OTHER
RACES ARE OUT THERE?
WHAT ELSE IS HSC GOVT HIDING?

But there was one article that made me curse, probably along with almost everyone else in human space:

HSC SCORES HUGE
ALIEN TECH BONANZA!
COMMUNITY SET TO LEAP AHEAD!

Janning phoned me about an hour later. At the time he called, I was having another attack of palpitations and breathing problems. I was still feeling that disturbing distance from myself, a weird pull away from the world of James Dunne, disgraced Service officer, and towards a simpler world, where Daddy worked very hard, which was why we never saw him, and Mommy would say that he was like the great and powerful wizards I read about in these old books. Colin told me I was such a *girl* for liking stories like that and that Daddy didn't come home because he was hiding from Mommy.

I liked stories; especially ones about heroes and knights and quests and mysterious secrets and riddles in the dark. I liked imagining myself as a brave knight, loyal and true, crusading for justice, smiting the evil hordes and restoring the light and winning the beautiful princess.

In later years, when Dad found me reading much the same kind of thing, aimed at an older readership, he would always threaten to rewrite those stories for me to reflect the world as he knew it, where good men found themselves constantly screwed over by their superiors, and where these superiors denied the good men the use of the tools they needed to carry on their great works. A world, in short, where fairness didn't count. Dad said a good knight in such a world would have to make do and fight the hordes of evil with a cheap pen and a rubber band and no shining armor, and even if the knight saved the kingdom, his king would take all the credit — and the beautiful princess — while the brave knight was banished, unemployed, into the wilderness.

Janning was talking; he sounded agitated: "James, there's been a change of plan. We're not going to Ganymede. I thought you should know."

I looked at the phone interface on the page. "Mr. Janning? What's—"

I heard a lot of voice-noise in the background. "We're being mobilized, son. The orders just came through."

"Okay," I said, "fine." But saying this, I was also rubbing at my chest, and wondering about the shortness of my breath. That pressing feeling in my skull was worse, assuming full-scale migraine dimensions. I should have been worried, but what I wanted right now was a good book, like the ones I used to read — sometimes two a day — when I was little, hiding away into obscure corners of the apartment so I could read by myself and not have to hear Mom and Dad fighting and Trish crying and Colin out in the yard bouncing a cricket ball against the wall.

"James — you okay? You don't sound quite yourself."

Sore head, weird feelings in my limbs, palpitations, difficulty breathing without pain, and a rushing sound in my ears. "I'm fine, I think. So how come we're getting mobilized?"

"You read the news?"

"Oh you mean that everybody thinks we're sitting on hot alien tech, and we might be a threat?" I laughed. "But we don't have anything!"

"Well, there's those glass ball things I suppose, but the point is they—"

I said, "They just want to swallow us up, and this is a good excuse, and besides, the alien technology might be worth something?" It was easy to imagine the government and the Admiralty going crazy blitzing the media with stark denials about any kind of technology or artifacts — saying how could there be any such material when there were no aliens and that whole information blitz had been an elaborate hoax?

Except, as the flood of media reports coming through the page's buffers suggested, the more the Service denied the existence of the aliens, the more everyone else believed. One report referred to "the Royal Interstellar Service's well-known creative approach to the truth in past scandals involving systematic cadet abuse..." and went on to list numerous incidents in the past decade alone that had made the Service look very bad indeed. Meanwhile, the Admiralty continued to "stand on the integrity and loyalty of its ancient traditions and fine men and women..."

It was all I could do not to fall down laughing again, but my chest hurt too much.

Janning interrupted: "The Asiatics are putting together a battle fleet. The Lords are appealing to the Unity for treaty-obligation assistance. No reply yet, as far as I know."

"The Asiatics?" For them it would be like swatting a bug. They could take us over, seize our "secrets", and absorb all our real estate, all without looking up from their tangled internal affairs.

Which brought me back again to Trish, living on Mars. Mars, including where Trish and Cory lived in the city of Viking One, was predominantly Francophone, and part of Unity Europa, even though the planet itself was in the Home System. Which was part of what made the whole concept of the "Home System Community" such a fraud. I imagined that the Asiatics would hardly care about Mars' complex political and security affiliations when the crunch came.

I found myself thinking of Trish and Cory as refugees, scrambling to get out of their house with some clothes and toiletries, heading for the port. They'd be frightened. Trish would already be feeling bad enough. Just lost her father, and fresh weirdness with her dead brother. It was too soon for my latest note to have arrived, but that wouldn't lighten her load, either. I was trying to deal with the thought of the Asiatics moving in with their typical approach of evacuating the world's existing population to make way for Metasphere citizens; it was enough to terrify me out of my self-indulgent introspection.

Trish.

Suddenly the pain in my chest, the shortness of breath, the headache — all of it was real. It was happening to me now. Not to someone standing off to one side of the stage, making arch comments about some poor wretch over there.

We were going to war. Those stupid media reports were based on nothing at all! Some "expert" said we could leap ahead with all our new alien technology! Where did these people get such information? They didn't know anything about the aliens we encountered. According to the reports coming through the Paper, the kinds of advances all sounded like stuff out of old vids! When people thought about aliens they thought about the aliens they knew, popularized through centuries of science fiction. The thought of actual, genuine creatures with intelligence and cultures and their own agenda was still beyond comprehension — and apparently beyond the interest of the sensationalist media, which only wanted a good story to tell and didn't mind paying for it. I read wild speculations about colossal mind machines that would boost our intelligence to the level of gods, of infinite energy generators, doomsday weapons, and devices that would let us travel faster than light without the need for hypertubes. It was all preposterous.

And now the Home System Community was at ground zero as every other major state and metastate decided to come and get us, just in case there was some small kernel of truth to all the media nonsense.

I said to Janning, my voice tight, feeling a full-blown panic attack boiling up inside me, "So we're going to fight off the Asiatics?"

"That's what I've been trying to tell you, Dunne. What's the matter? You sound strange."

"No, no, I'm ... well, I feel kind of peculiar, actually, but it's this other thing. My sister, she's on Mars. It's just..." I didn't know what to say. I was pacing about in the cell, holding Janning's page. I was sweating.

"Dunne, you're not having a bad reaction to the...?"

"Oh, no sir. Not that. I think that's going to be — look, you say we're mobilizing now? I can feel the power plant boosting. When do we hit the tube?"

"Shouldn't be much longer. We're rendezvousing with the *Queen Helen* Battle Group. I'll try to keep you posted."

The thought of *Queen Helen* stung, and I felt a fresh blast of pain over that whole wretched business with the late and unlamented Admiral Greaves. Thinking about her, that day, her grand scheme to purify the Service ... I had to sit. My head was spinning again. I didn't feel at all well.

"Sir," I wheezed, "call the Infirmary for me ... I'm..."

Twenty-Three

...light bars scrolling by ... immense, towering orderlies clad in surgical greens, faces made of bright planes and dark caverns — all grim expressions. Somebody was holding my hand — trying to hold my hand — telling me to relax, that it was all right. I had the feeling that I had to get off this ship. Somebody was screaming themselves hoarse — hacking gasping sobs — more screaming. I was paralyzed, unable to move, but I needed to get off this ship — walls were squeezing in, the ceiling grinding down, blinding light bars rushing past. Then a lift. The doors hissed shut. Orderlies stood around like Stalk elevators — I had unmatched views of flaring nostrils. Light bars stationary now, humming, blazing down on me. My screams shook the air. The doors hissed again. Light bars scrolling. I wished to Christ I could move, wished I could stop howling. Howling after Dad — I'm so sorry. It's all I can say. I let him down. Let Colin down. I'm so sorry, Dad. Can you hear me, where you are? An orderly said, "Son, I reckon they can hear you on bloody Mars!" I heard it like something in a dream — and I don't know what it means and I don't care. I just want to see my dad, tell him I'm sorry. Hot pain was boiling in my chest — screaming panic — needing NOT TO BE HERE — something's coming — GOTTA GET OFF THIS SHIP! — gotta find Dad, gotta tell him. Light bars, light bars flashing...

"So we meet again..." I said, trying to focus on Dr. Critchlow. My head felt like something dangerous and noisy wrapped in a cubic meter of construction foam.

Critchlow was studying a clipboard containing a fixed Paper display. "You picked a lousy time to have your little psychotic collapse, Dunne. Things are a little busy."

"Sorry, doc," I murmured, feeling the new drugs taking hold, smoothing things out. I was fascinated with the pattern on the ceiling tiles, feeling weak, wrung out, and wanting only to sleep for at least a month. My muscles, every one of them, ached like I had sprained my whole body. In the back of my mind flickered memories of my "collapse", as the doc called it. Down deep where my heart lay, I felt a cold shame. Service officers don't have these problems. Service officers grit their shiny white teeth and get on with the job. Stiff upper lip, and all that. We don't howl for the forgiveness of the dead.

My world spun, slow and heavy; the light was still too bright. I felt weak and fluttery, like I could subside into all that shrieking horror stuff again at any moment. Every time I shut my eyes, even to blink, I saw streams of images: Colin dead on that tree, black tongue sticking out of his purple lips and the stink of cold urine, cold shit, and stale semen in his pants; there was Dad, falling to his knees at the first sight of Colin that morning. I remember the way he collapsed, like he'd been shot. That look on his face. And then there was the look on Mom's face, when she heard. She didn't collapse; she stood and quietly imploded. And then the day she left us, looking in a lot of ways like she was glad to be going, to get away. Why didn't she collapse like Dad? Why couldn't she cry? Why couldn't I cry? And Dewey, at the Academy, late at night, when he was pissed, ordering me to suck his skinny little organ and he looked, even as he forced me, kind of vulnerable, like this was something he needed, but didn't know how to go about it like a normal person. He'd been brought up to bully people into doing things, into forcing intimacy. How often I was tempted to bite the damn thing off and spit it in his face!

The darkness upon darkness of the alien ship's reticula, winding like a vast intestine through that rock full of doom. I still found it hard to get warm, and sometimes dreamed of that heatless dark. I dreamed of swimming through those rocky tubes, freezing to death, barely able to breathe, terrified I'd be lost forever and become another crypt-dweller, and, breaking free, seeing a planet riding its orbit, and a god-sized Ferguson looming over it, with his knife out, only it wasn't a knife and…

I screamed, screamed enough to wake the dead. Sitting up on my bunk in the Infirmary, Critchlow and a nurse trying to push me back down, but I was hardly aware of them, just seeing Ferguson, smelling him, feeling his cold hands on my skin, the hot cut of his knife at my throat…

A voice yelled, "Nurse! Now."

There was a hard point of pressure on my shoulder. A feeling of oily warmth rolled through me. In its wake I slipped into a new comfortable darkness, like the womb.

When I woke later, feeling a little more like my old self but still fragile, a nurse told me the ship was transiting a long tube, headed for a rendezvous with the *Queen Helen* Battle Group. I noticed, with a weak dread, other Infirmary personnel rushing around, setting up extra beds, laying out sets of instruments, fabbing up supplies of monoblood products and drugs; a brisk, calm clatter of activity. Critchlow was distracted when he came to check on me. "Can you stand on your own?"

I got up to a sitting position, head not too woozy, saying, "So far, so good."

"That's great. Look, I really don't have the bed capacity for you if you're well enough to be ambulant."

"So it's back to the big house, huh?" Just what I needed, more solitary confinement, just me and my demons.

Critchlow smiled. "Not necessarily. I've got something more interesting."

And so saying, he glazed over for a moment.

I tried to stand. Standing was fun. I accidentally hit Critchlow as I pinwheeled my arms around. But I soon got the hang of this standing upright business.

I heard a ping in my head. A sign appeared in my field of view:

Installation of Mindstar Interface AC's product, MINDSTAR EXECUTIVE 3.0, was successful! Miss Riordan, I would recommend that you make a backup of my seed assembly and store it in a safe place. Please confirm that audiovisual display characteristics are within acceptable parameters, according to your preferences file. I hope you will be happy with me.

I stared. And stared some more. I got back up on the bed, and sat there, looking at this message. After some time, thinking, "*What the hell?*" I blinked my confirmation, and a relatively familiar headware interface presented itself.

Except it thought I was Lily Riordan. Even though at the level of tissue-lock, it should have taken one sniff of my non-Riordan DNA, proclaimed me an impostor, and shot off an army of alarmbots, probably knocking me out in the process.

Yet here I was.

"I know that look," Riordan said, appearing next to the doctor.

I looked at her, frowning, my pacified mind trying to make the connection. And then...

"Miss Riordan, your headware—"

She put a finger over her lips. "Shhh. Let that be our little secret, okay, Mr. Dunne?"

"You and ... Mr. Janning!" I was finding it very hard to think straight. "I don't, I don't understand. What's going on?"

Critchlow put a hand on my shoulder. "Mr. Dunne, Miss Riordan is going to personally supervise you until we get back to Ganymede. That means she's going to have you stay in her quarters."

"Doc, isn't that ... um, against regs?"

Critchlow looked at Riordan, "Now he worries about regs!"

Riordan said, arms folded, "You might have thought that before you shagged Admiral Greaves, son."

I blushed, hearing it put like that. "Well, hmm. But isn't it, you know, inappropriate for a junior officer of one gender to occupy the quarters of a senior officer of another gender?"

She said, still looking arch, "I'll actually be staying somewhere else, so fear not. Propriety will be served, Mr. Dunne."

That all seemed fine, if puzzling. "But why do I have your headware...?"

Riordan glared at me. Almost immediately an encrypted message appeared in my head. Her headware unscrambled it in a picosecond:

> Mr. Dunne:
> My headware contains the security overrides that let me access parts of the ship that are otherwise locked and sealed. My job description contains all the authorization I need for such access. I don't need probable cause. The Service has declared that if the safety of the ship is even remotely in doubt, I am entitled to use my own discretion over a wide variety of actions in order to protect her. I have deemed this to be one such instance, and am using my discretion to provide you with a suitably hacked copy of my headware. Mr. Janning was only too happy to be the conduit.
>
> It is not my place to provide you with instructions on what you should do next. I believe you will know what to do at the right time. Suffice to say, there are a lot of people on this ship with a profound degree of sympathy for your situation, Mr. Dunne, but are too terrified to let their feelings of solidarity be known. If you have any further queries, please put them in cryptomail like this, using my personal decrypt key, okay?
> L. Riordan

I looked up at her. "I see, ma'am. When do we start?"
Eclipse exited the tube and returned to real space.
"Whenever you're ready."

⊕⊕⊕

She left me in her quarters, with firm instructions not to touch her violin or she'd kill me. "You think Ferguson's scary? He's just a pathetic old bastard. Me, you should be scared of." With that, she stalked out the door to resume her patrols.

I sat at her desk and thought about cracking open an old book she had evidently been reading, a biography of Carl Philipp Emanuel Bach that looked dense and daunting. Instead I started exploring the features of her headware. She had bridge cloud access, I discovered right away, with both present mode and surveillance mode. I toggled the latter and got into the feed.

I appeared, sitting, off to one side of the "room." Rudyard was at the head of the table, chin resting on his hands, with Ferguson standing, hands behind his back, next to him. Rudyard looked tense and worried, though trying to mask it. Ferguson had his "let's kill everybody!" snarl going. He was loving this. Janning, smooth and professional, was in control of the Helm himself, I saw, with support from his team, who would be in their own cloud. In a different world, I could have been in there with them, helping compile the navigation data. Finney, sitting further down the table, relayed important comm traffic. At that moment, *Eclipse* and *Queen Helen* were swapping information about the immediate tactical situation and where *Eclipse* should go in the flagship's defensive perimeter and Janning's people were processing that and making the necessary adjustments. Bartlesby, on weapons, sat quietly disclosing the readiness of the ship's main gun, the turrets, power supply, loader systems, fire control, infowar capabilities. Critchlow sat at the end of this table, already looking angry, full of doom, providing infrequent reports on the Infirmary staff and facility readiness.

It was so quiet. So much of the real activity was occurring within the heads of the people gathered here. Comments were only made regarding significant changes. Habit, and training, and brain-mounted control systems, combined to cut the time needed for understanding and communicating down to a bare minimum.

The room we occupied felt smaller than the last time I was here. I kept wanting to hunch over, lest my head bang on the low ceiling. There were so many people in here, too — more than usual. There was a stifling, hot feeling. It was strange, too, to notice how Ferguson, standing, easily dominated the table while Rudyard, murmuring commands, looked uncertain, and like he hadn't slept in a week. His hair was a mess, perhaps unwashed, and I thought he needed a shave. It looked like he could feel the tightness in the room, the sense of airlessness and confinement. I had no idea where his physical self was. He could be wandering around loose, or jogging on a treadmill in the gym, or lying on his bunk in his quarters, sweating buckets, wondering if we could make a difference.

Perhaps wondering where the Asiatics were.

Queen Helen had a new commander, Admiral Charles O'Connor, a man who looked more like Ferguson's kind of officer than like Rudyard's. O'Connor was tall for a Service officer, filling out his whites like something from an ad; but behind his reassuring, fatherly charisma there lay the same steel-eyed predator I saw in Ferguson. Only O'Connor looked so charming you could wind up thanking him for killing you.

He appeared over the cloud, standing over the other side of the room from where I sat, invisibly watching. He stood there, cap under his arm, silver hair worn long enough to require brushing, his face stern.

"Captain Rudyard, XO Ferguson, men and women of *HMS Eclipse*..." he opened.

I saw Ferguson snap to attention. Rudyard looked like this was one more damned thing he could do without.

O'Connor continued, in a deep, serious voice so we'd know he wasn't kidding, "We move at 0700 tomorrow. The QH Battle Group will enter the same tube, with a view to emerging in Jupiter Space shortly thereafter. Our intelligence indicates the Asiatics are planning to neutralize the Community government seat on Ganymede, with secondary targets consisting of our communication infrastructure nodes. Government officials have already left Ganymede on a routine transport and entered a tube."

The time now was 0100 hours.

I wondered if I was the only one in the room who thought the Asiatics were being unusually dainty about their operational plans. They had the resources to mount at least two major Battle Groups; we all knew that. It would be no trouble for them to, say, go for Mars at the same time, or perhaps a couple of the bigger habs. Then again, Mercury and Venus had very few defenses, but who'd want to live there, let alone pay for the terraforming? Terraforming Mars had proved strikingly unpopular once the population realized their taxes would have to pay for it over hundreds of years.

And all that assumed we could trust what Service intelligence had found out. They had been wrong on other occasions. And it had been several months since the last big spy scandal hit the intelligence community.

Could I be blamed for thinking we were totally screwed already?

O'Connor went on, "And now, it is my great pleasure, to introduce you to our leader, Her Majesty Queen Helen, who has a prepared an inspirational message for us all." Even Ferguson looked pained at the prospect.

O'Connor stepped back and disappeared. The lights in the room dimmed. A circle of light appeared on the floor, and a tall, slim figure stepped into this circle. Queen Helen, High Commander of the Service, wore the dazzling white uniform befitting the Service's ultimate position, Spacecraft Command Officer Level 10. Her uniform was encrusted with decorations and festooned with commemorative ribbons, and she wore on her shoulder the patch of the Home System Service's first flagship, *Earthrise*: a blue crescent on a black field. Her short, dark hair was trimmed up neat; her violet eyes were set hard with purpose.

She said, "Men and women of the Royal Interstellar Service — good morning. By now you know your mission, and you will be preparing to carry it out. I know that you are feeling scared, that the forces arrayed against you are overwhelming. This is true. We are just one system, and a crippled system in many respects, with the loss of Earth and without the support of most of Mars, yet we still number in the hundreds of millions of souls. We are plentiful in population, if not in territory. And all of those souls are counting on you now, each one of you, from the lowliest SSO1 to the Admiral of the Fleet, Mr. O'Connor, to stand between them and the storm to come. Perhaps you think we have no chance against such an opponent. Perhaps you think the battle is already lost. Perhaps you are letting your own fears and petty concerns prevent you from seeing the real issues.

"More than your lives and your ships are at stake. What is at stake here today is our home. We had no say in what happened to Earth. By the time we could act, she was already gone. Now we face a new threat — but this time, we can act, and we will act, together, for the sake of our very home.

"Good luck, and good hunting."

She saluted, stepped crisply back out of the lit circle, and disappeared. Silence followed her departure. What does one say about an inspirational speech that fails to inspire?

Twenty-Four

I had six hours to stew in my own juices, stuck in Riordan's quarters, wondering what was next, and what my supposed last chance might involve. So far, not much.

Riordan's natural scent was thick in the air. I knew she wore no perfume. It was an intimidating feeling, sitting there in her room, surrounded by her stuff, artifacts of her casual presence. It was like she was there, sitting behind me perhaps, watching to see what I might do.

And what that might be, I did not know. What could I do? Riordan and Janning — and perhaps Critchlow and his people — were up to something, and it involved me. Again, I was being used, a tool to do a deed they dare not do themselves.

But what deed? And why now?

On a lark, I got back into Riordan's headware; I thought I'd noodle around some of the other features. She had a lot more gear in her rig than I'd ever seen. She must have had processor mesh webbed throughout most of her brain. Lots of the features were disabled, I found; I lacked most of the neuroid structure support she had.

There was one interesting feature: I could interrogate every door on the ship on whether it was open, closed, locked, unlocked — and who had passed through. For a while I looked around the ship, talking to doors, monitoring crew movements. It might be fun, I thought, to see where I'd been. So I found the door to the Brig. The door indicated I had gone in.

But not that I'd left.

This gave me pause. I sat and thought about this for a moment. It had to be a system glitch. So I had another look. Still no record of me leaving for the Infirmary, and no record of the orderlies coming to get me, either.

I had a look at Riordan's Brig records. There was a note saying I had been deposited in cell number one — and that I was still there.

Riordan's headware had access to a surveillance feed from the cells, so she could monitor activity in there. I tuned into that channel through ShipMind. The view was from overhead, and the image bulged to get the whole cell into the view.

"I" was lying on the bunk, sleeping.

I skimmed back over the accumulated record. The person on that bed used the bucket occasionally, used the fab, was heard to bitch about the vile water, scratched himself, sometimes sat on the edge of the bunk looking wretched, holding his head, talked incoherently to himself, slept some more. Vital sign info pulled from the cell's surveillance systems showed he was depressed and angry, but definitely alive. Interrogating the identity-checking system showed that it was definitely SSO1 Dunne, J. Unique, uncrackable ID code and everything.

Damn. Pulling out of there, I switched to Riordan's quarters. Visual surveillance showed her room, at this moment, was empty. Door logs showed that Riordan had entered a short while before, and left again, locking the door behind her.

She had been alone at all times.

I got back into a map of the ship, and traced the route from the Infirmary to Riordan's quarters. Every door between here and there was unaware that I had been with Riordan when she brought me here. In the Infirmary there was no record that I had been there recently, either.

The time was 0220 hours.

I phoned Riordan. She answered right away, "Riordan, go."

"What's going on?" Before she could answer, I went on, "What are you and Janning up to?"

Riordan asked, "You're still in my quarters?"

"There's no trace of my movements anywhere. The system thinks I'm still in the Brig. I've looked all over! What are you doing?"

"It's all right. It's nothing to be worried about. We—"

I was up and pacing. Panic was heating up within me. "I'm not gonna let you bastards use me. I fell for that once before, and it's not gonna happen again. You hear? You hear me?" I went on in this manner, my voice getting louder and shriller.

Riordan said, "Just wait there. I'll be right there and we can talk."

"I'm not going to be the fall guy for you! I don't know what it is but I'm not doing it, I'm not playing along!"

"Just settle down. Everything's all right. Just hold tight and I'll be there shortly, okay?"

I was screaming, "You're not gonna use me the way Greaves used me! I won't do it! Do your own bloody dirty work! Do it yourself!" And so on.

At some point, Riordan killed the connection, leaving me ranting to nobody.

She arrived a few minutes later. I was still pacing, feeling sweaty and tense. Riordan took one look at me. "I'm sorry, James."

I wasn't interested. "Why does your surveillance system say I'm still in the Brig? Huh?"

She walked up to me. She looked at me. It was a serious stare. "We're going into a possible combat situation in a few hours, James. You know that."

I stormed away from her, ranting, shouting abuse, hitting things. I felt incandescently angry. The prospect of actual combat did not concern me too much; I didn't figure I'd be much involved, and I didn't figure we'd last long. I'd be sitting around in my Brig cell, or stuck here in Riordan's quarters, instead of in the Helm cloud doing my job.

Riordan tried to get me to listen, shaking me hard. This took a while. At some point she said, "James — we can't go into combat with Ferguson as XO."

This surprised me. "What?" I stared at her. And, down in my bowels, I felt a slow tightness, as I began to get an idea of what was going on.

Oh no, not that…

"That's right. It's bad enough we're stuck with Rudyard, but at least he knows he's got problems. Maybe if we'd got back to Ganymede, he might have gotten himself some med leave or something, get his head sorted out."

"The captain's that bad?" It wasn't hard to imagine, knowing what I did about him, and his background. Chances were the thought of what he did to that planet was eating at him.

She continued, looking at the floor, face pinched with anxiety, "That bastard Ferguson, he's… Something's changed in him." There was something disturbing about the way she said it.

I said, "Get Critchlow to take him off duty. Easy."

"He's tried. I've tried. Rudyard says he won't stand in the way. He knows what Ferguson would be like as acting captain. Meanwhile, Ferguson says he'll kill anybody who thinks they can take him off duty."

"He said that?"

"To me, he said he knows what's going on: that the bleeding hearts on the ship want to get him. That we want to bring him down as if he were some rogue bull elephant."

Ferguson as a bull elephant gone nuts. Crushing everything under its giant feet as it rampages through the jungle. I could see that. But to say he'd kill to stay in his job…

"So what's changed in him?"

She stood back, arms crossed and looked away. "Miss Riley's stunt, mainly. Also the prospect of war — it's got his blood up, so to speak."

"But Ferguson's not likely to be acting captain, is he?"

"Critchlow and I think Rudyard's a risk. He's never had to take a ship into combat, except in sims. And in his present shape, he might … well he might fail under pressure. It's happened before, on other ships. Which means we need an XO who can be relied on, someone solid."

"Janning is next in line, isn't he?"

"Right."

So here it was, perfectly clear but unstated. My gut feeling was correct. Here I was: Boy Assassin for Hire. And conveniently, already thought to be nuts, so the conspirators get to maintain their deniability. Who'd believe me if I talked?

Or maybe they had that risk covered in their calculations as well, I thought, feeling queasy and cold. I looked at her, the anger now hard like cooling steel. "Find another sucker. I'm not touching this little game. No way."

She shoved me against a bookcase. Things rattled. Her hot blue eyes scalded me. I could smell bad coffee on her breath. "Mr. Dunne — do I need to remind you of your Oath of Service?"

I tried to push her away; she secured herself against me harder, forearm jammed against my throat. "Piss off!" I gurgled, but I was scared.

"We need you for a special mission of the highest importance, Mr. Dunne. The safety of the ship and her crew is at stake!"

I scowled back at her, as best I could. "Spare me! I'm already staring down the barrel of summary execution after a nice show-trial court-martial. My plate's nice and full, thanks."

"Mr. — James," she said, breathing hard, glaring at me. Her face was so close to mine, I could feel the tension coming off her like heat. She was quivering with it. A part of me began to think she really might be willing to hurt me to get her point across.

She continued, "You help us, and we will help you with your trial."

I laughed in her face, but it was all bravado.

She added, "I wouldn't laugh at the woman who can get the charges dropped, Dunne."

There was a long pause. I felt my breath struggling in and out, my feelings turning over. Staring at her, wanting to believe, but I knew we were talking about the Service.

And thinking, too, that I didn't want another run-in with Ferguson. Not now, not ever.

"No way."

She said, "We want you. And we'll make it worth your while."

It was too much like the Greaves business. "You want me because they already think I'm nuts. Nothing to tie anything back to you."

"You think you know what we're after?"

"I might be nuts, but I'm not stupid."

She allowed a small curl of a smile. "So what are we talking about?"

"Ferguson." I wanted to spit his name.

"What about him?" she asked.

"You want me to kill him. Do I get the prize?" I didn't want to think about the idea. My knees weakened. My guts churned.

She said, "What if we did?"

"I — you can't... I can't. Doesn't matter what you offer. I couldn't."

"Perfect crime, James. Everybody wins."

"No such thing, ma'am. Little fish always get eaten by the big fish."

"Dunne, we've got it all set up for you. You've seen that. My records are perfect. They're immaculate. They show you've been in the Brig for ages. You'll be there the rest of the voyage. You've got nothing to lose but your death sentence!"

I shook my head. "I can't. I can't do it. I just can't."

She eased off my throat. Immediately my legs buckled. She eased me into a chair and pulled up another. "After what he did to you?"

A voice leapt up inside me, wanting to deny anything happened, to say he wasn't such a bad guy. But I said, "That's ... that's why I can't." Big, swamping feelings surged around me. It felt like I was drowning, and starting to panic, taking gulping breaths. I wanted to get out of this room. It was too hard to deal with all this. I wanted her to go away and leave me be.

But I was also thinking about what she offered: charges dropped. No disgrace. No execution.

Just a life of knowing what I did. Maybe I'd convince myself I acted for a higher purpose. Rationalizing could be a merciful thing. I felt a tidal pull towards the idea.

I wouldn't have to face my sister, shamed and broken. I wouldn't have to think of letting down my father.

But Ferguson?

"I couldn't, ma'am..." I wanted to. I felt that deep in my guts, the urge to hurt him, fill him with gibbering terror. But that was a dream. There was no way I could tackle him, face him down, and hold my ground.

Because, in the back of my mind, there was the terrifying thought: *what if he did it again*?

"Do you want him to gain control of this ship in a combat situation? The way he is?"

"I can't murder another man!"

She said, leaning close, "The charges will be dropped, James. Think of it!"

"I am thinking about it! I am!" I yelled at her, wishing to God she could see what she was asking of me.

"We don't have long, James. We need the right command team before we enter battle — you do understand that, don't you?"

And all the while, I was trying to motivate myself by trying to think back to that night. Thinking about everything that had happened so far. About Sorcha's sacrifice, and the thought of her enduring torture.

The annihilation of an entire race of life forms despite evidence suggesting their sentience, their intelligence: cities underground, artifacts, space travel.

And that look on my father's face, when I couldn't stop crying about Mom leaving, the same look I saw for years: his disgust, his contempt, for his weak son, a very poor substitute for Colin. No matter what I did, or how hard I tried, in school after school after school, always trying to be Colin for Dad, and all I ever saw was that look of disappointment on his face. And, not that he had ever said this in so many words, I could never escape the feeling — one with which I had long struggled — that if I'd just done better, been a better kid, been more like Colin, Mom wouldn't have left.

It took Riordan a long time to settle me down. She said, at one point, rubbing my back, talking to me in a soothing voice, "Do it for yourself, James."

"That's very trite," I sniffed.

"So the Service has let you down. Boo-bloody-hoo! It's let us all down. And it's going to go on, just as it is now."

"Unless the Asiatics wipe us out, that is."

"One thing at a time. If we've got the right team on the bridge, we might have a better chance. Do this one thing for us. I guarantee I will get your charges dropped in return."

I said nothing. My brain felt like it was drowning in fear. It was all I could do to think straight. There was nothing in my head but a white noise of terror.

After a while, though, I found my voice. It was tiny and quiet. I had never felt more like a mouse. Something was shifting around in my head, making room for a sense of fatalism. In all probability, I was going to die when I got court-martialled. It was also fairly likely we wouldn't survive this war. So what did I have to lose?

"Tell me again why Ferguson needs to go." It was worth hearing the argument again, I supposed, though I knew as soon as I said that that I had just decided that I would do it. All the rest was formality. Besides, I didn't have the strength to argue. I thought I'd humor her.

She said, sighing, "*Eclipse* is an explorer ship — light military capability. Ferguson wishes we were a frigate, a full-blown warship. He wants to go to war, he wants all guns blazing. He told me this once, over drinks at a bar. I thought he was this rakishly interesting older man, I even kind of fancied him. Until he started talking about his destiny. He actually used that word. Destiny. He said he was destined to die in battle, a great warrior." She coughed up a bleak laugh. "He never expected he'd be stuck on *Eclipse* so long. Figured he'd move up to a warship of some kind. But he was already too old. The Service left him to rot here with us until retirement. But now he's got this big chance, a final shot at his glorious destiny. It's pretty bloody pathetic, if you ask me."

I had no idea about any of this, but it made a certain sense. "You really think he might freak out?"

She nodded. "Our main value to the fleet is as a sensor platform. We have fantastic sensors. But we're not all that fast. Our power plant coolant isn't what it could be, so we've got too much of an IR profile, despite all that nano stealth crap on the hull. Ferguson doesn't care. He would love to break out of the Battle Group and target the enemy, any enemy!"

"And he said he'd kill anybody who tried to pull him off duty?"

She looked sad and tired. "I could play you the recording I made."

"Which is where I come in, right?"

She didn't smile. "Check your personnel maps; he's not in his quarters right now. He's with Rudyard."

I nodded, feeling too weak now to protest. "I could wait for him." I could find his personal sidearm. The gun he had made me clean and polish so often. And I knew where he kept it.

"What happens," I asked, facing the real fear, "if it goes bad, and he ... and he..." Still I couldn't say it. So scared.

"What's this? A change of heart?" A faint hint of wry smile.

"Look, I'm too tired to argue. What happens if...?"

"Then we bust him for murder, and *accidentally* kill him while he's in custody."

"How do I know I'm not bait for exactly this scenario?"

She rubbed at her tired eyes. "If you do the bloody job right the first time, we won't need that scenario — and besides, doing it right the first time means fewer awkward questions later."

I sat and thought about this, and tried not to think about how easily I had agreed to be an assassin. Then again, it's one thing to agree to do it; quite another to follow through on it. And quite another again, to kill Ferguson. I felt a cold shudder just thinking about it. "I can't decide this now. I need more time."

Riordan grabbed my face in her hands. She said, "We hit the tube back to Ganymede in four hours, Dunne. We just don't have time for you to sit on your precious little thumb and ponder your navel fluff." She pushed me back, looking like she was losing patience.

"If I say no?"

Riordan stood, paced around. "You wouldn't like what happens in that option, Mr. Dunne."

"I want that guarantee in writing."

She stepped over to her desk, opened a drawer, and pulled out a small sheet of Paper; she handed it to me. It contained a fixed document, signed and sealed, laying out the deal. "That's the only copy there is, too. And you'll note the offer is only good tonight."

The acceptance square was highlighted, flashing, waiting for my thumbprint and signature. I skimmed over terms indicating that I would promise, should I survive, that I would not divulge any of the details of the operation to anybody, ever, on pain of harsh penalties left unspecified.

"I can't believe my Service career — hell, my whole miserable life — has come down to this."

"Just sign the damn thing," Riordan said, sitting on her desk, looking pretty disgusted herself.

"Give me a bloody stylus."

She handed one over. There were cold flutters in my gut as I took the thing. "What am I doing?"

"Fighting back. Giving this ship and this crew a chance."

Killing Ferguson. It was hard to imagine. I couldn't see it — couldn't see myself raising a weapon against him.

My hand shook.

Riordan was chewing the nails on her left hand, looking tense.

"But — " I said.

She said, "Do it."

I signed. Of course I signed, though it felt like someone else was in my body, driving my hand. The same force caused my thumb to leave an imprint in the flashing pixons. A notice came up, acknowledging my ID. Riordan took the document, looking it over. She sighed. "I'm really sorry, James. You've got no idea how sorry."

I quirked the corner of my mouth. "Uh-huh."

She let me out, to go and do my duty.

Twenty-Five

The first priority was to check Ferguson's location. Riordan's headware showed him still in the captain's quarters with Rudyard. They were probably going over tactical plans, conferring with the *Queen Helen* people, and getting ready for the tube.

The second thing was to set out for Ferguson's quarters on Deck D, port side. It felt like a long way. I don't remember what I thought about, walking over there, feeling numb with disbelief. The air was stuffy and dark. When other officers passed, I squeezed up against the wall so they could get by, and I don't remember saluting, but then neither did anybody call me on it. Everyone was in a huge hurry.

All the way there, I kept the personnel map running, so I could track Ferguson's movements. I kept remembering Riordan's image of him as a rogue elephant stampeding through the ship, trumpeting his fury. It made me smile.

I was walking up the passageway to his door when I noticed the Ferguson-icon move. Swearing, trying not to panic, I stood there frozen, watching him. He visited a nearby head, did his business, then moved quickly away. Watching his movements, I began to get a bad feeling about where he might be heading. He got in a lift, heading down.

Focus, just focus! I was close to his door. Interrogating the door and finding it locked, I used Riordan's access to open it.

The Brig was on Deck E. If he ran from the lift, he could get there almost immediately. The lift dropped him at Deck E. He took off, and it looked like he was running for

the Brig. What else was down on that level that would
warrant running in the middle of the night — except maybe
the Officer's Mess? It was hard to imagine anyone in a
hurry for space chunder. On the other hand, I remembered
that Ferguson loved his space chunder. Could he be just
in a hurry for a midnight snack?

I called Riordan. She answered right away, no doubt
watching Ferguson, too. "What's he doing?"

She said, "I don't know, but I doubt he's taking an
evening constitutional."

"Is he getting the feed from ShipMind showing me in
the Brig?"

"Yes."

"Is anybody else in the other Brig cells?"

"Nobody."

"So it seems likely he wants a word with me?"

He came to an intersection. The Mess was aft; the Brig
was forward. Ferguson took off forward.

Riordan said, "I think yes, he wants to pop by for a visit
before the shooting starts."

"Stall him!"

"I have an idea," she said.

He was nearly there. One more turn, up a side-passage-
way...

"Make it quick."

He was there.

Riordan said, "Done!"

I said, "What?"

"I changed the door access there. His keys won't open
the door."

The Ferguson-icon was standing at the door of my cell.
On Riordan's headware an alert flashed that Ferguson was
trying to unseal that door without the correct authorization.

The phone rang. Riordan went to say, "Don't — " but
it was too late. I answered. "Yes?"

Riordan hissed, "Shit!"

Ferguson said, "Lily? Is that you?"

I gasped. Of course — I would get Riordan's phone calls!

She stepped in, coughing a little. "Mr. Ferguson, good
morning. How can I help you?"

"Listen, love. I'm just down here at the Brig. I thought I'd have a word with our Mr. Dunne..." His voice was oily, full of phony goodwill.

"Uh-huh," she said, betraying no secrets in her tone.

"But I can't seem to unlock his cell door. Do you think you can shed some light on this, my dear?"

She affected a yawn. "Oh I'm sorry, sir. I just recently authorized a routine key-change program. Did you not get my note about it?"

"Not that I recall, but we have been rather busy just lately. Hmm. It's just that I need to speak to Mr. Dunne for a few minutes."

"You don't think," Riordan said, keeping cooler than I ever could, "you've caused that boy enough grief?"

Smoothly, missing only one beat, his voice dropped a tone, "Excuse me, dear, I don't follow your meaning."

"Mr. Ferguson, look. It's the middle of the night. I'm sure you can wait until after we hit the tube to bother poor Mr. Dunne. Let him have a bit of rest from your attentions, okay? You wouldn't want rumors to get around, would you?"

His voice changed. A nasty edge cut through his words. "Rumors, love?" He paused, muttering something I couldn't make out. "Just open the bloody door for me. Now."

"You threatening me, Mr. Ferguson?"

He killed the link. On the personnel map, I watched him leave the Brig area, heading back for the lift.

Riordan said, "I wouldn't waste any more time, James."

I took a big breath, fought down my nerves, and ducked into Ferguson's quarters. I didn't die on entry, as I had feared. Standing there, breathing hard, I felt strange: sort of dizzy, scared and exhilarated at the same time, like I was committing the worst sin in the universe, violating the holiest of holies, I was sure that God — Ferguson — would catch me and make me pay. And pay. For a long moment, I stood paralyzed, unable to breathe, let alone to get on with the task at hand. Those shelves full of the tawdry, cheap souvenirs from his travels, memories of places defiled, of sexual conquests — it was all huge and sticky and heavy with pain and noise and lurid colors; it gave off a choking sense of sleaze. The stuff was everywhere. I saw pictures of Ferguson with friends, most of whom were very young, and half-dressed. There were no disposables present, either.

Oh God. Feeling sick, disgusted and furious, I was starting to see how he might have felt frustrated stuck on such a boring ship, but it looked like he made up for it on shore leave.

The personnel map reported that he was in the lift, going up. As I watched, he reached Deck C, got out, and started running for Riordan's quarters. At the same time, I saw Riordan leave her quarters heading for a side-passage, perhaps hoping to intercept Ferguson with a surprise.

There was no time for daintiness — I trashed Ferguson's quarters. Before anything else, I swept the souvenir shelves, and then I remember jumping, stomping on things, yelling incoherently, feeling cheap ceramics and plastic crunch under my boots.

And then I remembered what I was doing here. His gun, the Proddi bimodal ten-millimeter. He kept it under his mattress.

Somehow I had so far managed not to look at the bed.

I felt my bowels weakening. Bending over, hands on my knees, I had to stop and take big gulping breaths. The room was closing in on me. My head wouldn't turn to face the bed. Sweating now, I was cold and clammy all over and starting to remember that which I'd tried so hard to forget, the things that had happened in the dark and the pain, and the taste of the standard-issue Service blanket as I bit down on it...

Trembling with panic, I felt my mind skittering, wanting only to leave. Primitive responses were rising up, ready to take charge...

On the personnel map, Ferguson ran into Riordan. She piped me a feed.

"Ah, Lily — just coming to, uh, see you..." he was saying, and looked surprised to see her step around a corner, almost bumping into him.

"I know, Ron. I thought we should have a wee chat, you and I."

His face showed he liked the sound of that idea, despite the urgency of his business. Something had made him run to that Brig. But here he was, looking at Riordan, and even I could see he still fancied her. There was a sickening expression on his otherwise severe, sharp face. He touched his moustache and smiled. "Is that so, is that so?" he said, eyes keen.

"That's right," Riordan said, her voice sounding like she was smiling. She took him by the arm, gently, like she really did have something interesting in mind.

"I do need to have a word with young Mr. Dunne."

"I won't keep you long, Ron."

She was looking at him as he looked down at her. He looked a tad suspicious, I thought, like he wondered if something was up, with all this informality.

But then he flashed his shark smile. "Of course..."

I returned to my current problem: the bed. Ferguson had left it made in impeccable Service fashion, corners folded exactly right, blanket tightness beyond reproach. Now I just had to lift the mattress and reach underneath...

Taking several breaths, I was trying to talk myself into it. It was only a bed. Only a bed. The real monster was outside somewhere — I knew that. But all the same...

Bending down, vast quantities of blood rushed to my head; the room spun. I was hot, dizzy, and almost fell.

"Bloody hell, get a grip..." I straightened up again, took more breaths, bent down again, and lifted the mattress...

Ferguson was saying, unamused, "What are you really up to, Lily?" Leaning over her.

Riordan wasn't worried. "I just think a little counseling would help you, Ron. You're obsessing over this Dunne. He's not worth it. He's just a 1!"

"He might be just a 1," Ferguson said, looking at her with a dark and fractured glare, "but he's also a proven spy and traitor, and an attempted murderer, in case you'd forgotten!"

The Proddi wasn't there. Shit... Standing there, stunned, I was ready to snap, if I hadn't already. I kicked the damn bed.

Then, not knowing what I was about to do, I hauled the mattress off the bunk, up-ended the bunk itself, threw aside books, pillows, a third-full bottle of genuine, non-fabbed Scotch. I tore up sheets of Active Paper I found on his desk, and pulled out all the drawers, throwing all this crap around the room. I don't remember, but I was probably screaming, a catharsis of rage and joy; all this destruction, and I was liking it a lot — until I opened the drawer on the bottom-left side of his desk.

Gleaming amongst other bits and pieces, documents, folders, and books, was Ferguson's knife.

Standing there, staring down at it, I saw it in the sight of my imagination, the blade covered in my blood. Part of me wanted to touch it, but another wanted to flee. "Oh..."

Suddenly, red alert klaxons came blasting over my headware.

"What...?" Standing, I was staring at the inert ceiling and the stupid white glare of the light bar.

It was a ShipMind notice from Rudyard, "We are under attack! Man your stations! Repeat: we are under attack!"

The klaxon continued to sound.

Under attack? How the hell could we be under attack? I flipped to ShipMind's vessel status channel. A vast cloud of fist-sized crackbots, Autonomous Informational Assault Devices, wrapped in high stealth and almost invisible to sensors, was headed our way, fast. There were perhaps a million of them, homing in on the whole Battle Group, seeking our heat, our space-time deformation, our ship-to-ship comm traffic, and the very molecules of our polydiamond armor itself. Already they were close enough to engulf the entire fleet. The ships that had launched the bots were nowhere in sensor range.

Eclipse joined the other ships in the group. We deployed close-in weapons defense systems, more than a dozen automated launcher turrets rose out of our hull and launched a monster storm of small explosive shells designed to home on the AIADs. Between the combined firepower of the Battle Group's dozen ships, over one million such shells were launched in the first minutes. Meanwhile, the ships' reflective white armor shifted black and sensor-hostile. Intership comm went to tightbeam lasers.

Nearby space lit up with fire as shells found targets.

Or most of them. The close-in defense systems kept firing. Deep in the core of each ship, automated weapons-grade fab systems were cranking out more ammunition. When the shells arrived at the turret autoloaders, they would still be hot from the fabs.

ShipMind reported, "Four AIAD units have made hull-contact. Prepare for emergency conditions."

I swore, grabbed the knife, and shoved it in my pocket. It was time to get the hell out of here!

Riordan broke the link. Last I saw, as I left Ferguson's quarters, he was running this way. She was heading for her quarters.

Vessel status showed the four crackbots limpeted on the hull. I knew they would begin their comm assault, doing their best to break into our infostructure, probably using quantum anticrypto systems. Powerful pre-programmed countermeasures would attempt to block their ferocious attack while the turrets would try to shoot the bots off the hull. Speed was everything. The enemy, if they gained control of ShipMind, and with it access to all ship's systems, could conceivably shut down this entire fleet in a matter of minutes without firing a shot.

Long-range sensors still showed no sign of the fleet that had launched this attack. I was starting to wonder if perhaps somebody back at Service HQ had sold our intended coordinates to the Asiatics.

As for me and my bizarre mission, I didn't know where to go or what to do. There wasn't much I could do but watch the battle unfold and keep tracking Ferguson. I stopped and took a breath. It would be fun to lock Ferguson out of his quarters.

God, the dumb things you think about in a crisis!

As I searched for the commands to do this, I saw him running up the passageway. He looked furious — until he saw me. He stopped cold, staring, blinking, baffled. It was a unique moment: Ferguson surprised and unprepared. "Dunne — is that...?"

I wanted to run. I had never felt a stronger urge to flee in my life.

But I stood there and faced him, shaking with fear. "Mr. Ferguson." My mouth was dry.

"But ... you're down, in the..." Ferguson was thumbing over his shoulder, to indicate the Brig.

"Quantum tunneling..." I said, showing the calm poise of madness. Strange how right now he looked like a scared old man. For a moment I stared, wondering what had changed.

"What?"

Hands in my pockets, I found myself walking towards him with a strange sense of detachment, knowing I'd finally lost it.

"Dunne, we're under attack. Get to you post."

"I have no post. Sir." I stood in his path.

"Well, listen. I need you to do a little job. It's the captain, Dunne. He's falling apart."

"The captain?"

"I've just come from seeing him. Man's a damned basket case. Won't let me get the docs to take him off duty. Says he can bloody well handle it."

I said nothing and stared at him. It was odd, seeing how small he was, how like a weasel.

"Dunne, you have to kill him."

"Kill him?" I laughed out loud. "You want me to kill the captain?" More laughing. Laughing fit to burst.

"Do this for me and I'll drop the charges, boy. You'll be completely free. You can have a transfer to the ship of your choice. The flagship! Just do this one thing. This one little thing."

I kept laughing. The irony was too much. And he looked so pathetic — scared, even. The great battle was upon us, and he wasn't in charge. The man who was in charge was falling apart. We were doomed, and he knew it! His only hope was the one man in the crew least inclined to do him a favor. If I laughed any harder, I'd wet myself.

"For Christ's sake, boy! I order you to kill the captain! Now get on and bloody do it!"

"No. Don't think so. Sir." Wiping tears from my eyes with my left hand. My right hand was still in my pocket.

The light bars flickered. Painful feedback noise screamed through our headware. I winced, gasping at the agony.

Ferguson, gritting his teeth, pointed at me, advancing a further step. "You can hear that? You've got headware?"

It was hard to gloat and smile when you've got piercing torture shooting through your brain. The enemy crackbots were starting to get through. Where were the bloody countermeasures?

"But we cleaned out all your headware. We took it all out."

Wincing, fighting flashes of pain, I said, "The headware fairy left me some under my pillow, Ron."

Then Ferguson put it together. "Riordan!"

I had my right hand on the cool steel of his knife. He was two steps away.

"That bloody bitch!"

I took another step forward, clenching my jaw, trying to keep my eyes open. Pain swooped through my brain like dying angels; terror howled in my guts.

Ferguson was suddenly distracted — bridge business. He said, "Launch the bloody counterswarm now, damn you! Target those crackbots! Break formation!"

While Ferguson was losing his own coherence, sensing his destiny slipping away, I found myself feeling calm, in the eye of a cyclone of madness. The pain in my head was bad, but I could handle it. Pain was life; life pain.

"Hey, Ron!" I said.

Distracted, he looked up and saw me before him. "Not now!"

I plunged the knife deep and hard, up under his ribs. It slipped through the layers of his uniform, skin, muscle, and pericardium with surprisingly little effort, less than I had expected. Like the blade wanted to cut his heart, like it couldn't wait. The blade went in up to the hilt.

"A lady made me a better offer, Ron." His hot blood was streaming onto my hand.

He looked astonished, but amused. "You're one of us ... now, boy," Ferguson said, staring at me, not blinking, almost smiling.

We were close enough to kiss. I twisted the knife. He shuddered, wincing.

So much blood.

Deep in the eye of my madness, I hardly noticed the screaming feedback in my headware. The lights were going. My headware was flashing emergency core crash warnings. There was one that mentioned shipwide personnel biocontrol access was being challenged.

Big deal. I had Ferguson.

At that moment I could have sworn I saw Colin standing behind Ferguson, leaning against the wall, one foot up behind him. He was watching the blood pooling around the old bastard's polished shoes. Colin gave me a wry smile and a thumb's up.

I laughed and cried. Colin wasn't there next time I looked.

"I'm a real Service officer now," I said softly, tears running down my face, as Ferguson died, heavy at the end of my arm.

He slumped and gurgled, "... knew ... you were ... trouble..."

His body fell off the knife. I dropped it on his blood-soaked chest.

I shook, and felt funny. My legs were weak; I had to sit down before I fell down. Sitting on the deck under the flickering, fading lights, next to the spreading lake of blood around Ferguson's body. It was getting hard to breathe; my heart was racing, fluttering.

The lights went. Darkness closed over us.

In the noise coming through my headware, a hissing, breaking-up warning: *Biostatic control interface violated. Recommend immediate hard system eject or risk organic system failure. Please confirm.*

I blinked my confirmation in the dark. My new headware began to unravel.

Twenty-Six

The Paper spoke the time in the cooling darkness, "The time is oh-five-twenty-four hours, Winter City Mean Time." There were no feeds from outside. ShipMind was offline. Primary environmental systems were offline; such air and heat and gravity that we had came from isolated backup power sources hardened against infowar attacks. The air was still; there was no background hushing sound from the ceiling vents or hum from the matter pumps. The power plant was down. *Eclipse* was adrift.

I heard voices in the distance, yelling.

Janning was coordinating repairs. Rudyard was in the Infirmary, supposedly curled up in a fetal ball, making strange chewing and swallowing motions. I wondered if I was the only one on the ship who understood why he was doing that.

Riordan had found me earlier; she took me back to her quarters, tucked me into bed, and made sure I kept warm to avoid shock. She said our counterswarm had blasted the enemy AIAD units off the hull, but they had already finished uploading their crippling code into our compromised infostructure, and had begun phase two of their programmed mission: undoing the ship's armor, breaking the chemical bonds. When the enemy ships came into missile range, they'd find nice, vulnerable holes in our armor. We could only wait and hope we could restore basic systems before they arrived to finish us off.

"What about the other ships?" I asked her, feeling my whole body trembling still in the wake of killing Ferguson.

I wanted to push off the blankets; she kept pulling them back over me.

"Pretty much the same condition we are, as far as we can tell."

She left for routine patrols. There were reports of enlisted men going berserk in the dark. Other officers were going through strange psychological crises, wandering the passageways, shouting, crying, calling out for their mothers. Riordan received word of at least three attempted rapes, and several assaults.

About two hours later Acting Captain Janning announced we had basic systems back online. The power plant was still down, but we could at least maneuver. Tracking tubes was out. A bunch of workerbots were out inspecting the hull and fixing the damage left by the AIADs. Environmental systems were up; air was circulating; heat was coming back. Lights flickered and came on, running at about three-quarters strength. Matter pumps were working, too, which meant that fab units would respond to orders so we could put aside the hard rations and bottled water. ShipMind would be up shortly, Janning reported. His image on my Paper made him look small and exhausted. In the window I saw people milling around him, passing back and forth, yelling things to each other. It looked like he might be in Engineering.

Twenty minutes later, ShipMind was back. I sat up in Riordan's bunk, waiting for my headware to snap back into luminous life. And then remembered I had removed mine.

I also remembered I still had the breakdown products from my previous headware slowly turning into cytotoxins.

I slumped, sighing. The crap around here never ended.

Shortly before 0800 hours, my Paper relayed a report from Janning: sensors were back. "That's the good news," he said, face grim.

"What now?" I muttered.

"The bad news is the Asiatic Fourth Fleet is closing on our location, moving at relativistic speed, coming in from three directions. Estimated arrival — thirty minutes. Our best estimate on power plant availability is at least another hour. Sorry, folks. We're doing our best down here. Meanwhile, we've redirected ten thousand AIADs of our own to close on the Fourth Fleet as fast as they can."

The Asiatic Fourth Fleet, according to ShipMind's files, consisted of at least twenty ships, twelve of which were rated at cruiser strength or better. At least two were thought equivalent to *Queen Helen*.

I called up ShipMind's vessel status channel on my Paper. It showed which systems were available, which weren't, and the status of the remainder. Without the power plant, we couldn't use our main gun, such as it was. Helm systems were capable of showing us a display of local hypertube weather, which revealed eight viable tube entry points within a thousand cubic kilometers. So many escape routes, if only we had the power plant.

The Asiatics were braking, dumping velocity hard. On IR they showed up like shooting stars.

They'd reach their missile range in twelve minutes.

At minus four minutes they disappeared off our sensors.

No IR traces; no other traces. One moment they were there, twenty powerful ships diving on us with evil intent and terrifying power, and the next — gone.

Our AIADs sent back word that they couldn't find any targets. Should they return to *Eclipse*?

Janning called them back.

He appeared on shipwide comm, looking puzzled and shaken. "Men, women, it now appears that the Asiatic Fourth Fleet will not be engaging us, after all. A minute ago, they completely disappeared off our scopes. We've been scanning across the band, and can't find a damned thing. No visible wreckage, no telltale emissions from tube usage. All of which is..." he swallowed, visibly uncomfortable with this idea, "a bit disturbing."

I punched up a display from the portside of the ship. Three of the other ships in our group were more or less functioning. One, the destroyer *Nelson*, was still adrift, and looked like she might stay that way. There had only been a brief, tenuous comm-flash from some portable unit that indicated shipwide rioting, and that the captain and XO were dead. The rest of the ships, including *Queen Helen*, were still slowly coming back up. I couldn't see *Queen Helen* from this angle; I was glad of that. I didn't want to think about her.

For that matter, I didn't want to think about any of it. As it was, I was still trying to accept that I had killed a man. It occurred to me that I should have resisted the urge to kill him; that I should have let him go. Ferguson was the most despicable person I had ever encountered, including that bastard Dewey, but by repaying his violence with violence of my own, hadn't I shown that he'd broken me more than I thought? I had murdered him. He hadn't threatened me, hadn't been actively trying to kill me at that moment. Sure he'd ... hurt me, once or twice.

And the horrible fact was that I felt good about killing him. In my guts I knew he deserved to die by my hand, and it was just. I'd liked it too much.

The stars out there were hard points of unblinking light, like accusing eyes. I stared back.

At 0845, something anomalous appeared two kilometers away from the ship.

Janning ordered Red Alert.

Whatever the hell it was, it was big, the size of a major asteroid, more than 10 k's across.

But it was made of God knows what... Sensor information wasn't helpful. I imagined the sensors frowning, trying to figure it out.

It was made of a peculiar light, and there were things moving, angles forming, shapes opening and closing.

The whole thing was changing shape as we watched, as if it didn't want you to see what it really was. Was it another ship? Was it — an unwelcome thought here — some kind of creature? What other possibilities were there? Was it alive? Was it a machine?

I imagined Mr. Grantleigh being fascinated, and listening to him pondering the "ontological difficulty" of it all.

Janning's voice came over ShipMind, "We have the power plant back up. We're leaving!"

I felt the walls thrum before I heard the rumble of the plant.

Then one of the Battle Group ships disappeared, just like the Fourth Fleet: gone without trace. No wreckage, no emissions, nothing.

Eclipse was moving — towards the object. In my belly I could feel the power plant cranking up. It made little difference.

Another ship from the Battle Group vanished behind us. And then another, the *Nelson*.

Vessel status showed us passing through the one-kilometer mark. The object filled the sky with its geometric lunacy; its frightening light was like nothing I had ever seen.

Distracted by the looming object, I had not noticed our other Battle Group ships winking out of this reality, one at a time. *Queen Helen*, apparently, was the last besides us to go.

I thought I couldn't possibly have any more fear left. I had to be all scared out after this night. But I was wrong.

I got up from the bed as Janning said that his attempts to contact whatever that thing was had gone unanswered. "Therefore," he said, "it is time to abandon ship."

Standing there, panicking good and proper now, I wrestled with the Paper, tearing it, trying to bring up the phone interface. "Mr. Janning!" I babbled when I finally got it running.

Half a kilometer.

"James? Is that you? I thought you..."

"Sir, what's my designated lifeboat? I had to dump my headware!"

"Look — just get yourself to Hangar Two, Deck E, remember. Got that? We'll sort something out then. Sorry, I can't talk."

He was gone.

I left, sprinting along the passageways, heading for the nearest lift I could find. And ran into another officer—

Ferguson!

He was standing right there in my path, watching me and scratching one of his ears. "Do watch where you're going, Mr. Dunne."

I almost fell over. I had never been so shocked in my life.

My heart was in my throat. Gasping, babbling, "No, no ... Mr. Ferg — no! Couldn't ... it..." I wanted to turn and run.

"Where do you think you're going, hmm?" he said, taking a step towards me.

"Who — who the hell are you?" I was fumbling my way backwards.

Ferguson scowled down at me. "You'll meet them soon enough, boy."

Thinking, thinking real hard. And then realizing, filled with blinding panic. "You mean, you're ... out..." Pointing, I indicated the object outside. The object that was reeling in this whole ship like a caught fish, even as I felt the floor tremble with the power plant running at more than its full capacity to get us out of here.

The Ferguson-thing grinned. Just like the real Ferguson, that grin. I bolted.

And ran straight into his chest; I bounced off, stunned, and I made an embarrassing squawk of fright. Staring up at that face, that stupid moustache I'd always hated.

"When you're quite finished, boy, I'd like a quiet word."

"What's going on?"

"What's going on? You stepped on our toes, you might say. And we really can't have that."

"Oh shit!" I shot away again, running in the opposite direction, I was sure of it — and again ran into his chest.

Wearily, it said, "You really must stop doing that, boy."

I could hardly breathe. "I've got to get to a lifeboat..."

"Don't you worry your poor little head. You'll get to your bloody lifeboat."

"Then..." Trying to breathe, I stared, baffled. "What's...?"

"This vessel was involved in a very nasty bit of business a short while ago. You killed an entire race of sentient beings."

Gulping, feeling dizzy. My bladder wanted to let go.

"That wasn't my ... I didn't do ... God, that sounds lame, doesn't it?"

"I am aware, Mr. Dunne, that you were not a whole-hearted supporter of the operation. That's why you are still here."

"Okay. I think I see. What about, what about the ... others?"

"Don't think about them."

I fell against the wall. "God... Oh my God..." I whispered, feeling fresh tears.

"The chaps who constructed me out of the rancid muck in your brain so that we could share this awkward moment, they were, er, cultivating the beings you bastards killed. I see you understand the idea of gardening. Well, those beings, they were like a plant about to mature and flower, if you'll excuse the metaphor." He looked annoyed, anxious to hurry things along.

I was holding my face, unable to think of anything to say. Nothing could excuse what we did, or make up for it.

And then I remembered. The alien ship we encountered, all that time ago. It had a drive section of a completely different design style and composition from the main body of the craft. It was as if there had been two cultures at work.

"It was you ... you..." I couldn't finish the thought.

He nodded.

"B-But what about the other ships, why didn't you just wipe us out...?"

"How to put this?" it said, more irritated now. "This vessel is to be a trophy."

A trophy. I couldn't begin to understand this. The only thing going through my mind now was the inadequacy of my oceanic sorrow. "I am so sorry." Crying now. "I am so ... bloody sorry." I don't know how many times I said it. But when I looked up, wiping my eyes, he was gone.

The ship was empty.

I hurried to the boat hangars. Vessel status showed that *Eclipse* had crossed the object's shifting outer boundary, moving more slowly now.

Hangar Two rang with my footsteps. It was cold. There were a dozen lifeboats here, each rated for ten passengers. Each boat was still clamped down. I found a manual control board near the entrance, wiped a thin layer of frost off it, and powered it up. My breath plumed. Breathing hard, I could feel the cold air burning in my lungs. Hurrying. Things hummed and clunked. Red lights came on in boat number one. Scrambling over to it, I climbed in and sealed the door shut. God, it was cold.

I tried not to think about all the *Eclipse* crew members who were not here, who were not climbing aboard these things, who weren't leaving, and whose bodies were not lying around. Critchlow, Riordan, and Janning: they had been my only friends in the end. I imagined they had been sucked away to wherever the other ships in the Battle Group went.

I punched the big autolaunch pad on the flightdeck. Space doors began to slide open. Atmosphere blasted out, crystallizing, turning to fog, and blew away.

That light drenched the hangar. It was too bright to resolve details or structures. It felt like a punishment just to see that light.

I launched. Automated functions got the boat clear, and dodged us away from the object. Or rather, the object let me go. Why was it letting me go? I didn't understand. And what the hell was that thing, anyway? Was it a ship? It had to be some kind of ship, but now that I've had time to think about it, that view is probably too limited. Maybe it was like those glass sphere things we found: many things at once, not an either/or thing like humans made.

I never thought I would be so glad to see the dark of empty space.

About three hours later, I felt my pulse return to something like normal. I could think again.

I was wondering: how far would these — what should I call them? I settled on calling them "Gardeners" — how far would they take their retribution against us?

Sipping lukewarm fab coffee, I had the horrible thought that instant annihilation might have been the more merciful way to go. These guys, whoever they were, they might be much more subtle in their punishment than mere humans could imagine.

Meanwhile, I kept coming back to this other troubling thought, as I drifted away into unexplored space: *What if there's nobody left to rescue me?*

Ah, but there *was* somebody...

Epilogue

Sometime after day 153 since escaping Eclipse

My sorrow for the annihilated aliens surprises them. "Why do you care?" they ask.

Petrified, I say, knowing this matters, "We were absolutely wrong to do that, and I'm sorry."

They leave me alone a long time, after I say that. Later they return, and say, "Come with us."

They dissolve me into their consciousness, like a grain of salt into hot water.

We go to human space.

I see it all as if I am flying through space on my own, without vessel or life-support. This is how things are inside their vehicle: there is no sense of being inside anything. They travel like a flock of birds, except they cross light-years with a thought. It's terrifying, exhilarating, wonderful. I once dreamed of walking among the stars, but not like this.

Sorcha would have loved it.

Human space has changed. I had feared they would wipe out humanity, scour it from the universe. They are, as I feared, more subtle. They have stationed one of their platforms in every system occupied by humans, orbiting local stars. Investigating ships disappear.

The Service is gone. The Home System Community and much of the Home System population, regardless of affiliation, have dispersed, fleeing in terror. Even the Unity's colony on Mars is dwindling. Nobody has dared claim those worlds.

The Gardeners tell me they have created a small, sealed universe for all the disappeared ships and crews, including Eclipse's crew; they say it's stocked with human-habitable worlds. The Gardeners plan to watch it and wait. They tell me they want to see if anything interesting grows.

"Why didn't you just kill them?" I ask.

"Life is too valuable, James. It's all we have to push against the darkness."

I say, "Even humans?"

They tell me, "Even humans."

"What about me, then? Why didn't you put me in your pocket universe thing?"

They say, after a long pause, "We're growing you. You show promise."

"But I killed a man."

"We know. We understand how you feel. We have plans."

I think about this, confused, full of something resembling terror, but lacking the visceral, physical component. It's unsettling. They say they are growing me, but it seems to me that I am already grown. "And then?" I say. "When I've done this growing? What will you do with me then?"

They only say, "We will see. We will see."

ACKNOWLEDGEMENTS

I would like to thank my wife Michelle and my parents for putting up with me and the ups and downs of the scribbling life; and my friends, particularly Martin Chapman, Michael Tan, and Lee and Lyn Battersby, good eggs all, who help me more than they know; and, of course, the top folks at EDGE Science Fiction and Fantasy Publishing.